Two Action-Packed Novels
of the American West!

SIGNET BRAND DOUBLE WESTERNS

BITTER SAGE
and
THE BUSHWHACKERS

SIGNET Double Westerns You'll Enjoy

BITTER SAGE
and
THE
BUSHWHACKERS

by

Frank Gruber

A SIGNET BOOK

NEW AMERICAN LIBRARY

Bitter Sage: Copyright © 1954 by Frank Gruber.
Copyright renewed © 1982 by Lois Gruber.
The Bushwhackers: Copyright © 1959 by Frank Gruber.

All rights reserved. For information address Mrs. Lois Gruber, c/o New American Library.

Published by arrangement with Mrs. Lois Gruber. *Bitter Sage* and *The Bushwhackers* previously appeared in paperback as separate volumes published by New American Library.

SIGNET TRADEMARK REG. U.S. PAT. OFF. AND FOREIGN COUNTRIES
REGISTERED TRADEMARK—MARCA REGISTRADA
HECHO EN CHICAGO, U.S.A.

SIGNET, SIGNET CLASSIC, MENTOR, PLUME, MERIDIAN AND NAL BOOKS
are published by New American Library,
1633 Broadway, New York, New York 10019

First Printing (Double Western Edition), May, 1984

1 2 3 4 5 6 7 8 9

PRINTED IN THE UNITED STATES OF AMERICA

BITTER SAGE

Chapter *1*

During The War Between The States, Sam Older rode
with the infamous Quantrell. He raided and looted and
killed and he was with his chief at the bloody massacre of
Lawrence. After the war when even the guerrillas re-
ceived amnesty and returned to peaceful pursuits, Sam
Older became an outlaw. He held up banks and robbed
trains.

Then Sam Older was killed and became The Great
American Legend, the man who was hounded into out-
lawry and stole from the rich to give to the poor.

The name of Wes Tancred, the man who killed Sam
Older, became an epithet.

The sheriff unlocked the cell door and pulled it open.
He said, "All right, Tancred."

Wes Tancred got up from the cot and looked uncer-
tainly at the sheriff. It was scarcely two hours since the
judge had delivered the sentence. It couldn't be so soon.
It was always a matter of days, weeks.

The sheriff held out a folded paper. "Here it is."

Tancred took the sheet, unfolded it. He saw the seal
in the upper right corner, the words, *Office Of The Gov-*
ernor, but the body of the letter suddenly became a blur.
There was no need to read, however. The sheriff told
him the contents of the governor's letter.

A full pardon.

"You were expecting it, weren't you?" the sheriff asked.
"It was part of the deal. . . ."

"Deal?"

"Ten thousand dollars reward—and amnesty." The sheriff held up a hand to stop Tancred's denial. "I know. You
said it at the trial. There was no deal." He turned away.
"Come on."

5

Tancred followed the sheriff into his office. There the lawman opened a wooden box and took out the contents. Twelve dollars and fifty-five cents, a clasp knife and a Navy Colt.

"Your property."

Tancred picked up the money. He looked at the knife, hesitated, then put it into his hip pocket. The sheriff shoved the revolver across the desk with the heel of his hand.

"Someday you'll be able to sell that for a good price. The gun that killed Sam Older."

"Can I go now?" Tancred asked.

"Why not? You're as free as the birds."

Tancred stuck the Navy Colt under the waistband of his trousers and started for the door. As he touched the knob, the sheriff said, "There are a bunch of reporters outside. You can sneak out the back way."

Tancred turned, crossed the room and went through a door. He missed the reporters who were waiting out front . . . and faced Helen Older.

She was only twenty-four but she looked thirty. She said to him, "Remember it, Wes Tancred. Think of it every day of your life. How you murdered him in cold blood, for ten thousand silver dollars."

He cried out hoarsely, "No, Helen, it wasn't like that. You must believe me. It wasn't like they said. I didn't plan it. I didn't make a deal. I—I'm not taking a cent of the money."

"Take it, Wes, you earned it. Take it and may the food you buy with it taste like ashes, the whiskey like vinegar. May everything you touch turn to blood. And think of Sam, think of him every day of your life. Listen—listen to his voice in the night. See him wherever you go and hear him, hear him always, cursing you for a blackhearted traitor . . . and *murderer!*"

She turned then and walked away.

Chapter 2

Life has to be lived.

Tancred rode the lonely trails. He saw Dakota and Wyoming, he rode through Kansas and Colorado. He went to Texas and Louisiana, Illinois and Kentucky, Ohio and Missouri. He visited towns and cities, he rode for days without seeing another human being. Countless nights he spread his blankets under the stars and stared at the heavens above. A thousand hours he tossed in a bed and could not sleep.

He had to live, so he worked. He worked as a laborer on the railroad as it crept across Nebraska and Wyoming. He went deep into the bowels of the earth in the silver mines of Colorado. He sold shoes in a store and once he read law in an attorney's office, but mostly he worked as a printer, a trade at which he had had some apprenticeship back in Missouri before . . . before he had killed Sam Older.

He lived.

Nine years dragged by and in the spring of 1876 a doctor in Michigan listened to his heart and tapped his chest and his lungs and said, "Get rid of the tension, get out in the sun and work with your hands. Forget everything that's ever worried you and relax. If not. . . ."

The doctor knew him as John Bailey. A lot of people had known him by that name and quite a few of them had talked to Bailey . . . about the blackhearted traitor who had killed the great Sam Older, the sneaking youth who had caught the most desperate man of his time by surprise and put a bullet through his head. Someone wrote a song about it and the man who called himself John Bailey heard it. It was an extremely popular ballad and men sang it everywhere. Men and women sang it. Bailey heard it a thousand times.

And the doctor told him to get rid of the tension! He did not know that John Bailey was Wes Tancred.

Well, one place was as good as another. And one job paid almost as much as another, so now in the spring of 1877, the man who called himself John Bailey looked over the log poles of the corral behind the stage station and saw a hundred miles of Kansas prairieland.

He watered the horses and he fed them. He rubbed them down and he hitched them to the once-a-week stage as it paused for moments every Thursday on its way to Kansas & Western a hundred miles to the south. He drove the relieved horses into the corral and rubbed them down and fed and watered them and tended them, and on Saturday he hitched them to the north-bound stage as it stopped for moments on its run to the Union Pacific two hundred and twenty miles to the north.

The job was an easy one and it kept him in the open. He slept in the shed by the corral when it rained and when the stars shone he moved out under them. And when there was no work to be done, which was most of the time, he sat in the sun and watched the sod-covered stage station.

And Laura Vesser.

Laura was twenty, a slim, fresh girl with the bluest of blue eyes and a freckled nose. She had lived here with her father at this lonely spot on the Kansas plains for six years. It was a sorry life for a girl, but Vesser had no relatives in the east with whom she could live and he had only one lung and could not live in the towns. So he kept this miserable sod-house and horse relay station for the stage line and wondered what Laura would do when his second lung was gone.

Perhaps. . . .

When John Bailey came along and indicated a willingness to stay and help with the horses, Vesser offered him pay from his own paltry wage and when Laura's eyes brightened every time she saw the hostler, Vesser felt more at peace with himself.

Yet . . . what was it about Bailey?

He wasn't old, but his eyes were weary and always there was a faraway look in them. He did his work and he was there and always his eyes watched Laura, but in six weeks he had spoken no words to her that he could not have said to her before strangers. And Laura's smile was sometimes strained.

Then one Wednesday morning the three men came out of the north and tied their horses to the corral poles.

They were whiskered and unkempt and none had washed for days. They were ravenously hungry and they ate every scrap of the food Laura cooked and set before them and no word was said about payment for the food. They asked for whiskey.

"I don't sell it here," Vesser told them.

"Who said anything about selling?" sneered the worst looking one of the trio, a man the others called Jethro. "We ain't got two dollars between us."

"We still want the whiskey," said the smallest of the three, a squat, ugly man with snaggled teeth.

Vesser shook his head. "I've no whiskey to give you."

Dave, the third man, who might have been the leader of the trio, a cold-eyed man in his early thirties, got up from the table and went into the lean-to where Laura did the cooking.

Angrily, Vesser started after him. The squat man sprang up from the table and cut off Vesser.

"Don't," he said.

Vesser swerved to the wall where a Sharp's rifle was suspended across two wooden pegs. Jethro came up as Vesser reached for the gun. He clouted him a hard blow with his fist.

Laura screamed and the squat man lunged for her, but Laura evaded his grab and made the open door.

Outside, Tancred was coming toward the station from the corrals.

"John!" Laura cried. "Those men. . . ."

The squat man came out of the stage station, a Navy revolver in his grimy fist.

"Don't make no play, bub," he said.

Tancred held up his hands, palms forward.

"I've no gun."

The squat man showed his bad teeth in a wicked grin. "Good thing you ain't got one."

Vesser came hurtling out of the stage station, propelled by Jethro who followed with Vesser's Sharp's rifle. He looked coolly at Tancred, then with a sudden hard blow, smashed the gun barrel over a rock, cracking it. He threw it to the ground.

"Just so we don't have no trouble."

The leader of the trio came out with a flask of whiskey. "Your cooking whiskey, I suppose," he remarked.

Vesser said, bitterly, "All right, you've had food and you've got the whiskey. Pile on your horses. . . ."

"Uh-uh," said Jethro. "Not just yet."

"There's nothing here to hold you."

The man with the whiskey regarded Vesser coldly. "The south stage stops here tomorrow, doesn't it?"

Vesser understood the question and made no reply.

The squat man said, "Dave asked you a question."

"I heard it," replied Vesser testily.

"Then answer him."

Tancred saw that Vesser would not answer and as the squat man moved in on him, Tancred said, "Yes, the stage comes through here on Thursday, usually around two o'clock in the afternoon."

Dave grinned wolfishly. "You've got more sense than he has." He inclined his head at his companions and headed for the corral. They followed. When they were out of earshot, Vesser said to Tancred, "You shouldn't have told them."

"What difference does it make? They can see it coming ten miles away."

"I know, but . . ."

"They'd have killed you, Dad," said Laura.

Vesser exhaled heavily. "They're going to hold up the stage."

Tancred nodded agreement.

Vesser's forehead creased. "The rifle's out of commission," He paused a moment. "I've got a revolver—if they don't search my bed."

"No!" Tancred said, quickly. "You can't fight them. Fighting is their business."

"John's right, Dad," said Laura, worriedly. "The company doesn't expect you to fight bandits."

"I can't just stand by and watch them hold up the stage."

From the corral, Dave called, "You . . . the hostler! Come here. . . ."

"Be careful," Tancred said to Vesser and turning, walked over to the corral.

The three men had opened the bottle and passed it around once. Jethro was taking his second drink as

Tancred came up. Dave ran his eyes up and down Tancred's lean figure.

"How many people does this stage usually carry?"

Tancred shrugged. "It varies. Sometimes five or six, sometimes only one or two. Once in a while there aren't any passengers at all."

"Mail?"

"I take care of the horses here."

"But you've got eyes," snapped Dave. "You know what a mail pouch is, don't you?"

"I've seen them."

"All right, does the stage carry them?"

"Yes."

"Think carefully, now," said the squat man, wickedly. "Does she also carry a strong box?"

"No."

The outlaw grabbed the whiskey bottle from Jethro, took a great swig then passed it on to Dave. With a sudden spring he leaped forward and hit Tancred in the face with the back of his hand.

"I asked you about a strong box?"

"And I told you."

The short man rocked Tancred's head with a backhanded swipe. "What about a shotgun guard?"

"Don't do that again," Tancred said, evenly.

The little man took a step back. "Why, he's got spunk," he said, mockingly. "He might even try to fight me." He winked at Dave. "Shall we tell him who we are?"

Dave shrugged. "He's a horse-handler. He's probably never even heard of us."

"Everybody's heard of Sam Older," chortled the squat man. He pointed at Tancred. "Even you."

Tancred said in an even, flat tone, "Sam Older's dead."

"Sure, but Dick Small ain't." The short one tapped his chest. "Or Dave Helm." He indicated Dave.

Nine years ago Dick Small had been a thin man about six inches taller than the one who now called himself Dick Small. And Dave Helm . . . this man wasn't Dave Helm, not in a thousand years.

Tancred looked at Jethro. "And I suppose he's . . . Wes Tancred."

Jethro took that as a deadly insult. "Why, damn your

soul to hell, don't you accuse me of me being that dirty traitor. . . ."

Tancred backed away. "How was I to know? Seems to me, I heard men talking about the Older gang and the name Tancred. . . ."

"Don't mention Older and Tancred in the same breath," cried the man who called himself Dick Small. "Tancred was a scurvy rat who wormed his way into the gang, then shot Older when he wasn't looking."

"For ten thousand dollars blood money," added Dave.

"I'm just a horse-handler," Tancred said. He looked at Dave. "Like you said."

"See that you remember it," Dave retorted. "And you'd better tell the agent who we are. Just so he doesn't try another fool play, like with that rifle."

"We mean business," snapped Jethro.

Tancred nodded and started away but Dave grabbed his arm and whirled him around. "You didn't answer Dick's question—about the stage carrying a shotgun guard."

"I've never seen one," said Tancred. He waited a moment. "Can I go now?"

"Sure," said Dave. "As long as you stay in sight." He nodded toward the stage station. "And I don't mean in there."

Tancred went into the corral. He busied himself currying the stage horses, but every now and then he glanced toward the three outlaws. They had hunkered down outside the corral, near their own horses, and were killing the bottle of whiskey.

After a while they started a noisy three-handed poker game and kept at it until late afternoon, when they finally broke up the game and demanded food.

Tancred went to the stage station and stopped outside the door of the lean-to. Laura was working inside.

"They want something to eat," he said.

"I'm fixing it now," Laura replied. Tancred hesitated and was about to turn away when she said, "I saw them hit you."

Tancred let out a slow sigh. "Yes."

She gave him a quick look. "I'm sorry I said that."

"Why should you be sorry about it? They hit me all right."

"That isn't what I meant. I mean . . ." She was flustered

as she tried to straighten it out. "I shouldn't have said *anything* about it."

Vesser appeared in the lean-to, coming from inside the cabin.

"I hid the revolver, John."

Tancred frowned. "Two of them claim to be members of the old Sam Older gang . . . Dick Small and Dave Helm."

Vesser whistled. "Then there's no question about them holding up the stage!"

"No, I don't think so."

A yell came from the men by the corral. "Hey—how about that grub?"

"It's ready," Laura said.

Tancred relayed the information to the outlaws and they came toward the stage station, going in by the front door. Before Dave entered he signalled to Tancred to follow.

The supper consisted merely of beans and cornbread, but to the ruffians it was good fodder and they ate it with enthusiasm. Vesser sat at one end of the table, morosely eating his food without raising his eyes from the plate.

When they had finished eating, Dave looked toward the kitchen. "You got another bottle of whiskey out there?"

"You looked," Vesser said, curtly.

"Just in the kitchen. I didn't look in here."

"Then search."

"I may do just that." Dave got up. He looked around the room, but the effort of searching did not appeal to him. He shrugged and headed for the door. "Guess I'll roll in. We may not get much sleep tomorrow night."

He went out and after a moment Jethro and Dick followed. Tancred got up from the table and his eyes met Laura's. She said, "What are you going to do, John?"

"I'm going to sleep."

Her eyes fell from his. "Of course."

"They'll be watching me," Tancred said. "There isn't anything I can do."

Vesser said, "I thought maybe you could ride up the trail ten-fifteen miles and warn the stage."

"Make no mistake," Tancred said, soberly. "They're hard cases. Even if I could get a horse and get away they'd take it out on you and . . ." His eyes went to Laura.

"I've got the revolver," Vesser reminded.

"I wish you didn't have it." Tancred hesitated. "You've fired a gun, Mr. Vesser. And you've probably hit your target."

"I'm better with a rifle."

"You're not better than they are," Tancred said, earnestly. "There's a difference in shooting at a deer and—and a man. You have an aversion to killing—any normal man has—and whether you'd want to or not, you'd hesitate before actually pulling the trigger on a human being. They won't. They're killers. As a matter of fact they told me that they once rode with Sam Older."

"That riffraff!"

Tancred stopped. Sam Older was a legendary figure. Even to people like Vesser and his daughter. He was Robin Hood, of Robin Hood and his Merry Men.

There was nothing more for Wes Tancred to say. He exhaled slowly and started for the door.

"Wait, John," Vesser said. "I want to talk to you." He turned to Laura. "Do you mind leaving us alone, Laura?"

Laura minded, all right, but dutifully she went into the lean-to kitchen. Then Vesser said, "Believe me, John, I don't want to talk to you like this. But I've got to. I've thought of it all afternoon and I don't know which way to turn. I've got to *know* . . . about you and Laura."

A shudder ran through Tancred. "I'm sorry, Mr. Vesser," he said, "I can't answer that."

"I said this was going to be awkward and in the regular course of events wild horses couldn't make me talk like this. Only now . . . with those men out there . . . I've got to know."

"So you're going to fight them!"

"A man's got to do what he's got to do."

"Knowing that they'll kill you?"

"Even knowing that." A fine film of perspiration appeared on Vesser's forehead. "What is it, John . . . what is it about you that I can't grasp? I've watched you and I've studied you for six weeks. In any case, whether it's those men out there or not, I haven't got long. A matter of months, that's all. And I can't go without knowing about Laura. I'd hoped . . ."

"No!" said Tancred.

"Why not? Oh, I've seen her look at you and I've seen

you watching her. Then, why not, John, why not? Is it because you're already married?"

"No, it isn't that. I'm not married."

"Then, what is it?"

"I can't tell you."

"But I'm backed against a wall. You can tell me."

"I can't."

Vesser went around to attack the problem from the flank, as he'd probably done over and over in his mind. "You were sick when you came here, John, I know that. But I've watched you—you're better. I don't think it's that. You stopped here because it's an isolated spot. I've thought of that. Perhaps . . . you're wanted. . . "

"I'm not wanted."

A groan was torn from Vesser's throat. "Are you in love with Laura?"

The pain in Tancred's chest was as bad as it had ever been before he'd come out here to the Kansas prairie. But that was good. It was the shell Tancred knew so well. Behind it he was safe.

He said, "If I could be in love with any woman, I could be in love with Laura. But I'm not in love with her . . . because it isn't in me to love any person on earth."

Vesser capitulated. "All right, Bailey, all right, but I wish to God I had never set eyes on you!"

Tancred went out of the stage station and Laura came out of the lean-to where she had listened at the door and heard every word between her father and Tancred. She went into his arms and sobs wracked her body and Vesser wept.

Chapter 3

Morning came and Tancred came out of the shed where he had slept. The outlaws, two of them, were still sleeping beside the corral. The third, Jethro, was seated on the ground, his back to the corral poles, cleaning his gun with a dirty rag. As filthy as the three men were about their own persons, their guns were cleaned and well-oiled. Guns were the tools of their trade.

Over in the lean-to there was a clanking of pans as Laura prepared breakfast.

"That's a sweet morsel over there," Jethro observed to Tancred. "If I was a woman's man, I'd put my brand on that." He chuckled wickedly. "I'll bet you've already lit the fire under your branding iron."

"I've got work to do," said Tancred, heading for the corral gate.

Jethro sprang to his feet. "You're going to get those horses ready for the stage, just as if nothing was going to happen?"

"My job is feeding and watering and taking care of these horses." Tancred went into the corral.

When he came out the outlaws were all up and in the stage station, eating their breakfast. No one had called Tancred. He went into the shed and with a quick look over his shoulder, moved far in to the manger that was used by the horses during bad weather. It was half-filled with hay.

Tancred moved aside some of the hay and exposed a weathered carpetbag. He stared at it for a long moment, then shook his head and covered it again with hay.

When he went outside, Dave was coming out of the stage station. "Your breakfast's ready." He smacked his lips. "That girl cooks all right."

Tancred crossed the yard and entered the station. Dick

and Jethro were just finishing their breakfast, but Vesser sat at the plain table, his corncakes barely touched.

Tancred sat down opposite him and Laura brought him cakes and coffee. He ate and spoke no word to her or to her father and when he finished eating he went outside.

He curried the horses in the corral until their coats glistened. He rubbed them down with wisps of hay and curried them again. But at last he could work in the corral no longer and he came out.

The man who called himself Dave Helm looked at Tancred and said, "It's eating out your insides, isn't it? I don't know why it should. You're only a horse wrangler and the stage line shouldn't mean a damn thing to you."

"It doesn't."

"They can afford to lose anything we take from them." He looked thoughtfully toward the stage station.

Trancred went into the shed and threw himself upon the dirt floor. After a moment he heard a step and rolling his head to one side, saw Dave standing in the doorway, looking down on him.

"I just want to tell you that we mean business. If the old jasper over there don't know it by now, you'd better go and tell him."

"I've told him."

"Tell him again. No—I'll tell him myself."

Dave clumped away.

The outlaws had their dinner at twelve, but Tancred went without his. At one o'clock he got out the harness and got his six-horse team ready. A cloud of dust to the north told him that the stage was on time.

They saddled up their mounts, tied them to the top pole of the corral. Jethro climbed to the top of the corral and studied the approaching stage.

He climbed to the ground.

"Ten minutes."

Vesser came out of the stage station. His revolver was in his hand.

"Look!" said the squat man.

"Be damned!" exclaimed Dave.

Tancred cried out, "Throw down the gun . . . please?"

Vesser came toward the corral. Jethro edged over to the right, Dave to the left and Dick remained in the middle. Vesser was still seventy or seventy-five feet away and he thrust out his gun as he walked and fired.

The bullet missed Dick by three feet.

Dick's first bullet didn't miss. Nor did Jethro's or Dave's. Vesser's gun went off once more but the bullet went toward the sky. Laura was rushing out of the house, screaming and sobbing . . . and Dave walked toward her fallen father and put another bullet into him.

By that time, Tancred was in the shed. He swept aside the hay from the manger, scooped out the carpetbag and tore it open. He plunged in his hand and brought out a holster wrapped about a gun.

He did not bother with the holster. Uncoiling it, he gripped the naked Navy Colt and stepped to the door of the shed.

His eyes went straight ahead, saw Laura on her knees, sobbing over her father.

Dave was the first to see him. Shock hit him as he saw the gun in Tancred's hand. Dick, looking at Dave's face, wheeled.

Tancred fired at Dave. The distance was seventy-five feet, but Tancred's bullet caught Dave square in the forehead. Then Tancred pivoted and fired at Dick, once. Jethro let out a scream of sheer terror. He fired, but the thing he had just seen, deprived him of . . . everything. His bullet went completely wild.

Tancred shot him down.

He did not look at the fallen men again. He went forward to Laura, who had rocked back to her heels. Her tear-stained face was taut, her eyes wild.

"I shouldn't have waited," he said. "But I . . . I couldn't . . . I couldn't fire the gun."

"Who are you?" whispered Laura in awe.

"My name," said Tancred, "is Wes Tancred. . . ."

"Tancred!" cried Laura, in shock. "The man who . . ."

"The man who killed Sam Older. Now, you know. . . ."

She continued to stare at him, hunkered back on her heels. Tancred turned and walked back into the shed. He put the revolver into the holster, wrapped the belt about it and put it back into the carpetbag. Carrying the bag he went out and picked the best of the outlaws' horses. He hooked the handle of the carpetbag over the saddle horn and swung up onto the horse.

When he turned it away from the corral, Laura was coming toward him.

"Wait, Wes, wait! You can't go now."

"I've got to," said Tancred. "The stage will be here in a few moments. Go with them."

"You can't go, Wes. Please. I'll go with you. I—I don't care who you are or what you've done. . . ."

"It's no use, Laura. I'm sorry. It—it wouldn't be fair to you. Wes Tancred is dead. He died nine years ago when he killed Sam Older. John Bailey is only a ghost. And a ghost is . . . nothing!"

He rode away from her and she watched him go.

Chapter 4

Abilene had its brief day as a boom town when the Texas cattle herds came to it, up the Chisholm Trail. Then the rails crept westward and Wichita had its day of glory and Ellsworth and Dodge City.

And then it was Sage City.

When Wes Tancred stepped off the Kansas & Western train at Sage City he looked to the north of the tracks and saw homes and shaded streets, a few stores; a town that looked like so many of the newer Midwestern villages. Then he turned and looked down South Street and saw a dozen saloons and gambling halls, a score of stores and shops, a street lined with hitchrails and churning with horses and wagons and humanity.

Trail town.

He stepped off the depot platform and started down the street. A cowboy came charging up the middle of the street on a cow pony, whooping and shooting at the sky and nobody on the wooden sidewalks paid any attention to him. A bleary-eyed man in Levi's, run-down-at-the-heels boots and huge Stetson reeled out of a saloon and took a header under the hitchrail into the dust of the street.

Tancred passed *Fugger's Mercantile Store,* the *Long-horn Saloon,* the *Sage City Hardware Company, McCoy's Saloon & Gambling Hall,* the *Boston Store,* the *Texas Saloon* and then he came to a two-story building with the sign, *Sage City Hotel.*

Tancred went into the hotel and a pimply-faced youth of about nineteen, who was polishing a brass spittoon behind the little counter, shoved a register toward him.

Tancred wrote the name John Bailey in the book, hesitated, then added, St. Louis, Mo. The youthful clerk studied the inscription.

"Two dollars. If you're going to stay a whole week it's ten."

"I'll take it by the day," Tancred said. He took out two dollars and dropped them on the counter.

The clerk studied a key rack and took down a key. "Number five. That's right in front."

Out on the street a gun banged twice. Tancred inclined his head.

"Doesn't Sage City have a marshal?"

"Oh, sure, we got a marshal and two deputies. We got a lot of laws around here."

Tancred picked up his carpetbag and valise and climbed the stairs to the second floor. He found that Room Number Five was the last door on the right. It was about nine by twelve in size, contained a cot, a washstand with a pitcher and bowl and a straight-backed chair. A row of nails on the wall served in lieu of a closet. The walls were rough wood, but painted with a single coat of paint.

Tancred took off his coat, poured water into the washbowl and washed his face and hands. Then he opened his valise and took out a clean shirt. He rolled up his soiled shirt and put it into the carpetbag. His hand touched a bundle at the bottom of the bag. He hesitated, then unrolled the bundle and exposed a well-oiled Navy Colt revolver. His face became bleak as he tested the gun, spinning the cylinder, trying the hammer and trigger, making sure that the cylinder was turned to the one empty chamber. Finally he re-wrapped the gun and put it back into the bottom of the carpetbag.

He put on his coat and descended to the lobby.

A sleepy-eyed man of about forty had taken over the desk. He was studying the ledger and did not seem very happy about it. "You're Mr. Bailey, the new guest?" he asked as Tancred came up.

"That's right."

"I'm the proprietor, Joe Handy. The boy gave you Number Five. I was saving that for Mr. Smith. Hong Kong Smith. He's checking in tomorrow." He looked inquiringly at Tancred. "Expect to stay here long?"

"That depends."

Joe Handy nodded. "Drummer?"

Tancred shook his head. "Can you tell me where I can find the *Sage City Star?*"

"Luke Miller's newspaper?" The hotel man frowned.

"You aren't, uh, going to work for Luke, are you?"

"That depends on him. He advertised for a man and —I'm looking for a job." Tancred looked shrewdly at Handy. "Anything wrong about that?"

"N-no, it isn't that. Only, well, Luke's got some of the people down on him. Not, me, though," Handy added hastily. "It's just, well, Luke's kinda outspoken."

"A lot of newspapermen are."

"It don't make them popular, though." The hotel man drummed his fingers on the desk. "Luke's place is right around the corner on River Street. You can't miss it."

"Thanks."

Tancred nodded and left the hotel. Outside he walked to the cross street and turned right. Then he saw the sign: *Sage City Star, Luke Miller, Editor and Publisher. Job Printing.*

Inside was a desk, heaped with newspapers and papers, and in the rear, a large two-page newspaper press, two job presses and several typecases. An elderly man was setting up type and Luke Miller was fussing and fuming over the newspaper press, his face dabbed with ink, his hands black to the elbows with the stuff.

He looked up as Tancred entered.

"Be with you in a minute," he called.

Tancred walked back to him. "My weekly repair job," Miller complained. "This newfangled machinery they been making since the war just don't stand up. Always something going out of whack." He picked up a benzine-soaked rag and wiped his hands. "What can I do for you?"

"You had an ad in the *Publisher's Auxiliary*," Tancred said.

Miller's eyes lit up. "You're a printer?" He thrust out his blackened hand and grabbed Tancred's. "Never thought a man'd come out here to this jumping off place!"

"You're here."

"That's because I haven't got any sense. How much pay do you want?"

"I'll leave that to you."

Miller winced. "Don't do that. I'll take advantage of you." He strode past Tancred to the littered desk and scooped up a copy of the *Sage City Star*. "Here's last week's sheet. Thirty dollars' worth of advertising in it."

"That doesn't seem like much."

"It isn't." Miller paused. "I may as well tell you the

rest. There's a boycott against me in town among the merchants. They don't like the things I write for the paper."

He exclaimed and held up his index finger. Tancred heard a burst of gunfire on South Street. "That's what I'm fighting."

"You mean there are people who approve of that?"

"Jacob Fugger approves of it. He approves of anything the Texas men want to do."

"I saw Fugger's name on a store," Tancred said.

"There's a lot of stores you didn't see it on," Miller exclaimed. "Places he owns or has an interest in. The bank for instance." Miller bared his teeth. "Fugger's our local tycoon, in addition to being the mayor of Sage City. In other words, he runs the town. That's why I'm carrying thirty dollars' worth of advertising instead of three hundred. And it's also the reason I'm doing twenty to thirty dollars' worth of job printing a week instead of a couple of hundred. And that's why I can't pay you more than twenty dollars a week."

"I don't see how you can afford to pay even that much."

"Well, there's some money comes in from subscriptions and sales of the paper. The people like the Star, even if the businessmen don't." Miller looked at Tancred. "I've told you the worst. Do you want the job?"

"When do I start?"

"Right now, if you want to. We go to press tomorrow and we're behind. Mose . . . !" He turned and called to the elderly printer. "Mose, this is our new man, Mr.—?"

"John Bailey," Tancred said, quickly.

"John Bailey, Mose Hudkins."

Tancred shook hands with the old printer. "A cousin of mine has a shop back in Sterling, Illinois," Hudkins said. "He had a man named Bailey working for him a couple of years ago. Young fellow."

Tancred shook his head. "I never worked in Sterling."

"This man's name wasn't John, though, as I recall. Thought you might be related to him."

"I have no relatives in the printing business."

"I've got one," declared Miller. "My wife. She's been helping out on Tuesdays and Wednesdays. That reminds me, Bailey, you'll need a place to live."

"I checked in at the hotel."

"You won't get much sleep there. Not with the Texas men in town."

"The proprietor wants my room tomorrow. A special guest. Mr. Hong Kong Smith."

Miller grimaced. "The grand Mr. Hong Kong Smith! So, he's to be with us again. One of the leading citizens of Texas. Brings up a half-dozen herds every season, but he doesn't come with the herds himself. Too rough for him. Takes a boat to New Orleans, then a steamer up the river to St. Louis and then from St. Louis to here by way of the Kansas & Western. Mr. Smith's a very popular man—in Texas. He brings northern gold to Texas. Pays five dollars per steer on the hoof and sells it here in Kansas for thirty dollars."

"Odd name for a cattleman," Tancred observed.

"He was a clipper-ship man before the war. Made a pile trading with the Orient. At least that's the story he's spread about himself. My personal opinion is that he made his money as a slaver, running slaves from Africa." Miller drew in a deep breath. "But he's quite a man, Mr. Hong Kong Smith. And so are the Texas men who bring his herds up the trail."

"If you have no objection," Tancred said, "I could put up a cot back here in the shop."

"I've no objection. I only wish I could put you up at the house. But we just don't have the room. And during the cattle season it's almost impossible to find a place in town. I'll stop in at the Boston Store this afternoon and have them send over a cot and some blankets."

"That'll be fine, Mr. Miller. And now I might as well get familiar with the typecases."

"You'll find some copy on the hooks. The big one's got straight matter, the small one ads."

Tancred took off his coat, hung it on a nail and walked to the typecases. Without hesitation he reached for a sheet of copy on the smaller hook. Miller, watching covertly, smiled.

An hour later, when Mose came to him, the newspaper owner said, softly, "I think we've got a printer, Mose!"

Chapter 5

Tancred left the newspaper shop a little after six and went to his hotel where he washed up. Coming down from his room he stood in front of the hotel a few minutes, then crossed the street to the Bon Ton restaurant and had a supper of fried steak and potatoes.

When he came out the street was more crowded than it had been during the day. More horses were tied to the hitchrails. He crossed to the hotel and went up to his room. It was stifling in the confined place. He opened a window and the street noises assailed his ears.

Up the street a cowboy yipped and emptied his revolver. The shooting was repeated by someone at the other end of the street. There would be no early sleep for the guests of the hotel.

He descended again to the hotel lobby and standing by the door watched the traffic on the street for a few minutes. Finally he went out. He strolled to the depot, stood there for a while, then returned to the hotel.

The tinkly music of a piano from the Texas Saloon next door caught his attention and on a sudden impulse he turned and went to the saloon and entered.

Although it was scarcely seven o'clock the place was crowded. A bar ran down half of one side of the room and the entire front section was given over to tables and various games of chance. A crowd stood around the main faro table.

At the rear of the room was a small raised platform on which stood a piano. A bleary-eyed oldster sat at the instrument, playing a fast tune.

Tancred found a spot at the far end of the bar and ordered a glass of beer from one of the four bartenders. He put the glass to his mouth and the piano player suddenly switched from his fast piece to a ballad.

Tancred drank some of his beer, but he did not taste

it. A girl began singing and he turned and looked toward the stage at the rear of the room.

She was in her early twenties, and wore a low-cut velvet gown. A beautiful girl with a fine voice. She sang her song and she sang it well. Tancred had heard it so many times during the past nine years but he had seldom heard it sung better.

The ballad was the saga of Sam Older and the man who had killed him. The words were mawkish and there was little truth in them. They told of a bold man who had been forced to become an outlaw, a man who stole and yes, who killed, but who did those things only from lofty motives. His wealth he gave to the poor, his gun was used only on behalf of the persecuted and the down-trodden. He righted wrongs. He was a fine man, Sam Older, and his men were loyal and true . . . save for the cowardly Wes, the youth befriended by Sam Older, who betrayed him for gold and laid him low by a shot in the back. The ballad of Sam Older ended with the verse, but the chorus, repeated, was the saga of Wes Tancred . . . Tancred, the outcast, the man shunned by all men righteous and true . . . the coward . . . the traitor, the murderer who would meet his end alone and cravenly and mourned by none.

Tancred had heard the song a thousand times, in cow camps, in railroad camps, deep down in mines. In towns and villages, in theaters and in saloons, on the streets and in houses.

He heard it now in the Texas Saloon, in Sage City, Kansas.

The girl finished the song and the applause was thunderous. She left the stage and was pawed by a Texas man or two, but she coolly brushed away their hands and worked her way through the crowds to the bar.

Tancred saw now that she had gorgeously golden hair, a smooth, fine complexion . . . and tired eyes of the palest blue.

She said to Tancred, "Your beer's gone flat. Have another." She signalled to the bartender. "Give the gentleman a fresh glass, Chippy."

Tancred nodded. "Can I buy you a drink?"

"You don't have to. I own the place."

"I'll still buy you a drink."

"Why? You didn't like my singing."

"I thought you sang very well."

"I was looking at you when I finished. You were the only man in ths place who didn't applaud."

"I've heard the song before."

"Who hasn't? But they still want it." She looked at him thoughtfully. "You're not a Texas man."

He shook his head.

"Gambler?"

"Printer."

"You work for Luke Miller?"

"You said that just like the hotel man," Tancred said.

"Miller's trying to put us out of business."

"He's a newspaperman and a newspaperman's job is to print the truth."

"What's the truth? Luke Miller wants to clean up Sage City. From his point of view that's probably the right thing. But I run a saloon. So do a lot of other people in this town. The saloon-keepers want an everything-goes town." The proprietress of the Texas Saloon smiled at Tancred. "You see, it all depends on where you stand. What's good for one isn't good for another. By the way, my name is Lily Leeds. It used to be Maggie Leeds, but Lily sounds better than Maggie."

"My name is Bailey."

A lean, sardonic-eyed man at Tancred's left turned. "Bailey, did you say? He wore a badge on which was the word, "Marshal."

"Mr. Bailey," Lily Leeds said, "Marshal Lee Kinnaird."

The marshal nodded, his eyes full on Tancred's face. "That wouldn't be John Bailey?"

"Why, yes."

"You worked for the stage line at Turkey Crossing?" Tancred hesitated, then nodded.

Marshal Kinnaird gave a low whistle. "I got a Wichita paper yesterday. It had a piece about you."

"Is it true?" exclaimed Lily. She made a small gesture. "People have been talking about it."

"I haven't seen the paper, so I don't know what it said."

The marshal pursed up his lips. "It said that three men killed Vesser, the station agent. It also said that the horse wrangler then killed said three men." The marshal paused. "With exactly three shots."

"That's shooting," said Lily. "And you're a printer now?"

"I've been a printer for quite a few years," said Tancred. "The job at Turkey Crossing was only a temporary one. Until last week I hadn't fired a gun in quite a while."

"Yet you downed three bad men with just three bullets," said the marshal.

"It was just one of those things."

"Was it?" Kinnaird frowned. "Bailey, John Bailey. I never heard the name before."

"Mr. Bailey," Lily said. "I'll buy you a drink."

"And I'll drink with you," declared Kinnaird.

Lily signalled to the bartender. "Chippy, drinks for Mr. Bailey and the marshal."

"A beer," said Tancred.

"Beer!" cried Lily.

Kinnaird smiled crookedly. "I think *I'll* have a beer."

Lily shook her head. "I won't. Beer's fattening."

The bartender brought the beers for the men and a small glass for Lily. It contained a liquid that looked like whiskey but was actually cold tea.

The marshal raised his glass to Tancred. "John Bailey." He quaffed some of the beer. "A printer."

"Who works for Luke Miller," Lily added.

Kinnaird grinned. "I'm still drinking."

"You're against Miller?" Tancred asked.

"The mayor hired me and he can fire me. And who do you think is the mayor of Sage City?"

"Jacob Fugger," said Lily.

The marshal looked covertly over his shoulder. "Jacob Fugger, who owns Sage City."

"He doesn't own the Texas Saloon," said Lily.

"But you're not on Miller's side," Tancred reminded.

"I'm on *my* side," Lily retorted.

Chapter 6

Jacob Fugger added the last digit in the column of figures and wrote down the sum. He looked at it a moment and pleasure seeped through him. The gross volume of his store had been very good, the lumberyard had sold an unusually large amount of lumber, the bank deposits were at an all-time high and two of three businesses that had rather substantial loans had made their payments and the third had met its interest payment. The hideyard had two hundred thousand buffalo hides ready for shipment and there were four carloads of buffalo bones on the siding and enough bones to fill up three more cars.

Business was good and Hong Kong Smith's first trail herd of the season had arrived. Much of the money that would be paid to Hong Kong Smith would find its way eventually into Fugger's hands, through one or another of the channels that Fugger owned or controlled.

There was only one fly in Jacob Fugger's ointment and he thought about it as he scanned the figures that told of the success of his numerous enterprises. Ten years ago, at the age of 45, Fugger had been a clerk in a dry-goods store, back in a small Ohio town. All he had had to look forward to was another twenty or thirty years of drudgery, the accumulation of a paltry few dollars every year by personal scrimping.

He was a withering, aging man at 45, without hope. And then, one night, there had been a burglary at the store. Five hundred dollars in cash had been taken. Fugger was not suspected of course. He had been at the store too long.

Yet a month later, Fugger left Ohio. He took the cars to St. Louis and then to Kansas City. He arrived there just as the first shipment of Texas longhorns was received at the stockyards. He learned that these steers had been driven north from Texas to the new railroad that was being built across the state of Kansas. The tracks were then at a little place called Abilene.

Fugger went to Abilene and for five hundred dollars bought a quarter interest in a small store. A year later he was the sole owner of the store in Abilene and since the railroad had gone on another hundred miles to the west, Fugger established a new store at the terminus.

Five years and five stores later, Fugger arrived in Sage City. From here the railroad headed due west, into Colorado. This was the closest it would ever come to Texas and here, Fugger decided, would be his last stand. Eventually, someone would build a railroad down into Texas, but that would not be for another few years and by that time Fugger would not care.

Heavy feet clomped up the stairs to the porch over the rear of the big store where Fugger did his bookkeeping. The huge head of Bill Bleek appeared.

"Van Meter's here," Bleek said, shortly.

"Send him up. There'll be some others, too. Let them in as they come, but don't let anyone else in the store."

"Just the usual?"

Fugger nodded. Bill Bleek stomped down the stairs and after a moment Van Meter came up. He was about forty, a smooth-looking man in Prince Albert and well-brushed derby.

"It's seven o'clock," he said.

"The rest'll be here in a few minutes."

"What's it about?"

"Hong Kong Smith's arriving in town tomorrow."

Van Meter nodded. "I thought he was due. His trail herd arrived yesterday."

"You've the money ready for him?"

"We've enough."

"He'll be paying his men. You know what that means?"

Van Meter grimaced. "We won't be getting much sleep. Unless . . ."

Fugger shook his head. "The money might as well stay in Sage City."

"It usually does."

"It won't if Luke Miller has much more to say. Smith can drive his herds to Ellsworth or to Dodge without much more trouble. And if he goes to one of the other towns, the Texas men will follow him."

A step sounded on the steps leading up to the veranda

and Fugger made a small gesture to the banker. The broad, placid face of Morgan Holt, the hardware man, appeared.

"Evening, Jacob," he said. "Hello, Horace."

"Thanks for stopping by, Morgan."

"It's no trouble. We're having a late dinner."

More steps creaked on the stairs and two men came up, Packard, the owner of the Boston Store and McCoy, who owned the biggest saloon in Sage City and had money in one or two other enterprises. Close on their heels came a pudgy man of about fifty, who wore a floppy black hat, a soiled white shirt and a long string tie. This was Judge Olsen.

Fugger then rolled out the ball. "I called you here to talk about Luke Miller."

"That's what I thought it would be about," remarked Packard.

Fugger regarded Packard without pleasure. "Perhaps I shouldn't have asked you."

Packard shrugged. "I can leave."

"And have you say we're all scheming behind your back?" Fugger snapped. "Stay. I'll say what I've got to say. It's been a long winter and we've got a short season ahead of us. Four good months, maybe five. We're businessmen and we've got to make the most of those few months."

"Amen!" exclaimed McCoy, the saloon man.

"The point is," continued Fugger, "what are we going to do about Luke Miller and his newspaper?"

"I don't see that we can do anything," declared Packard. "Luke's got a right to put out a newspaper."

"He hasn't got a right to slander anyone," retorted Fugger. He pointed to the judge. "Isn't that so, Judge?"

Judge Olsen cleared his throat. "A newspaper can't libel a citizen."

"Is the truth libel?" asked Packard.

"I think," said Jacob Fugger, "we can do without you."

Packard drew a deep breath and let it out heavily. "I think you can. But before I go, I want to say a few words."

"You don't have to."

"But I'm going to. I came to Sage City four years ago because I was looking for a new town, where I could settle down with my family. I brought money to this

town and I've made money here. I've built a home
and for five months of the year my wife is afraid to
step out of the house and I can't let my children on the
street, for the fear of a wild cowboy riding or shooting
them down. Sure, we've made money from the Texas
men, but we could have made it without them. The land
that the Texas cattle trample with their hoofs is the
finest farming land in the state. Farmers have come in
and more would come if they could settle down in peace.
The future of this area, as I see it, is not with the Texas
cattle drovers, but with Kansas farmers. . . ."

"Are you finished, Mr. Packard?" Fugger asked coldly.

"No, but I can see that I'm wasting my breath. Good
evening, gentlemen."

Packard stepped to the stairs and descended them.

"And now," said Fugger, heavily, "we'll get on with the
business. Judge, how much did you make on fines last
year?"

Judge Olsen squirmed. "Barely enough to get by."

"You made," said Fugger, "six thousand, two hundred
and forty-five dollars. Most of that money came from the
Texas men."

"I fine them as they come. The marshal and his men
arrest them."

"They're not going to arrest as many men this year."

The judge showed great displeasure. "But my office is
a fee office. There's no salary connected with it."

"We'll have to make other arrangements. The marshal
and his men can't arrest people for every trivial violation
of the city ordinances. A man has a right to enjoy himself
in our town. We'll let that word get around among the
Texas men and we'll have more herds coming here than
all the other trail towns put together."

"And what about Luke Miller?" put in McCoy, the
saloon man.

"He's got to be taken care of."

"How?"

"Leave that to me."

Morgan Holt cleared his throat. "Within reason, Jacob.
You're the mayor and we're the city council, but remember
we've got an election in a little while. And Miller's paper
gets to the people who vote."

"It may not be reaching them by election day."

Chapter 7

The noise of the Texas men carousing and brawling went on long after midnight and it was two o'clock before Wes Tancred fell asleep, but he was up shortly after six and by seven o'clock he was having his breakfast.

The waitress looked at him curiously but she waited until he was eating before she spoke of what was on her mind.

"You're John Bailey, aren't you?" she asked then.

"Why, yes."

"Is it true that you backed down Wyatt Earp, in Dodge?"

"Who's been saying that?" exclaimed Tancred. "I've never even met Wyatt Earp."

"Why, everybody in town's talking about you. How you wiped out that band of outlaws, singlehanded."

Tancred groaned. He hastened through his breakfast and went down to the print shop. As early as it was both Hudkins and Miller were already on the job. And they had heard about John Bailey. Miller had a copy of the Wichita paper in his hand as Tancred came into the shop.

"This true?" he asked.

Tancred took the paper from Miller and skimmed through the piece about the Turkey Crossing affair. It was a lurid account, as told by the driver of the stagecoach and the passengers who hadn't actually seen what happened, but who had seen the evidence and had received additional information from the hysterical surviving witness whose father had been murdered by the men whom retribution had overtaken so swiftly.

Tancred handed back the paper to Miller. "They didn't get this from me."

"But it's essentially true?"

"I worked for Vesser, the agent at Turkey Crossing until last week."

"You were a hostler?"

33

"I wanted to work outdoors for a while."

"Sick?"

"I was. I'm better now."

Miller looked thoughtfully at Tancred. "Is John Bailey your real name?"

"Does it matter?"

"You're a printer. As long as you can set up type your name could be Benjamin Franklin. Or Johannes Gutenberg. Only—"

"Yes?"

"Nothing." Miller got up and nodded to the rear of the shop. "I had your cot set up. Why don't you get your things from the hotel and move in?"

"I believe I will. They want my room for Hong Kong Smith."

Tancred nodded and left the print shop. He rounded the corner and strode to the hotel. As he reached it he remembered that there had been no soap in the hotel and decided to buy some. He was about to cross to the Boston Store, then saw the sign of the Fugger Store.

He was curious to see Jacob Fugger, who loomed so importantly in the affairs of Sage City.

He entered the store, saw a middle-aged woman behind the notions counter. He swerved away from it to go to the rear where he saw shelves of groceries. And then he stopped. Behind a counter containing clothing was Laura Vesser. He moved toward her.

"I didn't expect to see you here."

Her eyes were steady, but impassive. "I've been here for a week."

"Why Sage City? I thought you'd be going east."

"I've nothing in the east." She paused. "I heard you were here."

"I'm working at the print shop. I was a printer before I came to Turkey Crossing."

"It's a job. Like this one." The casual indifference in her tone caused him to look at her sharply. She said, "Is there anything I can do for you?"

He shook his head.

"If you need anything, Mr. Bailey," she went on, emphasizing the name, "Fugger's Store has it. Everything from shirts to shoes, groceries to—guns."

He nodded and walked stiffly out of the store.

Joe Handy was talking to a lean, swarthy man in the

hotel when Tancred entered. They stopped talking and both watched him as he climbed the stairs to the second floor.

It took him only a moment to get his things together and he descended to the lobby. The swarthy man was still at the desk.

"You can have the room now for Hong Kong Smith," Tancred told Handy.

The hotel man grimaced. "I can fix you up with another room, Mr. Bailey. Something just about as good."

"I've found another place."

"Sorry to hear that. I'd been proud to have you stay. Oh—Mr. Bailey, shake hands with Chuck Gorey. Chuck's one of our deputy marshals."

Gorey's hand was flaccid and clammy, entirely free of calluses. It was the hand of a professional gunfighter.

"How're you?" Tancred said.

"Good to find," replied Gorey, his pale eyes regarding Tancred appraisingly. "So you're the lad wiped out those bad men over at Turkey Crossing?"

Tancred made an impatient gesture. "Time I got to work."

"I'll walk with you a piece."

Tancred was not pleased but the deputy fell in beside him. As they came out of the hotel Gorey said softly, "I didn't think Miller had it in him."

Tancred looked at him sidewards. "What do you mean?"

Gorey grinned. "They *have* been pushing him around. Can't say's I blame him for sending for you."

"I'm working for Mr. Miller as a printer," Tancred said, coldly.

"Sure, sure."

"That's the truth, Gorey."

"Chuck, to my friends."

"Luke Miller hired me—as a printer—before he even heard of the Turkey Crossing thing."

"All *right*, Bailey."

A gun banged up the street. It was followed by a veritable thunder of gunfire, punctuated by the whooping of a score of men.

"The train's in," said the deputy. "That'll be Mr. Hong Kong Smith's boys welcoming him." He chuckled. "Now the old town will liven up." He gave Tancred a half

salute and turning headed back up the street toward the
depot.

Tancred continued on to the print shop. Packard, the
owner of the Boston Store, was leaving as he came in. A
frown creased Luke Miller's forehead.

"Fugger's declared war," Miller said. "He called a meeting of the city council last night. From now on Sage
City's an open town. Packard tried to talk against it and
Fugger ran him out of the meeting." He winced as the
thunder of gunfire on South Street came over.

"Hong Kong Smith's arrived in town," Tancred said.

Chapter 8

Hong Kong Smith towered well above six feet six in his high-heeled boots. He was about forty-five, tipped the scales at two hundred and seventy and down in Texas they said that you could hear his voice about as far as the ball of a needle gun would carry.

He came out of the Sage City Bank, his huge hat filled with coin. The score of Texas men who had brought the first trail herd of the season up the Chisholm Trail let out a roar. About a dozen fired their guns.

Hong Kong Smith shouted the Texas men into silence. "Come and get it, you dirty, mangy sons of Texas!"

He led the way across the street to the Texas Saloon, set the hatful of money on the bar. "Whiskey!" he roared. "Bring whiskey!"

A bartender brought a bottle and a couple of small glasses. "I said whiskey!" boomed Hong Kong, "and you call those glasses for men? These are Texas men!" He brushed the whiskey glasses off the bar.

A second bartender hurried up with two more bottles of whiskey and a water tumbler.

"That's more like it," growled Smith. He poured out a tumblerful of whiskey. "Let's do this businesslike. Who's first, beginning with A?"

"Adams," cried out a cowboy. "That's me."

"Adams," said Smith. "Forty-two dollars." He fished around in the hat, brought out four gold eagles and added two silver dollars. "Here's your money and—" He picked up the tumblerful of whiskey. "And this!"

The Texas man winced but drained off the huge amount of whiskey. He sputtered and choked and Hong Kong Smith slapped him on the back.

"Next man," he sang out.

"Baker," cried a Texas man.

Smith refilled the big glass of whiskey and forced it

on the man called Baker. He paid him his forty-two dollars, booming out, "You don't spend any of that. Not today, you don't. Today Hong Kong Smith pays the bill."

"Hooray for Hong Kong Smith!" yelled a man and the
ovation was taken up by every Texas man in the Texas
Saloon.

Lily Leeds came out of her office. Hong Kong Smith
whooped when he saw her. "Lily, my girl, you get prettier
every time I see you."

"Oh, it's you again," said Lily in disgust. "I should have
known."

"That's what I like about you—your sense of humor,"
roared Smith. He swooped Lily into his arms. "Give us
a kiss, Lily girl."

She slapped his face, but the big man crushed her to
him and forced her face up. He kissed her resoundingly
and when he released her, she rocked his head with hard
slaps. But Smith was impervious.

"Whiskey," he roared. "Whiskey for everyone in the
house. Hong Kong Smith pays the bill."

A half hour later every Texas man in Sage City was
drunk. They smashed four tables in the Texas Saloon and
broke the back-bar mirror. Then, with Smith in the lead,
they moved to McCoy's Saloon and pretty well wrecked
that.

By noon a half dozen of Hong Kong's men had fallen by
the wayside, but the rest carried on. The only difference
was that they were no longer in one group. A few men
were bucking the faro games about town, some kept on
with the drinking but had drifted to various saloons, one or
two here, two or three there.

Marshal Kinnaird and his deputies, acting upon instructions from Mayor Fugger, discreetly stayed out of the
way of the brawling men from Texas.

Chapter 9

Shortly before twelve Luke Miller brought a couple of sheets of copy paper to Tancred.

"Read that."

Tancred's eyes skimmed over the story, which bore the head, *The Devil and Texas Rule Sage City*. It was a strong piece, Luke Miller pulled no punches. Jacob Fugger, he said, catered to the lawless Texas men, because they were making him rich. The Kansas & Western Railroad paid him one dollar for every Texas steer that was shipped from Sage City. Through his bank, Fugger saw that the Texas Cowboys received hard cash in Sage City, instead of at their homes in Texas. And through his stores and saloons, Fugger saw that that money was taken away from them.

Fugger owned Sage City and he pulled the strings the way they suited him. Right now it suited him to let the Texas men run wild and the citizens of Sage City could expect only violence and bloodshed. The law would not curb the Texas men because Fugger owned the law.

Right now, if you were a Texas man and it suited you to insult a Sage City woman on the streets, that was perfectly all right. If you felt like breaking a few windows about town, no one would punish you for indulging your whim. Or, maybe your fancy ran to riding your horse on the sidewalks or into stores. Go right ahead, no one would stop you. As long as you paid your tribute to Jacob Fugger.

"What do you think?" Miller asked when Tancred finished reading the editorial.

"I'll set it up."

"After lunch will be all right . . . Fugger will never forgive me for that."

"He's not exactly your friend right now."

"Now he'll really put on the screws. But there's an

election in a month. My only chance is to try to rouse the local voters enough so they'll vote Fugger and his clique out of office. If they don't, I'm through in Sage City."

Tancred washed his hands and left the shop. He walked to South Street and crossed to go to the Bon Ton Café. As he walked along he heard angry yelling in McCoy's Saloon, then two quick shots.

A man catapulted out of McCoy's and made for the horses at the hitchrail. He mounted one and galloped up the street, emptying his revolver at the blue sky.

Tancred entered the Bon Ton Café and seated himself on a stool beside a giant of a man. Bill Bleek.

The waitress came up. "Hello, Mr. Bailey. What'll it be?"

"What've you got besides steak?"

"Steak."

"Then make it steak."

The girl went off and Bill Bleek turned to Bailey.

"Like Sage City?" he asked.

"A town's a town."

"Most people don't like Sage City," Bleek went on. "Too rough. Stranger in town got his teeth knocked out last week. Some broken ribs, too."

"I mind my own business," Tancred said.

"Like at Turkey Crossing?"

Tancred looked sharply at Bleek. "Who knocked out this stranger's teeth?"

"Me."

"That's what I thought."

"Bill Bleek is the handle. I work for Jacob Fugger."

"And I work for Luke Miller."

"That's why I'm talking to you. You got a good set of teeth and there ain't no dentist in Sage City."

"I won't be needing one," Tancred said with restraint. "Miller's paying me as a printer."

Lee Kinnaird came in from the street. He frowned as he saw Bill Bleek, but he quickly erased the frown.

"One of your Texas friends just killed a faro dealer over at McCoy's."

"So?"

"I thought Fugger might want to know."

"You're the marshal, ain't you?"

"Uh-uh, not any more I'm not."

"Since when?"

"Since about two minutes ago."

"Jacob know?"

"I'm telling you to tell him."

"Tell him yourself."

Bill Bleek looked at Kinnaird thoughtfully. Then he got up from the stool. "Well, since you ain't the marshal any more . . ."

He suddenly hit Kinnaird in the face, a savage back-handed blow that knocked Kinnaird backward over a table.

Kinnaird got to his feet, blood dribbling from his mouth. "Where's your gun, Bleek?" he cried.

"You know I don't carry one."

"Then get one."

Bleek regarded Kinnaird impassively. "So you can gun me? Uh-uh, I'll fight any man living with my fists, but I'm no gunslinger." His eye flickered to Tancred. "Hear that, Bailey?"

"I heard it."

"Lay a hand on me again, Bleek," said Kinnaird ominously, "and gun or no gun, I'll kill you."

"Get out of town, Kinnaird," sneered Bleek. "If you ain't working for Jacob, you're against him."

Bleek swaggered out of the restaurant. Kinnaird dabbed at the blood on his chin. "You saw that, Bailey," he said. "What do you think of it now?"

"When I get back to the shop, I'm setting up an editorial that I think expresses it very well." Tancred paused. "The title is, *'The Devil and Texas Rule Sage City.'*"

"Does the piece give the name of the Devil?"

"Jacob Fugger."

Kinnaird whistled. "I think I quit my job just in time!"

"What about the deputies?"

"Slattery's a Texas man himself. Only he can't go back to Texas because a couple of sheriffs want him. Chuck Gorey . . ." Kinnaird shrugged. "He says he talked to you this morning."

"Yes, he did."

"Is it true, what he said?"

"No."

"Sorry to hear that. I was kind of wishing it was true. But the Turkey Crossing thing—*that* was true?" The ex-marshal watched Tancred's face closely. "I'm not the marshal any more."

"They killed Vesser, the agent, in cold blood. I—I caught them by surprise."

"Three against one?"

"They weren't expecting it."

Kinnaird shook his head slowly. "I have a strange notion, Bailey—that I'd rather fight Bill Bleek's fists than go up against you with a gun."

"I'm a printer, Kinnaird," Tancred said doggedly.

Jacob Fugger entered McCoy's Saloon and bore down on Hong Kong Smith who was leaning heavily against the bar. Fugger did not glance in the direction of the faro table, where the dealer lay on the floor.

"Smith," Fugger snapped. "What's the name of the cowboy who shot Thatcher?"

"Who's Thatcher?" Hong Kong Smith asked thickly.

"The faro dealer." Fugger gestured toward the table.

"Oh, him," said Smith. "Never saw him before."

"He's Thatcher," gritted Fugger. "I asked you the name of the cowboy who killed him."

Smith became drunkenly cagy. "What do you wanna know for?"

"So he can be arrested."

"Nobody's going to arrest any of my men."

"This man's going to be. He's got to be, Smith. He killed a man."

"Self-defense. It was self-defense."

"All right, then he'll be acquitted. But he's got to stand trial. I go along with you, Smith. I go along with you pretty far, but I can't go along with you on killing. He's got to stand trial."

But Hong Kong Smith still shook his head. "Harpending won't stand trial, Fugger. He's a high-spirited man and he won't—"

"Is this Manny Harpending you're talking about?"

"One of the best boys in Texas, when he isn't loaded with whiskey. That's what got him in trouble at home."

"The story is that he killed two men in Texas," snapped Fugger. "And what about that marshal over in Newton, two years ago?"

"He tried to buffalo Manny and Manny's a high-spirited boy—"

"You said that. But I still say he's got to give himself up."

"He won't."

"Then he's got to be arrested." Fugger held up his hand. "There were witnesses—*you* were a witness, weren't you?"

"Yes, of course. I saw Manny—"

"All right, you saw the whole thing. You saw Harpending draw in self-defense . . ."

Hong Kong Smith suddenly guffawed. "Yes sir, I sure saw it. Manny shot the dealer in self-defense, that's what he did."

A gun banged outside the saloon and the batwing doors burst open. Chuck Gorey, gun in hand, plunged into the room. He saw Jacob Fugger and came over.

"Here you are, Mr. Fugger. What're the rules if a Texas man tries to kill you?"

A bullet tore through the flimsy batwing doors and crashed into the bar. Outside a raucous voice yelled, "Come on out and fight, you goddam Yank!"

"That's what I mean," said Gorey.

"That's Harpending's voice!" boomed Hong Kong Smith.

"Arrest him," snapped Fugger.

Gorey looked at him blankly. "Arrest him, did you say?"

"Yes. Disarm and lock him up."

A shudder ran through Gorey. "He's got a six-shooter and a rifle and he's fighting drunk. . . ."

Hong Kong Smith roared. "That's all right, Marshal, Harpending won't hurt you. Not much. You just go out there and take away his guns and tell him to march down to the calaboose, nice and quiet."

"Come on out, you goddam marshal!" yelled Harpending out on the street.

"Yeah, come on out and dance," cried a second voice. "We got the music for you. Listen!" A bullet came zinging through the door, then a couple more.

Gorey darted to the side of the door and risked a quick peek out upon the street. He turned back. "He's got some Texas men with him."

"You've got to talk to him," Fugger cried to Hong Kong Smith.

"Talk to him yourself," declared Smith.

"He's your man. He works for you."

"That don't mean a thing," retorted Smith. "He works for me on the trail, not here in Kansas. And even when he's working for you, you don't go up to a man like Harpending when he's roaring drunk and has just killed a man and ask him to give you his gun, pretty please. I'm Hong Kong Smith and I'm alive and prosperous today because I know how to get along with Texas men. I know *when* to get along with them."

Fugger gave Smith a withering look and went over to Gorey. "Now, look here, Gorey. Kinnaird quit when the shooting started. That puts you in line for his job. You go out there and arrest that man and you get Kinnaird's job. Otherwise, you can quit, too."

Gorey looked toward the door. "I'll go out there and kill him. I'm not afraid of any man alive—"

"You can't kill him. You've got to take him alive."

Gorey stared at Fugger. "You drive a hard bargain, Mr. Fugger." He bit his lower lip. "The marshal's job pays three hundred a month, doesn't it?"

Fugger nodded. "That's a lot of money."

Gorey hitched up his cartridge belt, drew a deep breath and started for the door. He faltered as his hand reached for the batwings, but he went through.

Harpending and three Texas men were on their horses, across the street from McCoy's Saloon. Their height gave them a clear view over the horses tied to the hitchrail in front of the saloon.

Gorey popped out of the saloon, throwing up his left hand. "Hold your fire!" he cried out. "I want to talk to you."

Harpending whipped his rifle toward Gorey and fired. The bullet tore through the brim of Gorey's hat.

Gorey waited for no more. He whirled and plunged back into shelter. Before he disappeared a bullet from one of the other Texas men took off the left heel of his boot.

Harpending and his friends were now the rulers of Sage City. They yipped and whooped and fired their guns at random, crashing a store window here and there.

Then Harpending decided to pay a visit to Jacob Fugger. He assumed that he would find him in the latter's store and rode his horse up onto the sidewalk with the intention of riding right into the store. But the doorway was not high enough and he dismounted, leaving the horse in front of the door.

That was the moment Wes Tancred stepped out of the Bon Ton Café, across the street from Fugger's Store. He saw Harpending, gun in hand, plunge into Fugger's place.

Tancred started swiftly across the street. One of Harpending's friends sent his horse forward to cut off Tancred.

"Where do you think you're going?" he demanded.

"Into the store, where else?"

The cowboy noted the lack of armament on Tancred. His code forbade him to shoot an unarmed man and while he hesitated as to how to stop Tancred, the latter went past him into the store.

Inside Fugger's Store, Harpending was advancing toward the rear. On the right, Laura Vesser watched his progress with trepidation. Two other clerks, one a middle-aged woman, the other an elderly man, were backing away before Harpending.

"I want to see the old coot," Harpending was saying. "He told the marshal to arrest me and I wanna know why."

Bill Bleek came down the stairs from the perch in the rear of the store.

"Get out of here, Harpending, if you know what's good for you."

"Well, if it ain't Mr. Fugger's errand boy," sneered Harpending. "And without a gun as usual."

"I don't fight with guns," Bleek retorted, "but if you'll put down your own gun, I'll break every bone in your body."

Harpending raised his rifle, took a careless shot at Bill Bleek. The bullet missed by inches but stopped Bleek on the stairs.

Laura Vesser could not repress a little scream and thus called Harpending's attention to her.

"Hey, what's this? Purtiest girl I've seen in Kansas." He swerved and headed toward Laura Vesser.

At that moment Tancred entered the store. Harpending did not see him. He continued toward Laura.

"I'm a ring-tailed civet cat," declared Harpending, "if you ain't got all the girls down at Ma Hanson's beat a mile. Here—gimme a kiss."

He had reached the counter and suddenly lunged across it. Laura dodged and started away behind the counter.

Harpending wheeled to follow and walked into the swiftly advancing Tancred. Harpending yelped in surprise, tried to lever a fresh cartridge into the chamber of the rifle, but Tancred grabbed it savagely out of his hands and threw it to the floor. Harpending went for his revolver, but it never cleared the holster.

Tancred's fist smashed into Harpending's face. He crossed with a savage blow into the midriff and as Harpending gasped and folded forward Tancred hit him the third and last time, a stunning blow on the jaw. Harpending collapsed.

Tancred stooped and grabbing Harpending by the belt yanked him up. Bleek came forward.

"If you ain't the goddamdest hero!" he snarled.

Tancred shot him a look of complete contempt and propelled the half-conscious Harpending to the door. He whipped it open with his left hand, then braced up Harpending with both hands.

"Here's your friend," he said to the Texas men outside the door.

He shoved Harpending violently forward. The Texas man caromed off one of the horses, hit the hitchrail and fell on his face in the dirt of the street.

The three friends of Harpending stared at Tancred in amazement. Harpending was their leader. His downfall filled them with consternation. One of them half pulled a gun on Tancred, but lacking Harpending's lead he let the gun slide back.

Tancred did not even look back. He went stiffly down the sidewalk, past the hotel. Chuck Gorey, having peered out of the saloon and seeing that Harpending had moved away, was coming cautiously out of the saloon. He stared at Tancred in amazement.

"Is that Harpending back there?" he asked.

Tancred shook his head carelessly, went past Gorey. Jacob Fugger popped out of the saloon and looked after Tancred.

Tancred continued on to the corner, turned and entered the print shop.

"What's all the shooting?" Luke Miller asked.

"Just the usual," Tancred replied. "Drunken Texas men."

But it wasn't more than then minutes before Miller

had the complete story from a visitor. Miller wrote it all down and made certain to give the copy to Mose Hudkins to set up. In the meantime, Tancred was setting up the type for Miller's editorial.

Chapter 10

The last copy of the *Star* was taken away from the press by Mrs. Miller, shortly after four o'clock. The publisher's wife was a plump woman of forty-five, who always criticized what her husband did and always stood behind him on his decisions.

A couple of boys who came in on press day were counting out bundles to deliver to stores and various places around Sage City where the *Star* was sold.

Miller picked up a damp newspaper and let his eyes skim over the front page. An ironical smile twisted his lips.

"And now, the explosion."

"I've read it," said Mrs. Miller. "You just can't take things easy, can you?"

"When a thing's got to be said, it's got to be said," replied Miller.

"But do you have to be doing the saying all the time?"

Miller shrugged easily. "I'm a newspaper man." He turned to Tancred. "What do you think of the Harpending story?"

"You wrote it."

"You wish I hadn't?"

"It was news, I guess, so it had to be printed."

Miller sobered. "I'd write it if it was about myself. If you print the news about other people you've got to print it about yourself," Miller said. "Well, the paper's out, so we might as well call it a day."

Mrs. Miller came over to Tancred. "If it wasn't press day I'd ask you over to supper, but on Thursdays we only have leftovers."

"That's quite all right, ma'am," Tancred said.

The Millers left the shop with the delivery boys who were also taking a bag of mail copies to the post office.

Mose Hudkins puttered about a few minutes, then went

home and Tancred was left alone in the shop. The cot on which he was to sleep was set up in the rear of the shop, but it was scarcely four-thirty.

He washed himself, then took a turn or two around the shop. Finally he left the shop and walked to the Texas Saloon.

Lily Leeds was either in her office or out of the saloon, but two of the bartenders were reading the *Sage City Star*. One of them came over to wait on Tancred.

"Man, oh man, I'd like to see old Jacob's face."

Bill Bleek climbed the steps to Fugger's office on the balcony of the store. He laid the paper on his employer's desk, then stepped back.

Fugger read the editorial in cold silence. When he finished he cursed once, bitterly. Then he read the rest of the paper, skimming through the social and personal items. Finally he swung his chair around.

"He's gone too far," he said to Bill Bleek.

Bleek nodded. "Well?"

"It's too late to talk to him. He's got to have a lesson taught him."

"Some broken bones?"

Fugger hesitated, frowning. "A lot of people like him." He shook his head. "No, don't hit him. Just a warning."

Bleek nodded. He walked down the stairs and out of the store to the office of the *Sage City Star*. He peered through the window and saw that the place was empty. He grinned wickedly and opened the door.

He went past Luke Miller's desk in front and stepped up to the printing press. He knew nothing of printing but even to his unpracticed eye this was obviously the machine that printed the paper.

It was too big, too heavy for one man to turn over without leverage, so he searched until he found a hammer and light-heartedly broke a few rods and bars that were not too massive and smashed a few teeth out on some gears and cogs.

He spied the typecases and pulled out the drawers, dumping the type in a heap, then kicking it about the shop. He knocked over a stock of newsprint, found some cans of ink and dumped them onto the newsprint. He knocked over the paper cutter and broke a bar on it.

That was all the real damage it seemed that he could

do, but on leaving he saw Miller's desk and with a heave
sent it crashing loudly to the floor on its side.

He left the shop, pleased with his work. He regretted
that Tancred had not been in the print shop.

The courtroom was a rectangular room over the marshal's office and the jail. It contained a half dozen chairs,
some benches and a plain wooden table with an arm-
chair at one end. Hong Kong Smith and a half dozen
Texas men were in the courtroom when Chuck Gorey
brought Harpending up the stairs into the room. Harpending was only half sober and quite unchastened.

Judge Olsen banged his wooden mallet on the table.
"Bring the prisoner before the bar," he said officiously.

Gorey nudged Harpending and the Texas man, having
seen his friends, whirled and snarled at the deputy marshal. "Don't shove me around!"

Gorey looked gloomily past the prisoner toward Hong
Kong Smith. "The judge wants you up front," he said,
with restraint.

Harpending swaggered up to the judge's table. "It was
self-defense," he growled. "I caught him cheatin' and he
pulled his gun on me."

"Just a moment, Mr. Harpending," Judge Olsen said.
"This has got to be done legal-like and according to Black-
stone. You got to be sworn in, to tell the whole truth
and nothin' but the truth, so help you God? Do you?"

"Do I what?"

"Do you swear to tell the truth?"

"You callin' me a liar?" Harpending asked belligerent-
ly.

"No—no," replied the judge hastily. "But you've got
to be sworn in. That's customary." The judge's worried
eyes saw Jacob Fugger and Bill Bleek entering the courtroom and he brightened. "See here, prisoner, you'll do
what you're told or I'll fine you for contempt of court."

Hong Kong Smith pushed forward. "Now, wait a minute, Judge. This man works for me and I'm going to see
that he gets a square deal . . ."

"He'll get it," snapped Fugger, coming forward.

"He'd better," growled Smith.

Fugger signalled to the judge. "Proceed with the trial,
Your Honor."

"That's what I'm trying to do." The judge fixed his

shifty eyes once more on the prisoner. "Now, do you swear to tell the truth, the whole truth and nothing but the truth, so help you God . . . ?"

"I just told you . . ." Harpending began to bluster again, but Hong Kong Smith dropped his huge hand on his shoulder.

"Do as he says."

"All right, I swear."

"Good," said the judge. "Now, let's see, You're charged with shooting one Henry Thatcher, said Henry Thatcher being now deceased. How do you plead, guilty or not guilty?"

"Not guilty," said Hong Kong Smith, calmly. "I saw the whole thing. The dealer pulled his gun on Harpending and Harpending shot in self-defense."

The judge sent a quick look at Fugger. The latter nodded. The judge exhaled in relief. "Were there any other witnesses?"

Hong Kong Smith signalled to his crowd. "These boys all saw it. Did't you, boys?"

The Texas men gave their answers in a single chorus. "We sure did!"

Judge Olsen nodded amiably. "In that case, I find the prisoner not guilty."

The Texas men, including Harpending, let out a whoop of approval. It took Judge Olsen a full thirty seconds of pounding with his mallet to bring them to silence.

"There's another charge against Mr. Harpending," he announced. "Disturbing the peace. I find the prisoner guilty as charged and fine him twenty-five dollars."

Hong Kong Smith scowled. "Now, wait a minute. . . ."

But the little judge pounded the table with his wooden hammer. "The prisoner will pay the twenty-five dollars, plus six dollars costs or go to jail."

Fugger signalled to Hong Kong Smith. The big Texas man hesitated, then reached into his pocket and brought out a fistful of money. "Here's your money, Judge, but I don't mind telling you that I don't like it."

Fugger stepped up beside Smith. "We can't turn him altogether free, Hong Kong. Not after what Miller printed in his paper today."

"The hell with Miller and his paper," snorted Hong Kong Smith. "I bring my herds to this town and I spend a lot of money here. I expect a few small favors in return. If I don't get them, I can take my business to Dodge . . ."

"Where Wyatt Earp'll make your boys toe the line," snapped Fugger.

"There're other places."

"Let's talk about it," suggested Fugger. "Dinner's almost ready. Let's go to my house and have dinner and talk things over."

Hong Kong Smith scowled. "You got anything to drink at your place?"

"I don't drink myself," said Fugger, coldly. "But I guess there's a bottle or two in the kitchen. . . ."

"That's more like it." Smith turned, waved to his men. "All right, boys, you can go now. Have fun and I'll see you all later on."

Harpending swaggered over. "Who's the damn Yankee who hit me when I wasn't looking? I got a score to settle with him." He whirled, grabbed Gorey's shirt-front in his fist. "It wasn't you, was it?"

Gorey looked steadily at Jacob Fugger. The latter shrugged.

Gorey said, "His name is John Bailey. You'll find him at Luke Miller's newspaper shop."

Harpending and his followers streamed out of the courtroom. Gorey turned to find Lily Leeds standing just inside the door, her eyes on him.

"After this," Lily said to the deputy marshal, "stay out of the Texas Saloon."

"I may have to come in now and then," said Gorey, thinly, "to see that you're running a clean place. I'm the new marshal of Sage City."

Lily turned and found Fugger coming toward her. "Is that true, Mayor Fugger?"

"Somebody's got to be marshal," Fugger replied, testily. "Kinnaird quit, so I appointed Gorey to take his place."

"Then Heaven help Sage City!"

Tancred was on his second beer when Lily Leeds came in from the street. She was about to go into her office when she saw Tancred.

"Come in," she said. "Bring your beer with you."

Tancred carried the glass into her office. It was a tiny room, furnished simply with a rolltop desk, two chairs, a

couch and an iron safe. There was a closet at the rear
where Lily kept several changes of clothes.

"I just came from the courthouse," Lily said. "Judge
Olsen tried Manny Harpending."

"And?"

"He killed McCoy's faro dealer in self-defense. A clear-
cut case, with a half dozen witnesses who saw the dealer
draw first . . . the witnesses being Mr. Hong Kong Smith
of Texas and various other Texas men who work for Mr.
Smith. But don't worry, justice triumphed. Mr. Harpending was tried on another charge, disturbing the peace,
and he was found guilty." She paused. "He was fined
twenty-five dollars and Mr. Smith paid the fine. Now . . .
about you. The train doesn't leave until morning, but I
don't think you ought to wait that long."

"I'm not going anywhere."

"You missed what I was trying to tell you. Harpending's free. He's a Texas man and all Texas men are proud.
You humiliated him and he's got to wipe that out."

"He can't taunt me into a gunfight."

"Are you so sure of that?"

Tancred hesitated only briefly. "Yes."

"I hope so, John, I hope so." Then she blinked. "Hey,
wait a minute, this is Lily Leeds." She looked at Tancred,
her eyes wide. "Well, whaddya know, I was worrying
about you."

"Don't, Lily."

A faint smile flitted over her lips. "I haven't worried
about anyone but myself in a long while. I'm twenty-four
years old. When I'm twenty-eight, Lily Leeds will disap-
pear. And somewhere, maybe in Chicago, New York or
even Paris, a widow will appear. A young widow of quality. She will have inherited a considerable fortune from her
deceased husband and she will marry even greater
wealth." She stopped a moment. "Just four more years."

Tancred nodded thoughtfully. "You'll make it, Lily."

"I know I will. Nothing matters, but that. It's the only
thing in this world that matters." She paused again. "And
you, John?"

He shrugged.

Lily shook her head. "You're a marked man. Violence
breeds around you. Oh, I know, you think you can avoid
it. Like now. You humiliated one of the worst men ever
to come out of Texas and you think you can avoid fight-

ing him . . . to the finish. And what was it at Turkey Crossing? What was the provocation there?"

"They killed a man who didn't have a chance."

"But wasn't there a girl there? The daughter of the station agent?"

"Yes."

"Yet you rode away after killing the outlaws?"

Tancred put down the emptied beer glass. "I guess I'll go and have some supper."

Lily laughed, but there was no humor in it. "I don't blame you. I just can't keep my mouth shut. But you won't stay away, will you? You'll come back?"

Tancred nodded and went out.

He had a supper of boiled potatoes, steak, apple pie and coffee and when he finished it was after six o'clock. He walked back to the *Star* office, his mind preoccupied and he was inside before he became aware of Bill Bleek's vandalism.

A groan was torn from his throat. He walked through the shop. The type was undamaged, but it would take all of them a dozen hours to sort it out so it could be used again. The press could be repaired, but new parts would have to be obtained and no printing press parts were available closer than St. Louis.

A cold rage seeped through Tancred. A physical injury to a person he could understand, but to destroy machinery and dump out type like this that would consume maddening hours of painstaking toil. . . .

Lee Kinnaird, standing across the street from the newspaper office, watched Tancred go into the shop. He waited a moment, then started across the street. He was halfway across when a pair of mounted Texas man swirled around the corner from South Street and bore down upon the print shop. One of the riders was Manny Harpending.

Kinnaird stopped in the middle of the street and the Texas men pulled up their horses.

"Where do you think you're going, Manny?" Kinnaird asked quietly.

"You ain't the marshal of this town any more," sneered Harpending.

"That's right, I'm not," said Kinnaird, calmly. "I quit this afternoon, because Jacob Fugger wouldn't let me kill you."

"I ain't afraid of you, Kinnaird," blustered Harpending. "Any time you're looking for a showdown. . . ."

"What's the matter with right now?"

Harpending moistened his lips with his tongue. He knew Kinnaird's reputation. A man had to be awfully good and very sober to draw a gun against him.

"I got no quarrel with you," Harpending growled.

"Then turn your horse and ride out of town—and stay away."

Harpending hesitated. The Texas man with him regarded him in astonishment. "You gonna let him get away with that?"

"This is Lee Kinnaird," snarled Harpending. "You fight him if you want to." He whirled his horse and sent it galloping away. His friend was close behind him.

Kinnaird relaxed. He glanced toward the print shop, then turned and walked back across the street.

Inside the print shop, Tancred stared down at the bundle in his carpetbag. A long slow sigh escaped his lips, then he closed the carpetbag and put it under the cot. He sent one more glance about the shop, then left and walked to South Street.

Fugger's Store was closed for the day. Tancred tried the door, then stepped to the street and picked up a rock as big as his fist. He heaved it through the glass of the door, then reached inside the aperture and shot back the bolt. He went inside and started automatically for the right, then swerved and went over to the left side. He put his foot against the grocery counter, gave a shove and knocked it over on its side. Stepping on it, he reached to the top of the shelving, gripped it firmly and backed away.

The shelves came over and merchandise spilled over the floor. Tancred got some bolts of cloth and dumped them onto the groceries, then performed the *coup d'éclat*. *He* found a barrel of blackstrap molasses and kicked it over so that molasses poured over the groceries as well as the bolts of gingham and muslin.

Most of Tancred's anger went with that but there was still a little left so he climbed the stairs to Jacob Fugger's office and emptied all the drawers of Fugger's desk onto the floor and kicked the papers around a little.

He was quite cheerful by that time and descended to the

main part of the store. Four or five people were standing just outside the door as he came out.

"Tell Jacob it was John Bailey," he told them, "and
I'll be at McCoy's Saloon for twenty minutes."

Chapter 11

It was fifteen minutes later when Bill Bleek came into McCoy's Saloon. He found Tancred at the bar with an untouched glass of beer in his hand. A happy expression was on the big man's face.

"I'm glad you paid back the visit, Bailey," Bleek purred. "It wouldn't have been half the fun if you hadn't."

"How are you going to fight?" Tancred asked.

"The way I always fight. For keeps."

Bleek peeled off his coat and tossed it on the bar. A bartender called for McCoy and the saloon-keeper rushed up from the rear. He sized up the situation instantly.

"Not in here, Bill!" he cried out.

"Jacob will pay for the damage," Bleek said. To Tancred, "Oh, he's really mad. The molasses, you know."

"That was for the ink," Tancred said.

Bleek nodded. "Oh, sure." He stepped toward Tancred, grinning.

Tancred smashed the heavy beer glass into Bleek's face. He followed instantly with his left into Bleek's stomach and was appalled by the muscular hardness of it. Yet Bleek reeled back. He wiped beer and blood from his face.

"All right, Bailey," he said. "But don't ask me to quit."

He sprang forward and threw his right fist at Tancred's head. Tancred rolled aside, lashed back. His fist connected but his body also encountered Bleek's left, a solid ramrod of sinew and bone.

Tancred staggered back and Bleek crowded forward. His right connected with Tancred's head, his left flailed into Tancred's stomach. A roaring filled Tancred's head and then Bleek's right exploded again on his jaw and the floor rushed up to Tancred. He fell to his knees and threw out both hands to brace himself against a complete

collapse. He remained there an instant—until Bleek kicked
him savagely.

Bleek had meant it. It was to be a fight to the finish. Total unconsciousness would not stop it. Bleek would
still kick in his ribs and batter his head.

Tancred dropped flat upon the floor, called on his re-
serves and rolled aside. Bleek's hobnailed boot grazed
the skin of his face and Tancred grabbed the foot and
twisted hard. Bleek crashed to the floor.

He landed hard and for a moment the breath was
knocked from him. He made his feet to find that Tancred
was up and grabbing at a nearby chair. Bleek lunged forward. Tancred smashed the chair over Bleek's head. It
shattered to splinters and Bleek dropped to his knees.

Tancred lurched forward, caught the bar's edge to
keep from falling and saw before him a bungstarter. He
grabbed it up, whirled and faced Bleek coming up. He
hit Bleek twice with the bungstarter and then it broke.

Bleek's face was streaming blood. His scalp was matted
with blood but he still came at Tancred.

"Stand still," he grated thickly. "Stand still and fight."

Tancred hit him, in the face, in the stomach. He hit
him four times and Bleek hit him once and Tancred staggered back. He didn't fall and his back touched the bar.
Bleek caught him there. He threw his arms about Tancred and put on pressure.

His fetid breath was foul in Tancred's face but the
pain was in Tancred's back, where Bleek's hands, locked,
were grinding into his spine.

He belabored the big man's head with blows, chopped
at his muscular neck with the edges of his open hands.
Bleek's grip grew tighter and Tancred could scarcely
breathe. With a tremendous effort he got the heel of his
left hand under Bleek's chin and forced it up an inch. He
got his right hand under the chin and muscled it up another inch. Then he slipped his left hand down to get a
firmer leverage and holding the head up with his left
hand alone smashed his right hand into Bleek's already
bloodied face.

It was a last ditch effort. There was no breath left in
his body, his lungs were threatening to collapse. He hit
Bleek's nose, his eyes, his cheeks. Again and again, savagely. A groan came from the other man's lips. Tancred
struck once more and Bleek let go. He reeled away,

blinded in pain and for a long moment Tancred could not follow.

Air rushed into his tortured lungs. He gasped and heaved. Then Bleek, by sheer instinct, lurched forward once more.

Tancred hit him. Bleek's stomach muscles had lost their rigidity. His fists sunk deep. Groans came from the bruiser. Bleek swayed but did not fall. Tancred smashed his face, over and over. Bleek's hands hung helplessly at his sides. His great body quivered.

Tancred stepped back. His fists weighed a ton each. He could not lift them to hit Bleek again. And Bleek was still on his feet.

Jacob Fugger stepped out of the crowd and took Bleek's arm. He turned him toward the door. And Bleek moved as Fugger led him out.

Tancred looked around a ring of quiet faces. Most of them were Texas men but there was now no hostility in them. There was no friendliness either.

Until Lee Kinnaird's face appeared. He stepped up to Tancred.

"Where do you want to go?"

"Miller's shop."

Kinnaird took Tancred's arm and led him out of the saloon. On the sidewalk he saw that Tancred could walk alone and let go of his arm. But he went with him to the print shop and helped Tancred take off his coat and bloodied shirt. He whistled softly as he saw the bruises on Tancred's body.

"You're hurt."

Tancred nodded and dropped heavily to his cot, but only to a sitting position. Kinnaird found a bucket of cold water, a towel. With an effort Tancred raised himself to his feet and soaking the towel in the bucket, sloshed his chest and stomach and arms.

Kinnaird watched and after a while he said, "That's the first fight Bleek ever lost."

"*I* don't feel like I won it."

"You didn't lose, so you won." Kinnaird paused. "He'll be after you again. If he can't beat you with his fists he'll try another way."

"I suppose so."

"And Manny Harpending? You'll have to fight *him* sooner or later."

Tancred dropped the soggy towel into the bucket of water. He exhaled wearily. "I've been thinking it was a mistake coming to Sage City."

"That's what I said, when I first came here."

"But you're leaving now."

Kinnaird hesitated, then shook his head. "That's what Fugger would like me to do, now that I've given him back his badge. But I've saved a little money and I think I'll stick around a spell."

The front door of the shop burst open and Luke Miller charged in.

"John! You're all right?"

"I'm all right," Tancred said, "but the shop isn't." He gestured about the litter on the floor.

Luke Miller groaned. "It'll take us a week to sort out the type."

Mrs. Miller came hurrying into the shop. Tancred expected her to bemoan the damage, but she scarcely looked at it. Her eyes were on Tancred.

"I heard what you did to Jacob's place," she said. "A barrel of molasses!"

"That was for the ink," said Tancred, pointing.

"I think we got a little the better of it." She reached for a printer's apron. "Well, let's get busy!"

Luke Miller chuckled. "That's a woman for you. She complains of every little thing that happens around here, then something serious comes along and she says, 'Let's get busy'!"

Chapter 12

The next morning Luke Miller boarded the eastbound train for St. Louis.

"I only hope they have the parts in St. Louis," he said before he left. "If they have I'll be back in three days, but if I have to go on to Cincinnati. . . ."

"Then we'll miss an issue," said Mrs. Miller.

"It'll be the first time." Miller frowned. "And the last."

He went off and Mrs. Miller, Tancred and old Mose resumed their monotonous sorting of the type. They worked steadily until noon and made scarcely an impression on the heap. Tancred ached in every muscle but oddly enough had greater mental peace than he had had in a long time.

What the talk was in town he did not know. There were two or three callers at the shop but Mrs. Miller went forward and talked to them in low tones. Shortly before noon she left and returned with a basket containing sandwiches and coffee.

After the lunch they worked straight through until six when Mrs. Miller called a halt. "I can't tell a 'b' from a 'p' any more," she declared. "There's only so much of this you can do at a time."

"We're more than half through," said Tancred. "We'll finish tomorrow."

Mrs. Miller and Mose went off. Tancred washed up and walked to the Bon Ton Café. He had scarcely entered when Bill Bleek came in.

His face was puffed and bruised, both eyes were blackened and the left closed entirely. He said to Tancred, "I can still lick you."

"I won't fight you again," Tancred declared. "Not with my fists."

Bleek made an impatient gesture. "Jacob wants to see you."

"I don't believe he can tell me anything I'd be interested in hearing."

"It's for your own good."

Tancred shook his head. "No."

"Jacob Fugger owns this town," Bleek went on. "Luke Miller don't think so but he'll find out. . . . I'll tell Jacob you'll be over."

"He'll have a long wait."

Bleek peered at Tancred from the one eye that retained vision. "Don't get Jacob mad at you."

He went out.

Tancred ate his supper and paid for it. As he left the café Jacob Fugger called to him from across the street. "You, Bailey, come over here."

Tancred looked at Fugger, then turned away deliberately. Fugger yelled after him, but Tancred continued on. Fugger looked after him, then went into the store.

Bleek stood just inside. "Find me Smith," Fugger said.

"He's next door in the Texas Saloon."

"Get him."

Bleek went out and Jacob Fugger turned and surveyed his store. The clerks were putting away merchandise, preparing to close up for the day. Fugger's eyes came to rest upon Laura Vesser. He studied her for a moment, then walked over to her counter.

"You're a very pretty girl," he said bluntly.

Laura regarded her employer in alarm. Until now, for all the attention he had paid her, she might have been a store fixture.

"Don't worry," Fugger went on. "I'm too old a dog to start that stuff. When I was young, I was too poor to get married and now I've got too much money. But I've noticed that there are quite a few men coming into the store since you're here. And they're buying things they haven't got any use for."

"I'm sorry, Mr. Fugger," began Laura. "I've sold them only the things they ask for. . . ."

"Sell them anything. It's none of your business if they can use the merchandise or not." He nodded shrewdly "Lee Kinnaird's been coming in a lot. He's taken up with that whatsisname who works for Luke Miller."

"John Bailey?"

Fugger grunted. "Bailey, yes. I forgot. He stopped that wild Texan from annoying you yesterday."

He pursed up his lips. "On your way home, would you mind stopping at the newspaper office and telling this, whatsisname, Bailey, that I'd like to see him. You go that way, don't you?"

"Why yes, I do, but . . ." Laura hesitated, then suddenly nodded. "Very well."

"Good. You might as well run along now. Leave things as they are."

Laura got her hat and jacket. Fugger waited until she had left the store, then suddenly shouted to his other clerks, "Close up now."

A few minutes later when the clerks had gone, Hong Kong Smith entered. He was almost sober

"That bruiser of yours said you wanted to see me."

"I guess I had something on my mind, but I've forgotten now what it was."

Hong Kong Smith bared his teeth in a grin. "I don't think you've ever forgotten anything, Jacob. Come on, what new scheme are you plotting?"

"This man of yours, Harpending . . . I haven't seen him around today."

Smith's eyes narrowed. "Neither have I."

"Has he left for Texas?"

"He won't be going back to Texas."

"Why not?"

"He doesn't like Texas any more," Smith chuckled. "Or maybe it's Texas that doesn't like him. If you know what I mean."

"I think I do."

"All right, let's stop beating about the bush, Jacob. What do you want with Harpending?"

"Do I really have to tell you that, Smith? I gave you a run-down last night on the situation here. All right, I'll spell it out for you. I want two or three men for a month or so, until things get squared away."

"Gunfighters, eh? Mmm, Harpending's all right, but I've got a man down in Texas who'd put two bullets into Harpending while Harpending was trying to draw a gun."

Fugger looked steadily at Hong Kong Smith. "Can you get him up here for me?"

"You can buy anything . . . or anyone . . . for money," said Hong Kong Smith.

Tancred was sorting out type when he heard the door open. He looked over his shoulder and exclaimed softly. Laura Vesser had entered the shop and was coming toward him. She said stiffly, "I'm here on an errand for my employer. He wants to see you."

"He'd stoop to anything!"

"And you?" she flashed at him. "I saw what you did to the store."

"But you didn't see what Bleek did here." Tancred pointed to the type he was sorting. "It doesn't look like much, but three of us have been sorting all day. And Mr. Miller's gone to St. Louis to get new parts for the press that Bill Bleek broke. If Bleek had known just a little more about machinery he'd have put the *Star* out of business for keeps."

"But why you?" cried Laura Vesser. "Why do you have to fight Fugger and Bleek? Miller's quarrel isn't yours."

"In all this world," Tancred said, soberly, "the thing I hate the most is a fight."

"Then why *do* you fight?" she flashed at him.

He said, "Sometimes a man can't help but fight."

She turned and went halfway to the door. Then she stopped, her head lowered. Finally she turned. "I'm sorry," she said, quietly. "My father's fight at Turkey Crossing wasn't your fight either."

She went out.

Tancred sorted out a few pieces of type, then took off his shop apron and put on his coat. He left the shop and walked to Fugger's store. As he came up to the place, Hong Kong Smith came out.

The big Texan gave him a hearty half-salute. "Good evening, Mr. Bailey."

Tancred nodded and went into the store. "I got your message," he told Jacob Fugger.

"Oh, Bailey," growled Fugger. "How are you?"

Tancred made a small, impatient gesture, to dismiss the trivialities and to indicate that Fugger should get down to the subject.

"They tell me you're a good man, Bailey," Fugger said.

"You didn't send for me just to tell me that."

"In a way I did," replied Fugger. "I like a good man. I like to have him on my side."

"I'm working for Luke Miller."

"How much is he paying you?"

"Enough."

"I doubt that. He can't afford it. He's got a hundred and eighty-two dollars in the bank and he still owes over six hundred dollars on his print shop equipment. His gross income last month was three hundred and fourteen dollars and fifty-five cents."

"You seem to know quite a lot of Mr. Miller's affairs."

"I make it my business to know everything. If Miller's paying you twenty-five dollars a week, he's drawing down about ten dollars a week for himself."

"He's paying me only twenty dollars a week."

Jacob Fugger snorted. "For a man of your caliber?"

"Mose Hudkins can set up more type than I can."

"A typesetter!" Fugger brushed it away. "Who's talking about setting up type? I saw you beat Bill Bleek with your fists. No man has ever done that before. And they tell me you're a fancy man with a revolver, and that's something Bleek's no good with. I can use a man with your qualifications."

"To kill Luke Miller?"

Jacob Fugger actually chuckled. "You like to call a shovel a shovel. Good. So do I. I'm going to smash Luke Miller. I have to put him out of business because he's threatening *my* business. That's the long and the short of it, I've got to get rid of Miller. I'll kill him if I have to, but I'd rather not. I just want him to close up his newspaper. I want you to work for me and I'll pay you fifty dollars a week."

"It's not enough."

"I pay Bleek only forty a week. How much do you think you're worth?"

"I imagine you're a man, Mr. Fugger, who believes everyone has a price."

"Yes."

"You're probably right. I suppose I have my price, too. I'll tell you what I'll do. I'll leave Sage City tomorrow morning . . ." Tancred paused, "if *you* will."

Fugger exclaimed angrily. "I'm not a humorous man, Mr. Bailey, I don't like jokes."

"You asked me my price and I told you."

"I made you an offer. I now withdraw that offer. Good night, Mr. Bailey!"

Tancred left the store and returned to the print shop. He donned his apron once more and resumed the monotonous job of sorting out type. He worked until midnight and when Mrs. Miller came into the shop in the morning, at seven o'clock, he was already at it.

"I can see now that it was a mistake letting you sleep here," she declared. "You must have been working most of the night.

"There wasn't much else to do."

"Well, you're not going to work tomorrow. Promise that you won't."

"It won't be necessary," Tancred said. "We'll have this all cleaned up by noon."

"Then you'll rest until Monday."

Rest . . . there was no rest for Wes Tancred.

Chapter 13

Saturday was the noisiest day Tancred had ever known in a small town. The cowboys really whooped it up from early morning, through the day and far into the night. Chuck Gorey, the marshal and his deputy, Slattery, remained in the jail most of the day and the Texas men ruled South Street. A faro dealer was wounded and two others suffered bad beatings. A half dozen windows were broken in various stores and one Texas man killed another in a duel.

Sunday morning was quiet. Tancred was awake before daybreak, but remained in the print shop until almost eight. Then he had breakfast at the Bon Ton Café and stood for a little while outside the restaurant. The street was virtually deserted. A church bell tolled north of the Kansas & Western tracks and Tancred blinked. He had not known there was a church in Sage City.

He realized that he knew very little of what went on north of the tracks and decided to take a walk in that direction. It was like entering another world.

There were no saloons on the north side of town, just a few stores that apparently catered to the residential trade, some of whom had businesses south of the tracks, but lived on the north side.

He passed the church, a small, gray-painted frame building. Soberly dressed men and women wearing fine dresses were going into the building.

He returned to the print shop and an odd restlessness kept him from relaxing. The type was all sorted, the print shop was as clean as he could make it and there was no copy on the hooks that he could set. He read some of the old issues of the *Star*, but could not keep his mind on what he was reading.

About ten-thirty he walked to the Bon Ton Café and

had a cup of coffee. When he came out Lee Kinnaird hailed him from across the street.

"Doing anything special?" Kinnaird asked as he came up.

"As a matter of fact, I'm having a hard time doing nothing."

"Then walk with me down there." He pointed to the south of town and Tancred, whose ears were becoming attuned to almost perpetual gunfire, realized that there was shooting out beyond the limits of Sage City.

"There's always a bunch of people out there on Sundays, doing target shooting," said Kinnaird, "and now with the Texas men here we might see some fancy riding and roping." He chuckled. "They even put on a bullfight for us last fall."

Tancred was not especially eager to associate with the uninhibited Texas men, but there was nothing else to do in town and he liked the company of Lee Kinnaird about as well as that of anyone he had met in Sage City.

They walked past the last house on the street to a stretch of flat prairie-land, where a dozen or more Texas men were showing off their skill with horses and the rawhide riatas they had brought with them from Texas. Off to one side another group of Texans were shooting at targets set up. Among the Texans were a few Northerners. As Kinnaird and Tancred came up, one of the latter, a man wearing a Prince Albert and a brocaded vest, was emptying a six-shooter at a board target, fully a hundred feet away. He hit the board each time.

Some of the Texas men were impressed, although one of them stepped up and calmly duplicated the Northerner's feat. The man in the Prince Albert smiled thinly.

"Put the target back a piece," he said.

A cowboy sprang for his horse standing nearby and galloped it to the target. Swinging down low on the right side of his horse he grabbed up the board and carried it back another hundred feet or so. Then he stopped his horse and waved the board.

"Far enough?" he yelled.

The man in the Prince Albert gestured the horseman back. "More!" he called.

The eyes of the entire group were upon him. The horseman rode back further, stopped and looked back. The Northerner pretended not to see him. The horseman accordingly galloped away some more and finally stopped, at a distance of more than three hundred yards from the firing line.

He cupped his hands over his mouth. "This far enough?"

The tall man in the Prince Albert nodded. "Try it there!" he called.

A murmur went up.

Kinnaird nudged Tancred. "Watch this, now."

The Texas men clamored around the tall man in the Prince Albert. "Nobody can hit a target that size with a revolver," shouted one of them.

"They probably can't—down in Texas," retorted the tall man.

"Any Texan can beat any Yank at anything!" howled an irate cowboy.

The tall man pointed at the speaker. "Five dollars says *you* can't hit that target."

"Five dollars says I can if you can," promptly retorted the cowboy.

"That's a bet!"

"And now," Kinnaird whispered to Tancred, "you'll have a chance to see Mr. Wild Bill Hickok . . ."

"Hickok!" exclaimed Tancred.

"The one and only. I heard he got in town yesterday, but I didn't know he was staying over. Guess he needs the money. They don't know they're up against Wild Bill. Watch . . . !"

Wild Bill suddenly thrust out a long-barreled revolver and without seeming to aim, fired. The cowboy on his horse, who had pulled over to one side, galloped up to the target and leaned down from his mount to look at the target. Not believing his eyes he dismounted and examined the target closely. Then he waved.

"He hit it!"

A shout went up among the Texas men surrounding Wild Bill Hickok. The man who had made the bet with him drew his gun. "I still got a chance," he said.

Manny Harpending rode to the firing line from the left where he had been putting his horse through its paces.

"You're a fool, Hodge," he exclaimed. "That's Wild Bill Hickok!"

All eyes went to Wild Bill Hickok. The latter bowed slightly.

Harpending jumped to the ground. "All right if I shoot in place of Hodge?" he challenged Hickok.

"Why not?" Hickok asked coolly.

Harpending drew his gun and took careful aim at the distant target. He fired and all around him could see a splinter fly from the board.

Wild Bill Hickok took a five-dollar gold piece from his pocket and handed it to Harpending. "You shoot very well, stranger."

"Good enough," said Harpending. He tossed the coin to his fellow Texan, Hodge.

"Care to move the target back another hundred yards?" asked Hickok.

"I can hit any target you can hit," snapped Harpending. But he did not look happy about it.

The target was moved back another hundred yards or so and a couple more Texans rode out to watch from the sides. Wild Bill Hickok smiled challengingly at Harpending.

"A small wager?"

"Now it comes," said Lee Kinnaird to Tancred. "I saw him do this in Abilene six years ago. Only then he fired almost six hundred yards. The target was a little larger, but I doubt if there's another man in the entire west who can hit any target at all at six hundred yards."

"Wasn't there a man named Bartles who shot rings around Hickok in a match during the war?" Tancred asked.

"I never heard of it." Kinnaird looked sharply at Tancred. "You're pretty well posted on shooters."

Tancred made no reply. The Texas men had crowded around Will Bill Hickok, making wagers with him. He covered more than a hundred dollars in bets.

He squared off, scarcely took more aim that he had previously and fired. Down near the target the Texas cowboys rode up. A shout went up.

"He hit it!"

A groan went up among the men surrounding Hickok, but Harpending, scowling, took up his position. He aimed and fired. The bullet kicked up dirt a hundred feet short of the target.

"Try it again," said Hickok.

Harpending emptied his revolver at the target, but failed to make a hit.

"Sorry, boys," said Hickok as he collected the bets. He jingled the coins in his hand. "I'll give you all a chance to get it back. Fifty dollars to any man who can hit the target."

"This is what I've been waiting for," said Kinnaird. He nudged Tancred and stepped up to Hickok. "I'll try fifty dollars of that, Mr. Hickok."

The smile faded from Wild Bill's face. "Uh, hello, Kinnaird, didn't see you."

"Shake hands with a friend of mine," said Kinnaird, easily. "John Bailey, Bill Hickok."

Hickok shook hands with Tancred. "Bailey, mm, the name's familiar."

"Mr. Bailey works on the Sage City newspaper. Let's see, the offer was fifty dollars to anyone who can hit the target, eh?"

"A fifty dollar bet," corrected Wild Bill. "Naturally, I'm not just *giving* money away. You've got to risk something, too."

"That wasn't the way I understood it," said Kinnaird. He hesitated, then noting the eyes of the Texas men on him, he nodded. "It's a bet."

He drew his revolver, took careful aim at the target and fired. The scorers examined the target carefully, then waved arms to indicate a miss.

Kinnaird counted out the money, as Wild Bill smiled thinly. "Care to try again?"

"There's a bit of a breeze," said Kinnaird, "makes it hard to figure at the range."

"Let's see Bailey try it," suddenly jeered Manny Harpending. "He's so good with a gun, let's see what he can do."

Tancred stepped back quickly and shook his head. "I haven't got a gun."

"Use the marshal's," cried Harpending. "Let's see if that Turkey Crossing story was poppycock or not."

"Turkey Crossing!" cried Wild Bill. "Of course. That's how I remember the name. John Bailey, eh?" He shook his head. ' The name was a new one to me, when I read about that in the Wichita paper and frankly, I . . ." He suddenly beamed. "I'll lend you *my* gun, Mr. Bailey. It shoots as straight as any gun can shoot."

"I haven't got fifty dollars," Tancred said, simply.

"Forget the fifty dollars," Wild Bill said, earnestly.

"I'm anxious to see you shoot." He tendered his revolver, butt first.

Tancred made no move to take the gun. Harpending moved forward. "Come on, Mr. Bailey, let's see you shoot!"

Several of the cowboys took up the chant. Kinnaird whispered to Tancred, "Maybe you'd better try it, Bailey."

"I've never fired a Frontier Model," protested Tancred.

"You're a Navy gun man, eh? Well, I don't blame you. They've never made a gun like them," stated Kinnaird.

"This is a good gun, Mr. Bailey," Wild Bill Hickok said, gently. "I wouldn't use it myself if it wasn't. The trigger pulls light."

Tancred swore softly under his breath, but still did not accept the revolver. Not until Harpending said with a sneer, "Yellow, Bailey?"

Tancred accepted the revolver from Hickok. He hefted it in his hand, then cocked the weapon and let it dangle loosely at his side.

A hush fell upon the augmented crowd of spectators. Tancred raised the gun, thrust it out ahead of him at arm's length and without aiming, fired.

The scorers rushed their horses to the target and one or two dismounted to examine the target closely. A sudden yelp of astonishment went up that carried back to the firing line.

"That's shooting, Mr. Bailey," said Wild Bill Hickok thoughtfully. "Did you say your name was Bailey?"

"John Bailey."

Tancred glanced at Manny Harpending. The Texan's sneer had gone. In his eyes was a look of doubt . . . and fear.

Tancred handed the gun back to Wild Bill Hickok and walked off. The cowboys moved aside to give him a clear passage. Kinnaird followed Tancred.

"That was the best thing you could have done!" he exulted. "Did you see the look on Harpending's face?"

Tancred nodded.

"I'll tell you, now," Kinnaird said, "he was going to go after you. As a matter of fact, I stopped him the other night."

Behind them a man came running.

"Mr. Bailey!" he called.

Tancred looked over his shoulder. The man was Packard, who owned the Boston Store. He stopped and Packard pounded up.

"I saw your shooting, Mr. Bailey," exclaimed Packard.

The former marshal grinned. "You saw mine, too."

"Yes, I did. The range was too far."

"Not for Bailey it wasn't. Or for Wild Bill Hickok."

"I know. If you don't mind, Mr. Kinnaird, I'd like to talk to Mr. Bailey alone."

"Go right ahead." Kinnaird started away, but Tancred detained him with an outstretched hand.

"I don't mind Lee hearing, Mr. Packard."

"I guess it really doesn't matter. Kinnaird's turned in his marshal's badge, which indicates that he isn't on Jacob Fugger's side at least. Anyway, it won't be a secret much longer. The fact is, Mr. Bailey, I've been talking to a few of the people around town and we're getting up a slate of candidates to run against Fugger and his crowd. Luke Miller's down for mayor and—well, we haven't got a name yet for sheriff of the county and I thought, in view of what I've just seen—"

"No," said Tancred, bluntly.

"The office is good for six or seven thousand a year."

"I'm not interested, Mr. Packard," Tancred said, shaking his head. "I'm a printer and that's all I want to be."

Packard was disappointed. "Would you like to think about it a day or two?"

"My mind's made up, right now. I can't think of anything that would make me change it."

Packard let out a slow sigh. "Well, it was a good idea. The marshal, of course, is appointed by the mayor and the city council, but the sheriff's office is an elected one and I'd hoped . . ." He shrugged. "Thank you, just the same, Mr. Bailey."

He went off and Tancred and Kinnaird walked on into Sage City. Both men were quiet. At the Bon Ton Café they separated and Tancred went on to the *Star* print shop.

Tancred was lying on his cot, looking at the ceiling of the print shop when someone rattled the door-knob. He sat up and peered toward the door, then exclaiming, got to his feet.

Wild Bill Hickok was outside the door.

Tancred unlatched the door and Hickok came in. "I've always been a curious man, Mr. Bailey," he said. "Guns are my business. I've practiced with them since I was kneehigh to a prairie dog. I do a lot of shooting and I've fired against some of the best men in the country. I haven't been beaten by any man in a good many years. But you beat me today."

"It was a lucky shot. And I didn't beat you, Mr. Hickok. Lee Kinnaird said he saw you hit a target once at six hundred yards."

"No man can do that all the time. But since you mention Mr. Kinnaird, didn't I hear you tell him you'd never fired a Frontier Model until today?"

Tancred hesitated, then nodded.

"In other words, you've done your shooting with a Navy Colt." Hickok's eyes became thoughtful slits. "There used to be some fellows over in Missouri, who were awfully good with Navy guns. Ran into them now and then during the war."

Tancred drew a deep breath. "What you're trying to say is that Quantrell's men used the Navy Colt exclusively."

"Yes."

"I rode with Quantrell."

"That's what I figured." Hickok held up his hand. "The war's been over a good many years. I guess everyone knows that I was on the other side, but in recent years I've talked to quite a few of the people who were with you and I've found a lot of them to be pretty decent citizens."

"Thanks," Tancred said, cynically.

"Mmm," mused Hickok. "When I was with Jim Lane in the early days I met a man who was awfully good with a Navy gun. In fact, he outshot me. Ted Bartles. Ran into him a few years ago. Said the boys over in Missouri put up a young chap to shoot against him, back in 'sixty-seven or 'sixty-eight. . . ."

"Donny Pence."

"Ah, you remember!" Hickok chuckled. "Donny was only nineteen or twenty at the time, but Ted tells me he shot rings around him. I guess you'd say that since Ted Bartles beat me and Donny beat him, that would make him just about the best man with a revolver in the country."

"That's possible."

"Bartles said this young Donny never aimed, just threw down his gun like he was pointing it at the target and fired. Wonder what ever became of young Donny."

"I'm not Donny Pence," Tancred said.

"Never said you was. Just talking about shooting. Lot of Quantrell's boys were awfully good with revolvers. Frank and Jesse James, the Younger Boys, Sam Older, Dave Helm." Hickok broke off and studied Tancred a moment.

"Brings back memories, doesn't it?"

"Not pleasant ones."

Hickok sighed. "Don't do to look back, I guess." He shrugged. "I've had my times." He grunted. "You saw what I had to do today to make a few dollars. As a matter of fact, I'm broke. I got married only two months ago and here I am now, away from home, trying to make a stake. I'm on my way to the Black Hills Country. Well, it's been nice talking to you, Mr. Bailey."

He extended his hand, smiling. Tancred shook hands with him.

Hickok started to go, then stopped. He looked quizzically at Tancred.

"There's a name keeps escaping me. There was a boy who rode with Donny Pence and the others during the war . . . some of the boys say he was a better shot even than Donny . . . you wouldn't remember who that was, would you?"

"No," said Tancred.

Hickok nodded. "It's not important. Good-bye, Mr. Bailey."

He went out, on to Deadwood, in Dakota Territory, where he would meet an obscure man named Jack McCall.

Chapter 14

Luke Miller was not on the Monday morning train. Mrs. Miller came into the shop, after going to meet the train, a worried look on her face.

"Apparently he had to go on to Cincinnati. That means he can't possibly return before Thursday morning."

"It wouldn't take more than four or five hours to put the parts into the press," Mose Hudkins said. "If we had the pages all made ready we could still get the paper out by Thursday evening."

"But we haven't got a stick of type set up!" exclaimed Mrs. Miller. "I can write up the local news, just as I always have, but we need more than that."

"I think I know what Mr. Miller would print on the front page," Tancred said. "The slate of candidates Mr. Packard and some other men are putting up against Jacob Fugger and his crowd."

Mrs. Miller winced. "That's going to mean more trouble."

"Especially since Mr. Miller's name heads the slate."

"No!" cried Mrs. Miller.

"He's the natural candidate for mayor," Tancred went on. "He's led the fight against Jacob Fugger."

For a moment Mrs. Miller looked crushed, but then she drew a deep breath. "I suppose you're right and if Luke were here, I'd back him . . . as usual. Do you suppose you could run over to Mr. Packard's store and get the list?"

Tancred nodded. "I'll go over right now."

He left the shop and walked to the Boston Store. It was a considerably smaller store than Fugger's big place and had only one clerk besides Packard.

Packard brightened when he saw Tancred. "You've changed your mind, Mr. Bailey?"

"No, I haven't. Mrs. Miller sent me over to get the

details about the candidates. Mr. Miller hasn't returned
yet and the rest of us are trying to get the paper ready
to go to press."

"You *are* going to get out an issue this week?"

"We're going to try."

Packard walked back to his desk and picked up a sheet
of paper. He handed it to Tancred. The latter glanced at
it.

"Miller for mayor," said Packard, "Fred Kraft for
judge, Herb Glassman for prosecutor, besides the six for
the council. We still haven't decided on a man for sheriff."

"I'd like to make a suggestion," Tancred said. "Lee
Kinnaird."

Packard's eyes narrowed. "Until last week he was a
Fugger man."

"He isn't any more."

"You're *sure* of that?"

"As sure as I can be of anything."

"Kinnaird is a very able man, there's no question of
that," said Packard thoughtfully. "Except for his former
affiliation . . ." He drew a deep breath and exhaled
heavily. "Give me an hour. I'll talk to the others."

"I'll start writing this up."

"Good. Oh—I've been thinking. Miller's not going to
get a great deal of advertising during the next few weeks
so I thought I'd take a rather large ad this week. A half
page. . . ."

"I doubt if Mr. Miller would accept a charity ad."

Packard grinned. "The only charity is for myself." He
waved about the store. "See any customers? The squeeze
is on me as well as on Miller. I've got to go after the
people Fugger can't intimidate, the few farmers, the
townsmen who can't be hurt by him. The *Star* reaches
those people and if I want to stay in business I've got to
get them into my store. Here, go see these people." He
pointed to the list of names on the slate. "Glassman's a
young lawyer who recently hung out his shingle. You're
already carrying a professional card from him, but the
others are all businessmen around town and all of them
are going to be boycotted by Fugger, so they'll need to
advertise to get a little business. Call on them."

"I'll do that, but I'll wait until later in the day, after
you've had a chance to ask them about Lee Kinnaird."

"I'll let you know on that within the hour."

Tancred returned to the *Star* shop and sat down at a table. He found Mrs. Miller busily scribbling at her husband's desk.

"Did you get the story?" she asked.

"Yes." He hesitated. "You're pretty busy. Would you like me to write it up?"

"I'd appreciate it if you would."

Tancred got a pencil and some paper and went to a table at the rear of the shop. He thought for a moment, then began to write swiftly.

He was still at it when Packard entered the *Star* office. Tancred got up and went forward.

"We've decided to accept Lee Kinnaird," the merchant said.

"I don't think you're making a mistake."

Packard smiled and took a sheet of paper from his pocket. "I brought along the ad I talked to you about and I also talked to the others. They'll all have ads for you."

"Ads!" exclaimed Mrs. Miller. "I hadn't even given that a thought."

"With Fugger laying the boycott on us we've got to advertise to stay in business. At least until the election." Packard paused. "If we lose that, we lose everything."

"We've *got* to win," declared Mrs. Miller.

Packard nodded. He left the shop and Tancred finished writing the story about the forthcoming election. When he finished it, he took it to Mrs. Miller. She scanned it quickly and when she finished she looked at Tancred worriedly.

"Isn't it a—a little strong?"

"I don't know. I tried to write it the way I thought Mr. Miller would write it."

"That's what I meant. It sounds just as if *he* had written it. I—I have a feeling that he would like it very much."

Tancred looked at her inquiringly. She nodded suddenly. "Set it up." Then, as Tancred turned away: "Oh—John, you write very well. How is it you haven't had a newspaper of your own?"

"I'm a printer."

"So is Luke. He was a printer for years before he bought his own paper. And I sometimes wish he was still a printer."

Tancred took the copy back to the type cases and began to set it up. Mose Hudkins was already working on the local news that Mrs. Miller had been writing.

When Tancred went to the Bon Ton Café for his lunch he found South Street even more crowded than it had been the previous week. The second trail herd had reached Sage City that morning and the cowboys were in town, roaming the streets. As yet they hadn't been paid, as they were not Hong Kong Smith's men, but the owner of the herd was expected to reach Sage City the next day and when he arrived and paid his men, the town could expect a repetition of the wild scenes it had seen the past week.

Lee Kinnaird walked down South Street and made a mental list of the enterprises that Jacob Fugger owned or controlled. There was of course the Fugger Mercantile Company, where Jacob made his headquarters. The Sage City Livery Stables and Corral were owned outright by Jacob as was the hay and feed business and the lumberyard down by the K & W tracks. The Fugger Produce Company which dealt in buffalo and cattle hides and shipped a hundred carloads of buffalo bones every season was another fully owned Fugger business.

Joe Handy was the nominal owner of the Sage City Hotel, but it was pretty generally known in town that Fugger had a large mortgage on the place and could foreclose at any time the fancy struck him. It was not generally known that Fugger controlled McCoy's Saloon, but the bank held a note of McCoy's. And the bank, of course, was Jacob Fugger. Horace Van Meter was the cashier, but he owned less than one-tenth of the stock. Fugger owned fifty-five percent and Van Meter never made a loan without first getting Fugger's permission.

Morgan Holt apparently owned his hardware store, but he was under some sort of financial obligation to Fugger so it could be rightly said that Fugger had control of that business too.

The largest single source of revenue to Jacob wasn't really a business at all; it was a simple agreement he had made with the Kansas & Western Railroad back in '71 when Sage City had sprung up from the prairie. The railroad paid Fugger one dollar for every steer that was shipped from Sage City. With the exception of the first year, when Jacob had spent a certain amount of money to put up the loading pens which were attached to the railroad siding, all of this revenue was clear profit. Fugger bought no cattle and he sold no cattle. Buyers from the Kansas City and Chicago stockyards came to Sage City in the spring and usually remained in the town until fall. They dealt directly with the Texas cattlemen. They bought the steers and paid the cattlemen . . . and Jacob Fugger received one dollar for every steer that was counted through his loading pens. In 1875 the railroad had paid Fugger for one hundred and seventy-two thousand steers and Fugger estimated that the number would reach the two hundred thousand mark in the current year.

The K & W paid Fugger a great deal of money every year, but it had a realistic attitude about it. It would probably receive much of the freight without Fugger's assistance, but it would lose much of it, too. The eastern Kansas towns that had once shipped a considerable number of steers gave the railroad virtually no such freight today. The western towns were closer to the origin of the beef trade. They cut down the traveling time of the trail herds by days. But there was competition for the herds. The Santa Fe reached Dodge City, a wide-open town, much liked by Texas men. The Santa Fe catered to the cattle trade.

Certain smart drovers even drove their herds past the K & W and the Santa Fe and went another three hundred miles north to the Union Pacific. The grass was good all the way and by leisurely traveling and grazing of the herds for a few weeks on the fine grass around Ogallalla they frequently put meat on the herds that meant extra dollars to the cattlemen . . . but no revenue to the K & W.

Fugger diverted many thousands of head of steers from going to the Union Pacific in the north. He cultivated the friendship of the Texas cattle drovers and encouraged many of them to bring herds to Sage City that might otherwise have gone to Dodge City or other points on the Santa Fe. The K & W railroad did not mind paying the dollar a head toll to Fugger of Sage City.

Kinnaird walked down to the railroad depot and saw a hundred head of restless, bawling steers milling around in Fugger's loading pens. A cattle train had been shoved onto the siding and was being loaded for an eastward trip.

A single box car stood on the west end of the siding.

Seeing some men working in and out of the box car Kinnaird strode over.

Kinnaird recognized two of the men as he came up. They were brothers named Strasser who had settled on the prairie south of town the year before. They were now loading furniture and farming implements into the box car.

"You're pulling out?" Kinnaird asked in surprise.

The older of the Strassers, a squat, heavy-set man of about forty, shrugged. "What else? We put in a hundred acres of wheat in the fall. A week ago it looked like it would run close to fifty bushel to the acre. Today there isn't a blade of it standing."

"Cattle!" snorted the other Strasser brother.

"But your farms were fenced in!"

"*Were* fenced in is right," said the other brother. "Them goddam cowboys broke down the fences. We go to see the marshal and the judge yesterday. The marshal says it's none of his business what happens outside the town limits and the judge says we was only squatters on the land and we had no right to put up fences anyway. All right, we know when we're licked. So do the rest of the farmers who settled here. They'll be pulling out one by one."

"Do either of you happen to read the *Sage City Star?*" Kinnaird asked.

"Sure, we both read it all the time. The editor, Mr. Miller, he was on our side, but he's only one man and— and we heard what happened to his paper last week. They broke up all his machinery and now he's out of business. So are we. We're going back to Illinois."

"You liked it here?"

"Sure, but we got families. We have to live where we can make a living."

"Would you stay in Sage City if, say, Luke Miller were elected mayor, if the county had a sheriff who would keep the cattlemen from breaking down the farmers' fences, and if there was a county judge who protected your rights as well as the rights of other people?"

The younger Strasser guffawed. "You're dreaming, Mister. That'll never happen around here, not in ten years."

"It might happen inside of two weeks," said Lee Kinnaird.

The older Strasser said, "Uh-uh. If Luke Miller was elected mayor of Sage City, Jacob Fugger would have him killed."

Kinnaird turned away from the farmers. Thoughtfully he started back toward the town. As he passed the depot a voice called to him.

"Mr. Kinnaird!"

Laura Vesser was coming out of the depot. Kinnaird brightened.

"Hello," he said, "what're you doing here?"

"Mr. Fugger sent me here with a telegram." She fell in beside him. "Who is Eric Stratemeyer?"

"He's a gambler. At least, that's the way he makes his living, but he's better known for . . ." Then he looked at her sharply. "Why?"

"I just happened to hear his name."

"This telegram that Fugger's sending . . . it was to Stratemeyer?"

Loyalty to her employer caused Laura to become evasive. "I didn't say that. I just wondered about Eric Stratemeyer . . . the name's rather unusual."

"Stratemeyer's an unusual man." Kinnaird nodded thoughtfully. "He's got a reputation for having killed about a dozen men."

Laura shuddered. "You said he was a gambler."

"He's a faro dealer. Most of the men he's killed played against him . . . and all of them drew guns against Stratemeyer. Stratemeyer's never killed a man except in self-defense."

Her forehead became creased as she frowned. "Some men were talking in the store this morning, about Wild Bill Hickok being in town yesterday."

"That's right."

"Is it true that someone beat him shooting?"

"What you want to know," said Kinnaird, "is if John Bailey has a chance against Eric Stratemeyer?"

She gasped. "I didn't say that!"

"You're taking the long way around, but that's what you're getting at, isn't it? Fugger sent a telegram to Stratemeyer and you have reason to believe that he's coming here to kill Bailey."

For a moment she kept her face averted, then she looked at him squarely. There was inquiry in her eyes.

He said, "Your last name is Vesser. You saw John Bailey in action."

She emitted a slow sigh. "I was there when he—when he killed those men, but it all happened so fast that I—I don't know what to think. He's made an enemy of Mr. Fugger and . . ."

"You're worried about him." A note of dullness came into Kinnaird's tone. He hesitated a moment, then shook his head. "I've talked to Bailey. I mean that just the way I said it. I've talked *to* him. But he doesn't answer. I don't know what he's thinking when I talk to him. I don't know anything about him. You knew him at Turkey Crossing."

She laughed shortly, without humor. "I saw him at Turkey Crossing. I saw him every day for six or seven weeks. I never knew him. I guess no one knows him."

Kinnaird nodded. "I saw him shoot against Wild Bill yesterday. He didn't beat him. It wasn't a contest. He hit a target that Wild Bill hit but he fired only once at the target. It may have been a lucky shot. I don't think so, but . . ." He shrugged. "That's John Bailey. He doesn't talk."

Chapter 15

Tancred stood at the bar in the Texas Saloon, a half-emptied glass of beer before him. Lee Kinnaird entered and stood inside the batwing doors, searching the room. He saw Tancred at the far end of the bar, nodded to himself and walked down.

"Evening, John," he said.

"Evening, Lee."

"Gil Packard talked to me this afternoon," Kinnaird said. "He said you suggested my name for sheriff."

Tancred made no reply.

Kinnaird, remembering his talk with Laura Vesser, frowned. "I accepted."

"I hoped you would."

Tancred took a sheet of paper from his pocket, unfolded it and handed it to Kinnaird. It was a proof of the article he had written for the *Star*. Kinnaird read it through carefully, then refolded and handed it back to Tancred.

"That's a pretty strong piece."

"It's intended to be."

"As a matter of fact," Kinnaird said, slowly, "I saw something this morning that kinda made me glad you put up my name for that job. I was down at the depot and talked to a couple of farmers who're pulling up stakes. They tell me that most of the others who've settled here the last year or two intend to leave."

"As long as Fugger runs Sage City there's nothing here for farmers."

"Sage City's all right for Jacob Fugger, but it's no good for anyone else. Yet the country around here is as good land as you'll find anywhere in the state. If we let the farmers come in, Sage City will remain a permanent town."

Lily Leeds came out of her office, looked at Tancred and Kinnaird a moment, then walked over to them.

"Hello," she said, to Kinnaird, then to Tancred. "You came back."

Tancred picked up his glass. "The beer's good."

"And you scared the hell out of Manny Harpending," Lily added, sarcastically, "so you think the Texas men will let you alone."

Kinnaird's eyes showed surprise as he watched Lily Leeds.

"I've no fight with Harpending," Tancred said, shortly.

"That's what you think," retorted Lily. "You humiliated him again yesterday and you think Harpending can let that pass. He's a gunfighter. If you back down a gunfighter he can do one of two things. He can run away . . . or he can kill you. Harpending can't run away He's got no place to run to."

"He's wanted in Texas," Kinnaird said.

Tancred drank the dregs of his beer. He nodded to Lily and walked off, heading for the door.

Kinnaird's eyes remained on Lily's face. He saw it redden with anger, saw her lips move slightly and barely heard the exclamation under her breath.

"Damn you!"

Kinnaird said, "It's like that, is it?"

For a moment Lily's eyes remained on the door, then Kinnaird's words penetrated and she flashed him a look. "What do you mean?"

Kinnaird shrugged. "Eric Stratemeyer's coming to Sage."

Her eyes remained clouded a moment, then suddenly narrowed. "How do you know?"

"Fugger's sent for him."

She darted another look at the door, through which Tancred had gone.

Tancred stood outside the Texas Saloon. It was a humid night and the thought of going back to the print shop depressed him. And Lily Leeds' scorn—which was not scorn at all—tugged at him. He turned north and walked to the railroad tracks.

He stood for a few minutes on the depot platform, looking at the north side of Sage City. Behind him, on South Street, was the noise of a dozen saloons and honky-tonks, the tinkling of a piano here and there, a voice raised in song, the shouting and whooping of carousing Texas men.

Ahead, was comparative quiet.

Tancred crossed the tracks. The street was dark, lighted only here and there by reflected light coming from a modest home. Tancred was not lonesome; he had lived alone too long for that. He had learned through the years to do with a minimum of talk and contact with people, but tonight a restlessness gripped him.

He walked for a block and crossing a street saw someone coming toward him. Tancred slowed his steps and watched a rectangular patch of light from a house. The person ahead entered the light and he saw that it was Laura Vesser.

She stopped. "Hello."

"The street's not a safe place for a girl at night," he said.

"I walk every night," she replied. "They keep pretty well on the other side of the tracks." She paused. "I haven't seen you here before."

"I haven't done much walking."

"You're living at the newspaper shop?"

"Yes."

She pointed over her shoulder to a house. "I've a room with Mrs. Martin. She works at the store."

"How do you like working in a store?"

She flashed him a smile. "It's the first job I've ever had and I—I like it."

"Fugger treats his employees well?"

Her smile faded. "I know you don't like Mr. Fugger . . . and I've heard other people complain of him. But he's been quite good to me. If it wasn't for . . ." She stopped.

"Yes?"

"He looks at me. Several times every day I—I feel someone's eyes on me and I look up to the balcony and he's standing there looking down at me." She shivered a little. "It makes me nervous."

"I don't think you'd have any trouble getting another job."

"But I like the store. It's just . . . I shouldn't have said anything. Mr. Fugger pays me well and the work isn't hard."

She looked over her shoulder toward the house where

she lived. Tancred's directness always disconcerted her. Now that she thought of it, she realized that every contact with him had not only disconcerted her, but caused her . . . pain.

She said, "It's time for me to go home."

"I'll walk with you."

"It's only a short way."

He nodded and fell in beside her. They walked a few steps in silence, then Tancred asked, "You're going to stay in Sage City?"

"I've no other place to go." She shot a look at him. "Are you going to stay here?"

"I'm not sure."

"You don't stay any place very long, do you?" She was unable to keep the tartness out of her voice and it silenced him. They walked to Mrs. Martin's house, a square box of a house with a picket fence surrounding it.

Laura opened the gate.

"Good night."

"Good night," Tancred said. He waited for her to move on into the yard, but she did not.

"I'm sorry," she said in a low tone.

"There's nothing to be sorry about."

"Yes, there is. I—I know who you are and I've been taking advantage of it."

"It doesn't matter."

She half turned, looked intently into his face. "It does matter. It matters a lot, doesn't it? I can't get it out of my mind. Wherever you go there's always someone who knows . . . oh, they may not know you, but they know about you. The night before last a man came to see Mrs. Martin. They—they're sort of friends and he comes here two or three a nights a week. He plays a guitar and he sings. He sang a song about Sam Older . . . and you. . . ."

"I suppose," Tancred said, wearily.

"You've heard the song? People who don't know who you are sing it when you're around?"

"I heard it the first night I came to Sage City. I've heard it a thousand times."

She shuddered. "How can you stand it?"

"You can get used to anything."

"No, that's not true. There are things you don't get used to. Things that—hurt."

"Good night," Tancred said, dully.

"Wait a minute." He stopped. "I—I think talking might help."

"It won't."

"How do you know it won't? You've never tried it. You've gone through all these years, from town to town, place to place ..."

"It doesn't matter." Testiness crept into his words. "Believe me, it doesn't matter."

He would have turned away again, but her hand came out and dropped on his arm.

"Why did you do it, Wes? Was it . . . like the song says?"

"No!" he exclaimed. "It's a lie. It's a lie that's grown so big that it's become the truth. Sure, I killed Sam Older. I've killed a dozen men, perhaps two dozen. Why not? It was all I knew." His voice became bitter, but the dam had broken and he continued on.

"I had a gun in my hand before I was six years old. We grew up with guns, all of us. In western Missouri, where I lived, they were raiding into Kansas in 'fifty-four and Kansans were raiding into Missouri. My father was killed by a Kansan when I was eight years. I was fourteen when the war started and I joined up with Quantrell when I was sixteen. The war on the border was . . . hell. We robbed and were robbed, we murdered and were murdered. Then, suddenly the war ended. I was eighteen years old in 'sixty-five and the only life I knew was violence and death. All right, some of Quantrell's men settled down. I did myself. I got a job in a print shop in Lexington. But they wouldn't let us alone. The Yanks were in the saddle and they made things miserable for us. Some of the boys—Sam Older for one—became outlaws. They made things even worse for the rest of us."

He paused a moment. "I was arrested twice for being an Older man—months before I actually joined up with him. I was kept in jail for six weeks the second time. It was too much. I joined up with Sam, in late 'sixty-six."

He stopped and exhaled heavily. "Yes, I rode with Sam Older. That part of the song is true. But the rest isn't. Sam was no Robin Hood. He didn't steal from the rich and he didn't give to the poor. He didn't go around helping poor widows. He . . . he was one of the worst of Quantrell's men. He killed without compunction. When the hue and cry went up for him he became like a—a mad dog. He turned on his own men. That's when I killed him."

He paused again, his mouth twisting bitterly. "But it was a fair fight—as fair as such things can be. I had the edge on him. Older was a good shot with a revolver. He could draw fast and he practiced all the time, but I—I had the knack for it. I could beat Donny Pence. Dave Helm and Dick Small were there and *they* know . . . they know that Older went for his gun first, that I didn't draw mine until his hand cleared leather. . . . Dave Helm and Dick Small know, but they couldn't talk. And soon it was too late. The legend started and it grew. Like the song."

The torrent of words stopped and Tancred stared at Laura Vesser, appalled. Her eyes were intent on his.

She said, softly, "I'm glad you told me."

His hand reached out, took hers. For an instant he gripped it tightly, then he pushed it away, almost roughly. "Good night." He turned and strode off into the darkness and Laura stood by the gate and watched him until he disappeared.

A smile was on her face as she went into the house.

Chapter 16

Luke Miller returned to Sage City on the Thursday morning train. On the train was a pale, drawn-looking man in his mid-thirties. He wore a gray derby, a gray Prince Albert with a gray silk vest. He also wore a broad belt with a holster that contained a nickel-plated, short-barreled revolver.

This was Eric Stratemeyer, whose reputation was known throughout the west.

Mrs. Luke Miller and Wes Tancred, who were at the depot, did not see Eric Stratemeyer. Their eyes were on Luke Miller whose arms were loaded with parcels and two or three wooden boxes. Miller set the packages down on the platform and kissed his wife.

"We'll have a paper next week," he declared.

"We'll have a paper this week," said Mrs. Miller. "We're ready to go to press as soon as the press is ready."

Miller exclaimed. "But how could you? When I left you had a mess of pied type and that's all."

"Just wait and see." Mrs. Miller smiled at Tancred. "Let's get these parts over to the shop."

Tancred was already gathering up an armful of bundles. Miller caught up the rest and they started for the print shop.

Inside the plant of the *Star* Miller stripped off his coat and rolled up his sleeves. "Let's get to work."

"Maybe you'd better read the proofs of the front page," Tancred suggested.

"No hurry. Just the usual local stuff, isn't it?"

"Not quite," said Mrs. Miller. "John's right—take a look at what we've got set up."

Miller caught up the page proofs. He had barely glanced at it, then he exclaimed.

"Mayor! Me?" He read on and as he read a gleam came into his eyes. "I see what you mean," he said, as he continued reading. Finally he looked up and drew a deep breath.

"Who wrote this?"

Mrs. Miller indicated Tancred. "Is it . . . all right?"

"It's great!" cried Luke Miller.

One of the *Star* delivery boys brought a bundle of newspapers into the Fugger Store and deposited them on the counter where Laura Vesser worked. She glanced at the headline and her interest was caught. She read Tancred's article, the frown on her face growing as she read.

Then the newspaper was whisked out from under her eyes by Bill Bleek.

"For the boss!"

Bleek started off with the paper, but began to read it and stopped. He read the entire article on the forthcoming elections, then looked up toward the balcony. He whistled softly, then shrugging, climbed the stairs.

Fugger had begun to total the results of the business of his various enterprises. He looked glumly at Bleek as the latter appeared with the newspaper.

"So they got out a paper, after all!"

"And it's quite a paper."

Fugger took the paper and began to read. A spot of red appeared on his cheeks, began to grow.

"So Miller wants to be mayor," he finally said.

"They were pretty close-mouthed about it," said Bleek, "but I got a hint of it a couple of days ago."

"Why didn't you tell me?"

"It was just a rumor and I couldn't check it. They offered the sheriff's spot to John Bailey, but he turned it down."

"That's crazy. The job'll be good for at least five or six thousand a year."

"He still turned it down."

"There's something about this Bailey I can't put my finger on," said Fugger. "And Miller, too. He's been twice as bad since Bailey's gone to work for him." He leaned back and the faint appearance of what might have been a smile on someone else broke his features.

"A man named Stratemeyer came to town today. . . ."

"I've seen him," said Bleek shortly. "You . . . sent for him?"

"Nobody knows that."

"Three people today told me that you sent for him."

Fugger made an angry gesture. "Stratemeyer hasn't been in here and he isn't going to be. He's going to deal faro for McCoy."

"And what about those gunfighters Hong Kong Smith's bringing from Texas? What're they going to do?"

"Where'd you hear about them?" snapped Fugger.

"Smith likes to talk when he's sober and when he's drunk he talks twice as much." Bleek paused. "You're going to fill up the town with gunfighters." He looked morosely at his employer. "Used to be *I* took care of all these things."

"You didn't take care of Bailey!"

"I can lick him," said Bleek.

"Can you?" sneered Fugger.

Bleek turned and walked heavily down the stairs to the store and out to the street. Fugger's eyes fell to his work, but for a long while he did not see the figures before him.

Bill Bleek was known to take two or three drinks of an evening, but he spaced them out and no one had ever seen him the worse for the drinks. No one had ever seen him sit in a game of chance in Sage City.

That evening Bill Bleek got drunk at McCoy's Saloon and he gambled. He sat in a poker game and lost fifteen or twenty dollars, then he played faro and won fifty dollars. He drank steadily.

And then he finally moved to the faro game of Eric Stratemeyer. Stratemeyer was widely known for his prowess with a gun, but it was also known that he ran an absolutely straight game and his table had a good play.

Bleek played for five or ten minutes and won a few dollars. Then he lost a ten dollar bet and doubled the next bet. He lost that and put out forty dollars.

"I'd better not lose this one," he muttered.

Eric Stratemeyer gave him a sharp look and slid the cards out of his box. "Queen wins, seven loses."

Bleek's money was on the seven. He reached out. "Pay me."

"Seven loses, friend," Stratemeyer said.

Bleek's reaching hand became a fist that darted across the table and exploded on the point of Stratemeyer's jaw. The gambler crashed backwards over his chair, hit the floor with a heavy thud. He scrambled clear and the cheap nickel-plated revolver was somehow in his fist.

The gun roared and a spot appeared in the center of Bill Bleek's forehead. Bleek swayed for an instant, then his body sagged to the floor.

Stratemeyer looked coolly around at the stunned witnesses. "Well?" he asked.

No one said a word.

Lee Kinnaird came into the Texas Saloon and saw Wes Tancred at the bar. He was watching Lily Leeds, who was at the back of the room talking to the piano player.

Kinnaird walked up to Tancred. "Bill Bleek just picked a fight with Eric Stratemeyer." Then, as Tancred looked at him inquiringly, "Bleek found out that a fist's no good against a gun. He's dead."

"Jacob will have a hard time replacing him."

"He's already been replaced," said Kinnaird. "Stratemeyer. Or, didn't you know that Fugger sent for him?"

Tancred shrugged. Kinnaird continued:

"Fugger sent a telegram to Stratemeyer. Laura Vesser told me about it." Tancred's eyes came to Kinnaird's face and the former marshal did not avert his own eyes. "Fugger's deep. It could be he wanted it to leak out that he'd sent for Stratemeyer."

"Possibly," said Tancred.

"You've heard of Stratemeyer's reputation?"

"Who hasn't?"

"I don't suppose it's occurred to you that Stratemeyer's being here has anything to do with . . . you?"

Tancred was spared the answering of that question. Lily Leeds had left the piano and the professor began to play.

An inadvertent tremor ran through Tancred. Then he relaxed and leaned against the bar.

Lily began to sing . . . the saga of Sam Older and the man who had killed him. She sang the song even better than she had sung it the last time Tancred had heard her. She finished to thunderous applause.

"That girl can really sing," Kinnaird said fervently to Tancred.

Tancred nodded.

"She puts a lot of feeling into it," Kinnaird went on. "Especially that song. I've heard her sing it a dozen times and she does it better all the time." Then he added, "Of course, it happens to be one of my favorite ballads."

Lily Leeds came up. "Like it?" she asked Tancred.

"I like your singing."

"Oh yes, that's what you said the last time. But you don't like the song." She smiled at Kinnaird. "But *you* like it!"

"I've always had a weakness for old Sam Older."

"Sure, he was your kind of man."

"I never met him, but I've talked too two or three people who knew him. They said he was a real curly wolf."

"And to think that a coward like Wes Tancred should kill a man like that!"

"Speaking of killing," said Lee Kinnaird, "Eric Stratemeyer killed Bill Bleek just about ten minutes ago."

She stared at Kinnaird in astonishment. "But . . . but I thought . . ." Her eyes darted to Tancred.

Kinnaird said, thinly, "You thought Fugger had sent for Stratemeyer. Don't discount that, yet. I was in McCoy's when it happened. Bleek was drinking—a lot. That's something he's never done before. And he was gambling. I was watching him and it seemed, well, like Bleek was working around to picking a fight with Stratemeyer."

"But why would he do that?"

"No one will ever know." Kinnaird pursed up his lips thoughtfully. "Except maybe Jacob Fugger."

Lily suddenly turned to Tancred. "Lee stopped me from saying it—that Stratemeyer's in town to kill you."

"Stratemeyer's a gunfighter," said Tancred, "and I don't carry a gun."

"Bleek didn't either," retorted Lily. "Maybe—maybe that's the point of the whole thing, a warning to you."

"Bleek wouldn't let himself get killed just to warn me!"

"But Fugger might have had him killed for that reason," suggested Kinnaird. He looked pointedly at Lily. "I forgot—you're on Fugger's side."

"I'm on my own side," cried Lily. "I've told you that before." She turned on Tancred. "I might even vote for Luke Miller. And you," she said to Kinnaird.

"If I'm elected sheriff," said Kinnaird, "I might have to close you up." He grinned lazily.

Chapter 17

Several days before election, Packard appeared before the town council of which he was still a member and demanded that there be at least one voting place north of the K & W tracks, in the "civilized" part of town.

The councilmen looked toward Jacob Fugger who made a negative gesture with his head. The council voted five to one against Packard. The voting was to be held in the only public building in Sage City, the courthouse, which also contained the marshal's office and the jail.

Packard then demanded that the saloons be closed while the voting was in process. He was out-voted again, five to one. He made one last request, that his faction be allowed three representatives at the polls. Fugger thought this over for a moment, then agreed. He did not see how he could do otherwise as the voting had to be public and too many people would take note of the fact if his adherents only were allowed to watch the ballot box.

The same day, Hong Kong Smith's fourth trail herd of the season reached Sage City. It was also his largest, with no less than thirty of his Texas hellions accompanying the herd. The cowboys who had brought up his third herd were still in town. They had just about squandered their salaries, but there was a whisper of free liquor on Election Day and they intended to take full advantage.

Hong Kong Smith rode out to his newly arrived herd, three miles from Sage City.

The cowboys whooped and surrounded him. "I'm sorry, boys," Smith announced. "I didn't expect you until tomorrow and the bank's closed for the day. But come in bright and early tomorrow and you'll have your money . . . and free drinks the rest of the day!"

A roar went up and guns banged. "See you in the morning!" boomed Smith. He mounted his horse and prepared to ride back to Sage City. As he cleared the camp, he discovered that a cowboy was riding after him.

"Mr. Smith," the man called. "I'm Dave Helm."

Smith pulled up his horse. "You got my message?"

"I wouldn't have left Texas if I hadn't," replied Helm. He was a lean, rather handsome man in his mid-thirties, a man who minded his own business as a rule and who was let alone by the wild Texas cowboys.

Smith nodded. "They don't know much about you in Sage City."

"You've got a sheriff here?"

"Not yet. They're voting tomorrow. There's a marshal, man named Gorey."

"I've heard of him."

"You're not afraid of him?"

"Of his gun, no. Of his badge, yes."

"Gorey takes his orders from Jacob Fugger—"

"—who owns Sage City!"

"And who does what *I* tell him to do," Hong Kong Smith said, importantly. "You haven't got a thing to worry about, Helm. Not a thing."

"I'm taking your word for it, but I've been around a long time. That's because I've always been careful." His eyes narrowed thoughtfully. "This election tomorrow . . . any chance of it going against Jacob Fugger?"

Hong Kong Smith chuckled. He closed one eye in a huge wink.

At seven A.M. Marshal Chuck Gorey hung up a sign outside the marshal's office. On the sign was scrawled, "Vote Here." Gil Packard, Luke Miller and Lee Kinnaird came across the street.

"Gonna vote bright and early," Gorey remarked.

"That's right," said Miller calmly.

They followed the marshal into his office. A wooden box stood on Gorey's desk. Beside it was a stack of ballots. "Help yourself," said Gorey, indicating the box and the ballots.

Packard shook his head. "We'll wait until the polls are officially open."

"They're open now," replied Gorey.

"Fugger was to have three men here," said Packard.

"Seems to me I did hear something about that," Gorey said. "I guess they'll be along. But if you want to vote, go ahead, nobody's stopping you."

"We'll wait," said Luke Miller. "If we expect to have others vote properly, we'll do so too."

Gorey's eyes narrowed. "You three going to sit here all day?"

"The city council voted to have three representatives of each slate of candidates preside over the voting."

"And you fellows picked yourselves?"

"Anything wrong with that?"

Gorey shrugged and left the marshal's office. Five minutes later Jacob Fugger came into the office, alone.

"You fellows don't trust anyone, do you?" he groused.

"You, least of all," snapped Luke Miller.

Fugger bared his teeth in a wolfish grin. "If it isn't the mayor," he sneered.

Miller's eyes flashed and he was about to take up the challenge, but Packard gave him a covert signal and the newspaper publisher turned his back on Fugger.

McCoy, the saloonkeeper, came in. He was followed a few minutes later by Morgan Holt, the hardware man, and Cece Tobin, who ran the feed and produce business in town, one of Fugger's enterprises. Fugger whispered to them a moment or two, then took his departure.

"We're ready when you are," Tobin announced then.

"Good," said Packard. "I suggest we do this with as little argument as possible. As each voter comes in he writes down his name, so we can check on possible repeaters."

"What if he can't write?" asked McCoy.

"If a man can't write he can't vote," snapped Packard.

"Whoa!" cried Morgan Holt. "You can't discriminate against a man just because he can't write his own name. That ain't right. Besides he don't have to write to vote. All he's got to do is put a cross before a candidate's name."

Packard looked inquiringly at Miller. The latter nodded.

"All right," conceded Packard. "We'll write down their names, then."

"Then let's vote," snapped McCoy.

He took up a ballot and made a few quick checks, then folded the ballot and dropped it into the slot of the ballot box. The others marked their own ballots.

A couple of the businessmen of the town came in during the next few minutes and cast their ballots, then there was a lull in the voting. A frown grew slowly on Miller's face, but it disappeared a few minutes before eight. Two or three people came in to vote and at eight o'clock there was actually a small line waiting to mark their ballots.

Miller remembered that the *Star* had announced that the polls would be open from eight to six.

A steady stream of people came in between eight and nine o'clock and Miller, glancing at the record book, judged that a hundred people had voted in the first hour.

A few minutes after nine o'clock South Street exploded. Hong Kong Smith's men rode into town in a body and whooped and yelled in front of the bank where Smith was getting the money to pay them. There was more whooping and shooting when the crew went into the McCoy's Saloon to receive their money and imbibe their first drinks.

For the next half hour there was only an occasional burst of noise as a cowboy spewed out of the saloon, but then there was a sudden rattle of gunfire and Packard, looking out of the window, suddenly gasped.

"They're coming here!"

Luke Miller left the ballot box and stepped to the window. A swarm of Texas men, led by Hong Kong Smith, was charging toward the jail.

Lee Kinnaird stepped through the door and found Chuck Gorey already there. Luke Miller came out behind him.

"Gonna fulfill our civic duty," Hong Kong Smith boomed. He saw the sign on the wall. " 'Vote here,' " he roared.

"You can't vote!" snapped Luke Miller.

"Who says we can't?" cried Hong Kong Smith. He turned to his cowboys. "He says we can't vote!"

A half dozen guns were discharged into the air and were scarcely heard above the roar of the Texas men. They surged forward, pushing Hong Kong Smith against Lee Kinnaird and Luke Miller. Kinnaird put his hand on Smith's chest.

"Don't crowd me, Smith," Kinnaird muttered, icily.

Smith's tongue came out and licked his lips. "I got as much right to vote as anybody." He appealed to Chuck Gorey. "Ain't that right, Marshal?"

Gorey shot a quick look at Lee Kinnaird.

"Seems I got nothin' to say about it," replied Gorey. "They got a committee of six to say who votes and who don't." He gestured to the group of poll officials, all of whom had come out by now. "Ask them."

"We're asking," said Smith.

"As far as I'm concerned you vote," growled McCoy, the saloonman. He was immediately seconded by Holt and Tobin.

"And we say you don't," declared Luke Miller, indicating Packard and Kinnaird. "Only legitimate residents of Sage City and Sage County can vote."

"What's a legitimate resident?" sneered Hong Kong Smith.

"People who live here."

"How long?"

Miller scowled. The question had never come up. In frontier towns everybody voted, even though they may have arrived only the day before.

"The intent of the law," Miller said, harshly, "is that people vote who have a permanent interest in a community. The length of time they have lived in a place isn't too important. The point is the voter must be a legitimate settler."

"We're settlers," howled Hong Kong Smith. "We're all settlers here, ain't we, boys?"

His men roared in the affirmative. Again there was a forward surge and the committee of six was forced back to the door of the marshal's office. Then Jacob Fugger came through the crowd. He was followed by Horace Van Meter.

"We can hold a council meeting right here, Miller," he said, as he came forward. He pointed to his members on the voting committee. "You're all councilmen. All right, do we let these *settlers* vote, or do we not?"

Miller capitulated. "Save your breath."

Sixty-two Texas men voted in the next half hour. When the crowd in the marshal's office thinned out, Luke Miller left. He walked down South Street to the corner and turned to his shop.

"You'd better go and vote now," he said to Hudkins and Tancred.

"I haven't been in town long enough to vote," Tancred said.

"You've been here longer than the sixty-two Texas men who just voted," snapped Miller.

Tancred whistled softly. "So that's what the noise was about!"

Miller nodded. "We're licked."

"Those sixty-two votes are enough to swing it?"

"About a hundred people voted before they showed up. We were running about fifty percent, maybe a little better. I think we'd have made it, by forty, maybe fifty votes. I figured on a total vote of possibly three hundred and I thought we'd swing about a hundred and seventy, maybe eighty of the total. But now. . . ." He shook his head.

"Have any of the farmers come in yet?"

"What farmers?"

"Quite a few are still around."

"They only come into town when they have to. The Texas men push them around."

"But they're on your side."

A gleam of hope came to Miller's eyes, but then faded. "They're too scattered."

"You were thinking of going after them?"

"Just for a moment. If we had enough men and horses. . . ." He paused. "The livery stable's got a dozen horses or more."

"It's Fugger's livery stable."

"All the better." Miller suddenly chuckled. "Wait here . . . !"

He dashed out of the shop. Tancred went back to his work. Ten minutes later Miller came in, followed by Herb Glassman, Fred Kraft and two other men. "Mose," he shouted. "Quick pull a proof of our subscribers."

While Hudkins was following Miller's instructions, the newspaperman turned to the men he had brought in. "We can't cover them all, but we can reach half of them, I'm sure. Those you talk to can tell the others."

Two more men came into the shop. By that time Hudkins had pulled the proofs of the subscription list. Miller skimmed down the list with a pencil, checking those names he felt sure were farmers.

"I count twenty-nine, but I don't know everyone. There might be that many more. Remember, it doesn't matter how long they've lived here—Fugger settled that. Every man who can come in, can vote. Now, wait a minute, let's not go over to the livery stable in a body . . . one or two at a time. Herb, you and Walter start now." He signalled to Tancred. "How about you, John? Care to ride into the country?"

Tancred took off his shop apron.

Chapter 18

Ten minutes later, astride a rented horse, Tancred rode out of Sage City. He took the south road, but once he passed the last house, he turned to the west and south, cutting across the prairie. His route took him across the grazing grounds of the Texas herds and he soon came upon a herd of more than two thousand longhorns, guarded by a few cowboys.

He skirted the herd, then put his horse into a swift lope that put the distance behind them. Yet he saw no signs of human habitation until he was more than three miles from Sage City. Then a half-buried sod house loomed up before him. It was a miserable house, built of logs and mud, with sod serving for roofing. Behind it was a tiny corral in which stood two work-horses and a single cow.

As Tancred rode up, a man came out of the sod house with a rifle in his hands.

Tancred held up his hand. "Do you read the *Sage City Star?*" he asked the settler.

The man looked at Tancred through slitted, red eyes. "I don't want no trouble. I'm pulling up stakes in a couple of days and I don't want no trouble with anyone."

"I'm not going to make any trouble," Tancred said. "It's just, well, they're having an election in town today and we're asking everybody to come in and vote."

"Vote for who?"

"That's for you to decide. Vote for whoever you please. The main thing is we want you to vote."

"I don't know nothin' about votin'," the man said, dispiritedly. "I'm a farmer. Least I thought I was"—he made a sudden, spiteful gesture with his rifle toward the east—"if those cowboys'd let me. I had a crop of wheat started and they turned their steers loose on it."

"That," said Tancred, "is what the voting's about. Some

102

of the people in town want to put a stop to things like that. And you can help, by voting."

The man cocked his head to one side. "Nobody cares about us farmers. Everybody calls us squatters."

"A group of people in town sent me out here," Tancred persisted. "They want to put a stop to Jacob Fugger's one-man rule of Sage City and Sage County."

"You mean I could vote *against* Jacob Fugger?" the squatter asked with sudden interest.

"You can!"

"And what'll Fugger do to anyone who votes against him?"

"There's nothing he can do. Besides, he won't know who's voted against him."

Tancred grabbed up his reins. "Think it over. But remember the polls close at six o'clock. Get in town before then if you want to vote."

He touched his heels to the horse's flanks and it bounded away. He looked over his shoulder and the farmer had turned and was looking after him.

It was ten minutes and two miles before Tancred found another squatter on the prairie. The man was a Swede and spoke only broken English, but his wife listened closely and questioned Tancred and before Tancred rode off she said to her husband, "You go and vote!"

By mid-afternoon Tancred had ridden thirty miles, in a wide circle and had found eight farmers. His circle had brought him close to Sage City again and his heaving horse told him that he could not ride much farther.

Ahead, was a herd of Texas longhorns. He circled to the left and saw that he would pass near a cowboy.

The man was slumped in his saddle. As Tancred came up he glanced idly at him and averted his eyes, but suddenly they darted back to Tancred, in sudden shock.

A shudder ran through Tancred. He pulled up his mount.

"Tancred," said Dave Helm.

The years disappeared. The man facing Tancred had been one of Quantrell's chief lieutenants, had commanded the troop of which Tancred had been a member. They had ridden side by side into Lawrence, at Centralia they had charged the Union cavalry together. At ghastly Westport they had stormed the breastworks of the Kansas militia. And then, after the war, they had ridden with the now legendary Sam Older. And Dave Helm—Dave Helm had been present when Tancred and Sam Older had faced each other in that crashing finale!

Tancred said, "Hello, Dave."

Dave Helm exhaled heavily. "It's been a long time, Wes." He shook his head. "How have things been with you?"

"Not good," Tancred replied, steadily. He gestured to the herd. "You're a cowboy?"

Helm shrugged. "Texas seemed like a good place, back in 'sixty-seven. I haven't been north until now."

"This is one of Hong Kong Smith's herds?"

"I work on his home ranch. You, Wes?"

"I haven't stayed very long in one place."

"I've heard a lot about you." Helm grimaced. "That damn song, they sing it all the time down in Texas. Made things kind of rough for you, hasn't it?"

Tancred made no reply for a moment. Then he asked, quietly, "What about you, Dave?"

"What about me?" Then Helm exclaimed. "Hey, you mean about that song? Hell, man, I was there when you downed Sam Older. Older was about the orneriest man who ever lived. The song . . ." He wrinkled his nose in disgust. "Try to tell someone it ain't true and they look at you as if you were crazy." He chuckled. "I tried it a couple—three years ago. Told the fella I was Dave Helm. He'd never even heard of me. Just Sam Older . . . and you."

"What's become of Dick Small?"

"I had a letter from him four-five years ago. He was running a grocery store over in Arkansas. Don't know what happened to Fletch McCorkle. I was never very friendly with him. Like I said, I stayed down in Texas. Wouldn't be here now if old Hong Kong hadn't sent for me. Somebody's been giving a friend of his some trouble. . . ." He stopped, his eyes narrowing. "You live here, Wes?"

"I've been here for a little while."

A perplexed frown settled upon Helm's features. "They know who you are?"

"No. I've used a different name since . . . since 'sixty-seven."

"The name wouldn't be . . . Bailey?"

Tancred nodded.

"I should have known!" exclaimed Helm. "Smith said you'd killed three men with just three bullets at a place near here . . ." Then he suddenly winced. "But you're not wearing a gun."

"I never carry one," said Tancred evenly. "I work as a printer."

"You—a printer!"

"If you'll think back, you'll remember that's what I was doing in Lexington when I first joined up with Sam Older."

"Yeah, sure, I'd forgotten." He grinned. "Nobody would suspect that Wes Tancred was a printer." A cloud came over his face again. "Texas is a big place, but it's not big enough to hide from Hong Kong Smith. They consider him a hero down there. He's given the ranchers the only hard money they've known since the war." He looked thoughtfully at Tancred. "By now you've guessed why Smith brought me up here."

"Me?"

Helm nodded. "Funny, isn't it?"

"Fugger's already brought in Eric Stratemeyer."

Helm whistled. "I've heard of him, even down in Texas."

"And there's a Texas man named Manny Harpending."

"Not in your class."

"Neither Harpending or Stratemeyer—or you, Dave—will make me take up a gun. I haven't carried one since the time of Sam Older."

"But the three men at that stage station here . . . or was that poppycock?"

"That was . . . one of those things. It won't happen again."

"You're sure, Wes? Nothing could make you take up a gun?"

"I can't think of anything that could."

Dave Helm showed relief. "I'm glad to hear that. I—I'd hate to think of facing you across a gun. And I don't mean that just because you happen to be good with a gun. You know that, Wes."

"I know it."

"It's because of . . . well, the past, Wes." He hesitated and the frown came again to his face. "I never came in, Wes. I'm wanted in Missouri and—yes, in Kansas, too.

I'm only safe in Texas and I'm not safe there if Hong Kong Smith is against me."

"So you'll take your orders from Smith?"

"I've got to."

"You'll tell him who I am?"

"I don't know the setup. He told me not to come into town today. Until they knew how an election was going."

"It may go against Smith—rather Fugger, who's on Smith's team."

Helm groaned. "That makes a hard choice."

Tancred picked up the reins of his mount. "Good-bye, Dave."

"Good-bye."

Tancred rode on.

Tancred re-entered Sage City shortly before four o'clock. Luke Miller, standing outside the courthouse, saw him ride up the street and signalling to him, came out into the street.

"Fred Kraft's back and Walter Colmes rode in just a few minutes ago. They said some people were coming in."

"I talked to a few and got some promises from some of them."

"Then where are they?" exclaimed Miller. "Only two farmers that I know of have come in to vote."

"There's still two hours."

"Most of the townspeople have voted. There's been quite a turnout, but I can tell you right now that we're still behind at least twenty-five or thirty votes."

"Do you want me to go out again?"

"Would it be any use?"

"I saw only eight people in my circle. I may have missed one or two, but not more."

Miller said, wearily, "Turn back your horse to the livery stable. Then come and vote. We may as well have that vote."

Tancred rode his mount to the livery stable and received a black look from the attendant. "You'd never have got this horse if I'd known what you were going to use it for."

"It's a good horse," said Tancred. "If you were going to sell it, what would you ask for it?"

"More money than you've got."

"How much?"

The man hesitated, "What do you want to buy a horse for?"

"Because I like this horse."

"Do you like it a hundred dollars' worth?"

"I might."

Tancred turned away. Out on the street he stopped. In spite of the fact that the town was filled with Texas men, there wasn't as much noise and commotion as there usually was.

He crossed to the Bon Ton Café, remembering that he had not eaten since morning. When he came out it was a quarter to five. He looked toward the courthouse, then recrossed the street and entered the Texas Saloon.

The place was crowded. A good deal of drinking was going on and some Texas men were wrangling among themselves, but it was not an unruly crowd.

He found a place at the far end of the bar, near Lily's office and ordered a glass of beer. He noted that the office door was partially opened and carrying his beer he went to it. He knocked.

"Yes?" called Lily from inside.

"John Bailey."

There was a pause, then she opened the door. "Come in."

He went in and she closed the door. "Have you performed your civic duty of voting?" she asked. "Isn't that what Hong Kong Smith called it?"

"I wasn't there, but I heard that he voted—along with sixty-some Texas men."

"It didn't surprise you that Jacob Fugger had an ace up his sleeve?"

"He's got a packful of aces," Tancred said. "Including one that he doesn't know about yet."

Lily looked at him in mock surprise. "Well! What do you know?" Then, as he looked at her inquiringly, "You, you actually said something that I didn't have to pull out of you."

"That bothers you."

She became serious. "Yes . . . things about you bother me. And I hate myself that they do." She looked at him boldly. "You know, don't you?"

He was silent and she exclaimed bitterly, "That drove you right back into your shell."

"Don't, Lily!"

"All right, all right," she said, forcing the usual note of asperity into her tone. "I'll put on a new face and go out there and sing for the boys. They've got to be entertained so they'll stay here and spend their money instead of going to one of the other saloons on the street."

"What are you going to sing, Lily?" Tancred asked, dully.

In the act of turning away from him she whirled and stared at him. Then she came closer. "John," she said, slowly, "there's something on your mind—something you want to tell me." She paused. "I—I have a suspicion as to what it is—it's—about that song?"

"I think you know."

"I've seen your face while I sang it and I . . . I've been thinking about you. The Turkey Crossing affair . . . your marksmanship against Wild Bill Hickok."

"Yes," he said, "I'm Wes Tancred."

She stared at him wide-eyed.

"I started to tell you about the ace in the hole that Fugger's got and doesn't know about—yet. That's it. I ran into Dave Helm. Hong Kong Smith sent for him—to kill me."

"Dave Helm was one of Sam Older's men!"

He nodded. "We were friends in the old days. But Dave Helm . . . is Dave Helm. He works for Smith."

"What are you going to do, Wes?"

"What can I do? Run . . ."

"I think you've done quite a lot of running in your time."

"Who would it help if I stayed? If Miller loses the election he's through. If he wins and it came out that Wes Tancred was working for him, it would hurt him."

"I sang that song to you," Lily said.

"You didn't know."

"Not the first time, but I sang it again when—well, maybe I didn't know, but I sang it deliberately, because I knew it hurt you, somehow."

"I've listened to the song before, Lily—a great many times. You can get used to a lot of things. You get a thick skin."

"You, Wes? You're telling me now that you have a thick skin?" She gripped his arm, savagely. "I said I was quitting in four years. I don't have to wait four years.

I've got enough—now. I can sell this place or I can just close it up and go with you."

"No, Lily," he said gently. "I've ridden alone too long."

She let go of his arm and the light went out of her eyes. "It's that girl, Laura Vesser. She's not your kind, Wes. She's—too fragile . . ."

A heavy fist banged on the office door and a hoarse voice shouted, "Miss Lily—come out and see what's happening."

Lily exclaimed in sudden anger, but stepped past Tancred and pulled open the door. "What is it?" she cried to the bartender who had knocked on the door.

"It's outside, there's about a thousand farmers come into town . . . they're going to vote!"

Lily whirled on Tancred. "You knew?"

"I spent several hours riding around, talking to some of them. And so did some other people on Miller's side. I thought they weren't going to show up, but they did."

He started to go out, then stopped. Her eyes met his.

"This is it?"

"I won't be here tomorrow."

The door was open and in the saloon proper a stream of men were pouring toward the front door. Lily laughed. "All right, then." He nodded and went out. After a moment she followed.

When Tancred reached the street, some of the farmers had already gone into the marshal's office, but at least twenty-five or thirty were outside, some on horses, some in farm wagons. All were armed. They were quiet, but their eyes were defiant as they faced the crowds that had poured out of saloons on both sides of the street.

Tancred pushed through the crowd of Texas men and townspeople and crossed to the farmers. He recognized one of the men as one he had spoken to that afternoon.

"We didn't think it was healthy to come in one by one," the man told Tancred. "We met outside of town and came in in a body."

"How many of you are there?"

"We counted before we come in. Forty-eight. And we're all voting the same."

Chapter 19

Luke Miller came into the print shop a few minutes before seven and found Tancred sitting on the cot.

"We won!" exulted Miller. "We won by twenty-seven votes. The farmers did the trick. Tomorrow there'll be a new council, a new sheriff, a new judge. . . ."

"And a new mayor."

"And a new mayor!" Miller clapped Tancred on the shoulder. "There are going to be some changes in Sage City. It isn't going to be Jacob Fugger's private town any more. I've got to go home now. We're having a meeting later. I just stopped in to tell you that we'd won, although I guess you already knew it."

"I figured you were in when I saw the farmers."

Miller starting off, stopped. "By the way, I don't think I saw you vote."

"I didn't. When I got ready there was too much of a crowd there."

"That's a fine business. You go out to bring in the voters and you don't vote yourself," Miller chuckled. "Well, your vote wasn't needed, as it turned out, but don't let any of our friends know you didn't vote."

"I won't," Tancred said.

Miller left the print shop and Tancred, drawing a deep breath, stood and drew out his carpetbag from under the cot. He stepped to the wall and took down his coat from the nail on which it hung. He put it on and without looking back left the shop.

It was almost dark outside and no one paid any attention to Tancred as he walked to the livery stable. He entered and found the attendant forking hay for the horses.

"Here's that hundred dollars," he said.

The man's mouth fell open. "What hundred dollars?"

"The price of that horse," said Tancred, pointing. "That's what you told me it was this afternoon."

The liveryman backed away. "I wasn't counting on selling any horse, not to you."

You said a hundred dollars," Tancred pursued. "That's more than the horse is worth, but I'm paying you what you asked. And here's twenty-five dollars for a saddle—any saddle you've got in the place."

The man hesitated, then suddenly shrugging, got a saddle and went into the stall. Ten minutes later, his carpet-bag dangling from the saddle horn, Tancred rode down the street.

The cowboys, having been held in all day, were cutting loose. They reeled up and down the sidewalks, churned into the streets. They shouted and cursed and sang bawdy songs and fired their guns at the sky, and at store windows.

Tancred was oblivious. He was astride a horse and no one singled him out for attack or abuse. He rode north to the railroad tracks, crossed and rode down the street, past the house where Laura Vesser lived. He did not see her, did not glance at the house as he went by.

Hunched down in the saddle he rode out of Sage City.

Dave Helm had lived so long in Texas he had gotten out of the habit of walking. Luke Miller lived less than two blocks from Fugger's Store where he had received his instructions and his directions, but Helm mounted his horse outside the store and walked it down South Street, then right, past the *Star* printing office and, counting, to the fifth house on the right.

It was a square little house of no more than three rooms. It was nicely painted and reminded Helm of the houses in Missouri that were so unlike the Texas homes . . . and which he had not seen for so many years.

Helm dismounted in front of the house and stepping on the little veranda that was raised a few inches from the ground, knocked on the door.

A man opened the door and looked inquiringly at him.

"Is this the residence of Mayor Miller?" Helm asked, politely.

"I'm Luke Miller, yes," was the reply.

"I'm sorry, Mr. Miller," Helm said. "There's nothing personal about this. It's a job of work, that's all."

He drew his revolver. Shock hit Miller. "No!" he cried, hoarsely. "Don't . . . please don't. . . ."

Helm raised the revolver and fired.

Miller fell back, his head and shoulders landing inside the house. Mrs. Miller, who had heard her husband cry out, screamed and rushed forward.

Helm exhaled wearily and putting away his revolver walked stiffly to his horse. He mounted it and turning, rode back to Fugger's Store.

He tied his horse to the hitchrail and crossing the sidewalk, knocked on the locked door. It was opened after a moment by Hong Kong Smith. Jacob Fugger, who had been hovering back, came forward.

"It's done," said Dave Helm.

Hong Kong Smith took out a huge white handkerchief from his breast pocket and mopped his perspiring forehead. He looked at Jacob Fugger.

"Satisfied?"

"He wouldn't have it any other way," Fugger said, defensively. "He kept crowding me all the time. He wouldn't stop, he kept after me. I didn't want to kill him. . . ."

"Oh, shut up," said Hong Kong Smith. He gestured to Dave Helm. "Come on, let's you and me get drunk."

"I don't touch the stuff," said Helm, morosely. But as Smith turned away, he added quickly, "Well, maybe one drink tonight."

He followed Hong Kong Smith out of Fugger's Store. On the sidewalk Smith started to pass the Texas Saloon, intending to go on to McCoy's Saloon, but a sudden impulse caused him to turn and go into Lily Leeds' place.

The Texas Saloon was more crowded than it had ever been in its four years' existence. They were standing two and three deep at the bar, but Smith grabbed a man by the arm and whirled him away. Another man he elbowed aside. And once he reached the bar he used his huge bulk to shove a space clear for Dave Helm.

A bartender, about to draw a beer for another patron, came over. "Yes, Mr. Smith?"

"Two glasses," said Smith, "and two bottles."

From another man there would have been a protest over the order, but they all knew Hong Kong Smith and the bartender promptly put two glasses and two bottles before Smith.

"Drink up," Smith said to Dave Helm.

Helm filled his glass and tossed it off in a single gulp. He sputtered and choked as the fiery liquid burned its way down his gullet and Hong Kong Smith giving him a hard crack between the shoulder blades only caused Helm to choke more. When he finally was able to control the coughing, Smith thrust a second glass into Helm's hand.

"Drink it slow, this time," he ordered. "It tastes better that way."

Helm sipped at the whiskey and a warm glow spread through him. The dullness slipped away and Helm had a third drink. He drank the last of it and then Lily Leeds stepped up on the little platform and began to sing.

She sang the song of Sam Older and Wes Tancred and there was a catch in her voice and a huskiness that had never been there before and men in the room became silent and listened. A man stopped whirling the chuck-a-luck cage and a faro dealer covered his box with his hands and stared at the layout before him.

At the bar, Dave Helm listened to the song and the knuckles of his hand whitened as his fingers closed about the glass in his fist and finally the glass collapsed and he let the broken pieces fall to the floor. His hand was wet with whiskey and blood and the whiskey burned into the cuts, but Helm scarcely felt it. His eyes were on Lily Leeds.

Lily finished the song and for a moment there was a dead silence in the crowded saloon. Then a man clapped and the others took it up until the room vibrated from the concussion. Lily, her face taut, her eyes stony, walked through the room to her office. She put her hand on the door to go in and could not. She couldn't go into the little room where Wes Tancred had revealed himself that afternoon. She could not go into the room . . . alone.

She turned to the bar.

Hong Kong Smith, who had drunk three times as much whiskey as Dave Helm, boomed, "Mighty good singing, Lily girl, mighty good."

Lily looked at the strained face and the piercing eyes of Dave Helm, which were on her. "You didn't like it?"

"I liked your singing, ma'am," replied Dave Helm. "I didn't like the song."

Lily stared at him. "Someone else told me that." Her eyes fell to Dave's hand. "You're bleeding!"

Helm opened his hand and looked at the blood on his palm. "It's nothing, ma'am, just a little cut."

Lily's eyes dropped to the floor, saw the little shards of glass. Her eyes came up to meet Helm's once more. "Why don't you like the song?"

"'Cause it ain't true, ma'am," Helm said, simply. "Sam Older was never no hero and Wes Tancred wasn't any coward. The song is a lie, ma'am!"

"You," said Lily Leeds, "are Dave Helm."

He made an odd little bow.

"You know him," Lily said. "You talked to him today."

"Wes Tancred, ma'am? Why, yes, he came along this afternoon when I was ridin' herd and we had a little talk."

Hong Kong Smith's huge right hand reached out and struck Helm's shoulder. "Who's that you're talkin' about? Wes Tancred . . . ?"

Helm wrenched his shoulder free of Smith's grip and faced his employer, a spot of color on each cheek. "Don't do that again, Mr. Smith!" he said, softly.

"This Tancred you're talking about," cried Smith. "You know him. He's here in Sage City?"

"Why, yes!"

"I'll be goddamned!" roared Hong Kong Smith.

Lee Kinnaird came along the bar. He was coatless and a star was pinned on the left side of his shirt. His face was sober, his eyes like those of an eagle, searching for prey.

He came up to the group and said, "Luke Miller was killed fifteen minutes ago."

"Oh, no!" gasped Lily. "Fugger wouldn't dare."

"He dared all right."

Hong Kong Smith pointed a thick forefinger at the star on Kinnaird's chest. "You didn't waste any time pinning that on."

Kinnaird said, "Fugger himself hasn't got the guts to kill a prairie dog and Eric Stratemeyer was in McCoy's all evening, so it was one of your hellions who did the job."

"Maybe," sneered Smith, "then again maybe it was your friend, what's he been calling himself?—Bailey. Shooting people when they ain't looking's in his line." He stopped, as Kinnaird's eyes bored into him. "Or maybe you didn't know your fine friend was the dirty coward, Wes Tancred."

"So that's why he's left town!"

"What?" cried Smith. "He's run out? That proves his guilt."

"It proves only that he's gone," retorted Kinnaird. "Mrs. Miller saw the killer. It wasn't," he continued firmly, "John Bailey."

Laura Vesser was in bed, but not asleep when Mrs. Martin knocked on her door.

"Yes?" Laura called.

Mrs. Martin opened the door far enough to poke in her head. "I didn't know if you were awake or not. I—I thought you might want to know—Mr. Miller, the newspaper publisher, has been killed."

Laura cried out in dismay. She threw back the bedcovers and swung her feet to the floor. "How—how was he killed?" she asked, fearfully.

"I don't know rightly. Mrs. Miller told the sheriff that someone knocked on their door and when Mr. Miller went to answer it, he was shot down without a word. But there's talk that a man working for him did the shooting. . . ."

Laura's hand flew to her mouth to shut off a low cry that was torn from her throat. "Not—John Bailey!"

"That's the one. He's been in the store. Only now they say that his name isn't really Bailey—it's Tancred, the notorious murderer."

"Wes Tancred isn't a murderer!"

Mrs. Martin let the bedroom door swing open in her astonishment. "You knew he was this man Tancred?"

"I knew him before I came to Sage City. I knew him . . . a long time."

Chapter 20

A half hour after Fugger's Store opened in the morning, Kinnaird came in. Laura was waiting on a customer and he stopped by the door and pretended to be examining some Levi's, until Laura had finished with her customer. He approached her then.

"You've heard?"

She nodded.

"What do you think?"

"It's not true—about Wes, I mean."

"Wes?"

"Of course. That's his name, Wes."

"I see," said Kinnaird, dully. "You've known who he was all along? Before you both came to Sage City?"

"Yes."

"You agreed at Turkey Crossing to come here."

"Oh, no. It wasn't like that. . . ." Laura looked at the sheriff in astonishment. "No, Lee. He told me who he was before he rode off, but that—that's all." Pain came into her eyes. "There was nothing between us, Lee."

"I suppose not," said Kinnaird. "Not if you say so, Laura. Only . . ." He shook his head. "I liked him." He looked at her, thoughtfully, a little worry creasing his forehead. "You, Laura?"

"What do you mean?" she asked, disconcerted.

"You liked him? Or perhaps it's more than just liking him."

"Oh, no!"

The quickness of her reply did not relieve Kinnaird. He sighed wearily. "I don't think he should have left town."

"But why not? He didn't do it, but because of his—his past, they'd accuse him of it."

"Oh, that's just talk. If it came right down to it, nobody could make that stick. Fugger's trying to, to cover

116

himself." He shot a quick glance at the balcony. "It isn't that. It's just . . . well, Miller counted on him. That's one of the reasons he got so tough with Fugger. He figured Tancred would back him up and he didn't."

"No, Lee," said Laura in dismay. "You're wrong. I know you're wrong. Mr. Miller didn't know who he was. I'm sure of that. He—he's not like that at all. He doesn't *want* to fight. He never carries a gun, even—"

"He had one at Turkey Crossing!"

"No, he didn't. I mean, he didn't carry it. Please—I was there. Father tried to get him to do something about the—the men beforehand. Wes wouldn't, tried to talk Father out of going against them. But Father wouldn't listen. He'd hidden this gun and then—then he ran out with it and before anyone could stop him—he was dead. It was *then* Wes shot them. He didn't pick the fight."

"That sounds just like here," Kinnaird said. "He wouldn't carry a gun, he wouldn't fight. But Miller knew who he was and counted on him."

"Father *didn't* know who he was! That's the point, Lee. For all Father knew Wes was just a man who took care of the horses . . . a sick man. I—he told me after it was all over who he was. That was when I . . ."

She winced and stopped.

"All right," Kinnaird said. He shot another look at the balcony, shook his head and went off.

After the door had closed behind him, Fugger poked open a little window on the balcony and called down, "Laura! Come up here."

Laura climbed the stairs and entered Fugger's office. "Yes, Mr. Fugger."

"I saw Kinnaird down there talking to you. What did he want?"

"Why—why nothing, Mr. Fugger!"

Fugger made an angry gesture. "Rubbish! You were leaning toward each other like a—a couple of love birds."

Laura gasped. "Mr. Fugger!"

"Don't Mister Fugger me," shouted Jacob. "What were you talking about down there, on *my* time?"

Laura drew herself together. "We were talking about—about what happened last night."

"About this Tancred fellow killing the newspaper-man?" sneered Fugger. "Another one of your fine friends, this Tancred. I must say you know how to pick them."

"If you're through, I'll get back to my work," Laura said, with sudden dignity.

"I'll tell you when I'm through! You forget that you're working for me. And you'll work in this town if *I* want you to work. If I discharge you for—for impertinence—there isn't another man in town who'd employ you. He wouldn't dare."

"I know that, Mr. Fugger." Laura nodded coolly and turning, started for the stairs.

Jacob Fugger opened his mouth to pour another blast after her, but changed his mind. He leaned forward, so he could watch through the little window.

He saw Laura walking stiffly down the stairs, saw how she held her head erect, saw the rise and fall of her bosom. A slow flush crept over his face. His tongue came out and moistened his lips.

Hong Kong Smith drank through the night. Once he slept for a half hour with his face on the table, but he awakened when a drunken cowboy bumped into the table. He knocked the man down with his fist and catching up a bottle from the table, put it to his mouth and took a copious swallow of the whiskey.

By morning Smith was stupid from liquor. McCoy tried to talk him into going to the hotel and get some sleep, but Smith threw the bottle at him. McCoy sent out for a big order of ham and eggs and put the food on the table before him. Smith wolfed down the food and demanded another order. It was brought to him and he ate it, then he had a couple more drinks and was able to get to his feet.

"This place stinks," he shouted. "Why don't you ever air it out?"

"The door's open now," McCoy pointed out.

Smith dragged a chair to the door, pushed through the batwings and planted his chair on the sidewalk directly in front of the door. He sat down heavily.

"Bring me a bottle!" he roared.

McCoy did not come with the bottle immediately and Smith dragged a long-barreled revolver from under his coat and fired at the batwing doors. The bullet tore through the flimsy wood and missed McCoy, hurrying forward, by inches.

McCoy charged through the door.

"You're going too far, Smith!" he said, angrily.

"What's that, you damnyank? Why, I'll buy your damn saloon and burn it to the ground."

McCoy made a tremendous effort to control himself. He handed the bottle of whiskey to Smith. "Here's your bottle!" He went back into the saloon.

Hong Kong Smith tilted the bottle to his mouth and drank deeply. Then he lowered the bottle and looked owlishly across the street. His eyes focused on the wooden sign over the Boston Store and he raised his revolver. Sighting drunkenly he fired. The bullet missed the sign by about ten feet, going off into space.

"Too high," muttered Smith. He depressed the revolver, took aim and fired again. Glass crashed as the bullet went through the window.

He was aiming a third time at the sign, when Gil Packard dashed out of the store. He saw Hong Kong Smith across the street and threw himself to the sidewalk. Smith fired a third time and again glass shattered, but it was the window of the Bon Ton Café this time.

"Lousy gun's no good," growled Hong Kong Smith.

He aimed again, but the sign of the Boston Store seemed to elude him and he swung the gun around and brought it to bear upon the window of the bank. He gripped his right hand with his left and holding it reasonably steady, pulled the trigger. The bullet crashed through the window of the bank.

Lee Kinnaird, who had heard the shooting, while he was inside the sheriff's office, came out on the street. Swearing under his breath, he started across the street. As he reached the side where Smith was, the Texan fired a fifth time. The bullet missed Kinnaird by inches and hit the courthouse.

Kinnaird ran forward and grabbed the gun in Smith's hand.

"What do you think you're doing, you drunken fool?" he cried.

He tried to jerk the gun from Smith's hand, but the big man held on to it with drunken strength.

"Lemme 'lone," he muttered. He jerked the gun free of Kinnaird's grip and swung the muzzle to point at Kinnaird. The latter, not knowing that the gun was empty, whipped out his own revolver and springing forward, smashed the barrel along the side of Smith's head.

Hong Kong Smith went over backward, rolling to the sidewalk. The blow that Kinnaird struck him was a hard one and Smith, rolling over, groaned and lapsed into unconsciousness. Angrily, Kinnaird stooped and jerked up Smith. He let the big man fall forward over his shoulder and grunting from the weight of him, carried him across the street, to the courthouse.

Gorey looked up as Kinnaird came in carrying the huge Texan.

"Who you got there?" he demanded, 'then recognized him. "Hong Kong Smith! What're you doing with him?"

"I'm putting him in jail."

"You can't! Not him. . . ."

Kinnaird carried the big man into the cell behind the marshal's office and dumped him onto a cot. Gorey came in after him. "There'll be trouble over this."

"He's made it," snapped Kinnaird. "The drunken fool was firing that gun all around. Almost hit me."

"That was here in town," protested Gorey. "I'm the marshal and you got no right—"

"As sheriff I've got the right to arrest a man anywhere in the county. Especially if the marshal of a town is no damn good!"

Gorey glowered at Kinnaird, but uncertain of his ground, decided to appeal to a higher authority. He left the couthouse and went to ask Jacob Fugger. But that worthy had already been informed of what had happened and was coming toward the courthouse.

He encountered Kinnaird coming out. "You can't arrest Hong Kong Smith," he cried.

"Maybe I can't," said Kinnaird, grimly, "but I did."

"Turn him loose!"

"He's unconscious. I had to crack him over the head."

Fugger cried out in horror. "There'll be trouble over this."

"For Smith. When he sobers up I'm taking him before the judge."

Fugger brightened for an instant, but then looked suspiciously at Kinnaird.

"What judge?"

"The only judge in the county—Judge Kraft!"

Fugger winced. "Kinnaird, I'll give you ten minutes to cool off. Then I'll be back."

"Better come with a gun," warned Kinnaird.

Fugger whirled away. He went straight to McCoy's Saloon. McCoy was bitter about Smith. "He took a shot at me."

"He didn't hit you."

"It wasn't his fault that he didn't. I saw the whole thing. He put a bullet through the bank window, among other things."

Fugger grimaced. "We've got to overlook what he's done. We—we need him and his business."

"I suppose we do, but how far can we let a man go?"

"He's never been this drunk before."

"His men have, plenty of them."

Fugger suddenly bared his teeth. "I'm not going to argue with you, McCoy. The point is, we've got to get him out of jail. When he sobers up and finds what's been done to him, there'll be trouble. He's a vindictive man." He looked around. "Where's Eric Stratemeyer?"

McCoy looked toward a room at the rear. "Sleeping."

"Wake him up."

"You're not going to send him against Kinnaird?"

"Not if I don't have to. Kinnaird's being unreasonable about the whole thing."

McCoy hesitated but went toward the office at the rear. He found Stratemeyer awake. "What's all the racket about?" the faro dealer asked.

"Hong Kong Smith's been shooting up the place," McCoy said. "The sheriff conked him and threw him in the calaboose and Fugger's outside now. He—he wants to talk to you."

Stratemeyer shrugged and put on his coat. He followed McCoy into the saloon.

"You," said Fugger. "I want you to go down to the jail and get Hong Kong Smith out."

Stratemeyer fixed Fugger with a cold look. "I haven't had much experience breaking people out of jail."

"Now, don't you go making trouble," Fugger complained. "I've had enough these last few days. I brought you here to town—"

"Let's get things straight," Stratemeyer said. "You sent for me to do one particular job—get rid of a man named

Bailey. He's skipped town. Maybe I scared him out, maybe I didn't."

"I'm not worried about that now."

"All right, you've got another job? You'll pay me a thousand dollars?"

Fugger swallowed hard. "You drive a hard bargain."

"They tell me you do, too," retorted Stratemeyer. "You want me to gun the sheriff?"

Fugger hesitated. "I'll let you know later."

"You do that, Mr. Fugger. In the meantime, would you mind sending over the thousand dollars you already owe me?" Stratemeyer smiled, a cold smile that sent a chill running through Fugger. He nodded and virtually ran out of the saloon.

On the street he encountered Manny Harpending and three or four Texas men. "Harpending," Fugger called. "If you're looking for your boss, he's in jail."

"I just heard that," exclaimed Harpending. "Who—who had the nerve to do that?"

"The sheriff. I asked him to turn Smith loose, but he said no Texas men could take Smith away from him."

"How about that, boys?" asked Harpending, appealing to his fellow Texans.

"We'll see about that!" cried one of the Texans.

"Mr. Smith's my best friend," Fugger pursued. "I don't think it's right that a man should hit him over the head with a gun, then drag him over to prison and say he's going to take him before the judge . . . a judge that happens to hate all Texas men. . . ."

Inside of twenty minutes, a score or more of Texas men marched on the jail. Kinnaird, pale but determined, met them at the door.

"Don't do anything foolish, men," he warned the Texas men.

"We're gonna take your jail apart if you don't turn old Hong Kong loose in thirty seconds," shouted one of the Texas men.

Kinnaird drew his gun. He was ready to make an issue of it and then Marshal Gorey appeared appeared in the doorway behind him. Kinnaird, hearing his step, started to turn and a Texas man close by sprang upon Kinnaird and smashed him on the head with his gun.

A roar went up and the Texans charged the jail, trampling and kicking Kinnaird as they swarmed over him. Gorey made no resistance and inside of a minute, Hong Kong Smith, only half-conscious, was brought out.

The mob paid no attention to Kinnaird, but when they left the jail, Kinnaird picked himself up, bleeding and bruised.

Tancred rode steadily through the night, until nearly dawn, when he stopped and staked out his horse on the prairie. Using his carpetbag for a pillow he stretched out on the buffalo grass and was asleep within a few minutes.

He awakened a few hours later and was soon in the saddle. He rode steadily all that day to the east and north and the following morning cut the stage trail. He followed it until late afternoon, when he crossed a shallow stream and sighted the stage station at Turkey Crossing.

The station attendant and his wife, a middle-aged couple, both came out of the station.

"Could I get something to eat?" Tancred asked.

"We was just going to have our supper," replied the attendant's wife. "You're welcome to sit down with us."

"And something for my horse?"

"I'll help you take care of him," volunteered the station agent.

Tancred unsaddled the horse and turned it into the corral with the stage-line animals. He rubbed the horse down with a handful of hay while the agent brought a measure of oats.

"You'll be riding on after supper?" the agent asked.

"I'd like to rest here, if you don't mind."

"There's plenty of room in the barn," was the reply, "and we don't see people here very often. Just twice a week."

"I know," said Tancred.

The agent looked sharply at him.

The supper was a plain one, but substantial, and Tancred, who had not eaten for two days, was grateful for it. When he had finished eating he walked outside and, after a moment, found himself heading for the little mound of earth, back of the station, that contained the remains of Laura Vesser's father.

He stood there for a few minutes and when he turned away he saw the agent, standing some fifty feet away, watching him.

"You knew him?" asked the man.

Tancred nodded. "He was a good man."

"That's what they told me. But me, I don't even keep a gun. Ain't nothing of value here but the horses and the company says I don't have to risk my life to keep them."

Chapter 21

Kinnaird, a bandage about his head and showing several cuts and bruises on his face, stood outside Fugger's Store as Laura Vesser came out a minute or two after twelve.

She exclaimed when she saw his face. "You're hurt!"

Kinnaird made a gesture of dismissal. "I was a hero this morning . . . almost." He took her arm. "I'll buy your lunch."

She flashed him a smile. "I've only a half hour."

"It'll be enough." He steered her toward the Texas Saloon, but as they got to the door, Laura pulled back. "I can't go in here."

"Nobody'll bother you," said Kinnaird.

"Couldn't we eat at the Bon Ton Café?"

"They've sent over some food. There's a—a friend here, wants to talk to you."

Dubiously, Laura allowed herself to be led into the Texas Saloon. As they walked through toward Lily Leeds' office in the rear, a whistle or two went up. Laura, keeping her eyes on the floor, flushed.

Lily Leeds was standing in the door of her office. She backed in. "How are you, Miss Vesser? I'm Lily Leeds."

A table had been set up inside the office, with chairs for three. Food was already on the table. Kinnaird closed the door. "How's this for service?"

"It's very nice," murmured Laura.

"Sit down," said Lily. "We'll eat while we talk."

Kinnaird pulled out a chair and Laura sat down. Lily and Kinnaird also seated themselves and began to eat, but Laura fidgeted with her food. She looked up suddenly and found Lily's eyes on her.

"I . . . Lee said you wanted to talk to me," Laura said, in some confusion.

"I wanted to meet you," declared Lily. "I've heard so much of you that I wanted to see what you were like."

"I don't understand," Laura said. "Who . . . ?" Then she looked at Kinnaird.

He shook his head. "Not me." He paused. "Wes."

Laura looked at Lily in astonishment. "Wes talked to you . . . about me?"

"Not exactly. He doesn't talk much—at least not to me. But he came in here before he left and told me he was going. I knew it was because of you."

Laura's eyes clouded. "Why should he leave town because of me?"

"Because he's in love with you."

Laura's hand twitched suddenly and she knocked over her cup of coffee. In the confusion of clearing up, she recovered herself. But if she thought Lily would be distracted by the incident, she was mistaken.

Lily said, "You see, I offered to go with him and he turned me down."

And then Laura felt the coldness that she had not known she possessed, until that morning when Fugger had gone too far, sweep over her once more.

"I don't believe I care to discuss that particular subject."

A look of grudging admiration came over Kinnaird's face. But Lily's eyes narrowed. "Where's he gone to?"

"Didn't he tell you where he was going?"

"No, he didn't."

Laura pushed back her chair. "I've got to get back to work."

"Just a moment," exclaimed Lily. "That fine employer of yours has been accusing Wes Tancred of killing the mayor and first thing you know he'll be sending out a warrant for his arrest."

"Not through me," said Kinnaird.

"He doesn't have to go through you, you know that as well as I. I want to warn Wes."

"I've got to go," said Laura, firmly. She started for the door.

Kinnaird grinned at the furious Lily as Laura went out. "Next time," he said, "you'll let me in on things."

"Don't be stupid, Lee," snapped Lily.

"You told me you just wanted to meet her. And then it turned out to be a cat fight."

"She's in love with him."

Kinnaird sobered. "But he's run out on her."

"No, he hasn't. She knows where he is. She's going to meet him later."

"I doubt that."

"Don't keep your fingers crossed. She can't see you, Lee. Not as long as there's Tancred."

Kinnaird said, harshly, "Maybe not, but *he* can't see *you* as long as she's around."

He went out.

When Laura returned to the store, Mrs. Martin got her shawl. "Hasn't been a customer in twenty minutes," she said. "I'll get something to eat."

She went out and Laura went to her counter. The other clerk was apparently out in the storeroom at the back of the store and she was alone in the store.

She looked up toward the balcony and gave a start. The little window was open and Jacob Fugger was looking down at her. He called, "Laura, come up a minute."

Frowning, Laura crossed to the stairs and climbed up. Fugger was standing by his desk, as she entered the office.

"Close the door," he ordered.

"There's no one in the store," Laura countered. "I want to listen for the door."

"Close it!" he snapped.

She closed the door and turned to find his vulture eyes boring at her.

He said, "You're a very pretty young woman, Laura."

She flushed. "Thank you, Mr. Fugger."

"Call me Jacob, when we're alone." His tongue darted out and flicked his upper lip. "A man like me could do a lot for a woman like you." He took a step forward and Laura said, desperately:

"I think I heard someone come in the store!"

Fugger sent an angry look through the little window, down into the store. "There's no one come in." He reached toward her, saw that his hand trembled and suddenly lunged for her.

"Damn you," he panted. "You drive a man crazy." He grabbed her arm, pulled her toward him.

"Mr. Fugger!" cried Laura. "Don't. . . ."

He wrestled her into his arms. "Throw yourself at a damn killer like Tancred, but a man like me . . . a rich man who could do things. . . ."

Laura struggled furiously to get out of his stringy

arms, but the old man found unexpected strength in his body. He crushed her to him, forced his hot face down to hers.

Laura screamed and struck him with her fist. His mouth touched her face and she shrank in aversion from his lips. Fugger released one of his hands to grab her face and force it up to his and that gave Laura her opportunity.

She wrenched away from him and slapped his face. Fugger staggered back, a look of incredible rage on his face.

"Why, damn you!" he mouthed.

He took a sudden step forward, raised his hand and clenching it into a fist, smashed her in the face.

Laura was knocked to her knees and remained on them for a moment. Then she picked herself up. Fugger stared at her.

"I'll be going now," Laura said, coldly.

She opened the door.

"Wait!" cried Fugger, in panic. "Wait—I'll apologize—I'll—"

Laura went out and started down the stairs. Fugger hurried after her. "I'll double your salary!" he called after her.

Laura continued down the stairs, walked through the store and went out of the front door. Fugger stood on the stairs looking after her. When the door slammed he began swearing low and furiously.

Chapter 22

The stage coach swirled up before the Turkey Crossing station in a cloud of dust and the middle-aged station attendant promptly began unhitching the horses.

Laura Vesser climbed down from the stage. She stood for a moment, her eyes looking off beyond the stage station.

Tancred came up, leading the fresh horses. He saw Laura, but did not speak to her. For a moment or two Tancred and the agent were busy, unhitching and hitching up the fresh team. The stage driver went around to the boot and took out a valise. He brought it to Laura and dropped it at her feet.

"Here you are, Miss!"

He climbed back on his perch, waited until Tancred hitched up the last trace. Then he shouted, "Hiyah!"

The horses sprang forward and the coach started off. Then the agent turned to Laura, his face perplexed. "You're staying here, ma'am?" Then, as she nodded, "There ain't no 'commodations here for people."

"I know," she said, "but my name is Laura Vesser and I'd hoped you could put me up until the next stage."

The agent gave a start and his eyes darted in the direction of the grave behind the station. He said in a sympathetic tone, "I think we might manage, ma'am."

Leaving her bag on the ground, Laura walked around the stage station, back to her father's grave. When she returned, the stage was several miles away and Tancred had already rubbed down and fed the tired horses. He was coming out of the corral and met Laura a short distance from the station.

He said, "Did you know I was here?"

"How could I know? You left Sage City without telling —anyone—where you were going."

"You've left—for good?"

129

"I'm going back east. I just stopped off here to . . ." Her eyes went to the mound behind the stage station.

Her eyes returned to his after a moment and she smiled faintly. "I want to wash up." She started away, then stopped. "You know that Luke Miller was killed right after you left?"

He could not conceal a start and she went on into the stage station. For long moments, Tancred remained standing where she had left him, then he finally turned and went into the barn. He sat on the edge of the horse manger, one leg swinging loosely and kicking the boards with its heel.

He sat there for a long time, until Waxman, the agent, came out and called to him, "Grub's ready."

He followed the other man to the station. The table was set and Laura was helping the agent's wife bring the food in from the kitchen. It was a better meal than usual, with hot biscuits, but it was eaten in complete silence by all four.

When he had finished eating, Tancred went out and took care of the horses. He worked for an hour or more, then came out of the corral and found Laura standing nearby.

"Who killed him?" he asked.

"No one knows who fired the gun. Fugger and Smith say it was . . . you."

"That's nonsense! Miller meant more to me than any man I've met in . . . in years."

"They say you killed him because he found out who you were."

"They know . . . everyone?"

"Yes."

He was silent for a moment, but a little frown grew on his face, a frown that had seldom come on his features, usually cold and impassive. "What do you think?"

"I don't think—I *know*—that you didn't kill him."

"What's Mrs. Miller doing?"

"What can she do?"

Tancred hesitated. "I thought perhaps she'd keep on with the paper."

"That's a man's job."

"Women have run newspapers."

"Not in Sage City, not with Jacob Fugger owning the

town." It was her turn to hesitate. "I—I had a quarrel with him." She bit her lower lip. "He struck me."

"Why?" cried Tancred.

She shook her head in confusion, was silent. Hard knots of muscle stood out on his jaws.

"I misjudged him. He *was* interested in something else than money and power." He drew a slow breath. "Who's mayor of Sage?"

"Who else?"

"How could he be? His term was up. Even with Miller dead. What about the city council?"

"What council?"

"So it's like that. But . . . Lee Kinnaird?"

"He arrested Hong Kong Smith and a mob broke into the jail and turned him loose."

"Lee?" exclaimed Tancred.

"He was hurt, but he's all right. He—he says you left Sage City because you were afraid that your staying would hurt Mr. Miller—when people knew you were Wes Tancred. . . ." She paused. "Good night—Wes."

She turned and walked toward the stage station. Tancred went back to the corral and leaning over the top poles stared sightlessly at the horses inside.

Later, when the light went out inside the station he walked back to Vesser's grave. He stood there in the darkness for long minutes and after a while his lips moved slightly.

Words came from his mouth, "There's no end to it!"

After a while he turned away. He walked toward the corral with certain steps and swinging open the gate went inside and found his own horse.

He led it out and saddled it in front of the stable. He looped his carpetbag over the horn and swung up into the saddle.

He rode past the stage station at a careful walk and did not see Laura Vesser standing in the dark open doorway. Laura watched him ride away, then went into the station.

Chapter 23

It was shortly after seven o'clock on Thursday morning when Tancred rode down South Street in Sage City. There were only a few people on the street at this early hour, but one or two stopped and stared at him, as he rode by, looking neither to the right or the left.

The waitress at the Bon Ton Café saw him through the window and came running out of the restaurant to look after him. Horace Van Meter, who was having trouble with his accounts at the bank and had gotten up early to work on them, stopped a dozen feet from his destination and whistled softly as he saw Tancred.

Tancred rode to the cross street and turned to the right. He stopped in front of the *Star* plant and looked inside. It was deserted.

He stepped away from the door and looked toward the Miller home. Then, drawing a deep breath, he started walking toward it.

He knocked on the door and it was opened by Mrs. Miller. For a moment she stared at him in astonishment, then a low cry was torn from her throat and she leaned against him. Tancred put his arm about her shoulder and she put her head on his chest and sobbed.

"I didn't do it, Mrs. Miller," Tancred said, quietly.

She raised her tear-stained face. "I know you didn't. It was . . . Jacob Fugger. I—I always felt that it would come to that, but Luke wouldn't listen. He was that way. He was afraid . . . I knew he was always afraid, but he wouldn't stop. . . ." She stopped and dabbed at her eyes with the skirt of her apron. Then she cleared her throat.

"Come in, John. I'll make some breakfast. . . ."

He followed her into the house. It was spotlessly clean, although the furniture was sparse and of poor quality; some of it seemed to have been made by Miller himself.

132

"Sit down," Mrs. Miller said, pointing to a rocking chair. "That was Luke's. . . ."

She winced, then to recover, bustled about the stove. "Coffee's ready and I'll have some eggs and ham in a jiffy. There's some fresh bread that I made last night."

She looked at him. "I didn't have much time to make home-made bread before, there was always so much work, but now . . . now, I've got nothing but time."

"What are you going to do . . . about the paper?"

"We owed some money on the equipment; they'll take it. The rest. . . . Mose thought perhaps I could sell it to the newspaper at Dodge or Ellsworth."

"No," said Tancred. "Keep the newspaper."

"But I can't run it—alone."

"I'll help you."

She stared at him. For a moment a ray of hope showed in her eyes but then it faded and she shook her head, "It wouldn't work. It would only be the same thing over again."

"Perhaps, but Fugger'll know it, this time," Tancred said.

A little shudder ran through Mrs. Miller. "But that's just revenge. And—and then you'll be like Luke—dead— and no one will be any the better for it."

"The town will," said Tancred. "And perhaps some of the people. People who've been frightened by Fugger, intimidated. I think," he added, slowly, "that was the way Mr. Miller thought about. He—he knew that he was risking his life and still—he kept on."

"I know." Mrs. Miller looked thoughtfully at Tancred. "We can get out a paper today," he said.

"We missed last week," she mused aloud, "and there's a lot of the local stuff still standing. We could do without the ads, or perhaps just run some of the old ones to fill up space. . . ." She turned suddenly and went to a shelf beside the stove. She took down a large key and extended. it to Tancred.

"Here's the key. After breakfast I'll find Mose and I'll come down to the shop myself."

Tancred unlocked the door of the *Star* shop and went inside. He set his carpetbag down beside Miller's desk, got some paper and a pencil. Words had been pouring through his mind and he began to write.

He wrote a heading, in large letters, *"Jacob Fugger Murdered Luke Miller."* Then below he began to write:

"Jacob Fugger, last week, murdered Luke Miller, the publisher of this newspaper. Fugger didn't fire the gun that killed Miller, but he pointed the hand that pulled the trigger and he paid for the bullet that killed Miller.

"Jacob Fugger has robbed and cheated the people of this community long enough. For his own selfish reasons he has aided and abetted trouble-makers and killers. The men who gallop the streets of Sage City, who fire their guns and injure and kill people are here because of Jacob Fugger. Fugger encourages and protects them and when a man dares to speak out against Fugger, he is shot down in cold blood. . . ."

He was still writing when Mose Hudkins came in and quietly went to the rear of the long room and began to work. A few minutes later, Mrs. Miller entered. Tancred got up and handed her the article he had written.

Mrs. Miller read it carefully. When she had completed reading, she nodded. "We'll use the biggest type we can."

An hour later Lee Kinnaird came into the print shop. "Can I talk to you, Wes?" he asked.

Tancred shook his head. "Later. We've got to get out a newspaper today." Then he grimaced. "Is it important, Lee?"

Kinnaird hesitated. "It'll wait."

He went out.

The were no other callers that day, although once when Tancred was in front he looked through the window and saw Gil Packard walking past on the far side of the street. Packard was looking toward the newspaper shop.

The boy brought the bundle of newspapers into Fugger's store and Fugger, who was standing just inside the door, grabbed them from him. He peeled off one paper and let the others drop to the floor. His eyes took in the headline and a groan escaped his lips. He read on, his face slowly turning pale.

At the back of his store, Gil Packard finished reading

the front page of the *Star*. He stood for a moment, staring at the newspaper, then got his hat and went out. He did not bother to lock the door behind him. There had been no customers in the store for two days and it was unlikely that any would come now.

Herb Glassman was standing up in his tiny little office, across from the courthouse, reading the paper when the door opened and Gil Packard came in. Packard pointed to the paper.

"What do you think?"

"He's committing suicide, that's what I think," said Herb.

"It took a lot to even come back to Sage City."

Glassman frowned. "Let's go over and see Judge Kraft."

They left the little office, crossed the street and climbed the stairs to the courtroom on the second floor. Judge Kraft was the only person in the big room and there was an open newspaper on the table before which he sat, although he was not reading it at the moment.

Mose Hudkins had cleaned up and left the shop. Mrs. Miller was washing her hands at the rear. She dried them on a towel. "Come to the house for supper," she said.

"Not tonight," replied Tancred. He indicated the cot. "I'll sleep here, but before I go to bed I've got to show myself around town."

"Is that wise?" Mrs. Miller asked, worriedly.

"I think it's necessary."

She hesitated, but she had committed herself and she had to go through with it. She said, "Good night, Wes."

"Good night, Mrs. Miller."

She went out.

Tancred picked up his carpetbag, which still stood beside the late publisher's desk and carried it to the cot at the rear of the shop. He set it down and opened it up and then he heard the door open. He whirled, then relaxed.

A group of men were coming into the shop. Gil Packard was in the lead. Tancred recognized the others as Judge Kraft, Prosecutor Glassman and two men who had been elected to the city council along with the others.

"Mr. Tancred," said Gil Packard, as the spokesman

for the group, "we're here because we've all just read this
week's *Star*."

Tancred regarded Packard narrowly. "Yes?"

"We represent the duly elected officials of Sage City
and the County of Sage. We were legally elected and
although we haven't as yet performed any duties we intend
to do so. . . ." He paused to moisten his lips. "That is,
on one condition."

Tancred waited. Packard shot a quick look around his
little group, saw that no one had weakened and drew
a deep breath. "On condition that you accept the job of
town marshal. . . ."

Tancred stared at them. "You know that I am Wes
Tancred?"

"We know it."

The door opened again and Lee Kinnaird came in.
Tancred said, "Lee, they want me to be marshal."

"Have they promised you any special kind of funeral?"
Kinnaird held aloft a copy of the *Star*. "I've just read
this."

"If necessary, we'll form a Vigilante committee," Packard said, angrily.

"Then you don't need a marshal," Tancred said quickly.

Herb Glassman stepped forward. He threw up his hand.
"Wait a minute, Tancred. There'll be no Vigilante committee. I'll go along with the rest on most anything—as
long as it's legal. But just because Jacob Fugger's broken
every law in the book doesn't mean that we should. . . ."

Judge Kraft cleared his throat. "Glassman's right, we've
got to uphold the law."

Kinnaird touched the bandage on his head. "Last
week I arrested a man named Smith. I did it quite legal-
like and he was taken away from me in a very *un*legal-
like manner." He pointed to Glassman. "Did you issue
any warrants, Prosecutor?" He whirled on Judge Kraft.
"Did you sentence anyone last week, Judge?" He turned
back to Tancred. "Don't do it, Wes. They'll let you go out
and face Eric Stratemeyer and Dave Helm and they'll
be behind you . . . a long ways behind. So far behind that
the bullets can't hit them."

Packard asked savagely, "Have you gone over to Fugger's side, Kinnaird?"

Kinnaird grinned crookedly and walked out of the

shop. When the door was closed the councilmen looked uneasily at one another. Tancred drew a deep breath.

"I've thrown it in Fugger's teeth. I've got to back it up . . . I'll take the job. . . ."

The councilmen shouted and began to converge on Tancred. He held up his hand. "I'll take the badge, but I'm warning you—I won't give it back until it's all over. I mean that, no matter how quickly you change your minds, I'll see it through."

"*I* won't quit!" shouted Gil Packard. "I promise you that."

Tancred walked back to the cot and reaching in, took out a heavy bundle. He unrolled it, exposing his Navy Colt. "This gun," he told his visitors, "is the gun that killed Sam Older. I'm telling you that now because it's going to be thrown into your faces . . . that I'm the man who killed Sam Older. Yes, I killed him. I'll tell you this, too. There was no deal. I received no reward for killing Older. I killed him to keep him from killing me. There are no charges against me—anywhere. That's as much as I'm going to say about myself—and Sam Older. I thought you ought to hear it from me."

He spun the cylinder of the revolver, saw that it was working smoothly and thrust the gun under the waistband of his trousers. Nodding to the councilmen he went past them and left the shop.

On South Street, Tancred crossed to the jail. As he neared the door it was opened and Chuck Gorey stepped out.

"Well, if it ain't Mr. Tancred," Gorey said, thinly.

"Give me your badge, Gorey," Tancred said. "You're through as marshal of Sage City."

"What?" gasped Gorey then his face turned a sudden crimson. "What're you trying to pull?"

"The city council's appointed me marshal," Tancred said in a deadly calm voice.

"What city council? I mean—they got no right."

Tancred held out his hand. "Give me your badge."

Gorey's eyes dropped to the revolver, the first time he had ever seen Tancred with a gun. A sudden whine came into his voice. "You're trying to make me draw on you . . ."

"For the last time, give me that badge!"

A palsy shook Gorey and he had trouble unpinning the badge. He handed it to Tancred, his hand shaking. Tancred took it and pinned it on his shirt. "Put your keys on the desk inside," he said evenly. "Then get out—and don't cross me, because if you do, I'll kill you."

He turned and walked away. Gorey stared at his back and the temptation to draw his gun and shoot Tancred must have been terrible. But something kept him from doing it; fear that Tancred, in spite of a bullet in his back, would still kill him.

Tancred walked perhaps thirty yards, then crossed the street. He passed McCoy's Saloon, the hotel and the Texas Saloon. Finally he came to Fugger's store. Without breaking his stride he turned in and opened the door.

There were two or three customers in the store, but Fugger was nowhere in sight. Tancred walked through the store and a sudden hush fell in the big room. He climbed the stairs to the balcony and pushed open the door of Fugger's private office.

Fugger sat at his desk, some account books in front of him. He gave a violent start as he recognized Tancred.

"You!"

"You're under arrest, Fugger," Tancred said evenly.

Sheer horror spread over Fugger's face. "What—what are you talking about?"

"I'm arresting you for the murder of Luke Miller," Tancred said. "You're coming to jail with me."

"You're crazy!" Fugger cried hoarsely. "You can't—"

"I'd rather kill you," Tancred went on, "but Luke Miller wanted things done according to the law, so come with me."

Fugger pushed back his chair and got to his feet. "Where?" he gasped.

"Jail."

"You'd put *me* in jail?"

Tancred stood aside and gestured to the door. Fugger swayed for a moment, then reeled toward the door. He went down the stairs, almost stumbling a couple of times.

Downstairs the customers and his clerks watched in awe as Fugger, followed closely by Tancred, walked through the store, to the door.

On the street, people came out of stores, watched as Fugger shuffled along. As they neared McCoy's Saloon, Fugger's steps faltered. Tancred reached out and gave him a shove. Fugger almost fell on his face. He cried out, recovered and almost ran ahead of Tancred.

Hong Kong Smith, half-sober, stared at Tancred as he passed. Then he turned to a cowboy. "Get Dave Helm and Manny Harpending." He saw McCoy's face over the batwing doors. "Get Eric Stratemeyer."

Fugger marched into the marshal's office and stopped. Tancred indicated the door leading to the cell in the rear.

"Not in there," sobbed Fugger.

Tancred opened the door and shoved Fugger in violently. Then he turned the key in the door.

As he came out of the marshal's office, Lee Kinnaird came up. "So you've done it!"

Tancred nodded. "I'll be back in a little while . . . to face them."

He walked down the street, cutting diagonally across, so that he reached the far sidewalk in front of McCoy's Saloon. Hong Kong Smith stood outside the door. His face was coldly savage.

"You've got an hour to get out of town," said Tancred.

"You've got about a half hour—to live!" retorted Hong Kong Smith.

Tancred went on to the Texas Saloon. He entered.

Lily Leeds was behind the bar, but when she saw Tancred her face paled and she walked to her office. Tancred followed her into the little room and closed the door.

"She found you!" Lily said.

"Laura? Yes."

"You love her, Wes! Then why didn't you go away with her? Why did you come back?"

"What else could I do, Lily? I couldn't run—any more. A man's got to make a stand somewhere."

"You can't fight them all. There are too many."

"I've got Fugger and he gives the orders. He'll be the first to die . . . and I think he's afraid to die." He looked at her sharply. "I just wanted to ask you one question . . . what's happened to Lee Kinnaird?"

"What do you mean, Wes?"

"He's . . . different."

"Oh, he had a rather hard time of it while you were gone. He arrested Hong Kong Smith."

"I know about that. That wouldn't change him."

"Well, maybe he thinks the situation is hopeless . . ." Then, as Tancred started to turn away, "Wait . . . !"

He stopped and looked at her.

She said, "He's in love with Laura Vesser. He . . . he hates you."

He let out a heavy sigh and opened the door. Lily cried out, "Wes . . . !"

He went out.

Chapter 24

When he came out of the saloon, Tancred saw a knot of Texas men gathered around Hong Kong Smith. It was a quiet group, however. They watched him as he crossed the street, but no one spoke, no one made a move.

He went on to the courthouse. Kinnaird stepped out as he came up. Behind Tancred, down the street, horses came galloping.

Kinnaird said, "Fugger offered me ten thousand dollars to turn him loose."

"He made me an offer once," Tancred said. "He said every man had a price."

Kinnaird, looking past Tancred, nodded. "They're coming."

Tancred stepped aside, made a half turn, to that he was facing Kinnaird and could look down the street. The horsemen had come to a halt in front of McCoy's Saloon and were dismounting. Hong Kong Smith and his other group had merged with them. The augmented force began to move on foot, diagonally across the street, toward the jail.

Hong Kong Smith walked in front. At his left were Manny Harpending and Dave Helm. On his right was Eric Stratemeyer, coatless, the cheap, nickel-plated revolver conspicuous in its holster. Behind the quartet came the Texas men.

Chuck Gorey came around the side of the jail, saw Tancred and stopped.

Tancred said, "I thought you might miss it, Gorey."

Sudden fear showed on Gorey's face. He started to back away, but Tancred halted him. "Stand still." He nodded to Kinnaird.

"Bring out Fugger."

Kinnaird waited a brief moment. "I can't. I let him out the back way."

141

"So ten thousand *was* your price!"

"No," said Kinnaird. "It wasn't the money. It was . . ."

"Never mind. It's too late."

He took another backward step and Kinnaird moved out of the doorway, across from Tancred.

A dozen feet away Hong Kong Smith stopped.

"Your half hour's up," he growled.

Gil Packard, Prosecutor Glassman, Judge Kraft and the other men who had called on Tancred a half hour ago, came around the corner and started across the street.

"Hold everything!" Packard called out.

Without looking at them, Tancred said, sharply, "Keep out of this. It's my fight."

Eric Stratemeyer pointed. "Is that the gun with which you killed Sam Older?" His voice was a taunt, the challenge from which there was no turning back.

"In spite of his faults," Tancred said, taking it up, "Sam Older never asked for the odds."

Stung, Stratemeyer sneered. "Look who's talking . . . the yellow-bellied coward who shot Sam Older in the back. . . ." He pursed up his lips and began to whistle the tune of the ballad of Sam Older.

Dave Helm said, suddenly, thickly, "Hong Kong, I didn't bargain for this." He took a quick step forward, made a half turn to face the Texas men. "I'll kill the first man who makes a move. . . ."

Still whistling, Stratemeyer's hand streaked for his gun.

He was fast, terribly fast, yet nine years ago, Tancred would have beaten him. But the years told and Stratemeyer's gun was in his hand, spouting flame and lead, when Tancred's came up.

It was the speed of the draw and the fast triggering that was so necessary to a professional gunfighter of Stratemeyer's calibre that beat him. He drew fast and he fired fast, but his aim was not true enough. He counted entirely on his speed. His first bullet missed Tancred by a hair's breadth and his second tore through Tancred's shirt and barely grazed his skin. There was no third bullet, for Tancred's caught him squarely between the eyes.

Tancred made his half-swivel, caught Kinnaird with his gun just clearing the holster. Kinnaird, in that last instant of his life, saw his fate and started to cry out. Tancred's bullet choked it off.

Harpending went for his gun only a fraction of an instant

after Stratemeyer, but he never quite got his gun out. Dave Helm's bullet caught him in the stomach and Harpending, gasping, folded forward.

Hong Kong Smith, the big, booming man from Texas, was suddenly paralyzed. His hands went halfway up and he babbled: "Don't shoot—don't shoot—"

His lips twisted into a sneer, Dave Helm stepped forward. He thrust out his gun so that the muzzle was almost touching Smith. He said, "This is the way I gave it to Luke Miller . . ." and pulled the trigger.

Tancred turned on Chuck Gorey. The ex-marshal stood, his mouth wide open in fright, his hand frozen, the fingers crooked, halfway to his gun.

"Go ahead, Gorey!" snapped Tancred. "Make your play!"

But Gorey could not move.

Then Jacob Fugger, the middle-aged book-keeper turned tycoon, hurtled out from between the jail and the adjoining building. There was a gun in his hand, and saliva drooling from his mouth. His eyes, the eyes of a madman, were straight ahead.

And straight ahead of him, his back turned to Fugger, was Dave Helm.

Fugger pulled the trigger. Tancred saw the bullet hit Helm, hurl him forward to his knees. He turned his gun on Fugger, but held his fire.

Slowly, with great effort and agony on his face, Dave Helm twisted around. His gun came up—thundered. Fugger let out an unearthly scream and hit the earth. His legs thrashed wildly.

Helm's tortured face came up. His eyes met Tancred's across the distance.

"Good-bye, Wes!" he choked.

"Good-bye, Dave," said Tancred, soberly. He started forward but Helm's eyes glazed and he fell forward on his face.

Not one of the Texas men drew a gun. Dave Helm's defection had stopped them. Or, perhaps, they were men, like Helm, who didn't like the odds—if they were against the other man.

Tancred stepped out and turned. He cocked his head to one side and watched Gil Packard come slowly forward. Shock showed on the merchant's face.

"It's over," said Tancred. He looked at Packard, then

at the Texas men who still stood where they had stopped
behind Hong Kong Smith.

He raised the gun that had killed Sam Older and realized that he no longer had any aversion for it. He felt
very tired, but an odd peace had come over him.

Then his eyes went beyond the Texas men, up the
street. Far away, past Fugger's Store, he saw a swiftly
running figure, a girl. Behind her, at the depot, was the
morning train from the east.

A half smile came over Tancred's face. He thrust the
revolver under his waistband and took off the marshal's
badge that he had pinned on less than a half hour ago.

"I won't need this any more," he said. He tossed it to
Gil Packard. Packard tried to catch it, but missed and
stooped to pick it up from the ground. When he straightened with the badge in his hand, Tancred had gone away.

He was walking down the street, toward Laura Vesser,
who was coming from the train toward him.

They met ten feet from the door of the Texas Saloon.
Lily Leeds standing in the doorway, looked at them
for a moment, then turned and went back into the saloon.

THE BUSHWHACKERS

———◆◆———

Chapter ONE

Quantrell looked around the ring of faces—at the blood-shot eyes of Bloody Bill Anderson, the saliva-dripping mouth of George Todd, the icy blue eyes of the youngster, Frank James, at the impassive face of big Cole Younger.

"Well, gentlemen," Quantrell said, "I'll leave it up to you. It's not much of a fort, but a hundred Union soldiers can give us a rough time of it."

"A hundred Yanks—pah!" sneered Bloody Bill Anderson.

"We'll lose some good men."

"I don't see that there's any argument," growled the savage George Todd. "We can't go back to Missouri and it's five hundred miles to Texas. We need the supplies."

"That's the only reason I'm even discussing the matter," agreed Quantrell. "We need the supplies."

"Then what're we waitin' for?" asked Cole Younger.

Wild Arch Clements turned from the edge of the clearing, trotted back to Quantrell and his group. "Reinforcements, Colonel!"

Quantrell and his lieutenants quickly moved to the edge of the trees. The unfinished fort—merely an earthen breastwork, five feet high—was two hundred yards to the west and south. A half mile away, approaching the fort from the north, was a strung-out detachment: thirty or forty blue-clad soldiers; two ambulances containing musicians, whose gleaming instruments were bared to the sun; and another ambulance containing two civilians and an officer.

"General Blunt!" exclaimed Quantrell. "I heard he was on his way here to take command."

"A general!" yipped Bloody Bill Anderson. "I ain't never killed me a general."

"You won't kill *this* one," snapped Quantrell. "We'll take him prisoner. With a general to dicker for . . ."

"Let's go!" howled George Todd, vaulting into the saddle of his horse.

"A general!" cried Arch Clements. "Let's capture us a general!"

A wild yell went up among the guerrillas, and there was a swift, reckless forward movement. Quantrell shouted for order, but was unheard. Still afoot, he was knocked aside as the guerrilla command swarmed out of the woods that had sheltered them and into the clearing.

In front of the earthen fort, in a double rank, stood some forty Union soldiers, ready to salute their new commanding officer as he approached. At sight of the two hundred-odd guerrillas headed for them, the soldiers broke and rushed for the protection of the earthen walls.

The guerrillas instinctively swerved away from the fort, to drive a wedge between it and the approaching detachment. They rode wildly, without formation, but every man was armed with a minimum of two Navy Colts. They rode with the reins between their teeth, a revolver in each hand.

General Blunt saw them coming. He stood up in his ambulance, began issuing commands, none of which were heard by his bodyguard. Blunt was new in Kansas; his men were veterans. They had fought Quantrell before— and they were alive because they had fled from him.

They fled now. They dispersed in all directions, some taking off for the open prairie, some galloping back toward the north, a desperate few riding furiously for the protection of the earthwork. Only a half-dozen men stood to fight it out. They died.

The members of the band were encumbered by their instruments. Bullets began banging on brass horns, cut through drums and smashed fifes.

A horse went down and his team mates began to plunge and rear, upsetting one ambulance. The bandsmen were spilled to the ground and were quickly dispatched by the guerrillas now wheeling and whirling, yelling and scream-ing, fighting and firing.

Thirty bandsmen died, as did five Union cavalrymen. General Blunt somehow got through the milling guerrillas and, under cover of a hot protecting fire from the breast-work, reached the confines of the new fort.

The guerrillas, just out of effective carbine range from the fort, began to plunder the dead soldiers and bands-men. Bloody Bill Anderson kicked a dying man in the face, stooped and picked up a large portfolio that lay on the ground. He tore it open, stared at what he saw and gestured to Quantrell.

"Charley, look at this!"

Quantrell rode over and took a rectangular piece of pasteboard from Anderson's hand.

His eyes narrowed. "It's a picture . . ."

"Lawrence! In front of the Eldridge House. That's me, there. . . ." Anderson pointed at one of the figures in the sketch.

Quantrell nodded. "A very good likeness, Bill. Al-though I can't say the same for this one of me."

"Looks *just* like you," chuckled Anderson wickedly. "And if I remember right, this happened just about like he's got it here." He looked sharply at Quantrell. "You think he was there?"

With the toe of his boot, Quantrell turned the dying man half over. He looked thoughtfully at the pain-distort-ed face. Slowly he shook his head. "If he was, he was hiding," Quantrell said. He stooped, reached inside the man's coat and took out a leather wallet. He opened it and skimmed through some papers and cards, finally stop-ping to read one: "JOHN HOVEY, *Fred Cowan's Illus-trated Weekly.*"

"A newspaperman!"

"A very good one, too," said Quantrell. "I've seen his sketches and battle reports in Cowan's paper."

"Well, this is one picture you won't see in it," growled Bloody Bill Anderson, reaching for the sketch in Quan-trell's hand.

Quantrell drew back. "No," he said sardonically. "It's

the least we can do for Mr. Hovey." He looked down at the dying man. "He didn't get a chance to mail it to the paper, so I think *we* ought to mail it for him."

Anderson stared at Quantrell, then began to chuckle. "All right, Charley; let's mail it to the paper. They can print it—after he's dead."

Carelessly he pointed one of his Navy Colts at the head of the dying John Hovey. He pulled the trigger.

Chapter TWO

It gets warm in Missouri river-bottom lands and sometimes after a good rain, or before it, the humidity rises into the nineties. On such days only the Negroes could toil in the fields, but the Negroes now were free, so they did not do much field work in mid-July. It wasn't necessary, when a good strong buck could pick up an easy fifty cents, or even a dollar, for a few hours of light work in one of the villages or hamlets.

Not more than four blacks were on the street of Raytown as Bokker stepped down from the stage in front of the express office. The agent remained inside, and since there were no other passengers, either coming or going, the stage pulled off, leaving Bokker on the wooden sidewalk with his valise.

He signaled to a Negro loitering in front of a nearby store. The man shuffled over. "I'm looking for a man named Grayson," Bokker said. "Bill Grayson. Do you know where he lives?"

"Yassuh," was the reply.

Bokker waited for the details and when they did not come, said gently, "Where?"

The man pointed down the street. "You goes right down this here road, to the first turn, 'bout a half mile. You go along the turn mebbe a mile, mebbe mile and a half. That's Cap'n Grayson's place. Spick 'n span, bran'-new white house."

"I can hire a rig?"

"Spec so. Mistah Lamon, what runs the hotel, has some car'idges."

"Thank you, Sambo," said Bokker. He picked up his carpetbag.

9

The Negro let him take a half-dozen steps before he said, "Tha's where he lives, like I told you, but if it's the Cap'n you want to see, he ain't there."

Bokker turned. "Where is he?"

The Negro pointed to a building across the street, a rather large two-story frame building, newly painted. It had a big sign across the veranda: *Raytown Hotel-Bar.*

"You find him in the bar."

Bokker did not bother to thank the Negro a second time. He crossed the street and climbed a short flight of steps to the lobby of the hotel. It was cooler inside, and off to the left, the bar, darkened, was even cooler.

A colorless man of about forty was leaning over the hotel desk, reading a newspaper. He looked up as Bokker entered.

"Afternoon, Stranger. Room?"

"Later." Bokker set his carpetbag valise on the floor near the desk. "A cold beer first, I think."

"Coldest this side of Westport. Yes, sir!"

Bokker went into the room at the left. It contained a fairly long bar, four or five tables and a good dozen patrons, some of whom were cool enough to wear their coats.

Bokker stepped up to the bar. "A big, cold beer," he said, "then a short one, right away."

The bartender, without comment, drew a large, foaming glass of beer and set it down before Bokker. As he quaffed the refreshing fluid, the bartender set a smaller glass of beer before him.

Bokker drained the large glass and exhaled contentedly. Then he picked up the short glass and looked around. Bill Grayson, one of those wearing a linen coat, sat at a table nearby, with a friend who was drinking beer. Grayson had a whiskey glass before him.

Bokker carried his small beer to Grayson's table. "Captain Grayson?" he inquired.

Grayson was about thirty, a relaxed, dispirited-looking man. He had long mustaches, but had not shaved in three or four days. He said, "Pull up a chair."

Bokker seated himself and addressed his attention to Grayson. "Have you ever seen me before?"

A flicker of interest showed for a moment in Grayson's eyes, then faded. "It's possible, sir. I have a poor memory for names. Unfortunate."

"It's Bokker, Captain Grayson, Phil Bokker. B-o-k-k-e-r."

"I'm afraid it doesn't ring a bell. Should it?"

"I thought perhaps it might."

"You're a commercial man, a—a drummer?"

"No, but I'd like to show you something. If you'll excuse me a moment."

Bokker rose and, setting his short beer on the table, left the bar. He returned to the lobby, found his carpetbag valise where he had left it. Stooping, he opened the bag and took out a large magazine.

The hotel man watched him without any show of curiosity. Bokker re-entered the bar and found Captain Grayson now alone at the table. His former companion had moved to a table some dozen feet away, where he sat huddled over his glass of beer, seeking to find in its amber color some chord of memory, or . . . clue to life. He seemed indifferent to his surroundings, but Bokker had an idea that a sharply raised voice at Grayson's table would rouse him very easily.

Bokker sat down. He extended the magazine to Captain Grayson and picked up his beer.

Grayson glanced at the magazine and began to leaf idly through it. *"Fred Cowan's Illustrated Weekly,"* he observed casually.

"Page eleven . . ."

Grayson's eyes flickered to Bokker. He leafed past page eleven, to page fifteen.

"You passed it," Bokker reminded him. "Page eleven."

Grayson turned back. "This picture?"

"Yes."

Grayson surveyed the picture and made just the right, although delayed, exclamation. "I say, this is about Quantrell!"

The type across the top of the full-page illustration read: *"Quantrell's Bloody Raid at Lawrence."*

It showed a guerrilla dragging a civilian by the heels into the dusty street of Lawrence, where Quantrell sat astride a great horse, passing judgment upon the victims. Two men stood beside the guerrilla chieftain, each with a sheet of paper in his hands. The face of the youth who was dragging the victim by the heels was wildly distorted, as were the faces of two other young guerrillas in the background, who were clubbing down another citizen of Lawrence with the muzzles of Navy pistols. Another was pulling his horse to its haunches, having apparently just ridden into the scene.

The clearest of all the faces in the picture, however, was that of the man who was thrusting a blazing revolver into the face of the citizen being dragged before Quantrell. At the distance the man's revolver could not miss, and it could be safely assumed that the man he was firing at died with a bullet in his brain.

There was a fairly long caption under the full-page sketch. It gave names of some of the principals in the scene of carnage and massacre. A box, made by routing out a square of the lower right-hand corner of the picture and filling it with black type, read:

This is the most astonishing picture of the year. It was drawn at the scene of battle by the noted illustrator-correspondent, John Hovey, and mailed to us AFTER HIS DEATH. Quantrell is the central figure in the portrait. It is reported that Quantrell murdered Hovey with his own hand at the Baxter Springs Massacre and with macabre humor mailed the illustration to us.

Bokker said, "You've seen the picture before?"

Grayson looked up from the magazine. "Can't say that I have."

"Weren't you at Baxter Springs?"

Grayson regarded Bokker mildly. "Whatever gave you that idea?"

Bokker exhaled with a touch of weariness. "You didn't ride with Quantrell?"

"Mr. Booker," Grayson said, "I served in the Confederate Army. Under General Jo Shelby, I'm proud to say. I also rode with him into Mexico and enlisted with Maximilian. I'm not ashamed of my war record. You, sir, you wore gray?"

"Look at the picture again," Bokker said gently.

Grayson picked up the magazine again, but glanced at the illustration only briefly. "This is a Yankee magazine."

Bokker decided to try a new line. "The war's been over for quite a while. There aren't any Yanks now, or any Johnny Rebs. Just Americans."

"The hell you say!"

Bokker sighed and picked up the magazine. "You don't recognize the portrait of yourself in this?"

"Me?"

"Third from the left—the caption says, 'Captain Bill Grayson.' "

"We covered a lot of ground," Grayson said easily, "but I don't recall that the Iron Brigade ever took a town named Lawrence. Not in Kansas."

"All right," said Bokker. "I won't press it."

"Never talk politics. Not my business." Grayson nodded carelessly toward the man at the other table, who had been with him when Bokker first sat down. "Lige's job."

The man named Lige couldn't have heard Grayson's soft-spoken words, but he had seen the nod in his direction. He got up and came over.

"Lige," Grayson went on, "this is Mr. Booker."

"Bokker," corrected Bokker. "B-o-k-k-e-r."

"Bokker," said Grayson. "Lige Thomas. He's our sheriff."

"Hoddo," nodded the sheriff. "Figuring to stay in Raytown very long?"

"Any objections?"

"No law against it. Only we had our share of trouble here during the war and we like things nice and quiet. Peaceful. Don't like trouble."

"There'll be no trouble from me."

" 'Course not. We don't go lookin' for trouble and we don't like people comin' lookin' for it."

Bokker got up, rolled up the magazine and, nodding to
the sheriff and Bill Grayson, walked out of the bar. In the
lobby he stepped up to the desk.

"I'd like to register now," he said to the relaxed man
behind the desk.

"Dollar too much?"

Bokker took a dollar from his pocket and plunked it on
the desk. The hotel man turned a register around and
handed Bokker a quill pen.

The date on the left-hand page was two days old and
contained only a single name.

Bokker wrote on the right-hand page: "Philip Bokker,
Beaver Dam, Wisconsin."

"Number three," said the hotel man, "upstairs, first
room to your right."

"Key?"

The man behind the desk frowned. "There's a hook on
the inside of the door. Guess there's a key around here
somewhere, but I ain't seen it for quite a spell."

"The hook'll do," said Bokker.

He picked up his bag and climbed the stairs to the second floor. The door of Room 3 was open and he went in.
Closing the door, he tried the hook and found it rather
loose, but he hooked it anyway. He took off his coat and
hung it on a nail in the wall, then sat down on the small
cot and opened the copy of *Fred Cowan's Illustrated
Weekly*.

He turned to page eleven and for the thousandth time
studied the last work of the late John Hovey. There was
no question, of course. It was six years since Hovey had
drawn his sketch and Bill Grayson had aged somewhat,
but it was still Grayson who stood at Quantrell's left;
Grayson wearing the butternut homemade tunic with the
large patch pockets that had been the unofficial uniform of
Quantrell's raiders.

Bokker's eyes went to the face of the guerrilla who was
in the act of shooting off his Navy pistol into the face of
the civilian being dragged toward Quantrell.

There was a touch of wildness in the young guerrilla's
face, yet . . . it was the face of Phil Bokker.

But Phil Bokker had not been at Lawrence, Kansas, with Quantrell.

Phil Bokker had worn a blue uniform throughout the war.

Bokker took a nap and when he awakened it was dark in his little room. He remembered having seen a candle and, striking a match, found it on the washstand, which contained a pitcher and a bowl of tepid water. He lit the candle, washed his hands and face and then went down to the hotel lobby.

Things were livening up in the barroom, but Bokker gave the room only a glance. He went outside and, standing on the raised wooden sidewalk, looked up and down the street, which consisted of less than two blocks of buildings.

His eyes finally focused on a restaurant across the street. It bore the sign: *Anne's Place—Eats*. He crossed the street and entered the restaurant. It contained a short counter and two tables. The only other customer was a whiskered oldster who sat at the far end of the counter, sipping a noisy bowl of soup.

Anne Moody, a fresh-faced woman in her late twenties, came out of the kitchen and set a glass of water before Bokker. "Would you like steak or chops, Mr. Bokker? Pork chops."

"You know my name?"

"Lige Thomas gets his meals here."

"I see. Mmm—how about the pork chops?"

She nodded and went into the kitchen. She put the chops on the fire and then returned. "I'd like to see that magazine, Mr. Bokker," she said.

Bokker regarded her curiously. "Captain Grayson didn't care about looking at it."

"Of course not. He wants to forget." Anne frowned a little. "My husband, Dick Moody, was with Quantrell."

16

"At Lawrence?"

"At Lawrence."

"I'd like to talk to him."

She shook her head impassively. "The bluecoats hanged him in September 'sixty-three."

"I'm sorry to hear that."

"He was stubborn. When General Ewing put out Order Number Eleven, he said he'd be damned if he'd leave. So they came out and burned our house. He—he killed two bluecoats before they got him." She paused. "You won't get much information in Raytown. Not from the menfolks."

"The war's been over four years. They all received amnesty."

"You don't forget in four years. . . . Excuse me, I've got to turn the pork chops."

She hastened into the kitchen, but did not return again until she brought out a platter containing two pork chops, potatoes and bread. The oldster, meanwhile, finished ladling his soup into his mouth, put a nickel on the counter and left. Bokker was the only customer when Anne brought him his food.

He said, "This was guerrilla territory during the war. I imagine quite a few of the men rode with Quantrell."

"Mr. Bokker," Anne said seriously, "what's your business?"

"I'm a farmer."

"You don't look like a farmer."

"I'm a farmer on Saturdays and Sundays. The rest of the week I'm a lawyer."

"A lawyer!" She showed concern. "What—what are you looking for in Raytown?"

Bokker looked toward the kitchen door, then turned an inquiring face to Anne. She hesitated, then nodded.

Bokker said, casually, "I'm handling an estate. It's rather complicated and I need someone who can identify a man who was killed at Lawrence during Quantrell's raid."

"An Abolitionist?"

"That word died a few years ago."

"A lot of Raytown people died during the war, more

than half the menfolks and some women and children. We—the people here aren't ready to talk to Abol—to Union people."

Bokker nodded thoughtfully. "I got the same idea from the sheriff."

"Lige was trying to warn you."

The frown came again to Anne's forehead and after hesitating a moment, she went back into the kitchen. Bokker began eating.

Anne remained in the kitchen until he finshed eating. As he rose from his stool, she re-entered the restaurant.

"An excellent supper," Bokker said. "How much do I owe you?"

"Fifty cents."

"That's not very much."

"I only charge forty cents to Raytown people. The fifty cents is for drummers and—and strangers."

Bokker put a half dollar on the counter. "I'll see you at breakfast time."

He left the restaurant and recrossed to the hotel. Someone was singing in the bar and Bokker stopped, of half a mind to go in and have a beer. He finally decided against it and climbed to the second floor. He struck a match to find his way to the door of Room 3, but it went out as he opened the door.

A voice inside the room said quietly, "Don't strike another match!"

It was a woman's voice. A chink of light came from the window, revealing a figure standing at the far side of the room.

Bokker stepped into the room and closed the door. "All right if I sit down?" he asked.

"Sit!"

Bokker groped and found the bed. He seated himself on it, letting his hand search beside the bed for his valise. It had been moved and he suspected that the woman—or girl—had ransacked it and probably held the Navy gun she had found in it.

She did not move from near the window, and Bokker could not distinguish her features. He could not even tell if she was young or old, pretty or ugly. He could, however, make out her form. It was slender.

She said, low, "Please don't talk loud. The walls are thin."

"All right," Bokker agreed. "What do you want to talk about?"

"The picture in the magazine. I've seen it."

"When?"

There was a trace of hesitation. "We—we have one. But I looked at yours a few minutes ago."

"Were you in the restaurant a little while ago?"

"Anne's place? No. . . . Why?"

"I had an idea Anne had someone out in the kitchen."

"Lige Thomas, probably. He and Anne are going to get married." The woman paused. "Did Anne question you?"

"A little."

"What did you tell her?"

"That I was a lawyer handling an inheritance case."

"Who? I mean, what's the name of the person whose case you're handling?"

"Bokker. Phil Bokker."

"That's you!"

Bokker shrugged and thought then that it was a useless gesture, since the woman couldn't see it anyway. He said, "I gave you my name."

"It's your own case you're handling?"

"No—no, I said that I *told* Anne Moody I was handling an inheritance case."

"It's not true?"

Bokker said quietly, "You're here because you want to tell me something, or you want to ask me some questions. Which is it?"

"Some questions first. *Why* are you here?"

"I came to see Bill Grayson."

"Why?"

"His picture's in the magazine—*Fred Cowan's Illustrated Weekly.*"

"All right," said the woman by the window, "your own picture is in it."

"That," said Bokker, "is what I'm trying to run down.

Why my picture was drawn showing me killing a man in Lawrence, Kansas, when I wasn't in Lawrence, Kansas."

"Can you prove you weren't?"

Bokker hesitated. "I can if Bill Grayson will talk."

"He'll talk."

"He wouldn't this afternoon."

"He won't talk to you directly. But—what did you want to know from him?"

"I want him to say I wasn't at Lawrence."

"All right, you weren't."

"*You* say so, but Grayson hasn't said so."

"He's saying so now."

"You're talking for him?"

"I'm his sister."

"He sent you here?"

"Let's put it this way. I know everything he knows and I can tell you what you want to know. I *think* I can."

"You know the picture? You've studied it?"

"I know it by heart."

"Quantrell's in the picture. He's dead. Bloody Bill Anderson is dead. So is George Todd."

"Arch Clements is dead, too."

"Who's still alive?"

"Fletcher Trow is in the picture. So is MacDonald Pierson. And Max Hildebrand."

Bokker repeated the names to remember them. "Fletcher Trow, MacDonald Pierson and Max Hildebrand. Your brother identified them?"

She did not answer that question, but countered with one of her own. "You weren't there, but you're in the picture—why?"

"*That's* what I'm trying to find out from Bill Grayson."

She was silent for a moment. Then: "He won't talk. You found that out this afternoon. You can't blame him. The Union Army's still running things around here."

"I haven't seen any bluecoats in Raytown."

"They're in Kansas City, and Kansas City isn't very far from here."

"The army's not bothering anyone."

"For the moment. But we've had our share of the Union Army. We don't want to stir up anything."

"I'm not trying to stir up anything," Bokker said seriously. "I just want to clear myself of a crime I didn't commit. I wasn't at Lawrence, Kansas, and I didn't ride with Quantrell. Not then, or any other time." He paused. "Was your brother with Quantrell at Baxter Springs?"

She did not reply for a moment; then, when she spoke, her tone was cautious. "Is that—where the artist who drew the picture was killed?"

"Yes."

"Bill wasn't there."

"You're sure?"

"He quit after Lawrence. So did a lot of others."

"What about Fletcher Trow? MacDonald Pierson? Max Hildebrand?"

"I don't know."

"You said you could tell me anything your brother could."

"Within reason."

"Can't I meet your brother somewhere?"

She exclaimed quickly, "No! Don't—don't try that. It'll make trouble. And it wouldn't be safe—for you."

Bokker drew a match from his pocket and reached to the floor to strike it. Apparently she could make out in the less than total darkness that he was stooping over.

She cried out and made a rush toward him. "Don't!"

He was starting to strike the match as her body hit his. There was a tiny flicker of flame on the floor, but it did Bokker no good. She was a bundle of fury, striking at him, kicking, fighting. Surprised by the savageness of her attack, Bokker was forced to defend himself. He caught an arm, but it was jerked free and her other hand raked his face. He caught that hand and she struck him with the freed hand. Her sharp, bony shoulder hit him in the chest; her knee almost drove the breath from him as it went into his stomach.

The tiny flame on the floor was out then and Bokker saw nothing of her face. For just a moment he won out over her, as his arms enveloped her. He felt her heart beating wildly, was aware that a tremor ran through her and then she was out of his grasp like a weasel, all sinew and muscle, without much bone.

Bokker lunged for her in the darkness, missed, then leaped to his feet and moved for the door. He was too late. She had whisked it open, was darting out.

Bokker followed. But only into the hall. Her flying feet were pounding the far end of the long narrow corridor. A door was whipped open and she was out, descending a flight of stairs into the darkness behind the hotel. Bokker knew that it would be a waste of time to go after her. She probably knew every nook and cranny of Raytown, and he was a stranger.

Besides, what good would it do to find her? She would tell him what she wanted to tell him and nothing more. He could not force her to talk ... as he might be able to force Bill Grayson.

Chapter FOUR

He stood in the darkened hall a moment, then, drawing a
deep breath, descended to the hotel lobby. The hotel man
sat behind the desk, paring his fingernails. He nodded to
Bokker as the latter crossed to the barroom.

The place was doing a thriving business. Several card
games were in progress and a half-dozen men stood at the
bar. Two or three wore wrinkled white suits and had mint
juleps before them.

Bill Grayson stood at the bar, in a little group of three,
which included Lige Thomas and a heavy-set man of
about twenty-five.

There was a small clear space at the bar, and Bokker
moved toward it, but before he reached it the big man
spread himself and covered most of the available room.

"Excuse me," said Bokker. He tried to move into the
space, but neither the heavy-set man nor his neighbor
budged an inch. Bokker signaled to the bartender.

"Beer."

The bartender shot a quick look at Bill Grayson, hesitated, then drew the glass of beer. There was a frown on
his face as he set the glass on the bar. Bokker waited for
his beer at the edge of the little group. When the glass
was set on the bar, he said, "Excuse me," and shouldered
the big man aside.

The man turned slowly. "You crowded me, Mister.'"

"I said excuse me!" replied Bokker coolly.

"Shovin' a man and sayin' excuse me ain't right,"
growled the heavy-set man.

Bokker swallowed his beer and looked at the other man
over the rim of the beer glass. He lowered the half-emptied glass.

He said to Bill Grayson, "He's going to do your fighting?"

Grayson had the grace to wince. "Don't know what you mean."

Bokker appealed to Lige Thomas. "What about it, Sheriff?"

"I warned you this afternoon, Bokker," snapped the sheriff. "We don't like strangers coming here, looking for trouble."

"I'm not the one making the trouble."

The big man was waiting for his cue. Lige Thomas gave it to him. He said, "I don't wear my badge when I'm having a little refreshment with my friends."

"My name," said the big man, "is Charr Mechem. I ain't ever been licked."

Bokker nodded. "And you rode with Quantrell?"

A sudden hush fell upon the men in the vicinity of the bar. Only in the background, at the far side of the room, was there still a hum of conversation.

Mechem's tongue came out, moistened his lips. His meaty hands reached out.

Bokker dashed the dregs of his beer into the big man's face, tossed the glass to the bar and smashed Mechem in the face. It was a hard blow that sent a shock up Bokker's arm, all the way to his shoulder. It barely caused Mechem to falter and Bokker knew then that this fight would be an ordeal.

He gave way before the big man, who outweighed him by at least thirty pounds. Mechem crowded in, swinging mightily. Bokker ducked, stepped back. A hand hit the small of his back, shoved him violently forward into Mechem's flailing fist.

The blow caught Bokker high on the left cheekbone, dropped him to his knees. A roaring filled his ears, but above it he heard Charr Mechem grate, "Get up!'"

Bokker climbed wobblingly to his feet and was promptly knocked down again. He rose only halfway, then threw himself forward into a tight clinch. Mechem heaved and swung from right to left to throw Bokker aside, but Bokker clung for dear life, while his head cleared. A rabbit punch clubbed the back of Bokker's head.

He gave way, striking at Mechem's face with his fist even as he broke. Mechem was hurt and let out a roar. He charged in, muttering curses, and Bokker hit him on the mouth and a smashing blow on the big man's throat that sent Mechem back, gasping and choking.

Bokker stormed in. He hit the big man in the stomach with everything he had and, as Mechem folded forward, brought an uppercut from his knees. Mechem reeled back on his heels, tottered, and Bokker hit him again. Mechem crashed to the floor on his back, rolled over and struggled to get to his knees.

Bokker made his great mistake then. He waited for his opponent to rise and a blow struck the back of his head and knocked him sprawling on top of Mechem. Both men struggled to clear themselves and Meechem made it to his feet first.

As Bokker got up, Mechem's fist smashed him down again. He got up a second time and Mechem's boot kicked him a savage blow on the forehead. Bokker went out.

He lay sprawled on his back, struggling for consciousness. Grayson called for a tall glass of cold beer and when the bartender gave it to him, stooped and dumped it over Bokker's face. It washed away blood and revived Bokker. He continued to lie on the floor, however.

Lige Thomas said, "I told you not to start trouble."

He stooped, grabbed a handful of Bokker's coat front, yanked him up to his feet and held him until he could recover. He said, then, "The Kansas City stage leaves in an hour. Be on it."

Bokker could not fight Mechem, Grayson, Lige Thomas and a half-dozen other former guerrillas who were probably in the bar of the Raytown Hotel. He walked, a bit unsteadily, out of the place, through the lobby and up to the second floor. He struck a match, found his room and lit a second match. Bill Grayson's sister had moved the candlestick to the floor near the window, but he found it with the third match.

He closed the door of his room, located his valise,

also near the window, and went through it. The girl had rummaged in it, but its contents were intact. He examined the Navy gun, found that the loads had not been tampered with and put it back in the valise.

He took off his coat and washed his battered face, dabbing tenderly at two severe bruises. Finally, he put his coat on and, carrying the valise, walked down to the lobby.

Lige Thomas was loitering near the front door, so Bokker assumed that it was not necessary to notify the hotel man that he was checking out.

There was a light in the express and stage office, and Bokker found the agent preparing some parcels to be shipped out on the stage.

For a dollar, Bokker bought a ticket to Kansas City, Kansas, and waited inside the station until the stagecoach arrived. There was one passenger aboard the stage, a middle-aged drummer, who was dozing fitfully in the seat facing forward. Bokker noted that Lige Thomas was outside the stage office.

Bokker seated himself opposite the sleeping drummer, his valise on the seat beside him. The driver cracked his whip and the coach rolled away. The drummer awakened for an instant, regarded Bokker through slitted eyes, then resumed his heavy breathing.

The lights of Raytown receded as the stagecoach bounced along a rutted road on the last lap of its journey to Kansas City.

A mile out of Raytown the speed of the coach decreased for a moment as it took a sharp turn. It was then that Bokker opened the door and stepped out into darkness, gripping his valise tightly in both hands. He hit the ground, made a violent somersault and landed on a patch of sweet-smelling clover. He lay still.

The driver of the coach was apparently heedless of the loss of a passenger; at any rate the coach noise progressed evenly and after a few minutes became faint in the distance. Bokker picked himself up. In the darkness he opened his valise and took out his Navy gun. He thrust it under the waistband of his trousers and looked back toward the dim lights of Raytown. As nearly as he could estimate it was around midnight.

The moon was three-quarters full, but somewhat obscured by hazy clouds. Yet it was light enough to distinguish shadows and Bokker set out across a field. He climbed a pole fence, walked through a meadow in which the lush grass was almost to his knees and then cut across a shallow ravine and came out in a stubbled wheat field. He was about parallel now to the village of Raytown, although a quarter mile or more to the west of it. A dog barked off to his left and Bokker veered to the right.

He went another quarter mile and then started obliquely to the left. A half hour of patient trudging over a couple of fields and through a patch of brush brought him out upon a well-traveled road.

He went down the road a short distance and came to a crossroad. He took the right fork. A house loomed up on the right, but it was dark. Its dogs, however, were wide awake and they set up a furious barking. Fortunately for Bokker the dogs were inside the yard fence which apparently was tight enough to contain them. He went on down the road, passed a heavy patch of woods and then came again to open fields. He estimated that he had traveled a mile or more down the side road, and stopped.

He thought for a moment that he saw a faint light up the road on the right, but it disappeared and did not come on again. He moved forward again, walking carefully in the dusty right rut of the road. After a few minutes he saw a cluster of large shadows on the right and knew that he was approaching the home of Bill Grayson.

Then, suddenly, Bokker heard a sound on the road behind him, the clop-clopping of horses' hoofs. In a panic he leaped to the cover of a bush at the side of the road.

The horses came closer. As did voices.

One of the voices said, ". . . I don't know. I've thought about it until my head's been ready to burst and I can't remember. There were too many other things to think about at the time. Just keeping alive."

"I know," said the second voice. "None of us knew

how it would come out. I, for one, never figured I'd live
this long. The things we did . . ."

"We were all crazy," said the first voice, "and the worst
one of all was Charley Quantrell. Because *he* had some
old scores to pay, *we* did things that still cause me to have
bad dreams. Damn that Bokker for coming around!"

That was the voice of Bill Grayson. The other voice,
which Bokker had not heard before, said, "It could have
been Charley who doctored up the picture. He was a
schoolteacher, you know . . ."

"He couldn't draw," replied Grayson. "I don't know
about Bloody Bill, but it wasn't his way. He went right
into a thing, settled it with the gun or knife. That's why
he and George were able to win out . . ."

That was as much as Bokker heard. The horses were
past him, and a dog at the house ahead suddenly began
barking. He was promptly joined by a half-dozen other
dogs and they set up a fearful racket.

A light went on in the house.

Chapter FIVE

Bokker came out from behind the bush and stood in the middle of the road. He was still standing there, when a revolver cracked and all hell broke loose at the house of Bill Grayson. A man's scream split the night air, another gun banged and another. The dogs went into a veritable frenzy of barking.

Bokker was tearing the Navy gun from his waistband as the horse came galloping toward him. He took a step or two to the right, cried out, "Hold it!"

Flame and thunder lanced at Bokker. A bullet tore through his coat sleeve and he thrust out his Navy gun and fired. The horse coming directly at him was suddenly riderless.

The animal shied away from Bokker, cut across a field on the left of the road. Bokker, running forward, skidded to an abrupt halt. Another horse was galloping down the road, away from Bokker and Grayson's house.

A woman's voice cried out near Grayson's house.

Bokker searched the road for the man at whom he had fired. He saw him lying in a huddle, moved cautiously toward him.

"I've got you covered," he said carefully.

The figure on the ground did not move, made no response. Bokker stepped up to him, got down on one knee. Dark as it was, Bokker knew that the man would not move again.

He got to his feet and went forward. The woman was still calling to the dogs, quieting them. When the racket finally died out, Bokker walked into the pale light cast by the light inside the house. He saw Bill Grayson lying on the ground and the woman came toward him, a carbine in her hands.

"Throw up your hands, you murderer!" she spat at him.

"Wait a minute," Bokker exclaimed. "It wasn't me . . ."

"Up!"

The frightened voice of a Negro called from the house. "Y-you need me, Miz Grayson?"

"Yes," replied the woman grimly over her shoulder. She moved forward, thrust the muzzle of the carbine within a foot of Bokker's stomach. "Drop that gun!"

Bokker let his Navy gun clatter to the ground. "You're making a mistake," he protested. "I came here to talk to Captain Grayson. It wasn't me who shot him."

"You can tell that to the sheriff! Mose, tell Donny to ride into town and fetch out Sheriff Thomas, then find a rope and come back here."

Five minutes later, his hands tied tightly behind his back, Bokker was herded into the house by a giant Negro and the woman, who still kept him covered with a rifle: the newly widowed Mrs. Grayson.

She was young, not more than twenty-two or three, a fine-looking woman with hair the color of dark taffy. She was wearing a long robe over her underclothes, but in spite of the loose robe, Bokker could make out her figure. It was excellent.

She gestured with the gun to a chair. Bokker hesitated, then seated himself awkwardly. "You're making a mistake, " he said. "I didn't shoot Captain Grayson."

Mose, who had taken possession of Bokker's Navy gun, sniffed at the muzzle. "Gun fired," he said laconically.

"I fired at the man who was with Captain Grayson," Bokker declared. "He came at me—shooting."

"I'd prefer you didn't talk until the sheriff got here," Mrs. Grayson said.

"I want to ask you just one question—where's Captain Grayson's sister?"

Mrs. Grayson regarded Bokker carelessly for a moment, then her eyes narrowed. "Bill has—had—no sister."

Bokker nodded. "Then it was *you* who came to my hotel room this evening!"

Mrs. Grayson inhaled sharply. "Do you know what you're saying?" She took a sudden step toward him, her hand drawn back to slap him. Then she caught herself.

"I forgot—you're a Yankee."

"How do you know I am?"

Her mouth set in firm lines. "I'm talking no more."

Lige Thomas entered the Grayson kitchen twenty minutes later. Charr Mechem and another man were with him, and Bokker could hear several more outside.

Lige Thomas came up to where Bokker sat in the kitchen chair, his hands behind him. "So you got off the stage!"

"Obviously."

Charr Mechem licked his lips. "You'd think he'd had enough."

His right fist flicked out and crashed against Bokker's jaw, knocking him and the chair to the floor. Bokker struggled up to his knees, licked away a trickle of blood that seeped from the corner of his mouth. Mechem stepped forward to smash Bokker again, but the sheriff gestured him back. "He's got to talk, Charr."

Bokker got to his feet. "It's easy enough to hit a man when his hands are tied."

"I can lick you any day of the week," growled Charr Mechem, "an' twice on Sunday."

Lige Thomas said, "You got a rough tongue, Bokker. Now, let's hear you use it to talk yourself out of this."

Bokker said, "I wanted to ask Captain Grayson some questions."

"You asked him enough in Raytown."

"I didn't get any answers."

Thomas scowled. "You figured you might do better with a gun in your fist?"

"I thought he might talk away from his friends."

"So now you got a murder against you."

"I didn't kill Grayson."

The sheriff turned to Mrs. Grayson. "You caught him with a gun in his hand?"

There was a slight hesitation before she answered. "Yes."

"There was a man with Captain Grayson," Bokker said doggedly. "And a third man was waiting for them outside the house."

"He's the one who shot Bill?" Thomas cried skeptically. "This third man?"

"That's right."

The sheriff's mouth twisted contemptuously. "I said good night to Bill when him and Hildebrand left the hotel together."

"Hildebrand?" exclaimed Mrs. Grayson.

"Yes, it's Max Hildebrand out there in the road."

"Then it's Hildebrand I shot," said Bokker. "He shot at me first. If I hadn't gotten him . . ." He held up his left arm, as well as he could, calling attention to the bullet hole.

"What'd you expect him to do?" sneered the sheriff. "You were layin' out there in the dark, waitin' for them. You opened up—"

"No," said Bokker stubbornly. "The third man fired at them first. Hildebrand turned to run away and I happened to be in his way." His eyes went to his Navy gun lying on the table where Mrs. Grayson had deposited it. "I fired only once. . . ."

The sheriff turned, caught up the revolver and flicked out the cylinder. He scowled. "You took this gun from him?" he asked Mrs. Grayson.

"He dropped it when I covered him. Mose picked it up."

The sheriff whirled back to Bokker. "You had time to reload."

"Did I, Mrs. Grayson?" Bokker asked quietly.

She hesitated, but finally shook her head.

"He couldda had another gun," suggested Charr Mechem.

Lige Thomas pounced on that. "We'll look for it when it's light."

Chapter SIX

There was a tiny room, with a barred window behind Lige Thomas's office. It contained a wooden cot and Bokker slept on it until daybreak. Shortly afterwards, there was much clomping of boots and harsh voices in Thomas's office.

After a while the door was opened and Thomas stuck in his head.

"C'mon," he said shortly.

A soldier wearing the shoulder straps of a major was in Thomas's office. "Major Holbrook, Provost Marshal," he said.

Bokker looked past him, saw soldiers outside the office.

"How are you, Major?"

Major Holbrook shook his head. "This is a bad business. The sheriff tells me—"

"Ah, yes, the sheriff," Bokker said.

Major Holbrook shrugged. "Very well, I've heard his version. Now let's have yours."

"Go ahead, tell him," Thomas prodded nastily.

The provost marshal made a gesture to Thomas to desist. "Let him tell it."

"I came to Raytown," Bokker said, "to ask Captain Grayson some questions—"

"*Captain* Grayson?" asked the provost marshal, emphasizing the title.

"Bill Grayson," Bokker shot a look at Lige Thomas and saw the scowl come over the sheriff's face. "I understood he rode with Quantrell and—"

"Whoa, there!" cried Lige Thomas. "You can't prove any such thing."

"He doesn't have to," snapped the provost marshal.

33

"It's common knowledge that Grayson—and probably every man around here—was a bushwhacker at one time or another." He held up his hand as Lige Thomas started to protest. "Let's not go into that, Sheriff." He turned to Bokker. "Go ahead. Why did you want to question Grayson? What did you want to learn from him?"

"There's a magazine in my valise, *Fred Cowan's Illustrated Weekly.* . . ."

"You mean this?" Major Holbrook stepped to the sheriff's desk and picked up the magazine, opened to the sketch of the late John Hovey. "A rather good likeness of you."

"So good," said Bokker grimly, "that you'd think the man who drew it had seen me."

"Apparently he had."

"I never met John Hovey and I was never in Lawrence in my life."

"That's just your say-so," interrupted Lige Thomas.

Major Holbrook's eyes glowed as he regarded the sheriff. "It seems to me, Sheriff, that you're awfully keen in pointing a finger at a man who was not a bushwhacker——"

"How do you know he wasn't?"

"For the moment, I'm taking his word."

"You'd rather take his word than believe the evidence?"

"What evidence?" asked the provost marshal. "Two men were killed and only one shot was fired from his gun. Mrs. Grayson admits hearing at least four or five shots altogether."

"He had another gun," exclaimed the sheriff. "He threw it away."

"Have your men found it?"

Lige Thomas scowled. "I'll be hearing from them any minute."

"Until you find a gun you've no case," snapped Major Holbrook. "At least not for the killing of Grayson. Hildebrand——"

"I'm not denying I killed Hildebrand," said Bokker. "He came at me shooting."

Major Holbrok nodded. "Sheriff, it's no secret that your sympathies are with the former Rebels."

"I was born and raised in this neck of the woods," growled Thomas. "These people are my friends. Most of them served in the Confederate Army——"

"Confederate Army, hell," exclaimed the provost marshal. "They were bushwhackers. I served here during the war. I know the kind of fighting they did. All right, the government gave them amnesty after the war. But that doesn't give them any right to keep on killing, or trying to kill, Union people." He pointed suddenly at Bokker. "You served in the Union Army——"

"Eleventh Wisconsin," Bokker said promptly.

"Forget it," said Thomas bitterly. "Two men were killed last night. A man was caught standing over one of them, a gun in his hand, but he can't be touched because he's a Union man——"

"Don't carry it too far," warned the provost marshal.

There was a commotion outside the door, then it was opened. Charr Mechem and another townsman entered. They were accompanied by a sergeant.

"Well, Sergeant?" snapped the Major.

"No gun," replied the sergeant. "But there was plenty of evidence that a man was waitin' outside the Grayson place; a man and a horse. They took off in one helluva hurry."

The provost marshal looked inquiringly at Lige Thomas. The sheriff gestured to Charr Mechem. "What about it?"

"It's like the blue boy says," Charr Mechem admitted grudgingly.

"Satisfied, Sheriff?" asked the provost marshal.

"It's your show," replied Lige Thomas angrily.

"Then do you mind if I have a few words with Bokker—alone?"

The sheriff stamped out of the office. The others followed. When Bokker and Major Holbrook were alone, the provost marshal held up the copy of the magazine. "What's the straight of this?"

"I don't know, Major," Bokker repeated wearily. "I

never knew John Hovey, I've never been in Lawrence and I never met a former guerrilla until yesterday."

"You weren't out here during the war?"

"No closer than St. Louis—and I was in the hospital there."

Major Holbrook frowned thoughtfully. "The picture couldn't be of someone who *looks* like you?"

"That was my first impression, but what do *you* think?"

The provost marshal studied the sketch. "It's an awfully close likeness of you, rather, the way you probably looked six years ago."

"I first saw the picture in 'sixty-four, a few months after it had been sketched. It looked exactly like I looked at the time. And there's no question about other people believing it's me. Last year I ran for prosecuting attorney in my county up in Wisconsin. My opponent dug this up and—well, it defeated me. That's when I made up my mind to run it down."

"And what've you found out so far?"

"Nothing—practically nothing. You heard what happened here yesterday. Two more of the men in the picture are dead."

"One of them you killed. The other . . . ?" The major looked inquiringly at Bokker.

"Fletcher Trow and MacDonald Pierson, who are in the picture, are still alive."

"How do you know?"

Bokker hesitated. "They were identified for me."

"By whom?"

"A woman—perhaps a girl. She was in my room last night at the Rayown Hotel. She *said* she was Bill Grayson's sister."

"What do you mean, she said? Is she, or isn't she?"

"Bill Grayson has no sister."

"His wife?"

"No." Bokker paused. "I didn't see the girl—it was dark as the inside of a pocket in my room. I did grab at her as she ran out, but that's all it was—a grab. Yet I got the impression that she was younger than Mrs. Grayson."

Major Holbrook shook his head. "It beats me. What're your plans now?"

"To find Fletcher Trow and MacDonald Pierson."

"Here?"

"No one knows where Fletcher Trow is."

"And Pierson?"

"She didn't say. He could have been the man who waited outside of Bill Grayson's home last night."

"Who's probably halfway to Texas right now." The Provost Marshal grimaced. "That's where they all go, every bank absconder, murderer, fugitive from justice. There's a lot of room in Texas."

"There isn't enough room in Texas—or anywhere else —to hide from me. I've got a picture of MacDonald Pierson and Fletcher Trow and I'll find them."

"You know," Holbrook said thoughtfully, "I think maybe you will."

Bokker took the evening stage to Kansas City.

Chapter SEVEN

Bokker got a room at the Federal Hotel in Kansas City and slept late the following morning. When he awakened he had breakfast in the hotel dining room, then strolled to the square opposite the courthouse. Kansas City had grown during the war, passing its twin city, Westport, in population. In fact, people were already calling the two towns one and using the name of Kansas City.

In the Square, the City Marshal, John Speer, held forth, leaving only now and then to get a glass of beer at a convenient saloon. In spite of the railroad having pushed west and south, Kansas City was still the jumping-off place, and the return port of call to which freighters, cattlemen, buffalo hunters and men who roamed the plains came periodically.

To these men guns were as much a part of their apparel as the trousers and boots they wore. They were, in fact, more important, as they frequently owed their lives to their guns. The talk, around Speer, was mostly of guns . . . and adventures with guns.

Bokker seated himself on the grass some distance from Speer and listened to the talk. He remained when the majority of the men adjourned to a nearby saloon, and he was still there when Speer and a few of his followers returned.

Speer eyed him thoughtfuly. "Stranger?"

Bokker nodded.

"My name's Speer."

"I've heard it."

"Haven't heard you sound off."

"Somebody's got to do the listening."

The marshal grinned. "A man that listens good is welcome anywhere." He grunted. "Anythin' special you're listenin' for?"

"Texas. I've been thinking of going there."

Speer's eyes narrowed. "Texas is no place for a *Union* man." He emphasized the word Union. "But it's a big state, a lot of room for a man to lose himself."

Bokker shook his head. "I'm not on the run." He paused a moment. "My name's Bokker."

"Bokker? Name's familiar." The marshal suddenly nodded. "Of course. You had some trouble over in Raytown." Speer stepped closer. "Join me in a glass of beer?"

Bokker got to his feet. "Don't mind if I do."

They crossed the street to a saloon. The marshal's face was creased in a thoughtful frown as they walked and he did not speak until the bartender had drawn beers for them and Speer had quaffed most of his rather large glass. Then he said, "The bushwhackers don't come into Kansas City very often. Only when they've got business to attend to and then they stay away from the Square."

"You were here during the war?" Bokker asked.

"Quite a lot."

"I don't suppose you got to know any of the—the guerrillas?"

"Guerrillas, hell, bushwhackers, that's all they were." Speer finished the rest of his beer and signaled for a refill. "At one time or another I guess I've seen just about all of the men who bushwhacked with Quantrell, Todd, Anderson. Yes, even those who were with Parker in 'sixty-two, before anyone ever heard of Quantrell."

The marshal drank some of his fresh glass. "You understand Kansas City and Westport were Union, but everything outside, in the brush country, was Secesh. Oh, there were people out there called themselves Union, but their menfolks did a lot of night riding. You understand these bushwhackers never had a real organization. A bunch of them would ride one time, another bunch another time. Then they'd take to the brush whenever we went after them. You couldn't prove any of them were bushwhackers. We knew the leaders, of course, and when we caught one of them, he had a short time of it, but the others . . ." Speer shrugged. "We'd have had to string up every man in about four counties. Not that we'd have hung many Union people if we'd done that."

Bokker nodded thoughtfully. "You knew Bill Grayson?"

"We had him in a dozen times. Always had somebody ready to swear that he was helping with the ploughing or butchering a hog."

Bokker hesitated. "And—Fletcher Trow?"

"I've seen him." Speer finished the last of his second glass of beer. "What do you really want to know?"

"MacDonald Pierson . . . I'm looking for him."

The marshal frowned. "He went through here like a bat out of hell the other night. One of my deputies saw him, but that was before we heard of the ruckus over in Raytown and there wasn't any reason to stop him."

"Which direction was he headed?"

Speer shrugged. "He didn't take the train, but that doesn't mean that he couldn't have got aboard across the river, over in Wyandotte—or further along the line. Gorey —that's the deputy who saw him—said his horse was pretty lathered. Rode hard from Raytown." Speer paused a moment, then said, "There's no charge against you, Bokker. Even Lige Thomas had to admit you shot Hildebrand in self-defense."

"Thomas, how come he's sheriff when the Union Army's in control here now?"

Speer grunted. "Thomas wasn't a bushwhacker. Oh, he's related to a bunch of them and he was born and raised in Raytown, but he enlisted with Sterling Price early in the war and remained with him right to the end. He's Secesh, all right, and a friend of all the bushwhackers. Like I said, we control Westport and Kansas City, but there are a lot of votes out in the county. There's some folks think that Secesh shouldn't be allowed to hold offices, but the army wants things to simmer down, and as long as Lige Thomas doesn't step across the line too far, they let him have his job." Speer spoke easily, carelessly and in the same tone and without pause, added, "Preston Kirk's in town, staying at the Federal Hotel."

"Preston Kirk?"

"From Lawrence."

Bokker said sharply, "I don't know anyone in Lawrence. I've never been there."

Speer toyed with his empty glass, then nodded as the bartender looked at him inquiringly. "I wouldn't advise you to go to Lawrence. It's six years, but they won't forget in sixty years what Quantrell did there." He paused. "I don't believe you were with Quantrell—the Raytown business proves that pretty well, but that picture in *Fred Cowan's Illustrated Weekly* would take a lot of explaining in Lawrence—and I don't think they're ready to listen."

"Do you think Preston Kirk would listen?"

"He might listen here—he might not in Lawrence."

Bokker nodded thoughtfully and dropped a dollar on the bar to pay for the beers. He forgot to pick up his change, which Speer noted.

At the desk in the Federal Hotel, Bokker asked for Preston Kirk. The clerk pointed at a man seated in a rocking chair facing the street windows.

Bokker took a vacant chair beside Kirk. "My name is Bokker, Mr. Kirk," he said. "I understand you're from Lawrence."

"That I am," replied Kirk. "Best little town west of Kansas City." He was about thirty-five, a thin man with a balding blond head. He wore a serge suit and a fat gold watch chain dangled across his vest.

Bokker unfolded the old copy of *Fred Cowan's Illustrated Weekly*. "I imagine you've seen this, Mr. Kirk."

Kirk started to reach for the magazine, then recognized the cover and drew back. "Everyone in Lawrence has seen it. I—I was there when it happened." He regarded Bokker through slitted eyes. "I saw my father murdered."

"Where were you at the time?"

Kirk scowled. "Underneath the sidewalk. I heard them coming down the street, saw what they were doing and I ran out of the store—yes, by the rear door. I got underneath the house and crawled all the way to the front, right under the wooden sidewalk. It was a good thing I went that far, too, because they burned down the store. I got a little singed, even under the sidewalk."

"You say you *saw* your father killed?"

"He was staying in the Eldridge House—he was an independent sort, wouldn't live with the wife and me. And he had a little money." Kirk paused. "He was active in the Abolition movement and Quantrell had his name on the list. For that matter, my own name was on it, but they didn't find me."

"The people inside the Eldridge House surrendered," Bokker said.

"Damned cowards," exclaimed Kirk. "Have you ever seen the place? Three stories and built like a fort. They could have stood off Quantrell for a week, but no, they surrendered. Not my father. A few of them fought as long as they could, but with the front doors opened to the bushwhackers, they had no chance. My father was wounded and dragged out to the street. There he was murdered . . . less than fifty feet from where I was at the time."

Bokker opened *Cowan's Weekly* to the Quantrell sketch. He tapped it lightly with his finger.

"The man who drew this, John Hovey—he was in Lawrence at the time?"

Kirk nodded. "He was in the hotel. He was brought out with the others, when they surrendered. His name wasn't on Quantrell's list, so they didn't bother him."

"If he was outside the hotel, he was in a position to see what happened?"

Kirk started to nod again, then suddenly exclaimed. He snatched the magazine from Bokker, stared closely at it, then raised his eyes to Bokker's face.

"Yes," said Bokker grimly. "My face—but I wasn't there."

Kirk looked at Bokker a long moment. "I don't know," he said slowly. "I really don't know. The way I was I couldn't see everybody. There was a lot of movement back and forth, a lot of—of shooting and yelling. But I've studied this picture so many times——"

"I've never been in Lawrence in my life!"

"Don't go there!" cried Kirk. "The people haven't forgotten. Your life wouldn't be worth a Secesh nickel." He looked again at the sketch. "Hovey was in a position to see everyone. . . ."

"I wasn't there," persisted Bokker.

"Then how'd he get your picture?"

"I don't know. According to the magazine people, this was sent to them, from Baxter Springs, Kansas. There was a note with it, signed with Quantrell's name. Whether it was actually written by Quantrell, or whether it was a forgery, they had no way of knowing. The note said that the sketch had been found on John Hovey on the battlefield . . ."

"They called it a battle?" sneered Kirk. "It was a massacre!"

"From your viewpoint." Bokker winced and added quickly, "From *our* viewpoint. I was in the Union Army myself—the Eleventh Wisconsin."

"In August, eighteen sixty-three?"

"From April 'sixty-one until July 'sixty-five."

"You could have had a furlough in 'sixty-three."

"I had one—in the hospital. I was wounded at Vicksburgh in June. In August, eighteen sixty-three, when Quantrell sacked Lawrence I was flat on my back in a St. Louis hospital. I can prove that."

"All right," conceded Kirk, "I'll take your word for it. Then tell me how your picture came to be here with these others."

"That's what I'm trying to find out. I've had these others identified. This is Quantrell—here's George Todd and Bloody Bill Anderson. They're dead. Bill Grayson—that's this one—was killed over in Raytown, a couple of days ago."

"By you?"

"No! By MacDonald Pierson. *I* killed Max Hildebrand."

Kirk shrugged. "I read about it in the papers, but you can never tell what the real story is. I thought perhaps——"

"The story in the papers was true."

Kirk pointed at another sketch in the old magazine.

"MacDonald Pierson," Bokker said. "Alive. And this other one is Fletcher Trow. Nobody seems to know much about him, but I've reason to believe he's alive."

Preston Kirk took the magazine from Bokker's hand and pointed at the likeness of Phil Bokker. "You say this isn't you—you weren't even in Lawrence at the time. Just for the sake of argument, let's say that's all true, but then—then who's the man who's wearing your face?"

Not even Major Holbrook, the Provost Marshal, had thought of that question. But it was the one that Bokker had asked himself for years. A man, wearing his face, was shown in the act of killing another man. If it wasn't Bokker—and that Bokker knew—who was it?

He said, "That's the man I want to find. I want MacDonald Pierson, Fletcher Trow, but most of all, I want to find *that* man!"

Chapter EIGHT

Carrying his valise, Phil Bokker boarded the morning train. The Kansas & Pacific Railroad started shortly after the close of the war, had crept into Kansas, but was now bogged down in the southwestern part of the state. The company was, however, doing an excellent business, shipping Texas steers to Kansas City and would soon have enough capital to continue its westward building.

Bokker had bought a ticket to the end of the line, railhead, a place called Pawnee City.

He entered the day coach and looked around for a seat. The coach was well filled and it was a moment before he found a vacancy beside an elderly man wearing a soiled sack suit. He started to put his valise on the rack overhead and then his eyes fell upon a man seated two seats away.

The man was facing Bokker and recognition came into his eyes.

"Bokker!" he cried. "Phil Bokker."

Bokker strode forward to grip the man's hand. "Paul Shay! It's six years . . ."

". . . since we had beds next to each other in the St. Louis hospital," exclaimed Shay.

He was a well-built man of thirty-odd. He wore a serge suit of excellent material. A derby sat rakishly upon his head and a fat gold watch chain spread across his brocaded vest.

Shay continued, "What in the world are you doing in Kansas?"

"I've got a ticket to Pawnee City."

"So have I. I'm going out to buy cattle for my company."

45

"You a cattle buyer?"

"Why not? It's a good business. That is, it ought to be, if I can buy any cattle in Pawnee City. I understand there's quite a bit of competition for the Texas trail herds. What's with you, Phil? I thought you'd be a big Wisconsin politician by this time."

"I ran for office last year. I was defeated."

The man seated beside Shay got to his feet. "I'll change seats with you," he said to Bokker. "You two are old friends—"

"Thank you, sir!" exclaimed Shay.

The man got his valise and carried it back to Bokker's seat. Bokker got his own bag and put it in the rack over Paul Shay. Then he sat down beside Shay.

"Now tell me about this cattle-buying job of yours, Paul. I've heard of these Longhorns the Texans are bringing north, over the—what is it? The Chisholm Trail."

"It's big business, Phil," said Shay. "There are several million Longhorns running practically wild on the plains of Texas. They're worth about three dollars down there for hide and tallow. But those same Longhorns brought to the railroad here in Kansas are worth twenty-five and thirty dollars a head."

Bokker nodded. "Is it true about those Texas men, that they're still fighting the North?"

Shay coughed gently. "As a matter of fact, I've only lately gone to work for the Midwest Livestock Company and this is my first trip. I've been warned, however, that the Texans are rather handy with their guns."

"You faced Texas Regiments during the war?"

"I was with Lyon at Carthage and Wilson's Creek. Ben McCullough's Texans gave us hell. However, they've had four years of Union Occupation. You'd think they'd be tamed by this time."

"I hope so," said Bokker, "because I may have to go down into Texas."

Shay looked at him sharply. "Why?"

Bokker hesitated. Then he reached for his valise, opened it and brought out the copy of *Fred Cowan's Illus-*

trated Weekly. He opened it to John Hovey's sketch and pointed at the picture of himself.

"Who does that look like, Paul?"

Shay barely glanced at it before he exclaimed, "Why, it's you, Phil."

"Read it!"

Shay scanned the article, then looked at Bokker, puzzled. "I don't understand. You were in the hospital when I got there in August, and you were there when I left in September. You *couldn't* have been at Lawrence."

"I wasn't, but that's a picture of me. It cost me the office of county prosecutor up in Wisconsin."

"But how, Phil? Your service record——"

"My opponent didn't spring this until shortly before the election, when there wasn't time for me to dispute it. Sure, I was able to prove—after the election—that I was in the hospital during August, 'sixty-three."

"That's the damndest thing I ever heard of." Shay scrutinized the sketch once more. "This fellow who drew it— John Hovey—is he an enemy of yours?"

"I never met the man in my life. According to the caption, Hovey was killed by Quantrell at the Baxter Springs Massacre. The sketch was mailed in by Quantrell himself—at least that's the way the magazine people recall it."

"Haven't they got the original?"

"There was a fire at the offices of the magazine early in 'sixty-five and they lost all of their files and records. But the same man's still editor and he says that a letter came along with the drawing. It was signed by Charles W. Quantrell and was to the effect that this had been found on the body of John Hovey after his death."

"And you say you never met Hovey?"

"Never. At least not by that name."

"Is it possible that someone could have *changed* the original drawing? Erased the face of the man drawn by Hovey and substituted your own?"

"I've considered that possibility, Paul, but who? I have no enemies."

"You're in politics."

"I wasn't, in 'sixty-three. Besides, the man who had the

opportunity to change it would have had to be one of Quantrell's men. Nobody knew me in New York—certainly no one at the magazine office. The change, if a change had been made, had to be done before the sketch was mailed." Bokker frowned. "You weren't in Kansas City yesterday?"

"I got in late last night."

"Obviously you didn't buy a Kansas City newspaper. My name's been splashed over it the last couple of days. I—I had some trouble over in Raytown, a village near Kansas City."

Shay regarded Bokker quizzically. "Trouble? Over—this?"

Bokker nodded. "Raytown's a hotbed of former guerrillas. Two of the men—probably three—who're in this sketch lived in Raytown."

"Lived? You put that in the past tense."

Bokker frowned. "That's what the trouble was. This man, Bill Grayson"—he touched the sketch of Grayson with a finger—"he was ambushed outside of his house."

"By you?"

"No. But I was there and I—well, I did kill his friend, Max Hildebrand."

Shay lowered his voice. "You're on the run now?"

"No," Bokker replied quickly. "I've been cleared." He paused. "Three men who were in this picture are still living. MacDonald Pierson . . . Fletcher Trow . . ."

"You said three?"

"The third—I *think*—is the man whose face was actually in this picture, the man whose face was changed to my own."

Seated opposite Shay and Bokker was a grizzled man in buckskin. His seatmate was a man of about forty, clad in gray Prince Albert, gray serge trousers and a gray derby. He wore a flowered vest and a gray cravat, in which was stuck a huge pin that was either a diamond or a very good imitation.

The man in gray leaned toward Paul Shay. "We've a long trip ahead of us. Would you gentlemen care for a game of cards?"

Shay looked at Bokker. "It's eight hours to Pawnee City."

Bokker shrugged. "If the stakes aren't too high."

The man in buckskins brightened. "I just sold me a load of buffalo skins in Kansas City."

The man in the gray costume produced a pack of cards. "I just happen to have some cards with me . . ."

Paul Shay smiled thinly. "If you don't mind, I'd prefer a new pack." He signaled to the conductor, who was collecting tickets a few seats away. When the man came over he said, "Is there a newsboy on the train? I'd like to buy some playing cards."

The conductor produced a sealed, fresh pack of cards from a pocket. "Just happened to have a pack with me." He grinned. "Big demand for cards on this train. That'll be a dollar."

Shay gave the conductor a dollar. The latter then got a table, made of two painted boards nailed together with a couple of crosspieces. The players laid this upon their knees.

Bokker had played much poker during his army days and had played several times with Paul Shay when they had both been in the hospital. He remembered him as an indifferent player, but such was not the case now. Shay dealt smoothly, played his cards with confidence and bet boldly.

The man in the gray Prince Albert, who gave his name as Charles Templeton, played them close—like a professional. The surprise, to Bokker, however, was the buffalo hunter. He talked a fast, reckless game, but bet his cards shrewdly and carefully. After an hour of playing he was forty dollars ahead. Templeton, the obvious professional, was the big loser, more than fifty dollars. Shay was a few dollars ahead and Bokker had contributed twelve dollars to the others.

It was about this time that Bokker became aware of the girl who sat across the aisle, two seats toward the rear of the coach. She was apparently in her early twenties, a beautiful girl with dark brown hair and the bluest eyes he had ever seen in a woman. She wore a brown suit of excellent material, topped by a dark green hat. She was reading a magazine, but Bokker's eyes, flickering toward her occasionally, met her blue eyes. Each time she dropped them to her reading.

A big pot came. Bokker, with three sixes, opened for two dollars. Shay raised him five. The buffalo hunter called the five-dollar raise and increased it five himself. Templeton, the dealer, merely called.

"One card," said Bokker.

Templeton looked at him quizzically and dealt the card.

"Two for me," Shay said.

"I like what I got," cried the buffalo hunter, Jed Jethro. "And I'll raise whoever bets."

Templeton grunted. "The dealer takes three cards. Apparently I'm low man. Opener?"

"Ten dollars," said Bokker.

"I'll double that," Shay said auietly.

"And I'll double *that!*" chortled Jethro. "Just like I said I would. Costs you forty, Mr. Templeton."

Templeton studied his cards long and carefully. "I guess I'm forced to call."

Bokker had drawn a fourth six. He started to count out forty dollars, then suddenly put back the money and tossed in his cards. "Beats me."

He sent a quick look at Templeton and thought that he detected consternation. The expression, however, if Bokker did see it, was a fleeting one.

Shay said, "I'll bet twenty dollars."

Jethro held up his hand. "Mind if I see your openers?" he asked of Bokker.

Bokker gathered up his discards, exposed three sixes. Jethro whistled. "And you threw in three of a kind?"

Bokker shrugged. "The bets are too high for three sixes."

"You said it," chortled Jethro. "I call the twenty and raise it forty."

Templeton grunted. "I'm low man, I guess, but I'll just see that forty and raise it"—he hesitated—"fifty dollars."

Paul Shay examined his cards once more. He scowled. "Costs me ninety to call."

"An' I get a chance to raise again," Jethro said smugly.

"I still think I've got the best hand," Shay said, but showed worry.

"Call, then," Templeton suggested. "But you'd better have it, because I don't mind telling you that I drew awfully well to my one pair."

"Ninety dollars," mused Shay. "That's a lot of money."

"That's about thirty buffalo," grinned Jethro. "And I don't mind telling you right now it's going to cost you about thirty more buffaloes."

"In that case," Shay said, coming to a sudden decision, "I call the ninety and—raise it a hundred!"

"Hey!" cried Jethro. "The man's got stuff! Well, I call that hundred and raise her two hundred."

"This started out as a friendly game," Bokker reminded.

"A man's got no friends in a poker game," Templeton said drily. "That's three hundred to me. Well, I just happen to have three hundred dollars more in my poke. If I lose, I'm broke."

Perspiration broke out upon Paul Shay"s face. "If I call you, I've got about forty dollars left. Well—easy come, easy go!"

He counted out six hundred dollars and put it on the line. The buffalo hunter, Jethro, somewhat worried finally, reached into his pocket and produced a buffalo-skin purse. It was heavy with gold coins. "I call," he said, dropping the purse on the table.

"All *I've* got," said Templeton, "is a full house, tens up."

Triumph came to Shay's face. "I can top that—four eights."

"Me," said Jethro, "I've got a king-high straight— only they happen to be all hearts—"

"A straight flush!" ejaculated Templeton. "That wins!"

"It sure does!"

"That's a very handsome pot," Shay said slowly. He hesitated, then nodded, "And as far as I'm concerned, it ends the game."

"I'm cleaned myself," said Templeton, the professional gambler.

"That leaves me and you," Jethro said, addressing Bokker.

Bokker shook his head. "I don't care for freeze-out."

"In that case," said Jethro, gathering up the money, "I think I'll go hunt me up a game in the next car."

"You've a nice stake," Templeton suggested. "You ought to save it."

"I can double it," Jethro said confidently. He stowed money into his pockets, then raised the board table and got up. "See you later, gents."

He climbed over the knees of the other men and headed up the aisle. Shay watched him go, glowering, then nudged Bokker. "Phil, like to have a word with you . . ."

Templeton got to his feet. "No sense you two leaving. I'm broke, but I'd just as soon go and watch our buffalo hunter friend awhile." He smiled brightly, got to his feet.

He was scarcely out of earshot than Paul Shay exclaimed, "We've been taken, Phil!"

"You," said Bokker. "*I* lost only twenty-two dollars."

"I dropped over seven hundred," groaned Shay. "And it wasn't my money."

Bokker winced. "You gambled with your company's money?"

"That's my trouble, Phil," said Shay worriedly. "I get in a game, I forget myself."

"You weren't like that when we were in the hospital together."

"I didn't have any money then." He was silent a moment. Then he said slowly, "Of course I can get money from the Pawnee City bank, for buying cattle, but I'll have to make up that seven hundred somehow."

"I've got about two hundred dollars," Bokker said, "if half of that will help you . . ."

"It wouldn't, Phil!" exclaimed Shay. "Anyway, I wouldn't take it from you. It isn't losing the money that makes me so damn mad, it's being a sucker. I have the feeling that the buffalo hunter and Templeton are working together."

"That's why I dropped out," said Bokker, "with four sixes."

"Four sixes!"

"I happened to notice that Jethro's hands were a little too soft-looking for a buffalo hunter."

Paul Shay half rose. "Why, the dirty . . ." His hand went under his coat toward his hip.

Bokker threw out a detaining hand. "Hold it, Paul! You're no gunfighter."

"I can shoot as well as the next man."

"You're still an amateur, Paul. I have an idea that Templeton's a professional. In gunfighting as well as card-playing. And Jethro's probably just as good—or bad."

"I've never backed down to a man yet."

"This isn't a question of backing down. They didn't force us to play cards."

Shay hesitated. "You're right, Phil. Anyway, they're headed for Pawnee City. I'll be seeing them again. And maybe . . ." He reseated himself, a gleam in his eyes.

Chapter NINE

Bokker's eyes flickered to the girl two seats away. She was standing up, struggling to wrestle a rather heavy carpetbag down from the overhead rack. Her seat companion was a middle-aged woman and facing them were two non-descript-looking men. One of these got to his feet.

"Allow me, madam!"

He thrust his hands up to the rack, one of them clawing at the bag, the other gripping the girl's wrist.

"I can manage," she said distinctly.

"No trouble, madam!" persisted the man.

He gripped at the bag with one hand, at her wrist with the other. He brought away her hand and the bag came down. It was heavier than he had expected and slipped through his one hand, bouncing the girl's shoulder and striking her in the stomach.

"You oaf!" she cried, in pain.

The man leaned over, grabbing both of her hands in his and caressing them. "Sorry, madam, I tried to help you, but the bag slipped." He continued to chafe her hands, although it was her shoulder and body that had been struck by the bag.

Angrily the girl jerked her hands free. "Let me alone!"

"Only tryin' to help, ma'am."

The girl leaned forward to pick up the bag. The man also stooped at the same time and their heads collided. The girl cried out in pain. Again the man reached for her hands, managed to secure one and began to massage it.

"Sorry, ma'am, guess I'm just too clumsy for . . ."

The girl, exclaiming, tried to free her hand of the man's grip. He clung to it. There was only one thing left for the girl to do. She swung her free hand and cracked the man's face with a stinging blow.

"What's the idea, girlie?" he snarled.

"You've pawed me enough," snapped the girl.

"Oh, yeah? Well, that's what you're used to, ain't you?"

Bokker got to his feet and took two quick steps forward. He grabbed the man by the coat collar, jerked him out into the aisle and gave him a hard, quick shove.

The man lurched forward, stumbled and hit the floor of the swaying coach. For just an instant he lay stunned, then let out a roar and scrambled to his feet.

He began to mouth curses as his hand went under his coat. Bokker, who had not expected gunplay, lunged forward. He struck out with his left hand, a flailing blow. It caught the arm of the man just as the hand came clear with a stubby revolver. The blow knocked the gun hand aside. Bokker, stepping in, smashed the man a savage blow on the jaw that again sent him to the floor, this time on his back.

The gun clattered to the floor behind the man. Bokker stepped quickly past him, one foot stepping on an arm. He scooped up the gun, continued on to the end of the car. He jerked open the door and threw the gun out and sidewards.

Then he turned.

The man he had knocked down was getting weakly to his feet. "Wasn't no call to hit a man," he whined. "I was on'y havin' some fun."

"Have it with someone else," Bokker said curtly.

"I wasn't hurtin' the lady."

"You weren't helping her any."

The man hesitated, then backed to his vacated seat. He reached up and got his bag down from the rack. Shooting a black look at Bokker, he went past him and out of the coach.

Bokker watched him go. He nodded to the girl and intended to go on to his own seat. The girl said, "Thank you!"

"It was no trouble, miss."

"I'm sorry you had to fight him. He—he might have shot you."

"I don't think so."

"Nevertheless, I'm grateful. I—this is my first trip away from home." She smiled nervously. "But I mustn't tell you my troubles."

Bokker waited a moment, then, when she didn't go on, he said, "You're going to Pawnee City?"

"Is—is it so terrible in Pawnee City?"

"I don't know. I haven't been there. But I understand it's a boom town and boom towns are apt to be wild."

"That's what they—they told me, at home."

"Where's that?"

"Ohio. A little place called Canal Dover. There's no chance there for a girl to make a living and when my father died—well, to make a long story short, I read an article in a Cleveland paper. It told about Pawnee City . . . said it was a—I think those were the words—a rip-roaring town, where everybody had plenty of money and the cowboys thought nothing of paying fifteen and even twenty dollars for a hat to take back to Texas. So I thought: Well, I *do* know something about making hats."

Bokker frowned. "You're going to Pawnee City to—to make hats?"

"The way you put it, it sounds ridiculous. But I've got to do something to earn my living. The little money I have would soon be gone if I stayed in Canal Dover."

Paul Shay came up behind Bokker and tapped him lightly on the shoulder. Bokker looked over his shoulder and saw Shay smirk. "This is my friend, Paul Shay, Miss . . . ?"

"Compton. Ruth Compton."

"Delighted, Miss Compton!" cried Shay.

"I," said Bokker, "am Phil Bokker."

"Miss Compton," continued Shay, "we've a double seat vacant opposite us. Since we're all going to the same place, why don't you come over and join us?"

Ruth Compton hesitated. Her eyes went to the door through which her recent neighbor had gone into the next coach. "Very well," she said, "I suppose I might as well accustom myself to the free-and-easy spirit of the West."

"Exactly," said Paul Shay. "There are no strangers in the West. Enemies, yes. Friends, positively; but no one's a stranger. Everyone talks to everyone else." He grinned. "So they tell me."

Chapter TEN

The bellowing of thousands of cattle, grazing on the plains near Pawnee City, was the signal for the passengers on the train to gather together their belongings. The train slackened its speed, the engine bell tolling.

Bokker carried his own valise and that of Ruth Compton, Paul Shay escorted Ruth out of the coach, helped her to the station platform.

It was an unpainted depot, built of fresh, raw lumber, as were most of the buildings on the single street that ran south from the depot.

Ruth stopped on the depot platform. Sudden panic seemed to grip her as she looked down the teeming street. Bokker did not wonder. There were six inches of dust on the street that was choked with wagons, horses and a seething mass of humanity.

Most of the buildings were one-story or one-story with false fronts to give the illusion of being two stories. There were probably three legitimate two-story buildings. No less than twenty of the buildings in the quarter mile of street were saloons.

Above the hammering of carpenters on new buildings being erected there rose the babel of voices—chattering, talking, yelling and screaming voices.

Somewhere a man howled like a wolf, punctuating his howl with a sudden burst of gunfire.

Ruth Compton exclaimed and shrank back against the steady arm of Paul Shay.

"It's great," enthused Shay, looking down the street. "More exciting than I dreamed it would be."

"You like this?" gasped Ruth.

"I love it!"

58

"I like a quiet town," said Phil Bokker.

"You, Phil?" cried Paul Shay. "Why, you breed trouble."

Ruth looked at Bokker in surprise. They had not touched on his adventures in Raytown during the journey to Pawnee City. Shay remembered now and winced. "Sorry, Phil."

"I think we'd better see if we can get rooms," Bokker said grimly.

They started down the street, Bokker still carrying Ruth's bag as well as his own. They were turning into the two-story PAWNEE CITY HOTEL when Shay became aware that it was Bokker who had carried the girl's valise.

"Here, let me help you with that!" he exclaimed, taking the bag from Bokker.

The lobby was small, with a saloon opening off to the left. A heavy-set man with a gold toothpick in his mouth stood behind the desk, frowning at the hotel register.

"We'd like rooms," Bokker said.

The hotel man sized them up, evidently speculating as to the relationship among the three. "How many?" he asked.

"Three," Bokker said quickly.

The man grunted. He scowled at the register. "I got a nice room at the front of the house with a double bed, but outside of that I ain't got a thing except one little room at the back."

"The big front room would be fine for Miss Compton," said Shay generously.

"Rather noisy, though," remarked Bokker. He frowned. "Is—is there another place in town rents rooms?"

"I got the only hotel in town," retorted the hotel man, "and if the lady takes the big room, I got to charge for two. I usually put two into every room, as it is. That's one thing this town needs, rooms for travelers. The cowboys don't mind bunking out on the prairie, but it's the commercial people, the gamblers, the cattle buyers, all of them's got to sleep indoors and there just ain't room for them all."

Templeton, the gambler, entered the hotel.

"Well!" he exclaimed. "Here we are again."

"We'll take the rooms," Bokker said. "Miss Compton will have the front room and"—he looked inquiringly at Shay—"I guess you and I will have to share the small room."

"That's nonsense," said Ruth Compton. "*I'll* take the small room."

"It's settled," said Paul Shay promptly.

"No, it isn't. As a matter of fact I—I don't think I can afford to pay double. How much is it?"

"Six dollars," replied the hotel man.

"Six dollars a week? I'm afraid that's too high for——"

"Six dollars a day, ma'am," was the correction.

Ruth let out an exclamation of dismay. "I can't pay six dollars a day for a room."

"Prices are high in Pawnee City," observed the hotel man. He looked inquiringly at Templeton. "You wish a room, sir?"

"Naturally. The best you've got in the house, sir!"

"Take the room," Bokker said angrily to Ruth. "For one night, at least. It'll give you time to look around."

Ruth's forehead creased in worry. "I suppose I'll have to, but . . ." She left the sentence unfinished.

Bokker signed the register for himself and Paul Shay, then hesitated and handed the pen to Ruth. She signed quickly.

The hotel man slid two keys acoss the desk. "Here you are, folks, and that's all I can do." He smiled at Templeton. "Unless one of my guests happens to be killed this evening, I'm full up."

Bokker again took up Ruth's bag, as well as his own. Shay carried his bag and the keys. They climbed the stairs to the second floor and Shay found Ruth's room, Number 5, at the front of the house. He opened the door, revealing the "large" room. It was about nine by twelve feet in size, containing an unsavory-looking bed, a stand with a pitcher and bowl and a small chair. Nails in the wall served in lieu of a closet.

"This is the *big* room?" cried Shay. "I wonder what we've drawn."

"We'll soon find out," said Bokker. He deposited Ruth's bag on the floor, nodded and walked down the hall. Shay followed closely. Their own room was Number 11. It was nine by six feet, with a narrow bed and washstand. It contained no chair.

Shay looked at the bed. "It's a good thing neither of us is very fat or we'd never make it. Do you turn much in your sleep?"

"Not that I know of."

Both men took off their coats and rolled up their sleeves. Shay poured water from the pitcher into the bowl and began to lave his hands.

"What do you think of the little lady, Phil?"

"I think she ought to start back for Ohio tomorrow morning."

Shay chuckled. "I'll admit that I don't think Pawnee City's the place for her, but don't forget she was handling herself very well with that mucker when you interrupted." He shook his head. "I've an idea that she's got more spunk than either of us realize. *You* suggest that she take the train home."

"You like her, Paul?"

Shay, splashing water on his face, did not reply until he reached for the single towel. "I like her—yes." He paused. "You?"

"I'm not going to fall in love with any woman," Bokker replied promptly, "not until I get my life straightened out."

"That may take a while, Phil," Shay said thoughtfully. "I've been thinking about your problem all day . . ." He grinned faintly. "Yes, while I was chattering. Suppose you find MacDonald Pierson and Fletcher Trow? What then?"

"They know the name of the man who was with them in Lawrence."

"And what if they don't tell you who it was?"

"They'll tell me!"

"Did Bill Grayson tell you?"

Bokker's eyes narrowed. Shay held up a cautioning hand. "I'm just trying to put the worst light on it, Phil. To show you what you're up against. You're a civilized man,

Quantrell and his bushwhackers were savages. Cutthroats and murderers."

"Not all of them," replied Bokker. "A former circuit judge rode with them. At least two men who'd been preachers——"

"One preacher stayed in Lawrence," said Shay, his lips curling in contempt. "The Reverend Alonzo Skaggs. They dragged his body up and down the street and finally set it on fire."

"I'm writing no brief on behalf of the guerrillas," Bokker said evenly. "I've more reason to hate them than most. And I know what they did on the border. But I also know what some Union men did—men who plundered with Jennison and Anthony—and Jim Lane. They were fighting the war back there in 'fifty-four. But the sacking of Lawrence was arson and murder. No one can condone it by any rules of warfare. What happened is too well known, too well documented to condone. That's why I've got to clear myself; because the picture of me in that old magazine shows a man who was one of the very worst of the guerrillas, a killer who murdered a man in cold blood. I've got to find that man—and clear myself. Until then——"

"Until then, you can't find yourself a woman and settle down," Shay said crookedly. "Fine, Phil, that leaves the field clear for me."

"Sometimes, Paul," Bokker said testily, "you're a hard man to like."

"Nobody likes me," Shay said cheerfully. "And my employers are going to like me least of all if I don't raise that seven hundred dollars for them that I lost in the poker game. Come on, hurry up and get washed."

Bokker stepped to the washstand, then looked over his shoulder. "Are we in a hurry?"

"Yes."

"Why?"

Shay chuckled. "I told you—I've got to raise that money. So I can buy some cattle and give the sellers earnest money."

"How do you figure to raise this money?"

"The same way I lost it."

Bokker exclaimed, "You're going to buck the professional games?"

"Templeton and Jethro were professionals. Only I didn't know it then. I'd like a return session with them."

"Don't, Paul," Bokker said earnestly. "You're in deep enough now. Don't make it worse."

"We'll see," Shay said evasively. "Now, how about some supper?"

"I'm ready."

They left the tiny room and started for the stairs. As they reached them, Bokker indicated Ruth Compton's room.

Shay nodded and stepped past Bokker to the door. He knocked on it.

"Yes?" Ruth called.

"We're going out to have some supper. Come along."

There was a slight pause, then Ruth said through the door: "Thanks, but I'm not hungry. I—I got pretty tired on the train and I'd like to get some sleep."

"All right, Ruth," Shay replied. "We'll size up the town for you."

He turned back to Bokker.

They descended to the lobby and Shay stepped quickly to the saloon and looked in. He nodded as he came back to Bokker. "It's all right."

They left the hotel and crossed the street to a restaurant run by a Chinese. They had a hearty supper of fried steak, potatoes, coffee and a gooey substance that was supposedly pudding.

When they came out of the café, it was getting dark outside. The street seemed more crowded than earlier. And it was noisier, if that were possible.

"She's going to have to be awfully tired if she can sleep through this," Shay said.

Just then a cowboy came out of the hotel across the street. He ducked under the hitchrail, sprang upon a horse and whirling it into the street, pulled out his revolver.

"Whoop-whoop-whoopee!" he screamed at the top of his voice and emptied his six-shooter at the sky. He sent his horse galloping down the street, causing pedestrians to jump out of his way.

A lean man stood at the edge of the high wooden sidewalk and smoked a thin cigar placidly. He wore a vest on which was pinned a star.

Phil Shay pointed at the star. "You're the law?"

"Some of it," the man replied laconically.

"And you let a man shoot like that?"

"He wasn't hurtin' anybody."

"He might have, though."

"Then I'd a run him into the calaboose. Strangers in town, eh?"

"We arrived on the train this afternoon," Bokker said.

The law man nodded. "Pawnee City's a good town. A live town. Two things you can't do in Pawnee City. You can't kill nobody and you can't cheat in cards. Understand?"

"But anything else is all right?" Shay asked sarcastically.

"Up to a point, mister. Up to a point."

"Well, you tell me when I get to that point," Shay said. He started across the street. Bokker followed.

"This town has possibilities," Shay remarked cryptically, as he entered the hotel.

Inside the lobby he turned automatically into the saloon, Bokker at his heels.

The place had filled up since Shay had peeked into it earlier. It was jammed now, a room some twenty-five feet wide by forty deep, holding a long bar, a dozen tables and more than fifty patrons. Three bartenders were behind the bar. A half-dozen gambling games were going on.

"Let me have that hundred now," Shay said to Bokker.

"For gambling?"

"What's the difference? You said you'd let me have it."

Bokker was loath to part with the money, but he had volunteered it on the train. He hesitated only briefly, then brought out a handful of money and counted out three double eagles and four ten-dollar gold pieces.

"I'll see that you don't lose it," Shay said, and moved toward one of the faro games.

Bokker stepped to the bar and ordered a glass of beer. He drank it slowly as he surveyed the room. The games of chance were boisterous, noisy. A man would leave a faro game, go to the bar and have a drink of whisky, then go back to the game, sometimes carrying a second drink with him.

Bokker wondered idly what the din would be like later on in the evening. He wondered, too, how noisy it was upstairs in Ruth Compton's room. The floor was thin, as were the walls.

Chapter ELEVEN

A heavy hand clapped Bokker on the shoulder. "Here you are, pardner!" boomed Jethro, the pseudo-buffalo hunter. "Wondered what'd become of you."

"Where's your partner?" Bokker asked pointedly.

"My partner? What partner?"

"Templeton."

Jethro looked at Bokker with assumed surprise, then chuckled. "You got wise, huh?"

"I didn't think you were a buffalo hunter."

Jethro grinned. "It was an honest game."

"I'm not complaining. I lost only twenty-two dollars."

"Which I'll be glad to give you back if you think I didn't win it fair and square."

"It was a cheap price for the lesson." Bokker nodded toward the table where Shay was playing faro. "Paul Shay thought *his* lesson was a little stiff. I'd keep away from him if I were you."

"Him?" sniffed Jethro. He shrugged and walked toward the table where Shay was playing.

Bokker put his glass on the bar and followed Jethro.

About a dozen men were gathered around the table. The dealer was an icy eyed man of about thirty. An unlit cigar was in the corner of his mouth.

"Make your bets, gentlemen," he droned. "Are you ready? I'm dealing." He slipped two cards smoothly out of the card case. "King wins, seven loses." He gathered up money from the layout, paid out money. He put a double eagle on a king and looked inquiringly at Paul Shay.

"Let it go," said Shay carelessly.

Money was scattered about on the various cards, all of them being played. The dealer dealt again. Still tonelessly, he said, "The king wins again, the trey loses." He added two gold pieces to Shay's.

"Copper your bets, gentlemen," the dealer said. "From soda to hock."

He slipped out two cards. "And the final king wins once more. " He added four gold coins to Shay's.

Jethro crowded in beside Shay. "Let's have a new deal now," he said. "A good deal."

The dealer regarded Jethro impassively. "Not in my game," he said coolly.

"My money's as good as anyone else's," retorted Jethro.

"It's good money," put in Shay. "I ought to know. It was mine before you robbed it from me."

A sudden hush fell upon the immediate vicinity of the faro game. It was broken by Jethro. "Say that again, mister!" His hand darted down below the level of the table. Bokker, behind Jethro, caught the arm and gripped it hard.

"Drop it, Jethro!" he said in the buffalo hunter-gambler's ear.

Shay said coldly, "The man doesn't want you in his game. Neither do I."

He rocked Jethro's head with a hard blow of his open hand, raked it back and gave Jethro the knuckles.

"Lemme go," cried Jethro with fine passion, "lemme go, and I'll cut out his heart."

The law man with whom Bokker and Shay had spoken on the street pushed his way through the crowd.

"Let go!" he said softly.

Bokker released Jethro. Shay already had his gun out and was pointing it at Jethro. "Now," said the law man, "what's the trouble?"

"The man's a card shark," Shay declared. "He robbed me of seven hundred dollars on the train."

"On the train," said the marshal, nodding. "I got nothing to do with that—not my territory."

"I'll kill 'im!" Jethro said hoarsely. "I'll kill him. Nobody c'n slap Jed Jethro around."

"*I* can," said the marshal carelessly. His hand came up

and smacked Jethro a resounding blow on the face. A murmur of approval ran through the onlookers.

"I told him I didn't want him in my game," the faro dealer offered. "That buckskin getup fooled me once, but it won't again."

"Mister," said Jethro ominously, "you got hardware on your chest. I got respect for the law when I'm in a town. On'y don't meet me outside of Pawnee City."

"I'll keep an eye peeled," the marshal said agreeably. "But suppose you start for the prairie right now. I don't want you sleeping in Pawnee City—unless it's down at the calaboose."

Jethro rubbed his face which had received a considerable massage. He said to Bokker, "Be seein' you." He half saluted Paul Shay, but gave the marshal only a dirty look before he left the saloon.

The marshal looked at Shay, then at Bokker. "Didn't take you long to get in trouble."

Paul Shay chuckled. "It wasn't any trouble."

The Marshal nodded and walked to the bar, where he ordered a glass of beer. Shay indicated the law man. "What's his name?"

"Tom Chaffee," volunteered the faro dealer. "And I'll give you some free advice—don't tangle with him."

"Chaffee's only the dep'ty," grinned a bystander. "If you want real trouble, take on Fletch Trow, the Marshal."

"Fletcher Trow?" exclaimed Phil Bokker.

"Yep," said the reply. "Fletch is a real curly wolf." The man winked at Bokker. "They say he used to ride with Charley Quantrell and Bloody Bill Anderson."

Bokker strode away from the faro game. He found Chaffee, the deputy marshal, with his back to the bar, looking over a half-emptied glass of beer.

"Where'll I find Fletcher Trow?" Bokker asked.

"Down at his office, I expect."

"Where's that?"

"Two-story log house on the corner of Kiowa Street. The calaboose is in back."

Bokker nodded his thanks and headed for the door. Outside, he looked to the right and left. The one cross street in the town was some hundred feet from the hotel. A two-story building, built like a blockhouse, stood diagonally across the street. Bokker crossed.

Fletcher Trow sat in a straight-backed chair, tilted back against the wall. He was a lean man of about thirty-one or two. There was a sardonic droop to the right side of his mouth.

"Trow?" Bokker asked abruptly as he entered.

Trow pushed back his flat-crowned Stetson, but showed no unusual interest. "You'll be Phil Bokker?"

Bokker's eyes narrowed. "You know me?"

"Been expectin' you." Trow made a slight gesture. "I had a letter."

"From Raytown?"

"I don't rightly remember."

"And you don't remember who wrote the letter?"

"I can't say I do."

"I don't imagine, then, that I'm going to get much information from you."

"Depends on what information you want. I'm a public official of Pawnee City. Anything you want to know about the town I'll tell you. I'll be glad to explain our laws to you."

"Your deputy already explained those."

Trow smiled thinly. "Chaffee? Good man, Chaffee."

Bokker said, carefully, "Do the people in this town know you rode with Quantrell?"

"Quantrell? Who's he?"

"Yesterday," Bokker told Fletcher Trow icily, "I talked to a man from Lawrence. Six years ago he was hiding under the sidewalk, across from the Eldridge House. He saw what went on."

"So?"

"He can identify you."

"His word against mine." The marshal brought the front legs of his chair down to the floor and got to his feet. "Ever hear of the word amnesty?"

"Every man who committed a crime during the war hides behind the word," Bokker said angrily. "But Kansas was a Union state. They still don't like Rebels. How'd you ever become marshal?"

"The job was open and the mayor offered it to me. I guess he thought I had the qualifications for it. I'm fairly handy with a gun."

"You've had enough practice!"

Trow waggled a forefinger at Bokker. "Let's don't get personal, Bokker. There's no United States Army here to back you up. Just the local law, that's all. And that's me."

The street door opened and Tom Chaffee came in.

"——and my deputy, Tom Chaffee," Trow added.

"He had a little trouble down at the hotel, marshal," Chaffee offered. "I could have brought him in."

"Anything serious?"

Chaffee hesitated. "No, but it could be, if you wanted it to be."

"Never mind, Tom. Mr. Bokker thinks he knows me from the war. Thinks I was with him and Quantrell——"

Bokker exclaimed, "*I* wasn't with Quantrell!"

Trow shrugged. "If you say so, Bokker. You see how those things get around? People even say *I* was with Quantrell."

"You were."

"Like I was saying, Bokker," Trow continued, "everybody was in the war and everybody talks about it. You can't tell the truth from a lie any more. Privates make themselves captains, captains generals. Why, a fella told me only the other day *he* won the battle of Gettysburg. Man from Georgia takes a trip up north these days and everybody calls him a bushwhacker and robber. They say the same thing about Sherman's boys down in Georgia. Just talk. Don't mean a thing. People say *you* rode with Quantrell. Hell, they say the same thing about me. And Tom Chaffee."

"Not me," said Chaffee. "I wore a regular blue uniform."

"And maybe I wore a gray? What's the difference? The war's over. Forget it."

"I can't," said Bokker. "People won't let me. My picture appeared in a magazine——"

"So did mine."

"But you were there and I wasn't. There's a difference."

"Is there, Bokker? Some fellows over in Clay County rode with Quantrell. So they tell me, anyway. Well, *they* became outlaws. *I* became a marshal."

"Take that marshal's badge," Bokker said, "put it on the outside of your coat and ride into Lawrence. See what'll happen."

"Nothing will happen. Because I'm not going to Lawrence," Trow said calmly. "I've got no business there. I've got no business in Kalamazoo, or in Kewanee, Illinois. Or a lot of other places."

"We've got business here," interposed Tom Chaffee. "Enough to keep us going day and night. Keepin' the Texas boys from takin' over Pawnee City."

The marshal nodded agreement. "And it's about time we started making the rounds." He adjusted the holster that held a long-barrelled Navy revolver. "Care to come along, Bokker?"

Bokker shook his head and left the marshal's office.

He walked back to the hotel, but had no desire to go back into the saloon. He climbed to the second floor. He noted the absence of a chink of light under the door of Ruth Compton's room and went to the room he was to share with Paul Shay.

He undressed and went to bed and then could not sleep. There was too much on his mind, too much noise came through the thin floor that separated the sleeping rooms from the saloon below. After a long time he dozed off and was awakened by a louder than usual commotion below.

It was quieted after a while and he was barely asleep when Paul Shay came in with a lighted candle. Bokker kept his eyes closed and Shay muttered and stumbled about the room. He finally crowded into the bed with Bokker and the latter was assailed by the whiskey fumes on Shay's breath. He finally slept, however.

Chapter TWELVE

Shay was dressing when Bokker awoke. Shay's eyes were clear, his hand was steady. "What a town!" he chuckled as he saw Bokker awake.

"You like this kind of life?" Bokker asked, putting his feet to the floor.

"You can't say it's dull! Busted one day, flush the next." Shay scooped up a double handful of money from the washstand on which he had heaped it. "I won back the seven hundred I lost on the train and three hundred profit." He began counting money. "Here—take half of it."

"Just the hundred I loaned you."

"If you hadn't given me the hundred, I wouldn't have won this," protested Shay. "You're entitled to half."

"I only want the hundred."

Shay shrugged. "Have it your way. Well, go back to sleep. No need of your getting up."

"I'm an early riser. It's after six o'clock."

"Only reason I'm up is that there's a trail herd coming in this morning. I want a chance to buy it. However, since you're up, let's get something to eat."

Bokker was already dressing and a few minutes later they left the little room. In the narrow hall, Shay nodded toward Ruth's room. "No use waking her."

They descended to the lobby and crossed the street to the restaurant. In spite of the early hour there were six or eight customers already in the place.

The menu was scrawled on a slate hanging behind the counter: *Breakfast, Hot Cakes, Ham, Eggs, Coffee. 50 Cents*. "We'll have it," said Shay to the bleary-eyed waiter. "And don't slice the ham too thin. Also, I like my hot cakes big."

He turned to Bokker. "I almost forgot—you found Fletcher Trow last night. How'd you make out with him?"

"I didn't. He was less talkative than the Raytown people."

"A man isn't going to talk himself onto a scaffold." Shay frowned. "I almost followed you last night. To tell you that Fletcher Trow is not a man to mix with."

"I talked to him. He can take care of himself."

"Did you hear how he became marshal of Pawnee City?"

Bokker shook his head.

"The Burke Brothers from Texas, who were real bad medicine, took over the town one day about six months ago. They killed the marshal and ran his deputy into a hole. Then they galloped up and down the street, shooting out the windows of the stores. Trow was in one of the stores. He was just passing through Pawnee City. A piece of glass hit him in the face. He went out on the street and took a shot at the older Burke brother. He winged him at a distance of over two hundred yards. Both of the Burkes then came at Trow, shooting. He put a bullet into the forehead of each. The mayor offered him the job of marshal. Trow didn't want the job, but the town council had a special meeting and made him an offer that he couldn't refuse."

"And Tom Chaffee? He was the deputy the Burke brothers ran out of town?"

"No—no. Trow brought Chaffee in. One of the conditions to taking the job. They've done great work, though. They've kept the town under control for six months—and nine marshals had the job in the year and a half before Trow took over. Four of them were killed by Texas men. The others quit—couldn't take it."

"I don't doubt that Trow knows the killing business," Bokker said testily. "He had plenty of practice during the war. And probably since."

"I don't want you to make a mistake, Phil," Shay said

earnestly. "This is Trow's town. The people are behind him. You can't go up to Trow and kill him——"

"I have no intentions of killing him," Bokker retorted. "I just want him to answer one question."

"He isn't going to tell you that," Shay said, "not unless you put a gun up against his wishbone—and maybe he wouldn't talk then."

"He'll talk," said Bokker. "I'll make him."

Shay's forehead creased. "You're my friend, Bokker. I'd hate to see you wind up in the Pawnee City Boot Hill."

A man at the far end of the counter paid for his breakfast and started for the door. Then he saw Paul Shay and stopped.

"Didn't think you'd be up this early."

Shay grinned. "I don't let my pleasure interfere with business. I figure to buy Winston's herd. Phil, shake hands with Clem Foster. *He's* figuring on buying the Winston beef."

"If it's prime," Foster corrected as he shook hands with Bokker, "and if the price is right."

"It'll have to be more than I can pay. That reminds me, I've got to see about my bank draft, Phil. You eat my breakfast. I'll have a double one later. See you, Foster."

Shay got up and went out of the restaurant. Foster remained behind. He shook his head as the door closed on Shay. "Quite a man, your friend. I didn't think he'd be up and around this morning, the way he was putting it away last night."

"Paul and I had beds next to each other at the hospital, six years ago," said Bokker. "I hadn't seen him since until yesterday."

"The company he's working for is new," Foster went on, "but I've an idea that Shay's going to do all right for them." He paused. "Unless he stubs his toe."

He nodded to Bokker and left the restaurant.

The two orders of breakfast came; Bokker finished his own and ate the ham from Shay's but was compelled to leave the rest. He paid for both meals, however. When he left the restaurant, Shay was riding out of a livery stable, leading a second saddled horse.

"Feel like a ride out on the prairie?" Shay called.

"I haven't had a horse between my legs in months," declared Bokker with pleasure. He sized up the animal, a rangy bay. He nodded in approval. "They've got good horseflesh out here."

"Let's ride," said Shay, handing the reins to Bokker. He sent his horse down the street at a swift run. Bokker mounted and set out after Shay.

He had difficulty catching up to his friend. Shay was an easy, smooth rider. He had apparently spent much time on a horse.

A wooden toll bridge spanned a river at the south end of the street. Shay tossed the bridge tender a quarter without stopping or even slackening his speed. Bokker came along and also tossed the man a coin.

A hundred yards south of the river, Foster, the cattle buyer, was jogging along on a black gelding. Shay slackened his speed. "Going to beat me, Foster?" he cried.

"I hate to tell you," Foster retorted, "but I bought Winston's last two herds. He won't sell to you until I've made my offer."

Shay fell in beside Foster. "In that case, there's no hurry."

A herd of seven or eight hundred steers was spread out a half mile before the three riders. Two or three cowboys rode slowly around the fringes of the herd, keeping it compact. A half-dozen other cowboys were gathered around the chuck wagon.

Foster, Bokker and Shay rode up to the chuck wagon.

A huge Texan left the group. "Thought you'd be out bright and early, Foster."

"I had to get up early to beat my friend here," Foster said. "He's with the——"

"Midwest Livestock Company," cried Paul Shay. "Our packing house is in Chicago and we can give you a better price than any of the Kansas City outfits." He grinned at Foster.

"If you can beat Foster's price," Winston said, "you've

got yourself eight hundred of the best Longhorns that ever
came up from Texas."

"The best?" asked Shay. He indicated the herd. "Look
kind of poor to me."

"Then you don't want my beef."

"Oh, I want it, all right. But there's no use fooling our-
selves. That stock is thin and the price has got to be a little thin."

"Mister," said Winston, "if you traveled seven hundred
miles, you'd be thin yourself. A couple of weeks grazing
will fatten them up into fine beef."

"All right," said Shay, "you keep them here, fatten
them up and in two weeks I'll give you thirty dollars a
head."

"Can't," retorted Winston. "I've got to get back to
Texas with my boys and bring another herd up before
fall. We can stay two days in Pawnee City, that's all." He
turned to Foster. "What can you pay, Foster—right now,
today?"

"Twenty-five dollars a head."

"I was hoping to get thirty. In fact, my partners back
home said they wouldn't be satisfied with less."

"Let me look at them," said Foster. He turned his
horse and rode it toward the outskirts of the herd. Winston followed afoot, but Shay, winking at Bokker, remained on his horse near the chuck wagon.

"We're going to have some company," he said, nodding
in the general direction of Pawnee City.

Bokker turned and saw two horses bearing down upon
the Winston camp. As they came nearer he saw that both
riders were well-dressed city men.

"Cattle buyers," said Shay.

Foster returned from the herd as the new men rode up.
He nodded to them. "Eight hundred head," he said. "I've
given my top price—twenty-five dollars."

Winston came up. "How are you, Mr. Peabody—Mr.
Cartwright?"

The men returned his greeting.

"I'll go twenty-six dollars," one of the men said, "delivery in two weeks."

"You got to take delivery today," cried Winston. "I just told these men that I've got to get back to Texas in a hurry if I want to bring up another herd this year."

The second new arrival shook his head. "I just stopped at the depot. They can't get any cars for two weeks. I'll go twenty-seven fifty, delivery in two weeks."

Foster showed sudden concern. "What's this about no cars for two weeks?"

"That's what the Kansas-Pacific man said twenty minutes ago."

"There's a string of empties on the siding right now!" cried Foster.

"Reserved," said the first cattle buyer. "Meeker says it's got to be first come, these days."

Foster turned back to Winston. "I'm sorry, Steve, if I can't get cars, I can't take the herd. It's impossible to get any herders in Pawnee City. Unless your boys can stay here two weeks, I'll have to pass up the herd."

Crestfallen, Winston turned to Shay. "What's *your* price—delivery today?"

"Twenty dollars," Shay replied laconically.

"Twenty dollars!" cried Winston, in consternation. "That's robbery."

"It sure is," agreed Shay, "but how many steers do you think I'll lose in two weeks? Every Pawnee in fifty miles'll get himself some free beef. Not to mention some white Pawnees from the town yonder."

Winston shook his head. "I can't stay here two weeks. I promised my partners I'd be back right away. Foster—I'll take your twenty-five dollars a head if you take the herd today."

"I can't. Shay's right. Without anyone to watch the herd, I'd lose half of it."

"I'm willing to take a gamble," Shay said. "I'll make it . . . twenty-one dollars."

Winston groaned. He looked at the other two cattle buyers. "Any better offers?"

Both men shook their heads. Winston turned back to Shay. "You've got yourself a herd," he said bitterly.

Shay reached into his pocket. "Here's five hundred dollars earnest money. As against eight hundred steers——"

"Eight hundred, more or less."

"More or less," agreed Shay, "but not too many less."

"It's robbery," exclaimed Winston, "but it's a deal."

"Drive 'em in to Pawnee City," Shay said, "to the loading pens."

"What's the use of that?" asked Winston. "If you can't get any cars?"

"I've got cars," Shay declared cheerfully. "Enough for this herd and a few over." He grinned. "I'm the man who reserved them."

Winston let out a howl. "Why, you lyin', doublecrossin' son of a thievin' Yank, you said you couldn't get any cars for two weeks."

"*I* said nothing of the kind," Shay retorted. "I said I'd take a gamble." He indicated the other cattle buyers. "*They* said they couldn't get cars for two weeks."

"I won't sell," cried Winston. "Here—take back your dirty five hundred——"

"You made a deal," snapped Shay. "These men are witnesses."

Winston appealed to Foster and the others. "Was it a deal?"

Foster hesitated, then nodded. "It was, but not the kind of deal I'd make . . ." He turned his horse and rode away. The other cattle buyers followed him.

Winston glowered at Shay. "All right, I said it was a deal and I'll let it stand. But you're not going to get any more cattle from me. And I'm going to be tellin' about this to some of the other Texas cattle drivers."

"You tell them," Shay said coldly, "and tell them also that I've got money to put on the barrelhead for good Texas beef. Now, if you'll drive this herd into town, I'll have your money for you at the bank."

He gave Winston a half salute and turned his horse. Bokker fell in beside him. They rode in silence for a little while, then Shay said, "You didn't like that deal?"

Bokker shrugged. "How you buy cattle is none of my concern."

"They'd cheat me if they had the chance," Shay said

testily. "I'm new here—I've got to get up earlier and be just a little sharper than the other fellows." He nodded vigorously. "I think I'm going to like Pawnee City. It's my kind of town."

Bokker made no response. Shay rode beside him in silence for a few yards, then exclaimed, "What're *you* going to do, Phil?"

"I have no plans—except to make Fletcher Trow talk."

"That's going to take some doing. I've been thinking, this other man, MacDonald Pierson . . . you said he was in Texas."

"They told me that in Raytown. I don't know if I can believe it or not."

"If he's in Texas, he's in a mighty big place. Here, at least you've got Fletcher Trow. He may talk and he may not. On the other hand, a good many Texans come up The Trail with cattle. Your Pierson is as likely to come as not. Trow's here and if Pierson comes, he'll be in touch with him."

"I've already thought of that."

"Have you also thought of settling down here? You've got to be doing something. You're a lawyer and I understand there's only one lawyer in town and he's the county prosecutor. He doesn't have too much time for private practice. Right now I need a bill of sale made out for me. I want it down in black and white the price I paid, the number of cattle."

"I'll make it out for you." A thoughtful expression came to Bokker's eyes.

In Pawnee City they went to the bank where Shay introduced himself to John Chandler, the banker. While they discussed their business, Bokker got some paper from the teller and wrote out a bill of sale in duplicate.

When Shay finished his business with the banker, Bokker handed him the bills of sale.

"Here," said Shay, "here's your fee." He tried to thrust a double eagle on Bokker.

Bokker shook his head. "Forget it, Paul."

"No," said Shay, "it's got to be strictly business between us."

Bokker hesitated. "All right, but a dollar's enough."

"The best lawyer," said Shay, "is the one who charges the highest fees. Five for making out a bill of sale is little enough."

Bokker accepted five dollars.

They left the bank and met Ruth Compton crossing the sidewalk to climb the three-stair flight of steps into the bank.

"I'm in business," she said. "I've bought a half interest in Mrs. Melcher's Bon Ton Millinery Shop."

"That's great," enthused Paul Shay, "but it's no good unless Phil draws up your contract."

Ruth smiled brightly at Bokker. "I was going to ask if you'd mind making out some kind of paper."

"I'll go with you to Mrs. Melcher's right now."

"I'll meet you there in ten minutes. I've got to cash a bank draft first."

"Good," said Bokker.

"I made a little business deal myself," said Shay. "Breakfast is on me. Suppose we all get together at the restaurant in a half hour."

Chapter THIRTEEN

Shay went off to return the horses to the livery stable where he had rented them. Bokker returned to the hotel and waited some ten minutes in the lobby, then strolled to Mrs. Melcher's Bon Ton Millinery Shop, a store some ten by fifteen feet in size.

Mrs. Melcher was a stout, redheaded woman, crowding forty. The store contained a modest assortment of hats, most of them gaudy creations of velvet, satin and silk. Ruth Compton had apparently just entered the store and was counting out bills onto the counter.

She stopped to introduce Bokker. "Mrs. Melcher, this is Mr. Bokker. He's agreed to draw up a contract——"

"A simple partnership agreement," Bokker corrected.

Mrs. Melcher regarded Bokker dubiously. "I didn't think we needed no lawyers in this."

"It's always best to have a lawyer draw up business papers," Bokker said. "A contract protects both parties."

Mrs. Melcher hesitated. "How much'll it cost me?"

"Nothing, Mrs. Melcher," Ruth said quickly.

"I'm representing Miss Compton," Bokker went on. "I think, therefore, that you ought to have your own attorney, Mrs. Melcher."

"Ain't no other in Pawnee City."

"Isn't the county prosecutor also engaged in private practice?"

"Mike Huntley?" Mrs. Melcher sniffed. "I wouldn't trust him to make out nothing. Spends most of his time in the saloons, playing cards." She looked at Bokker suspiciously. "When do I get my money?"

"I've already counted it out, Mrs. Melcher," said Ruth. "Here it is, five hundred dollars."

"For half of the business?"

"That's right."

With the money actually in her hands, Mrs. Melcher got pen and paper and Bokker seated himself at the counter and wrote out a simple partnership agreement. Mrs. Melcher read it twice and was still reluctant to sign it, but—fingering the five hundred dollars—finally did so.

"Well, Miss Compton," Bokker said then, "you're in business."

"And so are you," Ruth Compton said. "I'd like to pay you your fee."

"No," Bokker replied promptly. "This one is free."

"I insist—please!"

Bokker hesitated, saw that Ruth was serious and finally nodded. "Very well, then, I'll charge you the same as I charged Paul Shay for making out his bill of sale—five dollars."

She paid him the money. "Now let's have that party with Paul."

Bokker hesitated. "I've had my breakfast."

She looked at him sharply, but made no comment until they were out of the millinery shop. Then she said, "What's happened between you and Paul?"

"Nothing," Bokker replied a little too quickly. "Nothing at all. It's just—well, if I'm going to hang out my shingle here in Pawnee City, I think I'd better look around for office space."

She nodded. "Very well."

He watched her start across the street, then turned back toward the hotel. In the lobby, he found the hotel proprietor, Joe Wilkins, scowling over his register. "Morning, sir," he greeted Bokker. "Uh—I'm just looking over the room situation. Two trail herds are coming in either today or tomorrow and I've got a couple of telegraph reservations for rooms. Uh—could you tell me how long you expect to keep your room?"

"I couldn't say," Bokker replied. "You see, I'm thinking of settling in Pawnee City for a while."

Wilkins looked at him narrowly. "What for? You're not a gambler."

"I'm a lawyer."

"But we got a lawyer!"

Bokker shrugged. "There may be enough legal business in Pawnee City for two lawyers."

"Mike Huntley don't have enough to keep him busy."

Bokker said coolly, "I just stopped in to ask if you knew of a small office that I might rent."

"Be damned," muttered Wilkins. Then he shrugged. "Might be fun, at that. Yes, Mr. Bokker, I know just the place—Simon Maxwell's got a room next to his barbershop that he wants to rent. Right across from the jail. Make it handy for you. Be near your customers."

"Thank you," said Bokker and left the hotel.

He found Maxwell shaving a customer. "Sure," he said, "I got a room to rent. Here's the key, take a look at it. Right next door."

Bokker took the key, left the barbershop and went next door. It was an unpainted addition, more of a lean-to affair, attached to the barbershop. The front window had four panes, three of which were broken. Bokker unlocked the squeaking door and found himself in a room some ten by ten feet in size. A partition shut off a tiny room at the rear.

He returned to the barber. "How much?"

"How much can you spare?"

"Twenty dollars a month, on a six-month lease——"

"Lease? What's a lease?"

"An agreement that you'll let me have the place for that long a period."

"Oh, you can have it, all right. That is, as long as you pay your rent."

"If I don't, you can evict me. Have you got a sheet of paper?"

The barber rummaged around and found paper and a pen. He watched dubiously as Bokker wrote out a brief form. He read it, when Bokker handed it to him.

"Sounds just like a lawyer wrote it."

"I am a lawyer."

"Huh? Be damned!"

"If you'll sign, Mr. Maxwell, I'll pay you your first month's rent."

The barber signed the lease and Bokker handed him the money. The barber then showed some concern.

"I hope I done the right thing," he said. "I been shavin' Mr. Mike Huntley three times a week for the past six months."

"I'll let you shave me every day, instead of only three times a week."

The barber brightened.

In The St. Louis General Store, Bokker bought a small cot, a washstand, pitcher and bowl and two chairs. He asked about a desk, but finding they had none, settled for a kitchen table. He had the stuff delivered to his new office, then sought out a sign painter and a man to install new glass in the windows.

Toward noon Bokker was straightening out his office, while the sign painter was lettering on his newly installed windows:

> *Philip Bokker*
> *Lawyer*

A fleshy, red-faced man, wearing a rusty Prince Albert and a black felt hat, stepped into the office.

"I'm your competitor," he said.

Bokker started to hold out his hand, saw that Huntley had no intentions of extending his own.

"How are you, Mr. Huntley?" he said quietly.

"How long do you think you can hold out?" Huntley asked unpleasantly.

"Quite a while," retorted Bokker.

"You'll be leavin' before the month's out."

"Don't count on it."

"Want to bet?"

"No. I sit in a sociable poker game once in a while, but that's the only gambling I do. Same for drinking."

"It's going to be like that, eh?" snapped Huntley.

"It's going to be whatever you make it, Huntley."

"All right, Bokker, I tried to warn you. Don't say I didn't."

"You did!"

Huntley stamped out of the little office.

The sign painter came in, grinning. "That's fifty cents, Mr. Bokker."

"Thanks; here's your money. It's a good job."

"Our prosecutor don't like competition," the man continued. "Couldn't help hearing him."

"I'm sorry he feels that way."

"Oh, don't let it worry you. Well, not too much. Huntley's in with the mayor and his crowd, but Judge Paisley ain't payin' much attention to Huntley. He's a pretty square man."

Bokker nodded in satisfaction. "A lawyer can't ask for more than an honest judge."

He left the office and had lunch at the restaurant. Returning to his office, he was hailed by the barber.

"Mr. Bokker," the barber said unhappily, "I made a mistake. I shouldn't have rented you the place."

"Why not?"

"Well, business is good and I been thinkin' I might have to tear down the wall between the two places and put in another chair."

"You can do that," Bokker said, "in six months when my lease expires."

The barber winced. "Is that what that paper was for? I—I can't *make* you move?"

"That's right. Of course, if you want to go to court——"

"No, no, I don't want to go into any court," the barber said hastily. "Uh—what if I gave you your twenty dollars back and—and ten dollars to boot?"

"No," said Bokker. "I rented your place in good faith and I'm going to keep it. Tell Mr. Huntley that, will you?"

"Huntley? What's Huntley got to do with this?"

"Isn't he the one who changed your mind?"

The barber's forehead creased in worry. "N-no," he said. Then he turned back into his shop.

Ten minutes later Tom Chaffee crossed the street. He stood for a moment or two looking at the new lettering on the window, then opened the door and stood in the doorway.

"Going to do some lawing?"

"If I can get clients."

"Oh, we got plenty of crime in Pawnee City. On'y most of the people just up and plead guilty and pay the fine—if they can. If they can't, we keep 'em in the calaboose awhile. I s'pose you'll be comin' around now and tellin' the prisoners not to plead guilty?"

"No," said Bokker.

"How else you goin' to get customers?"

"In the way reputable lawyers get them."

"You a reputable lawyer?"

Bokker looked narrowly at the deputy. "The marshal sent you over?"

Chaffee grinned. "I do lots of things by myself. You'd be surprised." He gave Bokker a half salute and turned away. He did not cross the street to the jail.

Bokker frowned at the door, then got up and went out. He walked to the hotel, went up to the room he had shared for one night with Paul Shay and got his valise.

He descended to the lobby and found Wilkins, the hotel man, coming out of the saloon. "I'm giving up my share of the room, Mr. Wilkins."

"Don't do me much good. Shay's staying." His eyes went to the saloon door. "The way he's going he may be owning the hotel before long."

Bokker set down his valise and walked into the saloon. The space in front of the bar was vacant, but at least twenty customers were crowded around a table. Looking between two of the watchers, Bokker saw that Paul Shay was seated in the poker game. Also playing was Charles Templeton, the gambler from the train.

Two of the other players were faro dealers. A fifth player was obviously a cattleman. Shay had a considerable amount of money before him and was counting out a hundred dollars to add to the large amount already in the center of the table.

"I raise her a hundred," he said calmly.

One of the gamblers threw in his hand. "Too much for me."

The cattleman, however, called, as did Templeton.

"Three kings," said Shay, turning up his cards.

Templeton exclaimed, "On a four-card draw!"

The cattleman groaned. "Never saw such a lucky man."

"I wasn't so lucky on the train yesterday," Shay said cheerfully.

Templeton glowered at Shay. "You've made a couple of remarks about the train, Shay. You leadin' up to something?"

Shay pointed to one of the faro dealers. "Tell him what *you* said to *Mister* Jethro last night."

The gambler frowned. "I don't know anyone named Jethro."

"Oh, sure you do. You know—the fake buffalo hunter you threw out of the game."

"Mr. Shay," said the faro dealer. "I don't go looking for trouble."

"Say your piece," snarled Templeton suddenly.

"I lost seven hundred dollars on the train yesterday," Shay said.

"I lost money myself!"

"To your partner? The fake buffalo hunter . . ."

Templeton kicked back his chair, started to his feet. His right hand darted under the left lapel of his coat. Shay brought a gun up from under the table, where he had already been holding it in his hand.

"Draw, Templeton," he invited.

Templeton's hand came slowly back into sight. "You—you win, Shay!" he said hoarsely.

"You admit Jethro was your partner?"

Templeton made no reply, but his eyes threatened to pop from his head.

"I asked you a question," Shay pursued.

"Y-yes," conceded Templeton.

"Jethro left town last night," Shay went on, remorselessly. "I suggest you leave today."

Templeton started to gather up the money on the table

in front of him, but Shay made a gesture with his revolver. Templeton turned, leaving the money on the table. He walked stiffly out of the room.

"Now," said Shay, "let's continue the game."

"I'm sorry," said one of the faro dealers. "I need some sleep." He gathered up his money.

The cattleman stowed away his money. "I got to look after my herd."

Shay smiled thinly. "I guess I've got business to look after, too."

Shay got together his winnings. The crowd around the table disintegrated and then Shay looked up and saw Bokker.

"Oh, hello, Phil."

"Hello, Paul. I just dropped in to tell you that I've moved out of the room."

Shay regarded him sharply. "Why?"

"I rented an office and there's a small room in back of it. I've got to save money."

Shay seemed relieved. "Oh." He got up from the table. "Help yourself," he pointed to Templeton's money. "Twenty-some dollars of that is yours."

Bokker shook his head.

Shay grunted. "You're a hard man to figure out, Phil. You'd kill a man, but you're squeamish about little things. All right, you do it your way and I'll do it mine."

"That's good enough," Bokker said stiffly.

He walked out of the saloon. In the lobby he retrieved his bag and carried it down to his office.

Chapter FOURTEEN

Bokker was making up his bed toward the middle of the afternoon, when he heard the street door open. He stepped into the "office" and was surprised to see Ruth Compton.

"Curiosity got the best of me," she said. "Paul told me you'd opened an office."

Bokker made a small sweeping gesture to include the meager furnishings. "This is it. I sleep in the back room."

"That's what I'm doing at the shop," she said. "I'll need a good sleep tonight. I don't think I slept five minutes last night, with all the clatter and noise in the hotel." She paused. "I sold a hat."

"Just one?"

"Mrs. Melcher says some days she doesn't sell anything. Then, when a big trail herd comes, she may sell twelve or fifteen hats in a single day."

"A trail herd's here today," Bokker said, then added, "Paul Shay bought it."

"He told me. He—he also said you didn't approve of the way he bought it."

"Paul's business is none of my concern."

"I thought you two were old friends."

"We were in the hospital together, six years ago. We had beds next to each other. For about three weeks. I never saw him again until yesterday." Bokker paused. "I know very little about the man, what he did before the war, or since."

A little frown creased her forehead. "You've quarreled."

"It wasn't a quarrel."

"But you don't like him?"

89

Bokker made no reply for a moment, then suddenly shot at her, "You do." It was as much a question as a statement.

She replied without hesitation, "He's interesting. You never know what he's going to say—or do." She paused. "He told me about your—your trouble."

Anger swept Bokker. "He doesn't miss a trick, does he?"

"I don't think I know what you mean."

"He gives you *his* version of his own affairs—and there's nothing to them, the way he puts them. But the other man's——"

"No," Ruth said quickly. "He didn't make you out any villain. I—I understand your trouble."

"Do you?"

"Someone's done something terrible to you. It's only natural that you want revenge."

Bokker shook his head. "I'm not seeking vengeance. It's hard to explain."

"Why? Someone wronged you and you want to bring him to—to justice. Isn't that what you're trying to do?"

"No," Bokker said, "it's not as simple as that. I saw a lot of war. I saw things happen that were not right. And yet they weren't wrong. It was war. What Quantrell and his men did in Lawrence wasn't war. It wasn't right by any conceivable standards, by any rules of civilization. They looted and destroyed an entire town—they murdered almost two hundred men; they made a hundred and fifty widows and twice that many orphans. It was murder, murder of the foulest kind. The men who committed it should be made to pay for their crimes."

"You think every man who was with Quantrell should be executed?" exclaimed Ruth.

"No. Quantrell had over four hundred men with him. A good many had no idea of what was going to happen in Lawrence. They thought they were going into a battle—a raid at worst. They took no part in the looting and—and the murdering. But some of the men did. And they apparently enjoyed it, if the reports of the surviving witnesses are correct."

Ruth regarded Bokker steadily. "And it's your duty—*your* mission, rather, to find these—these murderers and kill them?"

Bokker exhaled wearily. "Is that what you think I'm doing?"

"Isn't it?"

"Wait!"

Bokker strode into the tiny bedroom, opened his valise and took out his worn copy of *Fred Cowan's Illustrated Weekly*. He returned to the front room and plopped the opened magazine on the table that served as his desk.

"Look at that picture."

Ruth bent over it. "It's—it's rather vivid."

"Look at the faces of Quantrell, Bloody Bill Anderson——"

"Here's your picture!"

"What do you think? Is it a good likeness?"

She stared at the picture, then turned to look full into Bokker's face. She was frowning. "It's—I just said, 'vivid.'"

"If I ever looked like that," Bokker said slowly, "I ought to be killed in the next moment. The man who has my face——"

"He seems to be enjoying what he's doing."

"Now you've got it!" exclaimed Bokker.

"But Paul says you can prove you weren't at Lawrence."

"I wasn't there, but someone was—someone who killed a man just like that and whose face the artist caught—'vividly,' as you say. So vividly that the real owner of the face wanted to remove himself from the scene of the crime. He did it by erasing his own face and putting in another. Mine."

"Wouldn't that be—rather difficult?"

"Not to a good artist."

"But he'd have to have possession of the original drawing, wouldn't he?"

"Yes. But there'd have been no difficulty about it if he'd been with Quantrell when this original sketch was found on the body of the dead artist. A half hour's work with a pencil—maybe only ten minutes—would have been enough."

"But he would have had to know you."

"He knew me."

"Who?"

"The man who changed the picture. No, I don't know his name. Not yet. When I find it out, I'm sure it'll turn out to be someone I know. Who . . . I haven't the slightest idea."

"And *when* you find out?"

"I'm going to kill him."

Ruth exclaimed poignantly, "But you've just spent ten minutes convincing me that you're not looking for revenge."

"I'm not. A man who did what this man in the picture did, a man who'd do such a thing and enjoy it, has no right to live."

"And you think *you* have the right to kill him?"

"No one else can kill him."

"What about the law? You're a lawyer."

"The law won't get this man. He's received legal amnesty. No one can touch him—no one, but myself."

"I think," Ruth Compton said slowly, "I think I'm beginning to dislike you."

She turned and started for the door. But before she reached it, a gun boomed out upon the street. It was a heavy, dull boom, not the report of a revolver.

Ruth gasped and took a quick step back. The gun boomed again. Then a loud yell came over. "Come on out!" the voice yelled piercingly. "Come on out and fight, you cheap tinhorn!"

Bokker grasped Ruth's arm, propelled her away from the door. "Keep back!"

He whipped open the door and stepped out onto the wooden sidewalk.

A man in buckskin sat on a horse some fifty yards away. He was reloading a double-barreled shotgun. Even as he snapped the gun together, the doors of a saloon bellied outwards and Paul Shay stepped out.

Two doors away, Charles Templeton, a revolver in his

hand, stepped from a doorway. He thrust out his hand, pointing the revolver at Paul Shay.

"Look out, Paul!" cried Bokker.

Shay had been moving out toward the hitchrail to get a better shot at the man on horseback, Jethro, the buffalo hunter-gambler. Attracted by Bokker's call, he whirled. He was caught between two fires, which he realized instantly. The blast of the shotgun, less than forty feet away, could cut him in two. And if he took time to shoot at Jethro, Templeton's bullet would cut him down.

Shay did the best thing he could do. He threw himself forward and down, under the hitchrail. Jethro's gun blasted, the buckshot going all around Shay, who was in no position to turn and get Templeton. Templeton made a quick step forward, depressed his aim.

Bokker's gun was in his hand. It roared and Templeton cried out and pitched forward, the gun falling from his hand. Shay sized up the situation instantly. He came to his feet in a lunge, thrust forward and fired at Jethro, just as the latter was throwing down for his second shot.

Shay's aim was bad, too hasty. Jethro's horse took the bullet. It screamed in anguish, reared up and went over backwards. Jethro slipped from the horse, hit the dust of the street. The shotgun was jolted from his hand. He dove for it.

Shay's second shot caught him, bent over the shotgun. He collapsed over the gun.

Shay walked out to the middle of the street, looked down at the dead man.

Bokker passed Templeton, saw that he, too, was dead and continued on out to the street.

"Thanks," said Shay.

Tom Chaffee came running, gun in hand.

"All right," he cried, "drop it!"

Shay looked at him, then down at the gun in his hand. "They tried to kill me."

"You can tell that to the judge," Chaffee said grimly. "Now, drop your gun. You, too, Bokker!"

Bokker dropped his revolver to the street. Shay, however, held his.

"Now wait a minute, Marshal. I was only defending myself."

"Drop it, Shay!" snapped Chaffee. "Drop it—or shoot!"

Men were coming out of stores, into the street. Fletcher Trow was running forward. Shay dropped his gun and held his hands, shoulder height, palms outward.

"I should have taken them in last night," Chaffee said to his superior.

Fletcher Trow stooped and caught up Shay's gun, then moved and picked up Bokker's. "Now you'll find out about law," he said to Bokker. "Pawnee City law."

"They would have killed Shay," Bokker protested.

"Sure, sure," Trow said easily. "Last night you and him ganged up on this one," indicating Jethro, "and today you crowded the other one." He nodded toward Templeton's body. "What did you expect them to do? Buy you a horse and buggy?"

Huntley, the prosecuting attorney, strode forward. "Lock them up, Marshal," he snapped. "I'll sign the complaint."

"You heard him," Trow said, pointing toward the jail. "Let's get going."

Paul Shay glowered at the marshal. "I'll say my piece to the judge," he promised.

Bokker and Shay marched to the jail with the marshal and his deputy crowding on their heels. In the marshal's office, Trow opened a door leading to the jail proper.

This consisted of two cells, with a narrow aisle between them. The cells were devoid of furniture. In one of the cells a drunken cowboy lay on the floor in a stupor. Trow opened the door of the other cell.

"Make yourselves at home."

Shay and Bokker entered the cell. Trow locked the door and left the cell block.

Shay exclaimed, "I thought they couldn't put a lawyer in jail!"

"They can, if a lawyer kills a man," Bokker retorted grimly.

"You saved my life. Templeton would have got me."

"And now, maybe, Fletcher Trow will get me."

"They got to give us a trial," Shay declared. "Looks like you're elected to defend us."

"You may as well know," Bokker told Shay, "I had words with Huntley, the prosecuting attorney."

"Oh, fine!"

"He doesn't want another lawyer in Pawnee City."

Shay snorted. "The cattle buyers didn't want another cattle buyer in town. They're afraid of competition."

"The cattle buyers didn't get us into this jam," Bokker reminded.

Shay suddenly grinned. "Things happen around me, don't they, Phil?"

"That's one way of looking at it."

They had been in jail no more than a half hour when Fletcher Trow came in from his office. "You're getting a quick trial," he said.

"Now, that's more like it!" cried Paul Shay.

"Is it?" sneered Trow. "It may mean a quick hanging."

"All we ask is a fair trial."

Trow unlocked the cell door. "Out and upstairs."

Tom Chaffee waited in the outer room, his hand resting carefully on the butt of his revolver. He followed the marshal and the prisoners out of the office and up a flight of stairs to the courtroom, which was above the jail.

Chapter FIFTEEN

Bokker was surprised when they entered the courtroom to find it jammed with Pawnee City people. Judge Paisley already sat behind his "bench," a table on a raised platform. He was in his fifties, a severe-looking man. Bokker hoped that the brief description he had received of him from the sign painter was an accurate one, for a quick glance around the room showed him only impassive, or hostile faces.

The judge looked only briefly at Shay, but his eyes came to rest upon Bokker. "You're an attorney, I understand?"

"Yes, Your Honor."

"You'll act as counsel for yourself as well as your fellow prisoner?"

"If the court permits."

"I see no objection. Prosecutor, will you read the charge?"

Huntley came forward. "The prisoners before the bar, who call themselves Paul Shay and Philip Bokker, are charged with the murder of Jed Jethro and Charles Templeton."

The judge looked at Bokker. "How do you plead?"

"Not guilty, Your Honor."

"That's ridiculous," cried Huntley. "They were seen by a hundred witnesses."

"That will do, Prosecutor," the judge said sharply. "Mr. Bokker, you understand, of course, that you are entitled to a jury trial."

"If it please the court, we will waive a jury."

Shay looked at Bokker worriedly.

96

Judge Paisley said, "Will the prosecution call its first witness?"

"Deputy Marshal Chaffee!" announced Huntley.

The deputy marshal came forward and was sworn in by the marshal, who apparently doubled as bailiff.

"All right, Marshal," Huntley began, "tell the court what you saw last night at the—the hotel."

Chaffee seated himself on a chair beside the judge's desk. He fixed his eyes on Phil Bokker. "The defendants got into a fight with the deceased, Jed Jethro. When I came up, Bokker had his gun in the—the victim's back and his partner, Shay, was threatening Jethro. They'd probably have killed him then and there if I hadn't happened to——"

"Objection, Your Honor!" exclaimed Bokker.

"Objection sustained," said the judge. "You, the witness, cannot assume what might have happened, or what was in the minds of the defendants or anyone else. You must confine yourself to stating what you actually saw."

"Why, I just told you, Judge," Chaffee said easily, "they was fixin' to kill——"

"Objection!"

"Objection sustained." Judge Paisley scowled at Chaffee. "I just got through telling you——"

"Oh, sure, Judge, sure," interrupted Chaffee.

The judge banged his gavel on the desk. "Your Honor!" he snapped. "When addressing the court."

"Sure, Your Honor. Like I was sayin', they was fixin' to——"

The gavel came down again. "Prosecutor, will you see that your witness confines himself to relating what he *knows*——"

"Your Honor," said Huntley angrily, "the witness is telling what he knows. The prisoners claim they were cheated in a card game on the train. They came to Pawnee City with the intention of attaining revenge."

Judge Paisley banged his gavel once more. "Prosecutor, you're supposed to be an attorney. Let's not have any of that from *you*. One more attempt to prejudice the case and I'll dismiss the charges against the prisoners."

"Your Honor," said Huntley with studied sarcasm, "as you said, I *am* a lawyer. I have appeared before a great many courts. I know the customs and procedures of courts and——"

"Proceed with your case!" interrupted Judge Paisley.

"I am through with this witness!" snapped Huntley.

Chaffee started to get up, but the judge waved him back. "Counsel for defense."

"No questions at present," Bokker said.

Paul Shay exclaimed, "Are you crazy, man?"

"No questions!" repeated Bokker firmly.

"Next witness," snapped Judge Paisley.

Huntley turned, surveyed the front row of spectators. A smirk twisted his mouth.

"Steve Winston!"

Winston, the cattle drover, came forward.

Shay grabbed Bokker's arm. "Not him, Phil!"

"I can't help it," said Bokker. "He has a right to call whatever witnesses he pleases."

"He'll crucify me!"

Winston was sworn in. A sardonic grin came over his features.

"Mr. Winston," began the prosecutor, "where were you at two o'clock this afternoon?"

"I was in the hotel bar, having a glass of beer."

"What happened while you were there?"

"I heard a gun go off, outside on the street, and then a voice yelled out, 'Shay, you dirty crook, come outside!'"

"And then?"

"Shay," said Winston, pointing at the prisoner, "got up from a poker game. He came toward the bar and said in a loud voice, 'Jethro, that's Jethro's voice. I guess he didn't think I meant it when I told him to leave town.'"

"The prisoner, Paul Shay, said that?"

"Yes, sir."

"Very well. Did he say anything else?"

"He drew out his gun and started for the door. He said, 'I guess I'll have to kill me a man.' After that he went outside. I—I followed. Up to the door, that is. I saw the whole thing."

"Tell the court what you saw."

"I saw him shoot Jethro."

"You saw him shoot Jethro. You're sure of that?"

"Of course. He said he was going to kill Jethro and then he went and done it. Right in front of my own eyes."

"Your witness," said Huntley, turning to Bokker.

Bokker stepped up to within a few feet of the cattleman. "Mr. Winston, what is your business?"

"Business? I haven't got any business," replied the witness. "I drive cattle. You know that."

"You drive cattle," pursued Bokker. "From where?"

"Texas. Where else?"

"I don't know. I'm asking you. Very well, you drive cattle from Texas to Kansas. Your own cattle?"

"Mine and my partners'. We buy Longhorns in Texas and we sell them here."

"What do you pay for the cattle you buy?"

Winston bristled. "What business is that of yours?"

"Your Honor," Bokker appealed to the judge, "I ask that the prisoner be ordered to answer."

"Does the price he pays for cattle have any bearing on this case?"

"I think it does."

"Very well, the prisoner will answer counsel."

Winston scowled at Bokker. "What was the question?"

"I asked you what you pay for cattle in Texas."

"They ain't worth much there."

"How much?"

"Three dollars, maybe four."

"Four dollars."

"That's in Texas," said Winston, frowning. "We got to drive them six hundred miles to Pawnee City."

"Of course. Now, will you tell the court what you receive for cattle here in Pawnee City?"

"That's my business!" exclaimed Winston.

"Your Honor——" began Bokker.

Judge Paisley pointed his gavel at Winston. "Once more and I'll hold you in contempt of court. You will answer the question of counsel."

"I protest, Your Honor," cried the prosecutor, "the

price of cattle has nothing to do with the murders committed by these men——"

The gavel came down loudly and Huntley, snarling,
moved back.

"Proceed," said the judge grimly.

"Isn't it a fact, Mr. Winston," Bokker proceeded, "that
you sold a herd of eight hundred steers to Mr. Shay only
this morning, for a price of twenty-one dollars per steer?"

"He cheated me out of four dollars a steer!"

"You *thought* he cheated you," said Bokker, "but you
made the bargain of your own free will. You signed the
bill of sale, did you not?"

"Yes," said Winston sullenly, "but them steers were
worth——"

"Twenty-one dollars," said Bokker. "You received
twenty-one dollars for steers for which you paid only four
dollars. In other words, you made a profit of seventeen
dollars per steer. It's true that you had to drive the steers
some six hundred miles to make that profit, but you did
make a profit, did you not?"

"If you call that a profit——"

"I do. You have just admitted that you believed Paul
Shay cheated you. In other words, you feel badly toward
Mr. Shay."

"He's a crook!"

"We'll pass that," Bokker said. "Mr. Shay is not on
trial for being a crook. But you are testifying against him
in a murder case . . . and you have admitted that you are
prejudiced against him——" Bokker paused, then said
suddenly, "No more questions."

Winston got up. As he passed Bokker to resume his
seat among the spectators, he gave him an angry look.

Huntley stepped up to the marshal, Fletcher Trow. He
talked quickly, excitedly, although in low tones. Trow listened, then shook his head. Huntley, scowling, turned
to the judge.

"The prosecution has no more witnesses. We believe
that we have proved beyond doubt that the defendants——"

"*I'll* decide that," interrupted Judge Paisley. "Mr. Bokker, do you have any witnesses for the defense?"

"Just myself, Your Honor."

"Take the stand, then."

Trow moved forward and swore in Bokker. Bokker took the witness stand. "Since I am a defendant as well as counsel for myself and co-defendant, I believe it would be best if I simply told what I know about this case."

"Do it the easiest way," the judge advised.

"Mr. Shay, myself and the men who were killed today, Jethro and Templeton, engaged in a poker game on the train coming to Pawnee City yesterday," Bokker said quietly. "I dropped out of the game after losing some twenty-two dollars. Mr. Shay continued and lost seven hundred dollars. Jethro, who was dressed like a buffalo hunter—and talked of being one—was the big winner. Mr. Shay, after the game, told me that he believed Mr. Templeton and Jethro were in reality partners. However, we did not see them again on the train."

Bokker paused. "Last night, Mr. Shay was playing faro at the hotel, when the man Jethro came along. The faro dealer referred to him as a professional gambler and would not permit him in the game. Mr. Shay then had words with Jethro and Jethro reached for a gun . . . I prevented him . . ."

"How?" asked the judge.

"By drawing a gun of my own and pressing it into his back. That was all. Jethro left and I did not see him again until today. This afternoon, I again was in the hotel when Mr. Templeton was playing cards with Mr. Shay. They had a quarrel over yesterday's game on the train. But nothing came of the quarrel. Not at the moment. Later this afternoon, I was in my office when I heard a gun go off. I also heard a voice yelling for someone to come out and fight. I stepped out of my office and saw Jethro on a horse, facing the saloon. Just then Mr. Shay stepped out. At the same time, Templeton, Jethro's partner, stepped out of a doorway, a gun in his hand. It was obvious that Jethro and Templeton had Shay between them. Both were armed and were obviously intending to kill Shay. I called out a warning to Shay and drew my own gun. I shot Mr. Templeton . . . and Shay shot Jethro."

"That's all, Mr. Bokker?"

"Yes, Your Honor."

"You may step down."

Bokker got up from the chair and resumed his position beside Paul Shay. The judge looked at the spectators, then fixed his gaze upon Bokker.

"Mr. Bokker, you are an attorney-at-law. I am surprised that you took the law into your own hands, not once, but twice."

"I had to act quickly, Your Honor," Bokker said defensively. "On both occasions. There wasn't time to appeal to the law."

"That is the mitigating circumstance," the judge continued. "Men should not be allowed to carry weapons. It leads to taking the law into their own hands. It is a regrettable circumstance, and I cannot advise too strongly that the legal arm of this city take steps to prevent citizens from carrying weapons. But since they have not done so, I cannot decide on that basis. I can only view the evidence and make my decision from it. It is quite obvious from what I have heard that the deceased, Jethro and Templeton, were intent on killing Mr. Shay. Mr. Shay had a right to defend himself. He did so. You, Mr. Bokker—you saved Mr. Shay's life. I abhor the fact of an attorney-at-law carrying weapons, but since I can do nothing about that, I can only declare that you acted within the rights of a citizen in preventing harm to another. . . . Case dismissed."

A sudden burst of applause went up in the courtroom. The judge banged his gavel on the desk once or twice, then shrugged and got to his feet.

Shay, meanwhile, had grabbed Bokker's arm. "Great, Phil—great! You did a magnificent job."

Fletcher Trow, smiling sardonically, moved up. "I shouldn't even have tried it, Bokker. But next time . . ." He smirked and turned away.

SIXTEEN

Bokker had scarcely returned to his office than Judge Paisley entered. He extended his hand.

"I want to welcome you to Pawnee City."

"Thank you, Judge."

The judge smiled. "I hope to see you often in my court. But not as a defendant."

"It wasn't of my choosing."

The judge shook his head. "That partner of yours——"

"Paul Shay isn't my partner!"

"I was under the impression that you were old friends."

"Acquaintances, Judge. But, frankly, I'm going to refuse Paul Shay's legal business from now on."

The judge regarded him quizzically. "He's a bit sharp." He held up his hand. "I heard about that cattle deal. He bribed the station agent . . ."

Bokker exclaimed, "How do you know?"

Judge Paisley shrugged. "Jenkins owed the bank three hundred dollars. He paid it off this morning."

"I should have known," exclaimed Bokker. "He was awfully sure that he would get that herd when we rode out to Winston's camp this morning." He frowned. "He had me make out the bill of sale."

"I think," the judge said, "Mr. Shay's going to get along in Pawnee City."

The judge's prediction seemed to be borne out during the next few days.

Shay bought another herd the following day and two days later a third. Bokker saw him in the company of the prosecuting attorney the next day and on the third day, Fletcher Trow and Shay came out of the restaurant together, talking like old cronies.

Bokker stopped in for a glass of beer at the hotel saloon and saw Shay playing cards with the prosecutor and the mayor of Pawnee City, Steve Longtree, who owned the hardware store. The mayor had a sizable sum of money in front of him and from his jovial attitude was apparently a big winner in the game.

Bokker, catching his eye, saw Shay wink.

And Paul Shay was becoming more than friendly with Ruth Compton. Bokker saw him go into the millinery store once or twice, and another time he saw the two riding past his office in a rented buggy.

Bokker, himself, had not talked with Ruth since the day of the trial. He was fairly busy himself. His defense of Shay and himself had impressed people in Pawnee City. Businessmen came to him to draw up contracts; he was the defending counsel in a law suit over a boundary line between two property owners and won the case. His opponent was Mike Huntley, the prosecutor, acting in a private capacity as a lawyer. Huntley showed considerable displeasure after losing his case.

Fletcher Trow did not avoid Bokker, nor did he put himself in Bokker's path.

Then, a week after Bokker arrived in Pawnee City, Tom Chaffee came to his office. "Got a prisoner keeps yowling he wants a lawyer."

"Huntley can't defend him?"

"Says he wants you."

"Very well, I'll go over and talk to him. What's the charge?"

"Resisting arrest."

"Arrest on what charge?"

"The usual, drunk—disorderly."

Bokker crossed to the jail with Chaffee. It was afternoon and the morning crop of prisoners, arrested during the night, had been disposed of. Bokker's prospective client was the only prisoner.

He was an unkempt-looking youth in his early twenties. A week's growth of beard concealed most of his features. Bokker was caught by the youth's pale blue eyes—and a bruise on his left temple.

"You sent for me?" he asked the prisoner.

"You're the lawyer?"

"Bokker's my name."

"Yeah, sure. You got to get me out of here."

"In this town, drunk and disorderly conduct is a misdemeanor——"

"They're charging me with resisting arrest." The youth touched the bruise on his temple.

"If you plead guilty, you'll be fined twenty-five dollars. At the very most, another twenty-five, if the judge sees fit to fine you for resisting arrest."

"Can't you get me out on bail?"

"There's no particular point in that. You'll only have to stay here overnight. In the morning——"

"In the morning I'll be dead!" cried the prisoner.

Bokker looked at him sharply. "That bruise——"

The prisoner made a gesture of dismissal. "That's nothin'. The deputy buffaloed me with his Navy gun. It's"—he looked nervously past Bokker toward the door leading to the Marshal's office—"it's the marshal," he whispered. "He recognized me."

"He's arrested you before?"

"No—no. He knows I know him from"—the prisoner's voice faltered "—from the war."

"The war's been over four years and more," said Bokker. "You weren't old enough then."

"The hell I wasn't!" retorted the youth. "I'm twenty-two."

"So you were eighteen in 'sixty-five."

"Sixteen in 'sixty-three, when we . . ." He did not finish.

Bokker's eyes narrowed. "In 'sixty-three, when Quantrell destroyed Lawrence?"

"Trow was there!"

"I know he was. And you?"

"I ain't sayin' I was and I ain't sayin' I wasn't. But the marshal was there and I—I know it. That's why you got to get me out of here."

Bokker looked thoughtfully at the young prisoner. That he had been at Lawrence he did not doubt. Quantrell's men had been young; it was common gossip that he had many fifteen- and sixteen-year-old boys in his bloody command; even boys fourteen. They had received an early baptism of blood and some of them had not returned to their farm homes after the war to resume peaceful occupations. The younger James boy could be no older than this youth before Bokker. And one or two of the Youngers of Harrisonville were not more than twenty or twenty-one even now. Yet they had been with Quantrell and were currently making a name for themselves as bank and train robbers.

Bokker said suddenly, "What's your name?"

"Uh—Smith."

"Your real name!"

"I'm tellin' you, Smith—uh—Bob Smith."

"All right, call yourself Smith," Bokker said impatiently. "Now, tell me what makes you think Fletcher Trow would kill you if you stayed in here overnight?"

"He's got to!" exclaimed the young prisoner. "I told you—I know who he is. I—I know what he done at Lawrence."

"A lot of people know that," said Bokker. "I know it myself."

"You wasn't there—you don't know all of it."

"What did Trow do in Lawrence, outside of killing people?"

"He was a captain. He made me——" Smith suddenly stopped. "I ain't a-goin' to tell you that. I'd be dead inside of an hour if Trow knew . . ."

Bokker had to restrain himself from reaching through the bars and seizing the young former guerrilla by the throat. He said carefully, "Have you got any money?"

"Yeah, sure. Here." Smith thrust a hand into his pocket and brought out a roll of greenbacks. Bokker counted the money.

"Sixty-one dollars. Enough for your fine, but not for bail if the judge sets it high."

"Get me out!" said Smith earnestly. "Get me out and keep the money. I've said too much already. Get me out and"—he came closer to Bokker and gripped the bars of the cell door—"Trow'll kill me, I tell you. You got to get me out."

"I'll do my best. I'll have to talk to the judge."

Bokker stepped to the door and went into the marshal's office. Tom Chaffee was seated behind Trow's desk, his feet up on it. The marshal, however, was not in the office.

Chaffee whistled tunelessly as Bokker went out.

Judge Paisley had a small office in the rear of the general store, but he was not in it when Bokker looked in. Bokker tried a couple of the saloons, a store or two and finally received word that the judge was down at the depot.

"Bokker," Judge Paisley greeted him, "you'll have a rest for a couple of days. I'm running down to Abilene on the afternoon train."

"You won't be holding court in the morning, then."

"I've no jurisdiction in Abilene—and that's where I'll be."

"I've been retained by a prisoner," Bokker said.

"That so? Anything important? The marshal hasn't made any report."

"It's a drunk and disorderly charge. Also, resisting arrest."

"Do the man good to sleep in jail a couple of days."

"I'd like to get him out on bail."

"A common drunk?"

"Yes."

The judge looked at Bokker curiously. "I've been trying these misdemeanor cases in the morning—the entire batch at one time. I don't like to convene court for one special case."

"I know—that's why I've asked for bail."

Judge Paisley frowned. "There's little enough co-operation between the marshal's office and the court. I don't want to antagonize Trow any more than I already have. . . . Very well, I'll set bail. Will a hundred dollars be all right?"

Bokker nodded. "The prisoner doesn't have that much. But I'll add some of my own money to it."

"You'll probably lose it. He'll get on his horse and leave Pawnee City the minute he gets out."

"I'll risk that."

"Very well. Come to my office and I'll sign a release order."

Ten minutes later, Bokker re-entered the marshal's office. Chaffee was still holding down the marshal's chair.

"Smith has been released on bail,—" Bokker said, handing the writ to the deputy.

Chaffee exclaimed, "Bail—a drunk?"

"Judge Paisley issued the writ."

Chaffee scowled at it. "I can't let any prisoner out without the marshal's say-so."

"Where is he?"

"Ain't seen him in a couple of hours."

"A writ is returnable immediately," Bokker explained. "You'll have to take the responsibility."

"Uh-uh, not me. I'm only the deputy."

"You refuse to honor this writ?"

"I don't refuse nothing. I'm just telling you that I don't have the authority to let a prisoner out of jail."

"If you can make arrests, you can let out a prisoner—with a writ signed by Judge Paisley."

Chaffee's face showed sudden relief as he glanced out of the window. "Here's Fletch!"

Chapter SEVENTEEN

Fletcher Trow came in from the street. He looked sharply at Bokker.

"He's got a writ from the judge," Chaffee explained, handing it to the marshal. "Says we got to release the prisoner."

"How'd he know we had a prisoner?"

Chaffee winced. "I—I guess I told him. The prisoner kept yammering about seeing a lawyer, so I——"

"You're taking a little too much on yourself, Chaffee!" snapped Trow.

Chaffee scowled. "I wouldn't honor the writ. Told him I didn't have the authority."

Trow tossed the writ to the desk. It was obvious that he was annoyed. It was more than mere annoyance, in fact. "All right," he said to Chaffee, "let him have the prisoner."

Chaffee picked up the large key from the desk and went into the cell block. He returned in a moment, young Smith at his heels. The prisoner kept his face averted, would not look at Fletcher Trow.

Bokker nodded and left the marshal's office. Outside, Smith said hurriedly, "Thanks, Mr. Bokker, thanks a lot."

"Wait a minute!" exclaimed Bokker. "I want to talk to you."

"Later. Uh—I want to get something to eat."

"Now," said Bokker firmly.

Smith shot a quick look over his shoulder at the jail. He frowned apprehensively, then followed Bokker across the street to the latter's office.

When he had closed the door, Bokker said, "Now, what is it you know about Fletcher Trow?"

"I can't tell you. If Trow knew——"

"He isn't going to know," snapped Bokker. "He'll get nothing from me. I'm not exactly a friend of Fletcher Trow's. Here . . ." He strode into his bedroom and caught up his valise, emptied of clothes, but still containing a few odds and ends. He carried it back into his office and set it on the desk.

He opened the bag, reached in—and froze.

The magazine was not in the bag. Yet Bokker knew that he had put it there the day he had shown it to Ruth Compton. He brushed the bag to the floor, whisked open the drawer of the table that served as his desk.

The magazine was not there, either.

His eyes met those of Smith. The youth looked at him, puzzled.

"I had something in this bag I wanted to show you. A magazine——" He stopped. "A copy of *Fred Cowan's Il-* with——" His eyes went to the window.
lustrated Weekly."

Smith's eyes widened. "The one with—with—

"The one with the sketch of Quantrell and his men at Lawrence. Fletcher Trow's in it."

Smith winced. "That—that's what *I* was going to tell you about."

"How long is it since you've seen the picture?"

"I dunno, a long time ago. Right after the war."

"You haven't seen it since?"

Smith hesitated, then shook his head. "It's four-five years ago, I'm sure."

"The picture," Bokker said carefully, "showed a number of guerrillas, some recognizable, some not. Here . . ." He caught up a pencil and pulled forward a pad of paper. "This is where Quantrell stood. Bloody Bill Anderson was here and here was Bill Grayson." A shudder ran through Smith. Bokker pushed the pencil into his hand. "Mark down the positions of the others— Fletcher Trow——"

Smith started to make a mark on the paper, then suddenly looked at Bokker. "You know a helluva lot about this." There was suspicion in his tone.

"I know a great deal," Bokker said grimly. "Go ahead. Next to Trow was McDonald Pierson."

A gasp was torn from Smith's lips. Bokker exclaimed softly, "You're MacDonald Pierson!"

"No!" cried Smith. "MacDonald is dead. He died in Texas."

"How do you know? Were you there?"

"No. I—I heard about it."

"Who told you?"

"I don't remember."

"Only three men who were in that picture are still alive," Bokker went on remorselessly.

"That's a lie! They never got Jesse James."

"Jesse James wasn't at Lawrence."

"His brother Frank was. So was Cole Younger and Jim and——" Smith stopped. "What're you tryin' to do—put a rope around my neck? Or get me a bullet between my ribs?"

"I'm not going to do anything to you. I got you out of jail. I put up money of my own—your sixty-one dollars wasn't enough. I'll see that Trow doesn't harm you. But I want the names of these men. Here . . ." Bokker grabbed the pencil from Smith's hand.

"This was Trow, this was MacDonald Pierson. . . . Who was next?"

"Max— Max Hildebrand."

"No, Max was over here. Think, Mac, the man next to you. . . ."

Smith took a quick backward step. "You're trying to trick me. My name—my name ain't Pierson!"

"You can stop that. I recognize you now. Without the whiskers, your face is that of Pierson. I've studied every face in that picture until I can draw it from memory. Who was next to you, Mac—the man who was shooting the man you were dragging up?——

"You said you knew everyone!" cried Smith.

"I know the faces. I don't know the names."

Smith—or Pierson—stared at Bokker. "Who—who are you?"

"You know who I am. My name is Philip Bokker and

I'm a lawyer. I got you out of jail and if you don't tell me now what I want to know, you're going back. I mean that, Pierson. I'll have your bail canceled and you'll go back into jail—with Fletcher Trow!"

Pierson would have talked, Bokker was sure of it. But just then the door was opened and Paul Shay entered. "Didn't know you were busy, Phil. Sorry. . . ."

"Do you mind, Paul? I'll see you in a little while."

Shay nodded and started to turn away. Then he stopped. "It's rather important, Phil. It'll take just half a minute. . . ."

He indicated the door. Annoyed, Bokker followed him outside, closing the door on young Pierson.

"What is it, Paul?" he asked.

"Trow," said Shay, "he's got something up his sleeve. Pumped me for about a half hour. Or, tried to pump me. I'm afraid he's up to something."

"So am I," said Bokker.

"Watch out, Phil!" Shay warned. "Trow's dangerous. Don't underestimate him. I—I've been getting rather friendly with him these last few days. He pretends to be a calm man, but he's like a coiled steel spring inside. Apt to explode any minute."

"Thanks for telling me. I'll watch——" Bokker's eyes went to the window. A cry was torn from his throat and he whirled and kicked open the door of his office. Pierson was no longer in it. Bokker plunged on into the little bedroom. The window was open and Pierson was just disappearing through it.

Bokker sprang from the window. "Stop!" he cried. He started to clamber after Pierson, then suddenly remembered that he did not have his gun. He turned back, knocked aside the pillow from the cot and grabbed up the Navy gun. He thrust it under the waistband of his trousers and then climbed swiftly through the window.

He hit the earth in the alley behind the row of stores. Pierson was no longer in sight. He had already turned into Kiowa Street, the single cross street in Pawnee City.

Bokker pounded toward the street, made a swift turn

and ran to the main street. Fifty feet away, MacDonald Pierson was vaulting onto a horse.

He let out a yip, jammed his heels into the horse's belly and it was off, galloping within a few strides. Bokker looked around for a horse. The closest was thirty yards away, almost in front of his office. He ran toward it, aware that Paul Shay whom he had left on the sidewalk, was running toward him.

"Phil" Shay cried. "What's up?"

"Haven't got time!" Bokker shouted.

He rushed to the horse, jerked the slip knot by which it was tied to the hitchrail and mounted swiftly. He turned the horse into the street and sent it after that on which Pierson was already a hundred yards away.

Bokker went a hundred yards and knew that he had lost. The mount he had taken haphazardly was heavy, clumsy, while Pierson's was a fleet Texas mustang. Bokker lost fifty feet in the first hundred yards. Another hundred yards or so and he was hopelessly outdistanced.

Seething, Bokker turned back.

Shay was standing in front of Bokker's office, arguing with a middle-aged farmer. The farmer saw Bokker and came to the rail as Bokker dismounted. "What's the idee takin' my horse like that?" the man demanded.

"Sorry," said Bokker, "I was in a hurry."

"I got a good notion to report you to the marshal," the farmer went on.

"Mister," said Paul Shay, "this is Mr. Bokker, a lawyer——"

"A lawyer!" exclaimed the man.

Bokker thrust a five-dollar gold piece into the man's hand. "This'll pay for the loan of your horse." He turned away. "Paul, I need a horse. A good one."

"How badly do you need it?"

"Plenty!"

"Then don't bother trying the livery stable. They've only got plugs to rent. Mmm—have you seen that bay I bought a couple of days ago?"

"That's what I was thinking of."

Shay hesitated, then suddenly nodded. "You won't find many faster. If it's really important, Phil—take it."

"I'm going to ride it hard."

"Go ahead. This—has something to do with——"

"The man I had in my office was MacDonald Pierson. I've told you about him."

Shay whistled softly. "Take the horse. It's over in the livery stable. Wait—I'll go with you so you won't lose time."

They crossed swiftly to the livery stable and Shay himself got his saddle and threw it upon a rangy bay in a stall. Bokker quickly tightened the cinches and mounting, started out of the stable.

"Luck!" called Shay.

Bokker stooped so his head would clear the door. He rode into the street and sent the bay into a swift trot. Once clear of the street traffic he let out the animal. Pierson had started off at a swift gallop. All of Quantrell's men had been fine horsemen. Pierson would know that he must not wind his horse in a prolonged gallop. Panic had sent him off at a gallop, but he would soon pull up and save his horse for a grueling later race.

Bokker decided to pace his horse. He let it out into a fast trot that ate up the distance yet left his horse with enough for a final burst of speed. Pierson had a good start on him, five-six minutes. Possibly seven. He could be two miles ahead of Bokker. Three.

It was a long head start.

Chapter EIGHTEEN

A mile out of Pawnee City and Bokker thought that he sighted the fugitive. He let out his mount a little. The spot on the prairie grew bigger and he suddenly groaned. It was a stunted cottonwood. He continued on to it, then pulled up.

The prairie from a distance seemed flat, yet it had a deceptive roll to it. You could see a fairly large object at a distance of two or three miles and miss one just as large only a half mile away. You saw the object on the summit of a swell, did not see it in the shallow valley.

Bokker dismounted. He could not afford to underestimate MacDonald Pierson. He was twenty-two, but at sixteen he had ridden with Quantrell. He had grown up in the border country. Horsemanship, outdoor lore was instinctive with him. Bokker could not assume that Pierson would continue in a mad flight, as straight across the prairie as a stampeding steer. Pierson knew his trade. He would circle and dodge, cover his trail and confuse it. Bokker was now two miles out of Pawnee City.

In two miles Pierson should have recovered from his fright. Bokker studied the ground around him. It was cut up by the hoofs of many cattle. Here and there a shod horse's hoofprint showed. Cowboys riding herd, trotting. No marks of a hard galloping horse, no fresh horse's prints.

Bokker climbed back into the saddle and made a wide circle, leaning low on the right side of his horse to study the buffalo grass sod over which he rode. He was losing time, but it was the only thing he could do. His first circle was a hundred yards. He widened it into a two hundred

115

yard circle. Coming back to the cottonwood he made his third circuit.

And then he struck the fresh trail of a galloping horse. It was headed west, slightly south. Bokker, had he continued, would have gone away from it at an angle.

He let out his horse again, watching the trail as he rode. It was a wearing ride, but Bokker, although no longer accustomed to the saddle, did not mind. He was going to come up with MacDonald Pierson. He knew that. After a mile or so, the trail of Pierson's horse turned again, west by north now.

Bokker turned with the trail. Pierson's trail continued to give way to the right. An hour after leaving Pawnee City, Bokker guessed that he had made a half circle. Pierson had started out due south and was now riding straight north.

No, he had turned again. He was now going east by north.

Bokker pulled up Shay's bay. There was nothing ahead of him, nothing but a vast stretch of prairie. Straight east was the railroad, a town nine or ten miles from Pawnee City, Acorn by name.

Bokker exhaled heavily and decided to take a big gamble. If he guessed wrong, he would lose Pierson. But if he was right, he would catch up with him in Acorn, possibly arrive there even before the former guerrilla.

He jerked his horse's head due east and sent it into a swift run. He let out the horse after a few minutes, into a gallop, pulled it up after a while and rested it a few minutes. Then he went into a swift trot.

The prairie lost its light. Behind Bokker the sun was dipping below the horizon. Shay's bay was laboring. Exclaiming under his breath, Bokker dug his heels into the animal's flanks, into its barrel. The horse broke into a run, its breath whistling.

A flickering light appeared ahead, after a few moments a group of lights.

"A little more," Bokker said to the horse.

The bay, however, had given all it could. Acorn was a

quarter of a mile ahead, a cluster of buildings huddled around a tiny depot on the Kansas & Pacific.

A mighty shudder ran through the horse. Bokker pulled it up and dismounted. He loosened the saddle and threw it to the ground. He took off the bridle and clapped the horse on a flank.

"Sorry," he said.

He started walking toward Acorn.

Full darkness had fallen when he reached the little depot. It was dark, but Bokker stopped on the platform to size up the hamlet. It consisted of two stores, a saloon and three or four houses. A wagon stood in front of one of the stores. Two horses were tied to the hitchrail and the rail in front of the saloon had four horses tied to it.

Bokker walked toward the store, stopped by the horses and felt each. They were cool, dry. He continued on to the saloon. The horses there were also cool.

Either Bokker had guessed wrong—and lost—or he had reached Acorn ahead of his quarry.

Bokker buttoned his coat over the Navy pistol, stuck behind the waistband of his trousers, and entered the saloon.

It was a small place, containing a bar not more than seven or eight feet long and two tables. A card game was going on at one of the tables, with four players. Another patron stood at the bar, hunched over a glass of beer.

Bokker stepped up to the bar.

"Evenin'," the bartender greeted him. He was an enormously fat man with a huge pair of walrus mustaches.

Bokker nodded. "A glass of beer."

The bartender drew a glass of foaming liquid. Bokker took a long pull at it, then holding the glass, turned his back to the bar to size up the card players.

He watched for a minute or two, sipping the rest of his beer.

"Ain't you the lawyer from Pawnee City?" the bartender asked suddenly.

Bokker turned. "Why, yes."

"Thought I recognized you. I was in court a couple of

days ago. . . ." The man frowned. "That judge is mighty free with his twenty-five dollar fines."

"He's a good man."

"For the county, maybe. You take that marshal of your'n; you'd think he was gettin' half the fines hisself the way he arrests people for hardly doin' anything. There I was mindin' my own business, havin' a sociable drink with some friends, when all of a sudden—wham—he comes up and says I'm under arrest and when I ask him what for, he clouts me one. Lucky he was wearin' that badge of his, or I'd have give him somethin' to remember me by." The bartender growled. "So I spent a night in the calaboose and had to pay twenty-five dollars to the judge in the morning."

"Who takes care of the law here?" Bokker asked.

"Nobody; that's one thing we ain't bothered with. 'Course, there's a sheriff, but he stays at the county seat—Bad Axe—fifty-some miles to the north. Ain't even seen the sheriff this year. He'll be around this fall, though. Election time. Then he knows us. Otherwise he leaves us alone. Had a little shootin' here, two-three months ago. I wrote the sheriff a letter and he wrote back. Bury 'em, he says. Hell, we already did that."

Bokker, his ears cocked, heard the clop-clop of a horse out on the street. He turned abruptly away from the bar, crossed quickly to the door and pulled it open. Light from the interior framed a horse and rider pulling up to the hitchrail.

"Don't reach!" Bokker called.

His gun was already in his hand. Pierson, astride a weary horse, cried out. His hand went for his gun. Bokker fired, deliberately missing Pierson, but sending his bullet within an inch or two of the former guerrilla's face.

"Damn you!" cried Pierson.

But he did not draw his gun. His hands went slowly up and Bokker ducked under the hitchrail and plucked the gun from Pierson's holster. He had the weapon in his hand before the shock hit him.

Pierson had left Pawnee City without a gun or holster. He had both now. Where had he picked them up?

"Where'd you get the gun?" he demanded.

"It was on the horse," the youth whined.

"And the holster?"

"Yeah . . . yeah!"

"You're lying, Mac. Just like you lied to me in Pawnee City."

Behind Bokker the door of the saloon banged open. The bartender's voice boomed out, "What's goin' on?"

"Private business," Bokker called over his shoulder.

"Don't believe it!" suddenly screamed MacDonald Pierson. "He's trying to kill me. Don't—don't let him!"

"That right, mister?" demanded the bartender.

A man came running from the store. Light flashed on a revolver in his hand.

It was Tom Chaffee, Deputy Marshal of Pawnee City. "Bokker!"

Behind Chaffee came a woman, a woman wearing a divided riding skirt.

Ruth Compton.

Chaffee said, "You'd better get that man back to Pawnee City, Bokker, or you'll forfeit your bail."

"He's going back," Bokker said.

Ruth came up and recognized Bokker. "Phil, what in the world are you doing here?" Then she sized up the tableau. "Not—again!"

Bokker replaced his gun behind the waistband of his trousers. He still held Pierson's, however.

"I didn't expect to see you here, Ruth," he said stiffly.

"I just got here a half hour ago. Tom—Mr. Chaffee rode over with me."

"Her partner skipped town," Chaffee explained.

"Mrs. Melcher?" Bokker said sharply.

Ruth bit her lip. "She said she had to visit her sister here in Acorn. I didn't think anything of it when she left this morning, but then this afternoon"—she hesitated—"a man came in with a bill. Mrs. Melcher hadn't paid for a single one of the hats that were in the store."

"You'd think only a man'd do a thing like that, wouldn't you?" chuckled Chaffee.

"Mrs. Melcher's here?"

"Uh-uh, not so's you'd notice. Sure, she rode this far, but she took the train here in the morning. In Kansas City by now."

"I've been a fool!" burst out Ruth Compton. "I've lost all my money."

"Perhaps I was at fault," Bokker said. "I should have insisted on Mrs. Melcher's showing you receipted bills for her merchandise."

"You couldn't have known," Ruth said. She turned to Chaffee. "I'm sorry I caused you so much trouble, Mr. Chaffee. I guess we may as well start back for Pawnee City."

"Kinda late to be traveling."

"But there isn't any place here to stay overnight."

"I'll be going back," Bokker said. Then he winced. "I forgot—I have no horse . . ."

"How'd you get here?" Chaffee asked.

"My horse gave out a short distance out of town." Bokker placed his hand on Pierson's mount. "I don't think this horse is good for another mile, either."

"I'd just as lief stay here," Pierson said quickly.

"You're going back with me," Bokker said firmly. "Get down."

Pierson slid to the ground, groaning as his feet hit the hard earth. He was stiff from steady riding. "I don't feel like ridin' no more today."

"You did a lot more riding a few years ago," Bokker reminded.

"Yeah, but then—" Pierson caught himself and grabbed at Bokker's arm. "Don't!" he said, under his breath.

"You'll ride?"

"Yes."

Chapter NINETEEN

Bokker turned to the fat saloonkeeper. "Do you suppose we could rent a couple of horses?"

"Ain't no livery stable here."

"I know there isn't, but still, is there anyone who'd let us ride a pair of horses to Pawnee City? I'd be glad to pay. . . ."

"How much?"

"Whatever's necessary."

The bartender pointed to the buckboard standing in front of the store. "That buggy's mine. Too fat to climb on a horse and I live out a piece. You want to drive that to Pawnee City—for twenty dollars?"

Bokker took money from his pocket and paid the bartender. "I'll take the train up in the morning and drive 'er back," the fat man said. "Just leave 'er in the livery stable in Pawnee City."

"Phil," Ruth said, "would you mind terribly? I'm not up to riding a horse. Do you suppose——"

"Sure," chimed in Chaffee. "The kid can ride your horse, and you can ride with the lawyer man in the buckboard."

Bokker swore under his breath. He was not going to let MacDonald Pierson ride with Chaffee. He said, "I've got a better idea, Chaffee. You let me ride your horse and Smith will ride Miss Compton's. You two take the buckboard."

"Thank you!" cried Ruth. "I'll ride my horse back."

"Make up your mind, Bokker," Chaffee said mockingly.

"I'm responsible for Smith," Bokker said stubbornly. "Judge Paisley released him in my custody."

"He wouldn't get away from me," Chaffee said. "Least, not very far."

"That's what I'm afraid of," snapped Bokker. Angrily he looked after Ruth who was walking back toward the store, where her horse was tied to the rail.

"Don't move!" Bokker said tersely to Pierson. He strode after Ruth, catching up to her out of earshot of Chaffee and Pierson. He caught her arm, whirled her around.

"Help me out," he said tautly. "That young ruffian's MacDonald Pierson, one of the men I've been looking for. I don't trust Chaffee. He may be in with Fletcher Trow and if he is, Pierson will never get back to Pawnee City."

"So you're still on that!" Ruth exclaimed bitterly. "I'd thought——"

"I can't help it," interrupted Bokker. "Trow had him in jail and I got him out, then he made a run for it. I caught up with him and I can't take a chance on his getting away again—or being killed. He's the weak link in the chain and I can make him talk. I *know* I can."

"And if he doesn't, you'll kill him? You'll probably kill him if he *does*."

Bokker exclaimed, "You can be pretty stubborn at times."

"I told you the other day what I thought of you. I've got enough troubles of my own."

"I'll help you with those," Bokker promised.

"Don't bother!"

Chaffee called, "What'll it be, Bokker? Buckboard or saddle?"

"I'll ride with the marshal," Ruth said coldly, "but that's all."

"I won't ask a favor again," Bokker retorted.

He stood by while she climbed into the buckboard. Bokker had an idea she would have struck his arm aside had he tried to help her.

Chaffee came over, walking behind Pierson. "There's the horses, Bokker." He chuckled again. "Nice night for a buggy ride—with a pretty girl. See you in Pawnee City."

He climbed into the buckboard beside Ruth, picked up the lines and clucked to the team of horses.

"All right," Bokker snapped at Pierson. "Climb aboard."

"You're not puttin' me back in jail?"

"After what you've done——"

"No!" cried Pierson. "I won't go."

"Get on that horse," Bokker said grimly, "or I'll put you on, face down."

The buckboard was turning beyond the store, where a trail of sorts meandered along toward Pawnee City, ten miles away. Bokker mounted one of the horses and waited for Pierson to clamber aboard the other horse.

He hesitated, "How's the road to Pawnee City?"

Pierson shrugged. "It's all right, I guess."

"You've been over it?"

"Once or twice. I mean, I rode over it yesterday and—once quite a spell back."

He turned his horse to head for the store. Bokker said, "The other way!"

Pierson wheeled his horse. "What?"

"We're not taking the road. The railroad tracks lead to Pawnee City."

"You can't ride them at night. Horses'd stumble on the ties."

"We'll ride beside the rails—on the other side."

Pierson swore. "Damn it, Bokker, you've got a rough way about you."

"You want to get back to Pawnee City alive?"

"What're you talkin' about?"

"There's a lot of things I don't like about you, Pierson. And I don't like some other things. . . . Chaffee being here in Acorn, for example."

"You heard what he said—he came over with the girl."

"That's what *he* said."

"*She* said it, too. Besides"—Pierson cocked his head to one side—"the deputy said you was sweet on her. The way you're talkin' now——"

"When did Chaffee say that about me?" snapped Bokker.

"When you went after her. He thought it was funny—
you bein' sweet on her and wantin' her to ride with him in
the buckboard."

"He'd have preferred riding with you," retorted Bokker. "Especially since I've got your gun. Which reminds
me . . . never mind, let's get going."

He signaled ahead and Pierson moved off past the
saloon and across the tracks by the depot. On the far side
of the tracks Pierson, with Bokker at his side, turned west.

"That gun," Bokker said, then, "where'd you get it?"

"I told you—it was on the horse."

"It wasn't," Bokker said positively.

"All right, I found it," snarled Pierson.

"On a dead man?"

"Damn you, Bokker," cried Pierson. "I can't make you
out. Whose side are you on—Trow's? You made out like
you was his enemy and then——"

"And then you chickened out on me. You were going
to talk if I got you out of jail, but the moment you were
out you became chicken. Perhaps you'd be more willing to
talk if I took you back and put you under Trow's protection."

"I've told you everything I know."

"No, you haven't."

"I don't get it, Bokker—what's *your* interest in all
that?"

"Pierson," said Bokker, "you're on a horse. I'll give you
this gun and you can ride that horse right now, anywhere
you please—if you'll tell me just one thing. One word.
The name of the man who was beside you in that picture
in *Fred Cowan's Illustrated Weekly*."

"I don't know, Bokker. I told you—it's years since I
saw the picture."

"But you did see it. And you were there in Lawrence.
You know who was with you in front of the Eldridge
House. You *know* who killed the man in the picture."

"What're you—a relative?" cried Pierson.

"No," said Bokker. "I have no relatives in Lawrence. I
never had any. And I've never been in Lawrence in my
life."

"Then what's your interest in it? Let it go—it's past and done with."

"Fletcher Trow doesn't think so. You said so yourself. You were afraid he'd kill you."

"Trow was one of Quantrell's captains, I told you that. He gave the orders for us—me, I mean."

"Bill Grayson was a captain under Quantrell."

"Yes, but he's——" Pierson stopped.

"Dead?"

Pierson did not reply.

"It was you in Raytown, Pierson, wasn't it?"

"I haven't been in Raytown since—since the war."

"You were there ten days ago. When Bill Grayson was killed."

"That's a lie!"

"Then how'd you know he was dead?"

"I heard—I saw it in the paper."

"You saw *my* name in the paper?"

Pierson hesitated. "Yes. That's—that's why I asked for you today. I heard you were in Pawnee City."

"Who told you?"

"I saw your name on your office, before I was arrested by Trow."

"You're lying again. I'm going to ask you that question once more, Pierson, and I want an answer. Who was——?"

"Hawkins!" exclaimed Pierson. "Harry Hawkins, that's who it was."

Bokker kneed his horse so it moved close beside Pierson's. He smashed out with his left hand and struck Pierson a savage blow in the face.

Pierson cried out in pain and rage. "I'll kill you, Bokker! Damn you, I'll kill you for that."

"Be lucky if I don't kill *you*," snapped Bokker. "I've had enough of your lies. Hawkins—that's the first name that came to your mind."

"It's the first and the last." Pierson dabbed at his mouth with his finger tips. "Nobody's going to hit me. Get down from that horse and I'll fight you."

"I'd beat you to a pulp!"

"Try it!" challenged Pierson.

Bokker was tempted to halt and accept the former guerrilla's challenge, but he did not think it would serve any purpose. He would beat Pierson into insensibility and then he would have to start all over again. A pummeling would not make Pierson talk.

None of them talked. Grayson had not talked. Fletcher Trow would not talk. And now, Pierson. Bokker was so near to the end of the trail and the last, thin curtain between him and the end stood before him like a sheet of steel ... because a man would not speak ... would not say a single name. Just one word.

Pierson's voice penetrated Bokker's thoughts. "Somebody's ahead."

Bokker's mind came back to the present. He pulled up his horse. "Wait!" he exclaimed.

Pierson stopped a few feet ahead of Bokker. The latter strained his ears. "I don't hear anything."

A streak of flame lanced the darkness ahead of him. The sharp, familiar crack of a revolver broke the stillness.

"They're going to kill me!" screamed Pierson. "You got to gimme a gun."

"Quiet!" snarled Bokker, whipping out his own gun.

A gun thundered again. A bullet whined within inches of Bokker.

A voice called out, "Bokker!"

Bokker fired at the sound of the voice—and gave away his position. In the almost total darkness the ambushers could not distinguish between Bokker and Pierson. And it was Bokker they wanted, not Pierson. A crash of gunfire followed Bokker's fire. More than one gun, more than two.

A bullet tugged at Bokker's coat sleeve, another tore through between his arm and side, taking along a strip of skin.

Lightning seemed to strike Bokker. There was a sudden blaze of varicolored lights in his brain, a crashing like thunder and then—total darkness!

Chapter TWENTY

A thousand little devils were prodding at the brain of Bokker. He writhed and groaned and the little devils merged and became one giant who rammed a red-hot bar of steel into him. He cried out in pain and became fully conscious suddenly and was aware of a vast aching in his head. He sat up and tentatively touched his head. His finger became wet.

He realized that he was sitting on the prairie, that a bullet had creased his scalp. How deep the crease was he could not determine. But he was alive—alive and conscious. The last he remembered, he had fired at the ambushers who had waylaid him and MacDonald Pierson. He had been hit. The fact that he had been shot only once indicated that his horse had bolted in the darkness. He had apparently clung to it long enough to elude the pursuers and had then tumbled into the buffalo grass of the prairie. It had been almost pitch-dark then and the would-be assassins had been unable to find him.

How long he had lain unconscious on the prairie he had no way of knowing. A moon was up, a faint crescent that dimly lighted the prairie. The stars were bright.

Bokker climbed unsteadily to his feet. The aching in his head became duller.

He was alive; that was all that counted. He looked up at the sky and picked out the North Star. It was as good as a compass for telling him the directions, but whether he was north or south of the tracks of the Kansas & Pacific he had no way of knowing. Wait—wasn't there a faint yellowness in the sky to the west and south?

Pawnee City, at night.

He began walking. His head throbbed, but pain had to

127

be borne. He trudged along. The yellowness in the west became lighter and after some time became faint pinpricks of lights.

A little while later Bokker heard a faint gunshot. Yes, that was Pawnee City ahead of him. He cut the railroad tracks, followed them for a little while, then circled so that he would enter the town from the south.

He crossed Main Street, at the outskirts of town and noted that there were still quite a few horses tied at the hitchrails. The stores, of course, were closed, but the saloons were still doing a thriving business.

Darkness had fallen when he had reached Acorn. They had left the little hamlet before nine o'clock. The return walk of almost ten miles had taken him possibly two and a half or three hours. That would bring the time close to midnight—but he would have to add to it the time he had been unconscious on the prairie. That could have been five minutes and it could have been five hours. No, not the latter, for that would have made it dawn now.

An hour or two.

He slipped between two buildings and made his way cautiously to the alley.

Counting the buildings from Kiowa Street, he reached the back of the little shack that housed his office. Instinct made him move with caution, even after he saw that the window through which he had followed MacDonald Pierson was open.

He was a bare half-dozen feet from the window when his nostrils were assailed by smoke. Cigar smoke. Fresh cigar smoke.

Someone was inside his place, seated or lying on his cot: someone smoking a cigar.

They were waiting for him. They had not found him on the prairie and had returned to Pawnee City to finish the job.

Bokker froze. The foot he had in the air at the instant he let down slowly, carefully. There was a creaking inside his room. Bokker squatted, placed his palms upon the ground and flattened himself out. The cigar smoke became stronger. Bokker, turning his head a careful inch or two,

was able to see the window. A black figure almost filled it.
Whoever was inside his room was standing by the window
looking out. It was too dark, however, to make out the
face of the man.

Bokker waited. A faint footfall came after a moment,
then a squeaking. The man had left the window and returned to the bed.

Bokker got up and moved quietly away from the window. He continued down the alley. He counted buildings
again and reached the little frame one occupied by the
Bon Ton Millinery Shop. Ruth Compton slept behind her
shop, as did Bokker.

He stood behind the millinery shop, frowning in the
darkness. He was in a precarious position. He was unarmed and hunted by a man, or men, who were trying to
kill him. A normal citizen could have gone to the marshal's office, or the jail, for help, but that was the last
place on earth that Bokker could go.

Trow was back of it, of course. But more than one man
had attacked him on the way from Acorn. Chaffee. . . .
Chaffee had been south of the tracks, driving Ruth Compton to Pawnee City in a buckboard.

Someone else had been with Trow—someone who had
known that he would be in Acorn and would be returning
to Pawnee City in the dark.

Bokker shook his head and changed his thinking. It
could have been Chaffee. Bokker had seen him leave
Acorn, yes, but Chaffee could have met someone a minute
or two out of the little hamlet. He could have changed
from the buckboard to a horse, gone swiftly ahead, cut the
railroad tracks and met Bokker and Pierson.

That line of thinking presented another problem, however. What had happened to Ruth Compton?

Bokker suddenly moved toward the window of Ruth
Compton's bedroom, behind her millinery shop. He
reached it. The window was closed, a shade inside was
drawn to the sill.

Bokker tested the window. The catch inside was locked,
but the window was a poor fitting one. A knife blade

could be worked in where the upper and lower windows met and force back the window catch.

Bokker found his penknife, opened it and slipped it between the two window halves. He found the catch, pressed hard to the left. His knife blade went through. The catch was open.

He drew a deep breath, gripped the window and raised it a fraction of an inch. It moved smoothly for a bit, then suddenly squeaked. It was a very faint squeak but to Bokker it seemed as loud as the scream of a dying cat.

He waited a moment, but there was no sound inside the room. He raised the window a full six inches in one quick movement and without a squeak, then repeated the procedure. Finally he had the window sufficiently high to permit his ingress into the bedroom beyond.

There was still the drawn shade, but Bokker decided against raising it. He pushed it inward carefully, threw one leg over the window sill and followed through. He stood then inside the room, his back to the open window, the shade covering him from the room.

Carefully he stooped and permitted the window shade to flap against the sill. He was inside the room now, in total darkness. The room was small, he knew, and would contain a bed, possibly two. He listened and heard breathing and locating the source of it, made out a deeper shadow that was a bed.

He took a step forward—and stepped on a loose board.

A gasp told him that the occupant of the bed had awakened. Bokker threw caution to the wind; he could not risk a sudden scream that would attract neighbors. The window was open, the walls were flimsy enough. A scream would bring people.

He lunged forward in the darkness. His knees struck a bed and he reached out. A scream started and Bokker, in panic, shot out his hands. They struck a face, smothered the rest of the scream. Then Bokker was very busy for a moment. Ruth Compton fought him. She was caught at a disadvantage but she had a lithe strength and she was fighting with every ounce of fury in her body. She bit at his hands, she raked his face with her nails, she struck him with her fists and she squirmed and heaved and tried to get out from under his weight.

"Quiet!" cried Bokker in soft panic. "It's me—Bokker!"

She fought harder.

"Ruth," Bokker continued desperately, "don't—it's Phil Bokker!"

She stopped fighting then, but her body was tensed. He held a hand over her mouth. "I was ambushed near Acorn," Bokker said, talking very fast. "I was wounded and I've just come back to Pawnee City. Someone's in my place, waiting to kill me. I—I haven't got a gun."

She could not reply, of course, and he tentatively raised his hand a fraction of an inch. If she tried to scream he would clap it down again. She didn't scream, however.

"Let me up!"

He sat down on the edge of the bed, inches from her.

"I've got to get a gun, Ruth," he said quietly. "You've got to help me."

"So you can kill again?" she threw at him.

"So I can keep from being killed. What—what happened after you left Acorn?"

"Nothing. What did you expect would happen?"

"Chaffee rode back to Pawnee City with you?"

"Of course—and I've been asleep for hours."

"But you must have heard shooting—you weren't so far ahead of us . . ."

"We heard shooting, all right," Ruth said, "but I've heard shooting every night since I came to Kansas. The marshal stayed with me all the way to Pawnee City—if that's what you mean."

"Then it was Trow." Bokker paused. "Trow and someone with him."

"You're still on that subject!"

Bokker stood up. He looked down to where he knew Ruth was lying.

The bed squeaked and Ruth's voice came from the darkness. "I don't like this, your coming into my bedroom at night."

An electric shock seemed to shoot through Bokker. He

reached out suddenly, his hand touching Ruth's night-gowned figure, brushing it. She pulled away instantly, but Bokker knew.

He said, "*You* came to *my* bedroom once."

"What?"

"In Raytown. It was you. . . ."

He heard her gasp. "Are you out of your mind?" she cried.

"Something about you bothered me right from the start. Your voice. You'd disguised it in Raytown and I didn't make the association because of the way I met you on the train—a lone girl, annoyed by a traveling salesman. It couldn't have happened better to lull any suspicion I might have had."

"I don't know what you're talking about!"

He reached into his pocket, found a match and flicked it into light with his thumbnail. In the sudden flicker of light he saw Ruth in a flimsy nightgown. Her hands were clenched into fists that she held before her breast.

He blew out the match. "Put on some clothes. We're going to talk."

"At this time of the night?"

"I've no choice," Bokker said. "I can't go to my quarters—I can't show myself on the street."

There was a moment's silence on her part, then she said, "Wait!" He heard her rummaging about in the dark and stepped back to the window. Reaching behind the shade, he pushed down the window.

He stood waiting.

It was she who struck a match this time. She applied it to the wick of a kerosene lamp and Bokker, turning, saw that she had put on a bathrobe or dressing gown. She was replacing the chimney on the lamp.

She straightened and saw the matted hair on the left side of his head, the caked blood and dirt on his face. She exclaimed softly.

"You've been hurt!"

"I told you I was shot."

She came swiftly around the bed. "You ought to have the doctor take care of it."

"I can't."

She looked around, her eyes falling upon a pitcher and bowl on the washstand. She went to it, got a towel and poured water from the pitcher into the bowl.

"All right," she said.

He crossed and sat on the far edge of the bed. She dabbed a towel into the water and washed the dried blood from his face. She worked carefully, her touch light. When she reached the vicinity of the wound, Bokker braced himself.

It hurt, but no sound came from him. He sat, his jaws clenched, until she finished washing his face and head. She went to a tiny dresser then, pulled out a drawer and brought out a sheet. She ripped strips from it, made a pad and bandaged his head neatly, securely.

He said, finally, "Thanks."

"I'd do as much for anyone."

There was still hostility in her tone. He said, "I guess there was no chance for us to be friends. Right from the start——"

"You didn't try," she accused.

"I tried," Bokker said. "I tried very hard."

"You came to Raytown to rake up old fires, dig up skeletons that were better left buried. You—killed two men."

"One," Bokker corrected.

"Two men were killed."

"I didn't kill Bill Grayson"—he paused—"the man whose sister you claimed to be."

She made a small gesture, dismissing the old lie.

He said, "Who are you?"

"It's too late for that."

"Is it?"

"You wouldn't stop," she said poignantly. "Even after Raytown, you went on. I—I didn't hate you at the beginning, but day by day——"

"Well, that much is out," he interrupted. "You don't have to continue pretending. You don't have to lie any more."

"Lie?"

"It's been nothing but lies," Bokker said. "You said you were Grayson's sister. . . . On the train you said you came from Ohio and had only two hundred dollars—and then you paid five hundred for a half interest in this place——"

"You made me lie!" she accused. "Your continual prodding and questioning. How could I remember what I'd said? You never left off questions, questions, questions. . . . I didn't know what I was saying or doing any more."

"Always," Bokker said, "I've wanted just one answer—one answer to one question. I couldn't get it from Grayson, I couldn't get it from Trow and I couldn't get it from Pierson."

"Stop it!" she exclaimed. "Stop it. I can't take any more." He saw then that she was near the breaking point. The hard surface she had presented to him from the first moment he had known her back in Raytown was all assumed. She had fought to maintain it—and was losing the battle.

Yet *she* was the weakest link; not Pierson as he had thought, but Ruth . . . Ruth Compton, or whatever her name was. She would tell him, she would talk if he pushed her just a little more. She would break, yes, but she would talk. She would spill out the name he had sought for so long.

Chapter TWENTY-ONE

She stood before him, slight and shivering, trembling and pathetic. She was sheltering and protecting a black-hearted murderer—but Bokker suddenly could not push her further.

He said gently, "I'll leave by the window."

He walked around the window, reached behind the shade and again raised the window. He heard her move then and he looked back. She was watching him, an almost dazed look in her eyes.

"Good night," he said.

She did not reply.

He pulled out the curtain, swung his feet out of the window and dropped lightly to the ground.

He walked quickly away from her window, but stopped in the alley.

There was still no safety for him in Pawnee City, not while it was night.

Yes, there was. There was a place where he would be safe. Several places, for that matter, but one in particular.

The Pawnee City Hotel-Bar.

He turned and walked swiftly down the alley. He had no trouble picking out the place from the rear, but when he tried the only door that opened on the alley, he found it locked.

There was, however, a narrow passageway between the hotel and the adjoining store. He slipped through it, paused a moment at the sidewalk, then stepped out boldly.

A cowboy was coming out of the hotel, but otherwise no one saw him. Bokker pushed past the cowboy, pulled open the front door of the hotel and was in sanctuary.

The night hotel clerk sat in a rocking chair, dozing. Bokker passed him and entered the saloon.

A clock behind the bar told him that it was ten minutes of three. A bleary-eyed cowboy hung over the bar. Another sat by a table, his head resting on it, sound asleep. At the rear of the room were at least a dozen men, most of them sitting or standing around a poker game. As long as the game continued the saloon would stay open. Bokker knew that.

He went toward the game. Before he reached it, Fletcher Trow, watching the game, turned. He grunted as he saw Bokker.

"Somebody caught up with you, eh?"

"Somebody did, yes," Bokker retorted.

Facing him, across the table, sat Paul Shay. He exclaimed when he saw Bokker.

"Phil, what happened?"

"I stopped one." Bokker's eyes fell and traveled swiftly around the table. There were only five players in the game; two were obviously professional gamblers, possibly house men for the saloon. Shay was the third player. The fourth was Mike Huntley, the prosecuting attorney and the final man was Longtree, the mayor of Pawnee City.

A few gold coins were in front of Shay, a thin packet of greenbacks. He suddenly pushed back his chair. "Just a moment, gentlemen," he said to the card players.

He walked to one side, signaling for Bokker to follow.

"What happened, Phil?" he asked when they were out of earshot of the group around the poker game.

"I caught up with Pierson—and then I was ambushed on the way back."

"Who—who, Phil?"

"Who but Trow? But there was someone with him."

Shay frowned. "After you left this afternoon, I went over to the jail. There was a man with him—big bruiser. Trow called him Mitchum, or Mitchell or something like that."

"Mechem?"

"Could be."

"Charr Mechem!" Bokker's eyes went back to the

group around the table. But Mechem was not there. He was probably in Bokker's bedroom, waiting.

"Have you seen Tom Chaffee?"

"Not in the last couple of hours. He dropped in around midnight." Shay suddenly winced. "I've been having the devil's own luck, Phil. I—I'm in the same spot as when we first hit Pawnee City."

"You've lost all the money you made?"

"Worse, Phil. What's on the table is all that's left of two thousand of my company's money. Less than a hundred dollars."

"You can quit, can't you?"

"A hundred dollars isn't going to save me. It's—it's my only chance to win it back." He hesitated. "I was wondering, Phil, if—well, if you could let me have some money."

"How much?"

"Whatever you've got, Phil. I'll pay it back——"

"If you win, Paul!" Bokker frowned. "I owe you for your horse——"

"You lost the bay?" cried Shay. "I paid three hundred dollars for that horse."

"That much?" Bokker winced. "I haven't got three hundred dollars, Paul. I've taken in some money this past week but I've spent money. I put some to Pierson's bail."

"What have you got?"

"Not more than eighty or ninety."

Shay groaned. "That's no money!"

Bokker looked toward the poker game. "It's enough to get into the game, isn't it?"

"You, Phil?"

Bokker nodded.

"It's a stiff game!"

Bokker shrugged. "As you said, eighty or ninety dollars isn't any money. I might as well lose it."

"All right, come ahead!"

They returned to the poker game. Shay announced, "Phil Bokker wants to sit in."

Bokker got a chair from an adjoining table and room was made for him.

"Well, well," exclaimed the mayor. "Two lawyers. Is that legal?" He chuckled at his own joke.

Huntley glowered across the table at Bokker. "Didn't think poker was your game?"

"I've played my share."

"Well, let's see some of your Eastern money," the prosecutor went on. "I know you haven't made enough in Pawnee City to sit in this game."

Bokker reached into his pocket and brought out a handful of crumpled bills and some coins. "I'll start with this." Actually it was all the money he had. He began straightening out the bills, while one of the professional gamblers shuffled smoothly and dealt the cards. "Draw poker," he said, "jacks or better."

"A good game," Bokker observed.

"It hasn't been for me," offered Shay.

"You've had a long streak, Paul," said the mayor. "You were into my store yesterday—a couple of feet, anyway."

"You've got it all back now—and more."

"I usually do get it, in the long run," Longtree said calmly. "I been in business here for quite a spell—and nobody's won my store from me yet."

"I'm going to try!" promised Shay.

Bokker looked at his hand. He had a pair of queens, an ace and two small cards. "I pass," he said.

The second gambler shrugged and indicated that he would pass. The mayor exclaimed, "Not me, I open. Let's see, twenty—no, make it ten. Don't want to scare out the counselor. Not yet."

"If you won't make it twenty, I will," retorted Shay.

Huntley shot an angry look at Shay, but threw twenty dollars into the pot. The gambler-dealer quietly slid in a twenty-dollar gold piece. Bokker studied his cards. "Well, let's see how they run." He put in twenty dollars.

The gambler at Bokker's left threw in his cards.

"And twenty back to you!" cried the mayor.

A slight twitch of Shay's mouth indicated his nervousness. He merely called.

"Stupid playing," growled Huntley. He threw in his cards.

The dealer put in twenty dollars, and Bokker, hesitatingly, finally put in twenty dollars more.

"Cards?" asked the dealer.

Bokker had already risked almost half of his stake. He was faced with a difficult decision. He didn't know the game of any of the other players, except possibly that of Paul Shay. He could play it safe and delay things—or he could gamble on a bold move.

"One card," he said.

He kept the queens, the ace and a nine. It wasn't good playing, but he reasoned that the others knew no more about the way he played than he knew about their game.

"Three," said the mayor.

"You raised me back with one pair?" exclaimed Shay.

"Why not? When you're lucky you draw, when you're not, you don't."

Shay counted out twenty dollars. "I'll take one," Shay said, annoyed.

"Two for the dealer," said the gambler.

"I connected," chortled the mayor. He counted out fifty dollars. "And it costs you fifty."

Shay studied his cards, swallowed hard and suddenly threw in his hand.

"Beats my two small pair."

The dealer threw in his cards. Bokker looked at his new card, saw that it was a nine, thus giving him two pairs, queens and nines. He counted his money. "Four dollars short, for a moment."

The mayor winced. "I didn't connect. All I've got are my openers, jacks—like I said." He chuckled. "Didn't believe that, did you?"

Bokker revealed his queens and nines.

The mayor shook his head. "So *you* weren't lying."

"I had tens and sixes," said Shay.

"You should have bet like you got them," the mayor exclaimed. "I don't think the counselor would have stayed with one more raise."

Bokker gathered in the money and scooped up the

cards. He shuffled and dealt. He looked at his hand. It was a complete bust. "I'm out," he announced.

It was the mayor who opened again, and again Shay raised him. Huntley stayed, as did the two professionals.

"Two," said the mayor, when it came his turn.

Shay again drew one card and Bokker, watching, saw his face twitch once more. Shay had not improved his hand.

"This time," announced the mayor, "the pikers can drop out. A hundred dollars."

"I'm out of money," Shay said. "Is my credit good?"

"This is a cash game," Huntley snapped.

The mayor held up his hand. "Tut-tut, Mike. We know Paul. All he's got to do is write out a check on the bank."

Huntley opened his mouth to protest further, but closed it and shrugged. The gambler on Bokker's right dropped out, but the one on his left called and raised it fifty dollars. He was promptly re-raised two hundred by the mayor.

"I call," said Shay tautly. "I'm three-fifty light."

"Sorry, gentlemen," announced the gambler. "I've got to go once more. A hundred to you, Mr. Longtree."

"And two hundred back to you!"

Huntley swore angrily and tossed in his cards. But Shay called. "I'm six-fifty short."

The gambler said, "I bet as much as I could on a small full house."

"Hey!" cried the mayor. "That's twice in a row my bluff got called." He exposed a pair of aces. "That's all there is."

Shay exposed a nine-high straight.

"I owe you six-fifty, Miller."

"A check will be all right."

"I don't believe I've got one with me."

"The bartender has."

Shay pushed back his chair. "All right," he snapped, "but deal me out a couple of hands. I need a drink."

He crossed to the bar.

Chapter TWENTY-TWO

Fletcher Trow brought forward his chair. "I'll play a hand or two."

"New blood!" cried the mayor. "I'd like to get some of your money, Fletcher.

"You'll work for it," Trow promised laconically.

Trow promptly won the first pot, a fairly small one, the mayor not even getting a pair, although he stayed for the draw and even tried a raise of twenty dollars.

Shay came back then. He tossed a slip of paper to the gambler, Miller. "I made it out for a thousand."

Miller counted out three hundred and fifty dollars. "There's your change, Mr. Shay."

Shay seated himself. It was the mayor's deal and he warned the other players. "I'm last this time, watch out."

Shay looked at his cards and passed. Huntley scowled at his own hand, hesitated, then opened the pot for five dollars. The gambler on Bokker's right merely called, but Fletcher Trow, next, raised it ten dollars. Bokker squeezed his cards and came up with three tens. He put fifteen dollars into the pot. Miller, the gambler, threw in his hand.

"I warned you," the mayor said. "I raise fifty dollars, just to get rid of the cheapskates."

"I'll see you," said Shay, "and raise you fifty."

"What kind of game is this?" cried Huntley angrily.

"A freeze-out," retorted the mayor. "If you haven't got the guts, Mike, drop out."

"I'm staying!"

The gambler stayed and Trow merely called. Bokker put in the extra fifty dollars.

"Cards?"

"Two," said Shay.

"Oh-ho!" exclaimed the mayor. "Holding an ace for a kicker."

"Maybe," replied Shay grimly.

Huntley drew only one card and scowled as he looked at it. Bokker felt certain that he had only two pairs, respectable pairs, however. The gambler took two cards. Fletcher Trow said laconically, "I like the ones I've got."

"Lady Luck's gone over to the marshal," observed the mayor.

Bokker drew two cards. One was a ten. He had four tens now.

"And three cards for the dealer," the mayor said cheerfully.

Huntley exclaimed, "You raised with a pair?"

"I've done it before—and I've connected," retorted the mayor. "Like now. Go ahead, you opened. Make your bet and whatever it is, I'll raise it."

"Fifty dollars," said Huntley, not too happy.

"I'll call to the pat hand," said the gambler.

"The pat hand raises a hundred," Fletcher Trow said.

Bokker, certain that the mayor would raise, counted out a hundred and put it into the pot.

Longtree, according to his promise, said, "And two hundred more. That'll get rid of the boys."

"I'm calling," said Shay, "and I'll raise it a hundred. That makes me one-fifteen short."

Huntley, disgusted, threw in his hand. "If everybody's going to be short in the pot, I might as well drop out."

Shay gave him a hard look. The gambler to Bokker's right said, "Something tells me that three nines isn't any good this time." He tossed his cards into the discard.

"I'm sorry," Fletcher Trow said, "but I've still got the best hand. I raise it three hundred."

Bokker had gone into the pot with around three hundred dollars. He had thirty-five dollars left to call Longtree's two hundred dollars. Trow's three hundred raise would make him short over four hundred and sixty-five dollars. But Shay had led the way. He had been short in the previous hand and was again short.

"I'm light for the moment," Bokker said, "for sixty-five."

"Another!" cried Huntley.

"I'm out," Mayor Longtree said suddenly, and threw in his hand.

"That leaves three of us," observed Fletcher Trow. "Paul?"

"I call the three hundred," Shay said. He looked across at Bokker, "and I raise you back, Fletch—three hundred."

"Put in your check," Trow said. He turned to Bokker. "And you, Mr. Bokker."

Bokker had no money in the bank. But neither, he knew, did Paul Shay. Shay had company money, but he had already dipped into it deeply. The bank probably wouldn't honor his check unless there was an invoice from the railroad company to cover a shipment of cattle.

Bokker said, "I'll make out my check after this hand—if I lose."

Trow exclaimed testily. "What kind of a game is this?"

"Freeze-out, the mayor said," Bokker retorted. "How much are you light, Paul?"

"Seven fifteen," Shay said angrily. "Are you calling?"

"I'm calling," said Trow, "with cash." He put out the money.

"I call," Bokker said, "short. Seven hundred and sixty-five."

"What's the use?" Trow snapped. "I could raise again, but nobody except myself is putting up the cash. I've got a queen-high spade flush."

"Beats three kings," cried Shay.

"Four tens," Bokker announced, showing the cards.

Trow, beside him, inhaled sharply. "You win, Bokker." He sat still for a moment, then pushed back his chair. "I guess I've had enough."

The gambler on the right stood up. "I'm tired; I need sleep."

"I'm not sleepy," the mayor said thoughtfully, "but the game's got out of hand."

"Mayor," Shay said carefully, "can you cash a check for me?"

Longtree frowned. "How much?"

already got two of your checks for fifteen hundred."

"I've got the money. The check'll be good."

Longtree hesitated. "You've lost quite a lot, Paul. I've

"A thousand—well, five hundred."

"You're short seven-fifteen in this pot," Bokker reminded.

"I'll give you a separate check, Phil. I'd like to play a little while longer."

"*I'm* through," Huntley said, getting up.

"How about you, Miller?" the mayor asked the gambler.

"If there's still cash in the game I'll play."

"There's cash," Shay said testily. He indicated the considerable amount in front of Bokker. "Win that and call it a night. You've already won a couple thousand from me. I'd like a chance to win some of it back."

"All right, Mr. Shay, I'll play."

The mayor had counted out five hundred dollars for Shay. "We'll play four-handed. A good game. But"—he paused—"no more checks, huh?"

"I'll quit if I lose this five hundred," Shay said angrily.

Bokker looked at the clock over the bar. It was after four o'clock. If he could keep the game going until six o'clock he was all right.

A half dozen of the spectators left as Huntley and Trow also went out. Seven or eight men remained, however, to watch the four-handed game.

The game became a more cautious one. Shay, with only five hundred, played carefully. Bokker was cautious, as was the gambler, Miller. The mayor tried once or twice to force a pot, but when he found that he could not make it stick, settled down to a hard, good game of poker.

Bokker's luck held. He drew well and won two pots in a row, lost three, then won three in a row. Shay's money dwindled. Bokker found himself with close to two thousand dollars when Shay was down to a little over a hundred.

The mayor dropped out of a hand after the draw, as did Miller. Bokker bet fifty dollars. Shay, who had drawn only two cards to Bokker's three card draw, called the fifty and counted out another fifty.

"Up fifty!"

Bokker looked at his cards. He had stayed with a pair of kings and had drawn another. He was sure he had Shay beaten, but if Shay went broke he would probably quit.

Bokker tossed his cards into the discard. "You win!"

Shay showed surprise, but gleefully raked in the pot. "I guess Lady Luck's turning."

At five o'clock Shay's luck really did turn. He won four pots in a row, two of them sizable. He had twelve or thirteen hundred dollars before him.

Then Miller said, "I'm beat. I'll play one more round."

The mayor yawned. "I think I'd better get a little sleep, too." He looked at Bokker. "Don't see how you do it, with that head."

"It doesn't bother," Bokker replied.

Shay, faced with only four more hands of poker, decided to bull the game again. He opened for twenty dollars and when he was raised twenty by Longtree, came back with a raise of a hundred. Everyone, suprisingly, stayed. Shay drew a single card, Bokker three, the mayor two and Miller one.

Shay bet two hundred dollars. Bokker, with only a pair of eights, dropped out. The mayor merely called, but Miller raised Shay a hundred and was promptly re-raised three hundred. Longtree threw in his cards and the gambler called. He had a king-high straight, beating out Shay, who had drawn one card to a low straight and had connected.

The hand had taken half of Shay's money.

Bokker did not stay at all in the next hand, nor did Longtree. Miller opened for twenty dollars, was raised a hundred and merely called. He checked to Shay after the draw and the latter bet three hundred. Miller called him—and won with a pair of aces.

There was no fourth hand. Miller won the third and

Shay wound up without a cent on the table. He got up heavily.

"An expensive night," he said, looking murderously at the gambler, Miller, who had been the big winner.

Bokker counted his money. He was almost eighteen hundred dollars ahead. Shay had not made out the check to him for seven hundred and fifteen dollars, but Bokker did not remind him of it.

The bartender came over. "Well, gentlemen, how about a last drink before I close up?"

It was twenty minutes after five. It would still be dark outside.

Bokker, about to put away his winnings, suddenly looked at the bartender. "This is more money than I'm used to having—and I haven't even got a gun."

"Nobody'll rob you—not in Pawnee City," said the mayor.

"I'd feel better with a gun," Bokker looked at the bartender. "Do you happen to have a Navy gun I could buy?"

"No, but I'll lend you one," the bartender said, "if it'll make you feel better."

Bokker peeled off two twenties from his roll of bills. "I'll feel better buying it and, here—the drinks for everyone and keep the change."

The last spectators of the poker game swarmed to the bar. The bartender served the drinks and brought out a somewhat rusted Navy Colt. But Bokker, examining it, saw that the caps on the nipples were good and that each chamber in the cylinder was loaded. He thrust the gun under the waistband of his trousers.

"Good night," he said to the group at large.

"I'll walk with you, Phil," said Shay. "I need the air."

Shay's usually ebullient spirits had seeped out of him. Bokker had never seen him so discouraged. They left the saloon and started down the wooden sidewalk toward Bokker's place. Shay walked slumped, listless, but Bokker beside him was taut, strained.

In the east the sky was becoming gray.

Shay said, "I'm through, Phil. I wrote out checks for

three thousand dollars that I can't meet, and I haven't got a dollar in my pockets. If it wasn't for——"

"Ruth?"

"Ruth?" repeated Shay. Then he exclaimed, "You think Ruth and I are——?"

"Aren't you?"

Shay was silent a moment. Then he said, "She's a good girl, Phil. If I wasn't the kind of man I am ..." He laughed hollowly. "She needs a man like you, Phil."

"Things between us have reached a low point," Bokker said cautiously.

"Don't be too sure. You never can tell about a woman." They had reached Bokker's office. Shay suddenly gripped Bokker's arm. "Phil, that money you won—eighteen hundred. I could pay off the mayor—well, almost. I can work it out—give me the eighteen hundred."

Bokker was taken aback. "I'll be damned!"

"It's just a loan, Phil," Shay went on. "I'll give you an I.O.U. It's just until I can buy another herd. Time's all I need. A herd's coming in day after tomorrow. I'll buy it——"

"You can't make that much profit on a herd."

"Yes, I can. I—I made thirty-two hundred on the first one I bought. I paid twenty-one dollars a steer and had the railroad agent make out the invoice for twenty-five. I'll do it again. I'll work out a deal and pay you off."

"Are you serious, Paul?" exclaimed Bokker. "You ought to know by now that I wouldn't be a party to any deal such as that."

"Then never mind how I make the money. Just lend me the eighteen hundred——"

"No," Bokker said firmly. "Money doesn't mean anything to you. You'll only get in a game again and——"

"You won that money!" snarled Shay angrily. "You didn't earn it. You won't be any poorer than you were a few hours ago."

"I've been poor most of my life," Bokker snapped. "Eighteen hundred dollars is a lot of money. All right, I won it in a poker game, but it's still eighteen hundred dollars."

"You won't help me out, then?"

"I don't think I owe you anything, Paul."

"Ah, hell!" snarled Shay, and whirled away. He clomped angrily down the wooden sidewalk.

And now Bokker was faced with it. Was the man still in his bedroom? Was he waiting with drawn gun?

Bokker drew the Navy gun he had bought from the bartender. He turned the knob of his front door, swung the door inward. He called into the dark interior.

"I'm coming in!"

There was no reply from inside. Bokker waited a moment, then entered. He stood inside the door, gun pointed at the door leading to the bedroom.

He sniffed the air. There was an odor of stale cigar smoke in the room. He heard no sound, however.

He called once more, "I'm coming in!"

There was still no reply. Bokker took out a match, struck it and then tossed it through the door into the bedroom. He followed instantly.

The room was empty.

The bed was mussed, there were cigar ashes and two cigar butts on the floor, the only mementoes of the man who had waited there for him earlier.

Bokker went to the window, drew the shade, then returned to the outer room and locked the door. He lit a candle in the bedroom and made up a bed on the floor.

Chapter TWENTY-THREE

Bokker slept three hours on the floor of his room and awoke stiff and sore in every muscle of his body. Or so it seemed. He got up, stretched and winced as pain lanced through his head. He had almost forgotten the wound in his head. He looked at himself in a tiny mirror over his washstand. He could use a shave, but was not in the mood for it. He washed carefully, then left his office to cross the street to the restaurant.

It was a few minutes to nine when he left the restaurant. He stood outside for a moment, then became aware that Ruth Compton was standing in the open doorway of her shop. He started across the street, but before he reached the far sidewalk, Ruth had gone back into her shop. The door, however, remained open.

Bokker started to pass, then she called from inside, "Phil!"

Surprised, he turned and entered the shop. She came forward, closed the door behind him.

"Paul's left," she said. "He's gone for good."

Bokker exclaimed, "He ran out!"

She nodded. "He was here a half hour ago. He—he told me about the checks that he'd written and he didn't want to wait until the bank opened at nine o'clock."

Bokker shook his head. "He finally used up all his tricks."

"You never really liked him, did you?"

Bokker looked at her sharply. Her tone was listless, containing a trace of—despair, was it?

He said, "*You* did, though?"

"Yes," she said, "I liked Paul. In spite of his—faults, I

149

guess you'd call them—I liked him. But I—I didn't call you in to talk about him." She stopped.

Bokker waited, expecting her to continue, but she averted her eyes from him and remained silent. He prodded: "Yes?"

"You're not an easy man to talk to!" she burst out. "You—you're always thinking of yourself and you don't see what's in other people."

"We won't get anywhere talking about Paul Shay."

"I'm not talking about Paul!" she cried. "I'm talking about—about me."

He looked at her, puzzled, but she still kept her eyes averted. She turned away from him suddenly, feeling him too close and went behind the low shop counter. Still without looking at him she said, "I'm taking the train this morning."

"Because of the shop?"

"What else is there for me? I can't pay Mrs. Melcher's bills."

"I'll pay them," Bokker said. "I mean, I'll lend you the money. I think you can make a success of the shop."

"No," she said, "I've made up my mind. I'm going home."

"To Raytown?"

"Kansas City, that's where I live."

"I suppose you'll meet Shay there."

Now she looked at him. Angrily, her eyes blazing. "You never stop, do you?"

"I'm sorry," he said stiffly. "We just don't seem able to carry on a normal conversation without getting into a quarrel." He nodded and headed for the door.

"Wait!"

He turned. "Yes?"

"You can't go like this. I—I'm taking the train in an hour. I didn't want to quarrel with you—not now. I'm—I called you in to tell you something entirely different, but . . . you've made it too difficult."

"Very well, let's try it again," he said gruffly. "And I'll try not to be—difficult."

"Come to Kansas City!" she burst out. "Come with me."

He blinked, astonished and she came toward him, only the counter between them. "This is no place for you, Phil. You've had nothing but trouble. Leave Pawnee City—take the train with me this morning."

Bokker suddenly started around behind the counter, but when she saw him coming she retreated in panic. "No—no, Phil. I—I didn't mean that. . . ."

"What *did* you mean?" he asked ominously.

There was no exit at the far end of the counter. It touched the wall partition. Ruth could retreat no further—and Bokker still advanced.

"No," she whispered. "No," even as he reached for her.

Her body was taut, but it trembled violently and as Bokker pulled her close to him, she became suddenly limp, yielding. A gasp was torn from her lips just before they met his. She responded to his kiss passionately, almost desperately.

But only for a moment. Then she was fighting him again, pushing him back.

"No!" she cried. "I won't—let it—happen."

"You can't love him," he cried. "You don't!"

"I don't—love you!"

He started to reach for her again, but saw her shrink and cringe from him. The hopelessness of—her character—swept through him.

"All right," he said dully. "I can't fight you. Not anymore. Go to him. Take the train and go to your Paul Shay. . . ."

He turned away. The aisle behind the counter was narrow. A magazine, lying on a shelf below the counter stuck out an inch or two. Bokker's leg brushed against it and knocked the magazine to the floor. He stepped over it, but even as he did, his eyes went down to the floor.

Gasping, he stooped and snatched up the magazine.

It was a copy of *Fred Cowan's Illustrated Weekly*—a battered dog-eared copy. His copy, the one that had disappeared from his office. He had handled it so many times his fingers had soiled and smudged it so that it was as recognizable to him as—as his own face in a mirror.

"Where did you get this?" he cried.

She saw the magazine in his hands then, and shock hit her. "Give me that," she screamed. "Give me that!"

She flew at him, tried to tear the magazine from his hands. But it was too late. The magazine had been turned to the page containing the Lawrence sketch. It was so familiar to him that his eyes immediately caught something in the illustration that was out of place. Something different . . . something that had been added to the picture.

A penciled drawing of a head in the upper right corner. A rough sketch, apparently made idly and unfinished, but recognizable.

The face of Phil Bokker. A second face of Phil Bokker.

The significance of the sketch sent a shudder through Bokker.

"Paul—*Paul drew this!*" he gasped.

The agony on her face told him that he had the answer at last. After so very long, he knew.

"Yes," he half whispered. "Paul Shay." The past hurtled through his mind. "Yes, it *could* have been Paul. He came into the hospital in August, after the raid . . . he was probably wounded in the retreat. And he left—he left in time to rejoin Quantrell before Baxter Springs!" The audacity of the man caused grudging admiration to filter through Bokker. "Only Paul Shay could have had the gall to go to St. Louis—to a Union hospital—after what he did at Lawrence."

"Go!" she said poignantly. "All right, go. You know, so *go . . . go!*"

He brought it down to the present. "No wonder we always fought. He was always between us. You loved him and you had to shield him—you had to protect him. Paul Shay, the blackest murderer who ever lived."

"He's my brother!" she screamed at Bokker. "He's my brother! What else could I do?"

"Your brother!" cried Bokker, almost reeling.

"It was war—and even if it hadn't been, he was my

brother. I didn't want to tell you. I wanted to get you out of Pawnee City before he came back. He's desperate. He's going to kill you and I—I don't want him to do that."

"He's coming back?" Bokker asked harshly. "When?"

"This morning—at noon. I wanted to get you on the train before—before——" She stopped, her eyes fixed on Bokker in shock. "I shouldn't have told you," she whispered. "I can see that awful look in your eyes again."

"Why is he coming back? Why did he leave before nine o'clock in the morning and why is he coming back at noon? Why doesn't he stay away?"

"I—don't—know."

"You're lying again. It's been nothing but lies—lies—lies—right from the moment I met you. Everything's been a lie. Nothing matters to you except—your brother!"

He whirled and clenching the magazine in his hand, strode out from behind the counter and out of the shop.

Seething inwardly, he stamped down the sidewalk. He was past his office before he realized that he had passed it. Angrily, he whirled back. And then his eyes flickered across the street. Fletcher Trow was standing in the doorway of his office.

Bokker cut across the dusty street.

Trow watched him as he came up. He leaned against the door jamb, almost aloof, impersonal, but Bokker knew that Trow was aware of the magazine in his hands seconds before he reached him.

"So it was Shay!" Bokker snarled. "It was Shay—and you knew it all the time."

"I saw you come from her shop," Trow said tonelessly. "I guess she told you. That's the trouble with a woman—she's got to fall in love with a man. Well, so you know. Only he's gone now, so it isn't going to do you much good." Trow was speaking deliberately, quietly, but he was choosing his words. "Of course you can start after him. Keep on looking for him and you may catch up to him sometime—maybe. . . ."

"It's over," Bokker said, "and you know it. You know Paul's coming back. You've been in with him all the time. You were playing with him last night in the poker game.

You've been with him all the way, Trow. Yes—you brought Pierson and Charr Mechem here. The whole thing was a scheme of yours and Paul's. Pierson was to lead me to Acorn, where I could be taken care of without any trouble to you—or Paul Shay. But it misfired and you staked out Mechem—or Pierson—in my bedroom."

"That's quite an imagination you've got," Fletcher Trow said quietly. "But I think I've heard about enough from you, Bokker. Enough to last me—quite a spell. . . ." He turned and walked into his office.

Bokker did not follow him. He walked down the wooden sidewalk. To the bank.

He entered and went through the low swinging door into the private compartment of Joshua Chandler, the cashier and president of the bank.

Chandler looked up at him. "Mr. Bokker," he exclaimed, noting the bandage about Bokker's head. "What happened to you?"

"Somebody tried to kill me, that's all. Mr. Chandler, your bank's going to be held up this morning!"

Chandler stared at him. "What . . . do you mean?"

"Paul Shay's going to hold it up . . ."

"But Shay's skipped town. He gave some checks to Steve Longtree last night—in a poker game. He has no money here, and I guess he couldn't face the music. Steve was in a half hour ago——"

"He's coming back!" Bokker said. "He's coming back at noon. He's going to take every dollar you've got in this bank."

"That's fantastic!" breathed Josh Chandler. "Why—why should he turn outlaw, a respectable cattle buyer?"

"A respectable cattle buyer! Paul Shay's a former guerrilla—a murderer——"

"Your friend, you're talking about your friend!" cried the banker.

"He was never my friend. He used me—he knew that I was after him and he worked on me—he worked on me every minute. To throw me off the track. He's a killer. He couldn't keep up the pretense any more so now he's coming out into the open. He's going to do what others of his old crowd are doing . . . he's going to rob a bank. *Your* bank, Mr. Chandler . . ."

"No, he won't!" cried Chandler. "I'm ready for him. I'll take no chances. Even if you're wrong about Shay, I'll take no chances. I'll have Fletch Trow——"

"Trow! Trow's in with him. Don't you understand? They're old friends—they rode together with Quantrell——"

"Oh, I've heard those stories about Trow. I don't know if they're true or not, but it doesn't make any difference. As far as Pawnee City is concerned Fletcher Trow's the best marshal we've ever had. What he did during the war—well, he's lived all that down."

Bokker stared at the banker in astonishment. "You still won't believe, will you? That those men were not guerrilla soldiers—they were *not* Confederates, fighting for a cause. They were bushwhackers—thieves, murderers!"

"Oh, come now, Bokker. . . ."

"Jesse James rode with Quantrell! So did Cole Younger and all his brothers—and Frank James and the rest of the Missouri boys. Were they fighting a war? Are they *still* fighting a war? Jesse James was a boy when Fletcher Trow was one of Quantrell's captains. Fletcher Trow gave orders to Jesse James and his crowd. They rode together and they murdered together. And they're *still* together. They're together today. Not just Trow and Shay, Mr. Chandler . . . a man named Pierson's here; he was one of Quantrell's men. So was Charr Mechem. He's here, too. They came yesterday. . . . *Why—why*, Mr. Chandler?"

"I don't know," Chandler said worriedly. "I guess—I don't understand things. I—I've heard stories about *you*, Mr. Bokker. Oh, it's been whispered, but nevertheless, more than one person's told me. They—they say *you* rode with Quantrell, too."

Bokker had the magazine in his hands, the magazine with the evidence *against* him. He could show it to Joshua Chandler and it would do only one thing—it would make

Chandler ever surer that it was Bokker who was in the wrong.

He said, "I can't do any more, Mr. Chandler. I've said my piece. Don't trust Fletcher Trow—or anyone . . . !"

He turned and walked out of the banker's office.

Chapter TWENTY-FOUR

Bokker stood across the street from Ruth Compton's millinery shop. He had been standing there an hour. She had not come out. The train came into Pawnee City, waited a half hour and took on its passengers and freight for the East. It went off at eleven o'clock and Ruth Compton was not on it.

Fletcher Trow, the Marshal of Pawnee City, passed Bokker, but did not look at him. Bokker saw him go into the bank. He saw Steve Longtree, the mayor of Pawnee City, go into the bank. Mike Huntley, the prosecuting attorney, had apparently also been sent for, for he too went into the bank.

At eleven thirty Trow came out of the bank. Again he passed Bokker. At a quarter to twelve, Tom Chaffee, carrying a shotgun and wearing two Navy guns, rode past Bokker and dismounted near the bank. He took up a position a few feet from the entrance. On guard. Against bank robbers? Or, for them!

Five minutes later, Fletcher Trow, wearing only his customary single revolver, rode past. He tied his horse to the hitchrail in front of the bank, but he did not go toward his deputy. He stood carelessly on the other side of the bank door.

The mayor and the prosecuting attorney were still in the bank.

A minute passed . . . two . . .

They came. They came from the north. They crossed the railroad tracks, rode down toward the bank at an easy canter.

There were three. Paul Shay, MacDonald Pierson and Charr Mechem.

Looking neither to the right nor the left, they rode up to the bank, and dismounted. Tying their horses to the hitchrail, they headed for the door of the bank. Before they reached it, Fletcher Trow turned and went into the bank.

The former bushwhackers were only feet behind Trow.

Tom Chaffee remained outside the bank.

Bokker was a hundred feet away. He took a last look at the millinery shop across the street, drew a deep breath and started for the bank.

A gun banged inside the bank!

Bokker's gun was in his hand. He started running toward the bank. And even as he ran he saw Tom Chaffee move forward to block the door.

"That's it, Bokker!" he called, when Bokker was still fifty feet away.

Another gun went off inside the bank. Glass crashed simultaneously.

The shotgun in Chaffee's hands was pointed at Bokker.

At the moment of the crashing of the glass, Bokker threw himself sidewards. The shotgun boomed and a tiny pellet stung his face. But he had missed the main part of the blast. Then his Navy gun barked.

Chaffee staggered. His convulsing finger pressed the trigger to the shotgun once more. The charge went across the street, breaking glass in a store.

Chaffee reached for one of his Navy guns. Bokker shot him again coldly, savagely.

There were men on the streets; they already knew what was happening, were converging forward upon the bank. Men were coming out of stores.

Chaffee went down and Bokker continued forward. The door of the bank burst open and MacDonald Pierson came leaping out. A wild cry rose from his throat.

The old guerrilla yell, the yell of the old Quantrell riders that had turned cold the blood of so many people in recent years.

Pierson did not even see Bokker. He rushed for the

horses. He fired indiscriminately at approaching Pawnee City men. They were firing back, of course. And inside the bank, a gun went off again and again.

Fletcher Trow came backing out of the bank. Crowding him was Charr Mechem—Charr Mechem, his face already bloody.

Paul Shay was the last man out. His left arm hung limp at his side, but his right hand held a revolver that he was firing into the bank.

Trow crossed swiftly to his horse. Mechem turned—and met a bullet from someone in the middle of the street. He cried out and pitched to his face.

Paul Shay whirled. His eyes, as if magnetized, went to Bokker's. His face was distorted.

"All right, Phil!" he screamed. *"You had to have it!"*

A bullet—not from Bokker's gun—struck him in the pit of the stomach. In agony, Shay bent forward. But he fought the death that was sweeping over him. He fought it and brought up his revolver . . . brought it up, to point at Bokker.

Even then Bokker held his fire. Something . . . something . . . would not let him kill Shay. Was it Ruth? . . . Was it because Shay was already dying?

Shay's gun thundered. The bullet, fired by Shay's dying hand, struck Bokker with savage force, turned him half around. A bullet, fired by Trow, already in the saddle, grazed Bokker. It would have killed him if Shay's bullet had not turned him around.

Bokker fired then. His bullet hit Shay, but it was not necessary. Shay was already going down. So was Bokker.

He fell to his knees, tried to get up again and couldn't. He did raise his gun . . . and through filming eyes saw MacDonald Pierson, the wild young bushwhacker who had pretended so admirably only the day before to be a craven coward. Pierson was on his horse. He could have gotten away, galloped down the street. But he had turned toward the scene of the carnage. He rode at Bokker.

Bokker squeezed the trigger and could no longer see Pierson.

There was more firing, more savage yelling and cursing and shooting. Mayor Longtree, blood pouring from a bad wound in his head, came out of the bank, a gun in his hand. It was his bullet that cut down the last man, Fletcher Trow—the best marshal that Pawnee City had ever had.

Boots swirled and pounded all around Bokker. He did not see them, heard only a roaring in his head, a pounding of his wildly stimulated heart. A hand touched him and a rough voice said, "He's got it—bad!"

Then another voice cried out, "Phil ... Phil ... oh, Phil!"

She was on her knees beside him. Her arms were about him, hugging him, holding him tight.

Bokker forced out words. "It's all right, Ruth, it's all right ..."

It was all right.